Xaphira of House Marelli

He stood there still, his mug unmoving in his other hand, holding Xaphira and letting her find her own balance. His smile was as broad as ever.

"Hello, Xaphira," the man known as Miquillon said warmly as hoots and hollers wafted up from below, cheers for her deft stunt that had almost gone awry.

"Hello, Quill," Xaphira replied. "It's been too long."

"I heard you were dead," he said, stepping back to give Xaphira room to swing her legs over the railing.

"You should know better than to hearken every rumor in the streets," she said sweetly as she settled to the floor beside him at last. A mug came sailing over the railing, flying between the two as they eyed one another. Xaphira refused to flinch, and Quill hardly moved either. "And more than that, you should know I'm not so easy to kill."

Her life lived in secret,
for the safety of her family,
and the future of her city.

Was it worth it?

THE SCIONS of ARRABAR TRILOGY

...

BOOK I

THE SAPPHIRE CRESCENT

BOOK II

THE RUBY GUARDIAN

BOOK III

THE EMERALD SCEPTER
August 2005

Also by Thomas M. Reid

R.A. SALVATORE'S WAR OF THE SPIDER QUEEN, BOOK II

INSURRECTION

GREYHAWK®

THE TEMPLE OF ELEMENTAL EVIL

STAR*DRIVE®

GRIDRUNNER

FORGOTTEN REALMS®

THE RUBY GUARDIAN

THE SCIONS of ARRABAR TRILOGY · BOOK II
THOMAS M. REID
Author of *Insurrection*

THE RUBY GUARDIAN
The Scions of Arrabar Trilogy, Book II

Distributed in the United States by Holtzbrinck Publishing. Distributed in Canada by Fenn Ltd.

Distributed to the hobby, toy, and comic trade in the United States and Canada by regional distributors.

Distributed worldwide by Wizards of the Coast, Inc. and regional distributors.

Cover art by Duane O. Myers
Map by Dennis Kauth
First Printing: November 2004
Library of Congress Catalog Card Number: 2004106771

9 8 7 6 5 4 3 2 1

US ISBN: 0-7869-3382-8
UK ISBN: 0-7869-3383-6
620-17669-001-EN

U.S., CANADA, ASIA, PACIFIC, & LATIN AMERICA	EUROPEAN HEADQUARTERS
Wizards of the Coast, Inc.	Wizards of the Coast, Belgium
P.O. Box 707	T Hofveld 6d
Renton, WA 98057-0707	1702 Groot-Bijgaarden
+1-800-324-6496	Belgium
	+322 467 3360

Visit our web site at www.wizards.com

For Norma Murray Reid
1945-2002
Safe journey, Mom.

To Phil, for putting up with all my shenanigans this time around—I really owe you. And as always to Teresa, who did *everything* else while I was trying to finish. I owe you even more.

A special thanks to Ed Greenwood, generous colleague and true friend, who always, *always* finds a way to help, no matter how busy he might be. At the very least, I owe you a cold one.

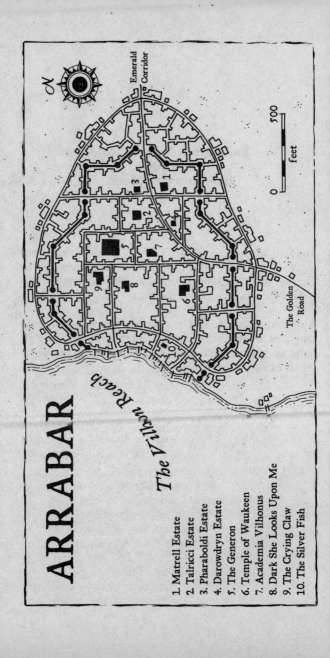

ARRABAR

1. Matrell Estate
2. Talricci Estate
3. Pharaboldi Estate
4. Darowdryn Estate
5. The Generon
6. Temple of Waukeen
7. Academia Vilhonus
8. Dark She Looks Upon Me
9. The Crying Claw
10. The Silver Fish

The Vilhon Reach

Emerald Corridor

The Golden Road

N

0   500
         feet

PROLOGUE

1 Tarsakh, 1373 DR

Marcon Hastori flinched and stifled a gasp as his surroundings shifted, changing in a single, startled breath to a moonlit ring of towering stones atop a low hillock. A heartbeat before, he had been standing in one of the rigid stone corridors deep inside the Palace of the Seven, listening to Senator Dwonlar Aphorio explain to him how he was needed for "a matter of utmost urgency and secrecy." Upon Marcon's reluctant nod of acquiescence, the senator had made an odd and complex gesture in the air between the two of them and the hallway had rapidly and completely faded away in a single, startled breath.

Marcon really hated magic.

The smoky, stifling air of the castle had been replaced by a humid, earthy breeze that

wafted lazily over the uneasy guard. The zephyr was
hardly cool, but Marcon shivered anyway, clenching
his halfspear warily as he peered about. His gaze
scanned past the circle of standing stones to the land-
scape beyond, wondering what need the senator had
of him in the middle of nowhere and in the darkness
of night.

The light of Selûne set the area beyond the hillock
aglow in an eerie way, illuminating a broad expanse
of open ground that was covered in low-lying mist.
Near the wide, flat mound supporting the standing
stones, a river flowed, though Marcon could really
only make out the near edge as a darker shadow, running in a more or less straight line. Full moonlight
glimmered off ripples in the water, and judging from
Selûne's position in the sky, the river sat to the north
of the hillock.

Marcon had no idea where the senator had brought
him.

Wishing that Aphorio had chosen someone else
to serve as assistant, Marcon followed the tall, muscular man down from the top of the hill, noticing
for the first time that the senator led him in the
direction of a second, steeper hill stretching off into
the darkness. Then flickering torchlight caught the
guard's eye from the distance, near the base of that
mound. For a moment, Marcon hesitated, his heart
racing and his palms sweating. But Aphorio didn't
slow, either unaware of or unconcerned about the
presence of others, so the guard steeled his resolve
and kept pace.

Serving at the pleasure of the Seven Senators
of Reth meant it was Marcon's duty to aid them in
whatever capacity they deemed necessary. If that
included being magically whisked away from the
Palace of the Seven and traipsing through a mist-
filled field in the middle of the night, so be it. It was

not Marcon's place to question such strange doings, and he would abide.

But that didn't mean he had to like it.

Among the Seven, Dwonlar Aphorio was responsible for the city's defenses and was considered the most eccentric of the ruling members of the city. Though he was judged as handsome by most with his lustrous, wavy black hair and prominent, chiseled jaw, the gods had apparently wasted their gift on the man. He sometimes spent days at a time in his personal quarters, alone or with apprentices, supposedly using divination magic to ferret out potential threats to the city or developing new arcane defenses to stave off such attacks. It was whispered that he never slept and could go for days without eating. Such tales unnerved Marcon, despite the fact that he knew them for nothing more than speculation. Few in the palace interacted directly with the reclusive man and could thus neither refute nor substantiate the fanciful stories. Marcon, it seemed, had become an exception that night.

He didn't have to like it at all.

Together, Marcon and Senator Aphorio crossed the open space between the two hills, heading directly toward the flickering light of the torch. The breeze from before, atop the hill, did not reach down there, did not disturb the mists. Only two men's slow, careful paces caused the vapors to swirl and flow around them, thick enough to obscure even the grass that grew near to knee high. The fog smelled both sickly sweet and foul to the guard's nostrils, adding to his sense of unease. He wanted to be away from there, and could sense that something dark and menacing lurked in the ground beneath their feet, waiting. It did not welcome them.

Soon enough, Marcon and the senator drew close enough to the light of the torch to make out several figures huddled together in a circle, gathered around something on the ground, something the guard could not see at first. Then the figures parted respectfully, allowing Aphorio to pass, and Marcon realized that they were the senator's apprentices, seven of them, all dressed in the same black and crimson that the senator himself, always wore. They bowed their heads as Aphorio approached, making room in their midst next to a gaping hole in the ground.

Marcon saw the turned earth along the hole's perimeter, evidence that it had been freshly dug. It was deep and long, and it almost seemed to tunnel into the side of the hillock. The guard's foreboding continued to grow, and he held back, truly afraid. Aphorio moved forward confidently, peering into the depths of the scarred soil eagerly.

"Excellent," the senator said, turning and smiling at his underlings. "Well done," he added. Then Aphorio turned to Marcon and motioned for him to step forward. "Come and look," he encouraged the guard, holding one arm up invitingly.

Marcon hesitated, feeling death radiating from the slash in the ground. He wanted to turn and run. "What is it?" he asked, his voice wavering uncertainly.

"An incredible find," Aphorio crooned, turning back and peering down again, leaning forward so that his hands rested on his knees and he could crane his neck for a better look. "It's history. Come. Have a look."

With dread making his legs weak, Marcon took one cautious step closer, then another. Finally, when he was able to see past the edge of the cut earth, he leaned forward and gazed where Aphorio pointed. The glow of dull yellow-white caught his eye.

Bones.

"W-what is this place?" Marcon said, trying to take a step back, away from the hole. He peered at the mound, which he could see stretched away as far as the faint light of Selûne would show him, though it was not round, as he had suspected before. It was a great long thing, straight and steep.

A barrow.

"A battlefield!" Marcon wailed, stumbling back another step. "You've unearthed the slain! No!"

Suddenly, with dreadful realization, Marcon knew well the place upon which he stood. He had never seen it before that very night, but he had heard it described often enough. The Fields of Nun, it was called, the site of the final, decisive battle of the Rotting War, where fell magic had brought the plague to all of Chondath. It was said that just as many warriors died of horrible wasting diseases as by sword and bow. The description of a great stone circle watching over the battlefield and the barrow tombs was unmistakable. As his eyes swept up and along the steep-sided, elongated hill before him, Marcon recalled in an instant the horrible stories of how it came to be.

The dead had lain thick upon the field of battle that day, many of them with festering sores and rotting flesh. The slain could not be buried by hand for fear of the plague spreading. Instead, great spells had been employed to furrow the earth into huge channels, like mountain giants tilling the soil with their own massive plows. The warriors who had died in the fighting were scooped into the furrows with more magic, buried as one.

Since that time, the field had lain fallow, for no farmer would come near. Visitors fell sick and died from crossing the ground. It was a place of death, a grim reminder of the terrible magic of the Rotting War. And Senator Aphorio and his brood of apprentices had dug into the very heart of its malicious remains.

Panic gripped Marcon. The sickly sweet smell of the mist assaulted his nose, making him gag. He turned, staggering, ready to sprint back to the standing stones, to find a way home to Reth, away from the death.

"Take him," Aphorio commanded, his voice casual and unconcerned.

Marcon shrieked in misery as hands grabbed at him, snatching at his tunic, his wrists, and his shoulders. Marcon felt his halfspear, forgotten in his panic, wrenched free of his grasp. He twisted away, savage, primal, and terrified. The hands were too strong, their grips like steel vises in the carpenter's workroom or tongs the smith employed. They halted his retreat, pulled him backward, off balance, dragging him down to the ground, kicking and thrashing. The guard was pushed to his knees, forced to face the hole in the ground.

Senator Aphorio turned away, back to the rent soil, and began to chant, gesturing, as he had done before, in the hallway of the Palace. Marcon watched, wide-eyed, wondering what terrible magic the man was calling forth. He dared not think about his own role in the ensuing rite.

Marcon felt the rumble well before he heard it. A low, throbbing vibration in the ground, as though all of Faerûn groaned, began at his knees and ran through him, fueling his terror. The guard yanked against the hands that held him fast, pulling against those grips of iron, but he was overmatched. He opened his mouth to plead, to beg to be released, but the words died in his throat.

The earth erupted as the senator stepped back, still gesturing. Bits of soil and rock were thrown skyward and showered down, pelting Marcon's face and arms. He cringed, blinking, caught between the stinging dirt in his eyes and the morbid need to see what had surfaced.

The thing that stood, its lower half still in the hole, was taller than two men. It was nothing but bone, dirty yellow and caked with mud and roots, but it was not the skeleton of any creature Marcon had ever known. Its skull was wide and flattened on top, and its snout was long and filled with rows of teeth as sharp and as deadly looking as any dagger. A pair of horns protruded from that forehead, slightly forward and curved up toward the glow of Selûne. Two long arms ended in skeletal, slender hands that were mostly claws. Two more hands fanned out to either side as part of what must have once been vestigial wings. All four flexed eagerly as the demonic thing stared at Marcon balefully, with twin globes of sickly green shining in the skull's eye sockets.

Suddenly, Senator Aphorio gestured right at Marcon and uttered a word the guard did not understand. He realized then, too, that the apprentices were no longer there, restraining him. He leaped to his feet, spinning to run, but the skeletal monstrosity was too fast, lunging at him.

Marcon was knocked sideways off his feet as the creature's claws raked his back. Liquid pain radiated through the terrified man as he tumbled to the ground and came to rest faceup, looking up at the demonic skeleton looming over him. Quick as a cat, the skeleton pounced, stabbing at Marcon with both of its wickedly clawed hands. The guard flinched and tried to fend off the attacks, but he was too slow. He felt the knife-like claws sink into his chest, his gut, sliding all the way through his body and penetrating the ground beneath him. With each agonizing blow, he wanted to cry out, but his breath had left him.

The guard turned away, his eyes welling with tears of pain and terror, just as the skeletal beast's head snapped down. Jagged teeth sank harshly into the flesh of Marcon's neck and shoulder, sawing through muscle and tendon. Marcon did cry out then, a pitiful whimper in his own ears that faded to a burbling gasp.

Just as quickly as the skeleton had appeared, it was gone, leaving Marcon lying motionless on the battlefield, his life force ebbing away into the tainted soil. He tried to move, to feel his wounds, but he had no strength left in his body, and all he accomplished was a feeble trembling.

Aphorio's face loomed into view, all sharp angles and shadows from the single torch flickering off to one side. The man peered down at Marcon with an eager, disconcerting smile. "Try to relax," he crooned, reaching out and patting the guard on one cheek. "It won't be long, now," he added. Turning to one of the apprentices, the senator said, "Fetch the decanter. Quickly, now. I don't want him dying on us before we can finish the transformation."

Marcon watched in a pain-rimmed daze as the apprentice disappeared from view and returned a moment later, a large crystal container held before him in both hands. The container seemed to glow with a faint green light.

Or perhaps, Marcon realized in a brief moment of clarity, the contents inside are glowing.

The mortally wounded guard had no idea what was about to transpire, but he wanted no part of it. He began to struggle anew, trying to turn away, to crawl from the field before any more of Senator Aphorio's foul magic could further harm him. But his arms would no longer move, and a cold chill began to creep in, numbing his extremities.

Marcon sobbed in frustration and terror. "Please," he croaked, begging anyone who would listen.

Ignoring him, Senator Aphorio took the decanter from his apprentice, removed the stopper, and waited, watching Marcon struggle feebly. The apprentices, perhaps sensing that the guard's life was fading, gathered in close, watching expectantly.

Marcon looked from one impassive face to another, not understanding such cruelty, terrified of what horrible fate awaited him. He tried again to roll over to escape their cold gazes, but the exertion only succeeded in bringing on a coughing spell—great, wracking hacks that brought with them stinging pain all through his middle. When they finally subsided, Marcon found it hard to breathe. He sensed death closing in, and he was afraid.

He closed his eyes and began to pray to Tempus for the courage to face it.

"Watch closely, now," Senator Aphorio said, as though he were a professor lecturing his students. "It will begin very soon."

As if to make the man a prophet, Marcon felt a rush of heat through him, and he broke out in a cold sweat. Almost immediately, his joints began to ache, and he began to shake, as if a great fever were surging into every corner of his body. Coupled with the dull, burning pain in his wounds, those new sensations overwhelmed him, and he cried out as his prayers were interrupted.

The plague.

The terrible disease of the battlefield had taken him, Marcon realized. He was thankful that he would die before the worst of the affliction could consume him. He prayed that it would, as he felt the fever and chills grow in intensity.

"There," Aphorio said, his voice filled with delight. "Do you see?"

Marcon opened his eyes to see the senator pointing at him knowingly. There was a smile on the man's face, and Marcon hated him.

"And now for the infusion," Aphorio said, and he tipped the decanter over, pouring its contents out upon Marcon.

The guard cried out again and squirmed, futilely trying to evade the concoction, which spilled out not as a liquid but instead as a thick, green, glowing vapor. The heavy, syrupy fog wafted down and oozed over Marcon, coating him in its glow. He tried to swat at it, make it drift away, but it insistently clung to him.

Almost immediately, Marcon began to feel the potion's effects. A strange sort of coldness settled into him, a sensation of sluggishness that suggested he was drifting away, leaving his body. At first, the guard thought that he was dying, that he was making the final journey to Warrior's Rest. But his mind did not escape from his mortal shell as he expected. Instead, it began to recede into a corner of himself. He felt his limbs grow heavy, felt control of his body lessening. He sensed his consciousness coiling up, becoming a mere spectator as his body was consumed and devoured by both the plague and the greenish glow. His heartbeat slowed and stopped, as did his breathing. Yet he remained there, seeing through filmy eyes all that took place around him.

"There," Senator Aphorio said, smiling broadly. "The transformation is complete. Now we can get him back to the city."

Suddenly, Marcon knew.

No! Not this!

Marcon tried to scream, but the sound that came out was a mere moan in his ears. He frantically tried to flail his arms, tried to reach out and claw at those despicable, staring faces, but his body no longer obeyed his commands. In his heart, he sobbed again, for he knew what they had made him.

Marcon Hastori, former guard of the Palace of the Seven in Reth, was a zombie.

CHAPTER 1

16 Tarsakh, 1373 DR

Letius Fordallin of the Iron Lion Mercenary Band swatted away the buzzing, biting flies that swarmed around the hunk of sunmelon he held; then he took another bite. The sweet, golden fruit practically melted in his mouth, it was so ripe, and its juices ran down both his chin and his arm as he gnawed on it. The flies wouldn't be denied, however, and finally, after he had eaten his fill, Letius tossed the bright orange rind aside, into the bushes, and reached for his waterskin.

Tilting his head back, the mercenary soldier unstoppered the skin and let some of the water spill out over his sticky face, washing away the remains of the sunmelon juice. The water ran down his neck, under his leather jerkin, and into his shirt, though that was already so damp from sweat that a little more was hardly noticeable. Letius's horse whinnied when it felt some of the stray water splash off the man's face and onto its withers, but the well-trained animal did not move. Finally, when he had removed the last vestiges of the sticky residue from his face and hands, Letius capped the skin again and let it drop back down to hang from his saddle.

Letius turned back to watching the men on the opposite side of the glade where he had been stationed. They were oblivious to him, hard at work sawing or chopping through the trunks of the trees. Already, they had felled more than two dozen large shadow-tops, which other men then trimmed, removing the trees' branches. Still other workers, assisted by teams of horses, were in the process of dragging those logs away, down the path in the direction of a nearby river, where they would be floated down to Hlath, milled into lumber, and used or sold there.

Letius yawned, feeling drowsy from both the noon-day sun and the food in his belly, and he thought of dismounting and settling in a shady spot for a brief nap. He abandoned the notion, though.

Sergeant Kukras'll have me scrubbing kettles for a tenday if he finds me sleeping, the soldier thought. Tempus, I hate this wretched guard duty.

Sighing, the mercenary wheeled his horse around and began to ride along a track, away from the tree-cutting, casually guiding his mount. The trail he followed was little more than a deer run, a narrow path that wound its way through the endless stretches of tangled suth trees that clogged the forest floor. He was supposed to be watching for hostile forces sneaking through that section of the Nunwood, mercenaries hired by noble families of Hlath attempting to sabotage their rivals' lumber operations in the area. Though he didn't doubt for a

moment that there were troops out there somewhere—
dueling mercenary armies were just a fact of life in
and around the Nunwood—he didn't see how they
could possibly manage to work their way through
the tangled growth in any sizeable numbers.

It didn't really matter, anyway, for like most of
the armies for hire along the northeast coast of
Chondath, the Iron Lion Mercenary Band regularly
switched sides in the endless games of one-upmanship
played out by the nobility. One month the company
might be working for the Lobilyn family of Hlath,
protecting their logging interests, and in the following month, when a larger sack of coin dropped
into Captain Therdusple's hands, the band would
most likely be serving House Lobilyn's most hated
neighbors. Sometimes, when Captain Therdusple was
particularly clever, he could play one side against the
other, convincing each family to pay them to ruin
their counterpart. With so many changes of fealty,
the armies themselves seldom even fought. Most of
the time, their captains met and negotiated an "outcome" based on how much coin had changed hands
and which noble houses were most likely to up the
ante for favorable results.

Fools, Letius thought, laughing to himself. They
waste their coin fighting. Then he sighed. But we're
the bigger fools, for we waste the chance to fight, and
thus waste our lives on meaningless guard duty, for
the sake of that coin. No one ever wins. What's it all
for?

The soldier must have been almost out of earshot
when he heard the shout from back in the logging
camp, for it was very faint. He hadn't realized he
had ridden so far away, and cursed himself for idle
musings. Finding a slightly wider spot in the trail,
he spun his horse around and bolted back down the
track, headed toward the logging site.

When he broke through into the glade, Letius spied a horde of men, many of them astride horses of their own, surrounding the milling cluster of loggers, who had obviously been rounded up by the newcomers. Though the strangers brandished weapons—mostly axes, crossbows, and halfspears—they seemed content to herd the workers.

Letius expected as much, and rode forward, a grin on his face. He would, of course, seek out the invading band's captain, or the most senior officer otherwise, and direct him toward his own captain, who was encamped perhaps a quarter mile back the way the invaders seemed to have come. It was as he had always done, usually with a laugh, a coarse joke about the coin squandered by foolish nobles, and a shaking of hands.

One of the enemy soldiers spotted Letius's approach and wheeled his mount about, giving a shout to his comrades to follow. He galloped toward Letius, who held his hands in the air, showing that he held no weapons. The other man, who looked to be a barbaric northerner—with a thick black mustache and twin braids of hair flying back from each temple—never slowed his approach, and half a dozen others came with him, strung out behind.

When the northerner was perhaps twenty paces away, he raised his axe menacingly. Letius's smile vanished, and he hastily fumbled for his own short sword, which was still sheathed in the scabbard on his saddle. At the same time, Letius spun his horse around, intent on rushing back into the cover of the forest. His mind awhirl in confusion and fear, the mercenary hoped that he could evade the onrushing foes in the suth tangles.

It was not to be. One of the riders charging hard toward Letius fired a crossbow, and the bolt slammed into the lone soldier's arm. The missile's tip passed completely through his bicep, embedding itself into his ribs. Letius's arm was effectively pinned to his side, and he dropped his sword in the process.

The wounded mercenary roared in pain and yanked reflexively on the reins with his good arm, drawing them back too sharply. His horse reared up, kicking its forelegs high into the air and unseating Letius. The mercenary landed on his back with a painful thump, knocking the wind from his lungs.

The northerner slowed his own horse's approach and circled around the gasping Letius, but instead of finishing the kill, the man reached out and took hold of the riderless horse's bridle. Letius looked up in fear and pain as the stranger began to lead his horse away. The casual way in which the foreigner seemed to have claimed the mount gave Letius a cold chill. He coughed and tried to speak as his body worked to regain its air, but when he began to struggle to sit up, with only one arm to aid him, a second enemy rider loomed above the downed soldier, halfspear raised high overhead.

"Wait!" Letius cried out feebly, throwing up his good arm to ward off the impending attack. "Let us parlay!" he begged.

There was a sudden fire in Letius's belly as the halfspear jammed down, skewering him to the ground, right through his midsection. Letius gasped, falling back, his good hand closing around the shaft of the halfspear in a vain effort to pull it free. He blinked repeatedly, feeling tears welling up in his eyes, both from the burning pain in his stomach and the bewildering fear that washed through him. He just didn't understand, and his mind was having trouble recognizing that he had been wounded.

"I—" he started, trying to make sense of what had just happened. "My captain," he mouthed, his voice a mere croak. "Parlay," he whispered, feeling the pain in his belly spreading.

Tempus, it hurts. Please.

"Leave him," the northerner said to his companions from a distance, his accent thick. "Let the others find him like that." Then the man leaned down from his saddle and peered at Letius. "If you live to see your brethren again," he said, his voice filled with contempt, "tell them that Reth claims this section of the Nunwood for its own and that the greedy, scheming folk of Hlath, of all of Arrabar, are no longer welcome here." Then the northerner spun his horse and, leading Letius's mount by the reins, rode away, his companions following.

Letius lay gasping, staring at the brassy blue sky overhead, clutching feebly with that one hand at the halfspear pinning him to the ground. He knew a man could linger for days with a belly wound before dying. Maybe someone would come. He prayed to Tempus they would. Flies began to swarm around him in the sweltering heat of the day.

...

"But why?" Lobra Pharaboldi asked with a choking sob from behind a black linen handkerchief she held delicately to her mouth. Occasionally, she dabbed it at her intensely dark eyes, red-rimmed and glistening with tears. The color of the fine cloth matched the heavy black velvet dress she wore, a cumbersome funereal outfit that made her uncommonly porcelain skin glow like summer moonlight, even though there was little enough illumination in the chamber at the moment.

Servants had draped the entire sitting room of the Pharaboldi estate in black, suitable for mourning, and had set up a handful of flickering candles.

The periphery of the solemn chamber seemed to shift and waver in their glow, which cast their uneven light haphazardly upon the pair of caskets arranged near the great fireplace. The effect made the shadows at the corners of Falagh Mestel's vision seem alive and restless. The tall, slender man did not much care for the dimness of the chamber, but the elegantly dressed woman huddled against him on the overstuffed couch had insisted they meet there. In the interests of getting her to agree to hear what Grozier Talricci and his partners had to say, Falagh had acquiesced.

Might as well humor her, he thought idly, running a single index finger along his thin black mustache. There's nothing worse than crossing a grieving wife.

"Who knows the dark thoughts of the greedy and grasping among us?" Grozier answered solemnly, pacing back and forth in front of the couple, his cape swirling about the somber doublet of black brocade he wore with each turn he made. A matching hat, rather ridiculous in appearance but of suitable style for the occasion, was canted at an angle atop the man's tight gray curls.

He looks like a burned peacock, Falagh decided, though he could hardly blame the man. Mestel's own outfit was hardly less foppish, though he had thankfully abandoned the jaunty hat, choosing instead to leave his perfectly trimmed blue-black hair uncovered.

Grand Trabbar Lavant, whose bloated bulk spilled over the sides of the high-backed chair he occupied, sat off to one side, letting Grozier hold center stage for the moment. The priest of the Temple of Waukeen seemed to be the most self-assured of the three, studying his own slipper-adorned feet in a knowing way. Falagh began to understand that Lavant, and not

Grozier Talricci, was the true guiding force behind
all that had transpired before Lobra's involvement.

Both the Waukeenar and Grozier seemed to ignore
the wizard they had brought with them—or rather,
who had brought them both there. Grozier had called
him Bartimus, right before telling the man to find a
quiet spot and stay out of the way. The paunchy fellow
sat in a corner in the shadows, constantly pushing
his spectacles up his nose and muttering to himself
with a foolish half smile on his face. Every time Lobra
sobbed aloud, Bartimus winced and stared, as though
she had interrupted some deep contemplation.

Falagh chuckled very softly to himself, finding the
wizard a bit amusing, in a ridiculous sort of way.

"Why did he have to kill them?" Lobra asked, flopping back against the seat next to Falagh, sweeping
her lustrous black wavy hair behind one ear with
her other hand, her face a look of helpless pain.

At the earnestness of her second question, Grozier
Talricci turned and knelt down in front of Lobra.
"Perhaps Vambran Matrell somehow considered his
family superior to yours and in his arrogance, could
not bear the thought of what he considered to be some
lesser scion courting his sister. Or perhaps he simply
wished to sabotage the alliance his uncle and brother
had made, desiring control of House Matrell for his
own, and found murder"—and with that word, he motioned in the direction of the twin coffins resting in
state—"to be his most reliable and straightforward
tool. Whatever the scurrilous dog's reasons, he has
affronted all of us."

Lobra glanced toward the caskets and shook her
head miserably. Falagh reached over and gently took
his wife's hand in both of his, giving it a comforting
squeeze and pat. The gesture caused Lobra to turn
back to him, staring into his eyes desperately, as
though she needed him to tell her that it was all

going to be undone, that Anista and Denrick weren't truly dead at all. Falagh had already tried every imaginable soothing gesture he could think of to assuage her pain, but she would not be placated. So he only returned her gaze, saying nothing. She fell against his arm, buried her face against his shoulder, and succumbed to her sobbing again.

"We all grieve for your loss, of course," Grand Trabbar Lavant said from his high-backed chair. Falagh turned to look at the heavyset priest, who had his hands folded together, his fingers interlaced across his ample stomach. The Grand Trabbar continued to stare at the floor in front of him with that thoughtful, if somewhat distant, mien. "To have both a mother and brother taken from you at the same time is a terrible tragedy ... simply terrible. And with the man most directly responsible for it running free, well ..." Lavant said, leaving the thought hanging.

Lobra sat up again, wiping the fresh tears from her cheeks with her handkerchief. Falagh could see her visage of misery transformed into one of hatred, and she shifted away from him and toward the front of her couch, sitting regally. The woman settled her hands into her lap, though she held them clenched into delicate fists.

Very good, Falagh thought, recognizing the priest's subtle manipulations. Move past what's done, and address what is still to be done.

The Grand Trabbar rose ponderously from his seat and carefully smoothed his gem-studded cream and crimson robes about himself, then he moved to stand next to Grozier, who still knelt in front of Lobra.

"If you want to see justice done, consider our cause," the priest said, resting one hand on the kneeling man's shoulder so he could bend forward slightly and emphasize his words. "With your help, we can not only see your mother's and brother's vision continue to move forward, but we can take steps to rectify this horrible grievance committed against you by House Matrell."

"But I cannot make these decisions!" the woman wailed. "I know nothing of managing these affairs. Mother always—" and Lobra choked on her words, her body shuddering in another silent sob as she covered her face with her handkerchief again. Falagh patted his wife's back as she shook in sorrow.

When Lobra had regained her composure once more, she continued with a sniff. "Others have always handled things. And I am not next in ascension, anyway; Jerephin is the head of the House, now."

"Lobra, sweetheart," Falagh said at last, finding it the right moment to add his own encouragement to the words of the two men beseeching his wife. "How many years has it been since anyone heard from Jerephin? Five, six?"

"Yes, but—"

"No 'buts,' darling. Jerephin is not here to make decisions, and he may never come back. The House needs a leader. You can do this." Falagh reached out and took Lobra's chin in his hand, turning her to look at him squarely. "You must."

Falagh could see the uncertainty, the hesitation, playing across Lobra's face as she considered his words. It was clear to the man that she did not have the first inkling about what she should do. She desperately wanted to have others make those choices for her.

Yes, Falagh mused silently, almost smiling. Let us help you decide. And the Mestels can be rid of the bastard Matrells once and for all.

Finally, her lip trembling, Lobra Pharaboldi turned back from her husband and faced Grozier and Lavant. She sat up a little straighter, forcing a look of determination onto her face. The grieving woman took a deep breath and, with a gentle pat from her husband to reassure her, gave a slight nod.

"Yes," she said, her voice nearly cracking. "You still have House Pharaboldi at your disposal. Let the plan go forward."

Falagh could see Grozier visibly relax his shoulders at the words, and the Grand Trabbar stood up straight again, nodding.

"Excellent," the priest said as Grozier climbed to his feet beside him. "We now have almost all the funds necessary to—"

"You *will* make him pay," Lobra said, causing the Grand Trabbar to snap his mouth shut in surprise at the interruption. "Vambran Matrell *will* account for his crimes," the woman added, giving both men in front of her a level look.

"Certainly," Grand Trabbar Lavant said sagely, folding his hands across his midsection and resting them on his stomach again. "We already have a few plans in place to deal with—"

"Promise me," Lobra cut in again, rising to her own feet, her eyes wide with intensity. "Promise me right now that you will punish him. I want him to hurt. Promise me."

Neither man spoke for a long moment, taken aback by the sudden fire in Lobra's countenance. Finally, the Grand Trabbar nodded.

"Good," Lobra replied at last, seeming to wilt from her former rage. "Then I trust that you and my husband can work out whatever arrangements are necessary. I must go and rest now," she said, her voice small and distant. She began drifting absently toward the door leading out of the room.

"Of course," Grozier said, almost too quickly, making Falagh frown.

Hoping to find the upper hand in negotiating with me, the scion of House Mestel thought. I think not.

"Yes, Lobra, darling," her husband urged. "Go rest. These gentlemen and I will finish up." And Falagh motioned for a servant who had appeared discreetly in the doorway to take care of his wife.

"Now, gentlemen," Lavant said as soon as Lobra had departed. "We have some details to attend to."

"Do not think me the wretched, grieving fool, Waukeenar," Falagh said, giving both men a piercing gaze. "My mind is not addled with grief over the loss of those two," and he waved casually in the direction of the coffins. "If you are to see one copper of my wife's wealth, then you are going to have to convince me that House Matrell will no longer be a thorn in your—or our—sides again. Ever."

Grozier seemed taken aback by the man's forceful words, and his mouth worked silently for several seconds, vainly seeking words that would assure Falagh.

"That is precisely why we also need *your* assistance," Grand Trabbar Lavant said. "If we are to eliminate Vambran Matrell's meddling—indeed, if we are to eradicate the mercenary's entire household—we are going to have to take some very clever, subtle steps."

"My help?" Falagh asked, ignoring Grozier and giving the priest his full attention. "What do I have that you want?"

"Why, your family's naval might, of course," Lavant replied, a hint of a smile on his face. "In all its wondrous forms. I think it's time Vambran Matrell met with a tragic accident at sea."

Falagh began to stroke his mustache again, unable to avoid a smile himself. "Yes, of course," he said at last. "I think I might know how just such a catastrophe could occur."

. . .

"It would seem that your financial woes have been alleviated, then," Grand Trabbar Lavant said, casually examining a finely wrought statue of a mermaid lounging upon a shard of rock jutting forth from a frothy sea. "Lobra was not so hard to convince. We told her what she wanted to hear." The sculpture was of silver inlaid with emerald and lapis, and it sat upon a pedestal in an alcove in one wall of Grozier's drawing room.

Bartimus watched from across the chamber as the priest plucked the delicate mermaid from her perch and studied the craftsmanship. Lavant held it in the light of a nearby lantern hanging from a hook set into the wall and peered closely at the underside, possibly looking for the artist's symbol etched into the silver.

The mage longed to return to his study, for he had research that still beckoned him before he would retire for the night. He knew, however, that he would have to magically return Lavant to his own quarters in the temple beforehand, so he stood patiently and waited as the other two men discussed their meeting with Lobra Pharaboldi.

"Yes, so it would seem," Grozier agreed absently. "She was never a bright one, but that was almost too easy. And Falagh was more than happy to offer additional Mestel resources, wasn't he?" the man added, sipping at a mug of chilled wine while he sat in one of his two most comfortable chairs.

Bartimus loved those chairs, with their deep cushions and matching footrests, but he had not been invited to sit, so he stood in a corner, leaning against a bookshelf and watching enviously.

I need to get a chair like those for my own rooms, the mage thought. Good for reading.

"Well, I expected the Mestels to jump at any chance to upend the Matrell household. Obiron the

bastard became quite an insult to his half-brother
Aulaumaer Mestel, because of all the success House
Matrell enjoyed. Old Manycoins has always wanted
to see Obiron's descendants dropped right back into
the sewers whence they crawled, a fitting end to their
upstart ways. So yes, Falagh was eager to get in good
with his great uncle by contributing to the downfall
of House Matrell."

Grozier nodded and shrugged.

"And yet you are still unhappy," the Grand Trabbar said reproachfully, replacing the statue and
turning to face his accomplice. "Our army is in the
field, sweeping all rivals out of the Nunwood. Sufficient funds are in place now to control the logging
industry. We can move forward with our plans, but
you sit there and brood."

Grozier snorted as he took another swallow from
his mug, then he set the vessel down rather abruptly
upon a side table, sloshing some of the dark liquid
onto his hand. "That whelp Matrell has ruined my
reputation in the city," the man said in disgust, rising
and beginning to pace. "I went from being the architect of a magnificent business alliance, standing on
the verge of greatness, to a near-prisoner in my own
estate, all in a matter of three days. Now next to no
one will consider doing business with House Talricci.
All the creditors are demanding immediate payment
for my other ventures."

"A minor setback, nothing more," the Grand Trabbar replied, moving to sit in the other comfortable
chair. "With such a sizeable army already in our
control, these new funds are more than enough to
keep the mercenaries loyal to us for the entire campaign year. Remember, it is not a simple plan we've
constructed, and you must have patience.

"We've made it seem like the city of Reth has
finally thrown down the gauntlet at Hlath, indeed

all of Arrabar, over logging rights. You know that
soon enough, Hlath will be forced to respond. All we
need now are to get the druids angry enough at both
sides to divert the Emerald Enclave's attention from
anything else. With a full-scale war raging all along
the coastal border of the Nunwood, our own lumber
operations elsewhere will be in high demand. Your
coffers will begin to fill to overflowing soon enough
with the high price of lumber, and when that happens,
the creditors will be clamoring for your investments
once more. Nothing remains frozen for long in the
business dealings of Arrabar."

Grozier snorted. "That's easy for *you* to say," he
replied dryly, still pacing. "Your role in all of this
has been carefully cleansed so no taint is visible.
Underlings stepping beyond their bounds, business
associates blundering without your knowledge. The
whole city isn't clamoring for *your* head on a pike
right now."

"You're fortunate your head is not already *on* a
pike," the priest scolded, folding his fingers in his
lap. "You could still be locked in the cells at the
bottom of the temple. At least here, you are safe
and untouchable. You have doubled the guards, as
I suggested?"

Grozier waved the question away impatiently. "Yes,
yes, the estate is safe. No one is going to slip onto the
grounds without being seen. And Bartimus here has
even established some magical alarms to inform us
if someone tries anything more subtle."

"Then all you need to do is be patient until the
furor dies down. None of the other Houses in the
city truly care what you have done. They only cry
for justice to keep attention away from their own
dealings, equally questionable operations that should
not suffer the harsh glare of public scrutiny. You're
simply the news at the moment, nothing more."

"I suppose you're right," Grozier said at last, slumping down into his chair once again. "But it burns me nonetheless. I do not take well to humiliation. House Matrell needs to feel a little of that for a change."

"And they will; I assure you," Grand Trabbar Lavant said, leaning forward and placing a hand upon his ally's arm. "They will have their due. We will make sure of it."

"But how?" Grozier asked, looking disgusted once more. "Hetta's brood seems to have nothing better to do than to attempt to spy on us and everything we have in motion. And I cannot believe that Kovrim Lazelle hasn't proven to be more of a thorn in your side."

"Do not worry about Kovrim, or Vambran," Lavant said coldly. "I already have signed the orders to have them both shipped on a mercy mission to a sister temple in Cimbar. With Kovrim away on campaign, he can't snoop around in my affairs. Once Mestel's 'friends' deal with the two of them, they won't be a problem any longer."

"Good," Grozier said, though he still sounded grumpy to Bartimus.

"You will also be glad to know that my latest divinations seem to confirm what I foresaw the last time we spoke. Everything is falling into place for even more support for our cause."

"Truly?" Grozier asked, an eager gleam appearing in his eyes. "And you have the backing in the temple to take advantage of it?"

"I believe so," Lavant replied. "We will know soon enough. In the meantime, we must get a better handle on what House Matrell is up to if we hope to take advantage of any weaknesses. Divide and conquer is our motto, but even with Vambran and Kovrim out of the way, Hetta and her gaggle of women can still be a problem. We need someone on the inside to convey information back to us on what, exactly, they

are planning, so we can mete out suitable counter-
strokes."

Grozier began to nod even before the priest was
finished. "Yes, I have been thinking about that. I
think I know just who will help us."

"I thought that might be your answer. Will she
cooperate?"

"Oh, yes. I'll insist on it." Grozier answered, smiling for the first time all evening.

...

Darvin Blackcrown stared down at the lights of
the city from his perch atop the vine-covered walls of
Academia Vilhonus in the Governor's District. From
such a vantage point atop the bardic college's main
library, he could observe much of the lower city, all
the way to the docks, as well as the Generon to the
north. In contrast, Darvin's own hiding spot was deep
within the shadows of two eaves of an upper floor of
the building. No one would think to look up from the
library grounds some forty feet below, but even if one
did, one would see nothing but shadows.

It was Darvin's favorite retreat, that spot atop the
library, and he rested there against the steeply sloped
roof, content. He kept his feet braced against a crum-
bling chimney and reclined against the tiles—still
warm from the sun despite the nighttime hour—just
staring down at the city. No one could bother him
there.

Are you alone? came a voice in Darvin's head.

So much for not being bothered, the man thought
wryly.

Yes, he replied, glancing over at the Generon for a
moment.

You haven't visited in several days, the voice said,
a hint of irritation present.

Darvin sighed but tried to keep his own irritation out of his thoughts. *I've been busy,* he responded. *Too many people looking for me.*

Do the others suspect anything?

No, Darvin answered. *Talricci still trusts me. He has no idea.*

Good. The voice was silent for a few moments. *Are their plans still moving forward?*

As far as I know, Darvin replied. *They went to meet with the Pharaboldis tonight, trying to convince the woman to help them.*

Excellent, the voice said, and pleasure radiated through the mental connection. *And how are you staying useful to him? How are you making sure he needs to keep you around?*

Darvin nearly laughed out loud. *Don't worry about that,* he replied. *Keeping the Matrell family off his back is work enough. I'm making myself very useful.*

All right, the voice replied. *Stay close, but don't let him suspect. I need to know if there are any more snags.*

Have I let you down, yet? Darvin asked, feeling a little put out at being tutored like a schoolboy. *Don't worry; Lavant is keeping things right on schedule. And he knows I report it all back to you.*

He'd better. This will all fall down on his head if it doesn't work.

Darvin shrugged. *If you say so. Is there anything else?*

No. Just don't be a stranger.

Darvin smiled. *I sort of thought you wanted to keep your involvement with this a secret.*

I do.

Then trust me to stay away when there's a chance someone might follow me.

All right. I'll check with you again in a few days.

Fine, Darvin replied, but the mental connection was already gone. Darvin sighed and glanced back over at the Generon again.

Then the man the rest of the world knew as Junce Roundface settled his head back onto his interlaced fingers and began once more to watch the city below.

CHAPTER 2

10 Mirtul, 1373 DR

Mulled wine sprayed over Xaphira Matrell as a hurled mug shattered against the wall just behind her, but the woman ignored it. Even the slightest distraction would likely earn her a split lip or black eye. The hulking dock worker who had cornered her needed little excuse to take a swing, and from the size of him— he was easily a head taller than she—any punch that connected would definitely leave a mark. As it was, the bald fellow was grinning stupidly, flashing a smile that showed several missing teeth. He had both meaty fists up and clenched, eager to fight. He seemed oblivious to the rest of the tavern brawl raging behind him. Xaphira eyed the brute warily, balanced on the balls of her feet, watching for that first sign, that first flicker of flexing muscle, that signified an attack.

It had been about a dozen years since Xaphira had last visited The Silver Fish, and the *rathrur* hadn't changed much in all that time. It still stank to high heaven, the drink was still watered down, and brawls were still a regular occurrence. For a moment, the mercenary officer wondered if even the patrons were the same since the last time she had paid a call to the place.

Now I remember why I haven't come in so long, Xaphira thought wryly, twisting and easily ducking beneath the first great sweeping punch delivered by her foe. *The regulars never were much for welcoming outsiders.*

Xaphira saw a second punch coming and side-stepped again, letting the huge fist rush past her cheek before she stepped inside the man's reach and planted a solid jab right into his nose. She heard the snap of crunching cartilage from the blow, but his head did not otherwise move much. The woman danced back out of reach again as her adversary blinked a couple of times. A trickle of blood appeared from one nostril, but he didn't seem to notice.

Waukeen, he's big, Xaphira thought. *Why did he pick me?*

If anything, the fellow seemed to smile all the more. He took a step toward her, swinging again.

Xaphira ducked to avoid the punch and glanced out at the rest of the room. Everywhere, men and women were scuffling. One stocky woman, still wearing her blacksmith's apron, grabbed a younger man by his collar and belt—a stable groom, judging from his clothes—and sent him flying through the air to crash into a table where several other patrons were laughing. The table collapsed from the blow and sent drinks flying.

Recovering her balance, Xaphira stood upright
again and watched as another dock worker grabbed
up a wooden bench and lined up for a swing against
the back of her own foe. Moments before, the two of
them had been sharing frothy tankards and laughing uproariously at the crude song the minstrels had
been performing.

Stupid bards, Xaphira thought, grimacing in disgust as she watched the bench shatter across the back
of the behemoth in front of her. Half the crowd always
loves their songs, and the other half hates them. No
better way to start a fight than to let a musician sing.
And these two don't even need *that* much of an excuse,
she realized, watching as the big fellow blinked in
confusion at the new attack, half turning to see what
had hit him. His former drinking partner just let out
a joyous shriek and grabbed another bench.

Seeing her chance, Xaphira went very low and
launched herself into a roll that moved her out of
the corner and past the two dock workers. The maneuver got her out of the immediate confrontation
between the pair, but it also put her into the middle of
the common room and the fracas roiling throughout
it. In one smooth motion, the woman tumbled into a
crouch and came up on her feet. She found her balance
just in time to spot another body flying through the
air directly toward her, a skinny runt of a man with
bushy muttonchop whiskers.

Xaphira could not react quickly enough to completely evade the living projectile, though she altered
her center of balance just enough to avoid taking
the worst of the collision. As the pair of them went
down, Xaphira spied the blacksmith back along the
skinny man's path, laughing as she finished the
follow-through on her throw. Then the mercenary
officer and the man were in a heap on the floor of
the *rathrur*.

Grimacing in frustration, Xaphira rolled out from beneath her counterpart and dodged sideways. The man struggled to his hands and knees just as a table came crashing down on top of him. She heard him grunt in pain as the heavy table knocked him flat, but she didn't stay to share in his fate. She kept on rolling until she was well out of the way then sprang to her feet again, looking for shelter from the rapidly expanding brawl. By that point, most of the patrons had either succumbed to the commotion or where in full riot, and platters, mugs, benches, and chairs flew in every direction. Xaphira spotted a relatively quiet corner near the stage. At the moment, it was occupied by the three minstrels, who cowered behind a half wall where a door led into a private section of The Silver Fish. She darted in that direction.

One of the three musicians saw her coming and let out a shriek. He fumbled for something in one of the voluminous sleeves of his gaudy shirt, producing a dagger just as the mercenary officer arrived. The bard clumsily jabbed at the woman, who narrowed her eyes as she shifted her weight enough to evade the ill-aimed blow. Xaphira then drove the heel of her palm against the back of the fellow's balled fist, shoving the dagger right along the path it was already taking, giving it enough extra momentum that she easily embedded it into the wood of the half wall.

"Fool bard," Xaphira muttered to the man, who stared at her wide-eyed. "Don't you know the difference between a tavern brawl and a real fight?" When the terrified fellow didn't respond, Xaphira made a sweeping gesture with her hand out toward the middle of the taproom, where the fisticuffs was still in full rage, though she never took her eyes off her counterpart's. "Do you see anyone else with real weapons in hand?"

The bard gave one quick shake of his head.

"That's right. At the moment, it's just a bunch of idiots having fun the only way they know how. But the moment you draw steel in here, all the rules change. And you're not ready to play by those rules, believe me. Now keep your head down before you get it taken off by a table."

Xaphira turned away from the minstrel and back toward the fighting. Beside her, the musician swallowed hard and shrank back even further into the corner, almost seeming to try to hide behind her. Snorting once in disgust, she scanned the perimeter of the room until she spied what she was looking for.

A middle-aged man stood leaning on the railing of the second-story balcony that ran along the entire length of the opposite side of the common area. He was watching the commotion with a bemused smile on his clean-shaven face, holding a mug of something as he rested his folded arms on the balustrade. His thick, curly brown hair was thinning a bit on top, and his skin was ruddy and wrinkled from long hours in the sun. The laces of his tan shirt were loosened, and the fabric was faded in certain spots, showing the darker outline of an absent breastplate. The blade on his hip showed a well-worn grip, a pair of sapphires set in the pommel. Xaphira remembered it, and him, even after almost twelve years.

Quill. You've hardly changed at all, she thought.

When the man noticed he had caught her eye, his smile deepened, an expression of genuine joy, and he casually raised his mug in a toast and gave Xaphira a nod. The woman returned the smile and began to map out a way to reach him.

Unfortunately, the stairs were on the far side of the room, which meant she would have to cross through the middle of the fight. Her original behemoth of an adversary was still clumsily sparring with his drinking mate, both of them with sloppy grins on their faces. From the look of things, the rest of the room had all but given up tangling with those two, for numerous groaning or comatose bodies had formed a rough ring around the pair. Everyone still standing wisely chose to remain well back of the makeshift barrier.

Shrugging her shoulders, Xaphira stood and began to sprint forward, headed directly toward the second fellow, who had managed to find yet another intact bench and was happily swinging it from side to side, keeping his larger companion at bay. When he saw Xaphira approaching, he set himself and drew the bench back, ready to swat at her with all he had. The mercenary gauged the distance, and when it looked about right and the brawler began to swing, she leaped high into the air.

As Xaphira sailed across the open space toward the two dock workers, she kicked out with both feet, planting them directly on the surface of the bench. The jolt of her weight and momentum reversed the bench abruptly, sending it back into the wielder's face. She had anticipated the shift, and she kicked hard off the bench, sailing to her right and landing on a table.

But she didn't stop there. Without pause, she launched herself across the table and up, angling her body toward a large post along one side of the room, one of a series of columns that supported the ceiling high overhead. With yet another great kick, she managed to push off the column, driving herself higher into the air, up toward the balcony of the second floor. As she reached the balustrade and planted her feet along the edge, she reached out and grabbed for the top of the railing.

Her momentum failed her there, though, and her fingers barely brushed the smooth wood without

managing to get a grip. Xaphira felt herself beginning to teeter back away from her perch, and she was
just beginning to windmill her arms and twist her
body back around to recover some semblance of dig-
nity with her fall, when she felt a hand close tightly
on her wrist. She felt the tug of being pulled upright
and spun back to face her rescuer.

He stood there still, his mug unmoving in his other
hand, holding Xaphira and letting her find her own
balance. His smile was as broad as ever.

"Hello, Xaphira," the man known as Miquillon
said warmly as hoots and hollers wafted up from
below, cheers for her deft stunt that had almost
gone awry.

"Hello, Quill," Xaphira replied. "It's been too long."

"I heard you were dead," he said, stepping back to
give Xaphira room to swing her legs over the railing.

"You should know better than to hearken every
rumor in the streets," she said sweetly as she settled
to the floor beside him at last. A mug came sailing
over the railing, flying between the two as they
eyed one another. Xaphira refused to flinch, and
Quill hardly moved either. "And more than that,
you should know I'm not so easy to kill."

At that, Quill began to laugh, a hearty guffaw
accompanied by a slap of the railing. "Aye, that," he
said at last. "There's no one harder to down than the
Ruby Terror of the Reach."

Xaphira pursed her lips in mock indignation,
but before she could spout a proper protest at the
moniker her old unit had bestowed upon her, Quill
wrapped her in a bear hug. The cheers from below
grew louder, accompanied by more shouting, and
another mug crashed into the wall next to the em-
bracing couple.

Finally, Quill pulled back. "Let's find someplace
quiet to talk," he said, motioning to one of the alcoves

that lined the second story of the *rathrur.* He led the way inside. "And safer. You may still be the Ruby Terror, but your face remains too pretty to be bouncing mugs."

Xaphira followed the man into the alcove, which was little more than a tiny closet with a table and a pair of benches, all firmly attached to the walls. The thick curtains were enough to muffle the worst of the noise from outside and below, though. Xaphira sat down opposite her old friend and just looked at him.

Still the same, she thought again, though she noted that many of the lines in Quill's weathered face had deepened in the past twelve years, and his eyes had a different look to them. Sadness and wisdom, she decided.

"I won't even ask where you've been all this time," he began, settling onto the bench opposite Xaphira and just looking at her in an appraising sort of way. "Though whatever you've been at, it's suited you."

Xaphira felt herself flush a tiny bit, remembering all over again the shivers he once gave her whenever they found time to be alone. The memories took her back in a rush.

"And you haven't changed a bit," she replied, smiling warmly.

"You're the worst kind of liar," Quill said, smirking, "but I'll let you get away with it just this once." The smile left his face, then, and the man leaned forward and rested his elbows on the edge of the table, folding his arms in front of himself. "I missed you. I always wondered—" His gaze flinched away as he stopped himself from finishing the sentence, and Xaphira felt pangs of guilt wash over her. She knew it would come to that eventually, that she would have to answer for disappearing all those years ago, without a word. It still hurt.

"I'm sorry," she said.

Quill began to dismiss the issue with a wave of his hand. "No promises were made," he said. "We both know the soldiering life is like that."

"I know, but—" Xaphira began, but then she, too, stopped herself. She wanted to tell him the whole story, explain to her old companion why she had fled the city of Arrabar nearly a dozen years before, to prevent her nephew from being framed for murder. But she couldn't. There was still too much at stake, still a chance that events from before could come back to plague her and her family.

"I had to leave in a hurry," the mercenary officer revealed. "If events had permitted, I would have gotten word to you. Someday I'll explain it all."

Quill nodded, and Xaphira thought she could see his shoulders straighten the slightest bit, as though a burden had been lifted. "I always knew you were alive," he said, though Xaphira wasn't sure she believed him. "And I wondered—but by Tempus's axe, it's good to see you!" he bellowed, reaching across and grasping her hands in his own. His touch was both firm and gentle, a mixture of hearty friendship and the hint of something more, something Xaphira remembered all too keenly. He gave her hands one extra squeeze, leaving no doubt he remembered, too.

"Quill," Xaphira said, pulling her hands away. It would be too easy to get lost in his touch, and she wanted to, but it would have to wait for another time. Her family was in danger, and she needed to focus on other things at the moment. "I need some help." She almost winced, then, when the barest hint of hurt flashed in Miquillon's eyes. He understood that she had not come back just to see an old friend, an old lover. The pain was brief, though, gone again and replaced by that warm smile once more.

"Anything," he said, perhaps a little too matter-of-factly. "Name it."

"I just need some information," Xaphira replied. "I need to find someone who doesn't want to be found."

Quill scowled. "If someone wants to stay hidden, it could be difficult to track them down. You, of all people, should know that."

Xaphira started, realizing the implications behind the man's words. *How long did he search for me?*

"If anyone knows a way to do it, you'd be the one," the mercenary said, reaching out again to take Quill's hand. She held it gently, letting him know that she understood the pain her disappearance had caused him. "I know you still have the best information, even after all this time." She laughed and added, "Or you wouldn't be the Quill I remember."

Quill gazed at Xaphira for a long moment, almost to the point where she began to feel self-conscious. "How much do you remember?"

"Enough to know I like what I see right now," Xaphira replied, and she meant it. "But I still have obligations, Quill, things that go all the way back to nearly twelve years ago. I never forgot. But I had to disappear."

Quill nodded. "Who is it?" he asked. His eyes were warm, with no reproach visible at all.

Xaphira sighed in relief. "His name on the streets is Junce Roundface." The woman noticed the man across from her start slightly. He knew of whom she spoke. "No one knows him, or where he spends his time. Or, at least, no one's talking."

Quill nodded again. "I've heard of him. Dangerous character. Not someone you want angry with you."

"Well, I'm pretty angry with him, and I want to find him. Can you help?"

"Maybe," Quill replied doubtfully.

Xaphira could sense his reluctance. "It's important," she said earnestly, leaning forward. "He's crossed my family, and I've got a score to settle with him."

Quill took in a deep breath and nodded a third time. "All right. I think I might know someone who can get you where you need to go. I'll try to arrange a meeting. Come back tomorrow night."

Xaphira smiled, feeling a surge of hope that she might finally track down the man who was tormenting her family. So long as Junce Roundface roamed the streets of Arrabar, the Matrells were in danger. It was time to put an end to that.

"Thank you," Xaphira said, giving Quill an appreciative smile. "I owe you."

"Yes, you do," the man opposite her replied, getting a devilish grin on his face. "And I intend to make you pay," he added.

Xaphira smirked and shook her head in wry amusement. Then, as she rose to leave, she leaned across the table and gave Quill a kiss. It was just a quick peck, all she would allow herself for the moment, but it rekindled a fire that she had not felt burning in many years. The warmth felt good. "I've got to go," she said breathlessly and slipped out through the heavy curtains.

Behind her, the man she knew as Quill stared after her departing form, a worried frown on his face.

• • •

Pilos Darowdryn's slippered feet made a soft *swish-swish* sound on the thick carpet that ran the length of the hallway leading to Grand Syndar Mikolo Midelli's personal quarters. While he didn't exactly hurry—moving too fast with a full pitcher balanced on one's tray was a certain recipe for mishap—the Abreeant priest also did not dawdle. Mikolo would be ready for bed soon, and he did not like to wait for his nightly dose of warmed milk. Pilos was not about to disappoint the highest-ranking priest in the entire Temple of Waukeen if he could help it.

As he walked, Pilos casually eyed the rows of ornate artwork flanking him. Magnificent paintings, fine needlework wall hangings stitched with thread-of-gold and other precious materials, bas-relief wood carvings highlighted with gold and silver leaf, statuary decorated with precious stones, all representing aspects of the Merchant's Friend and her faithful, either hung from the wall or glowed within magically illuminated alcoves. The young priest had seen them all many times, but each trip down the lengthy hallway brought with it an awareness of some new nuance, some previously unnoticed facet of the displays that caught his eye and made him catch his breath in delight. The opulence was truly a fitting tribute to Waukeen in all her splendor.

At the far end of the passageway, two ceremonial guards stood smartly at attention on either side of the wide, deeply stained wooden doors leading into the Grand Syndar's private quarters. The duo was dressed in highly polished adamantine chain shirts, over which they had donned white-and-blue striped tabards. Each guard held a halfspear perfectly vertically, the butt of which rested next to his respective right foot. Though largely ceremonial, the guards were veteran soldiers, seasoned in the temple's mercenary forces for quite a few years before being given the honor of warding the Grand Syndar's well-being.

The Abreeant knew the two guardsmen well, and as he passed between them and pushed open the twin doors into the high priest's chambers with his rear end, he gave them a respectful nod and murmured, "The Lady's blessings on each of you." Then he was through the portal and pushing the doors shut again with one foot.

Mikolo Midelli's rooms took up almost an entire wing of the temple, with numerous windows and shaded balconies opening to the outside, suitably trellis-covered to let in the breezes but not the heat of the sun. They had been further screened to keep in the multitude of tropical birds that were permitted to roam freely inside the chambers. The hallway Pilos had navigated was the only means of ingress to the chambers, and it opened into a large sitting room dominated in the middle by a large pool with a rather ornate marble fountain. A number of overstuffed divans and throw pillows were scattered around the perimeter of the pool.

Pilos crossed the room diagonally, heading toward the Grand Syndar's study. "I brought your milk, Reverent One," the younger priest called out as he approached the doorway. He intentionally spoke loudly and clearly, knowing all too well that Mikolo had grown somewhat hard of hearing in more recent years. As he passed through the inner doorway into the study, he added, "I'll just set it over here on the table, and I'll—"

Pilos started in mid-stride, nearly dropping the tray as he pulled up, staring at the desk situated in the far corner of the room. The Grand Syndar was there, as Pilos had expected, but the aged priest was slumped awkwardly over the top of the desk, his head lolling on one arm.

"Grand Syndar!" Pilos yelled, practically tossing the tray on the table as he dashed across the space toward the desk, heedless of the milk that sloshed out of the pitcher. He reached the elder priest and gently took hold of the man's shoulders, pulling him upright. The younger man was astonished at how thin and frail Mikolo felt, how little he weighed.

The Grand Syndar slouched back as Pilos righted him. A string of drool ran from the corner of the high priest's mouth to the table, and his eyes, usually so clear and amber, seemed glazed, staring at nothing. Desperately, Pilos felt for signs of life. The Grand Syndar's heart still beat, but it was slow and weak.

Without thinking, Pilos extracted a stylized coin from within his robes and placed his other hand upon his leader's brow. Closing his eyes, the younger priest began to mutter a prayer, the words familiar and delivered by rote. He felt the tingling presence of his goddess flow through him and down his arm, passing into the still form of the most influential man in the entire temple.

There was no visible effect.

"Guards!" Pilos screamed as loudly as he could while he tried to lift the man from his chair. The younger priest had both arms around Mikolo's chest and was just beginning to drag him out from behind the desk when the two soldiers who had been flanking the entrance burst into the study. When they spied Pilos struggling with the Grand Syndar, they both approached hesitantly, spears held before them, unsure of what they were seeing.

Realizing it appeared that he was assaulting Mikolo, Pilos said, "He's very ill! One of you, help me, the other go fetch a high priest. Quickly!"

Though unused to accepting orders from a mere Abreeant, both guards recognized the urgency of the situation, and neither one of them delayed a moment. As one spun on his heel and dashed back out of the chamber, the other set his halfspear aside and came on.

"Take his feet!" Pilos instructed. "Help me get him to his bed."

Together, Pilos and the guard, Atabi by name, carried the ill priest out of his study and into his sumptuous bedchamber. They crossed the floor, strewn with finely stitched carpets and throw rugs, to the large bed that sat near one screened-off window. Very carefully, the two men laid the Grand Syndar down atop his light covers. Pilos grabbed up several pillows and propped the aged priest's head up and tried to position him so he appeared comfortable.

Atabi stepped back and stared, his brow furrowed in worry. "What happened?" the guard asked.

"I don't know," Pilos replied, checking the ill man's vital signs once more, hoping his hands weren't shaking so visibly that the soldier would notice. "I found him like this at his desk. I have no idea how long he was there. A healing orison did nothing." Pilos felt his heart thudding madly in his chest, though he hoped his barely controlled anxiety was not visible to the guard.

Pilos had just decided to try another healing spell, one that was more powerful, but just as he was reaching for his holy coin, there was a commotion out in the antechamber. Several voices, all raised in alarm and clamoring one atop the next, began echoing in the sitting room as the doors banged open. Pilos felt relief wash through him. The arrival of older, wiser priests lifted a burden from the younger man that he had not realized he was feeling until that moment.

The priest spun around just in time to see a cadre of high-ranking Waukeenar enter the bedchamber, led by Grand Trabbar Lavant. The rotund high priest strode purposefully across the floor, his eyes focused intently on Mikolo lying atop the bed, while the others crowded in behind him. Some of them were terribly flustered and gesticulated and babbled animatedly as they followed Lavant toward their ill leader.

Pilos had to work to keep from scowling. He found the fat priest to be both condescending and vaguely unsettling in his demeanor, especially toward novice priests such as Pilos himself. And the way the others seemed to be deferring to him discouraged the younger man all the more.

Surely some of the others are more effective in the healing arts than Lavant, Pilos thought. Why do they let him dominate the situation?

Now is not the time, the younger priest reprimanded himself. The Grand Syndar's health is at stake.

Grand Trabbar Lavant stepped past Pilos without so much as a glance, and the other high priests shouldered their way past the young Abreeant, as well. The pudgy Waukeenar placed a hand upon the aging pontiff's brow and reached for his holy emblem, which hung from a chain against his bulging stomach. The other priests fell into an immediate hush.

"I attempted a healing orison before you arrived," Pilos said, stepping up beside the Grand Trabbar. The superior priest's only response was a slight smirk, and he continued his prayer.

Pilos sighed and stepped back again, wanting to give the more veteran clergymen room to aid their fallen leader, regardless of his own misgivings.

When Lavant finished his spell and opened his eyes, Pilos could see his face grow more somber. Whatever spell he had attempted, the Grand Syndar showed no improvement.

Immediately, the other high priests began to mutter among themselves once more, their faces grave and ashen. Everyone in the room realized the situation was dire.

"We must establish a healing circle," Lavant announced, silencing all talk. "Gather the materials at once. Quickly." As priests began to hurry urgently back out of the bedchambers, talking in muffled voices, Lavant turned back to Pilos and Atabi. "You were wise to fetch us," he said, looking from one to the other of them. "The Grand Syndar is very ill and needs our strictest attention." The rotund man turned to the guard. "You and your companion are to return to your station and prevent anyone other than myself and the other high priests from entering. Do you understand?"

Atabi nodded resolutely and spun on his heel to carry out his orders.

"And you, young priest," Lavant said, not even deigning to call Pilos by name, "must return to your own chambers and speak nothing of this to anyone. It would not do to upset the temple at large with this dire news. Not, at least, until we know more."

Pilos began to protest. "But I am needed by his side! I must—"

"You must let us do our holy work," the Grand Trabbar interrupted, adopting a steely gaze that made it clear he would brook no further argument from an underling of Pilos's stature. "I understand your concerns, but what the Grand Syndar needs now is our expert ministrations, and there is little you can do to aid us in that. Now return to your quarters, and when there is news, I will send someone to fetch you."

Pilos opened his mouth as if to resist further, but he snapped it shut again, knowing too well that he could not argue with a Grand Trabbar long and expect to come away unscathed. Reluctantly, in torment, he turned away and plodded toward the doors leading out of Mikolo Midelli's chambers, knowing full well he would hear little from any of the high priests once he was out of their sight.

CHAPTER 3

The first fingers of sunlight were just reaching through the line of shadowtops to the east when Emriana rode into the orchard. Honey took an easy pace, and the girl gave her dun filly free rein, content to let the horse make its own way while she enjoyed the coolness of the morning. Back in Arrabar, Emriana would never have been up that early in the day, but whenever the Matrells spent time at their country estate, the girl always liked to rise at daybreak and get in a ride. With no refreshing sea breezes able to reach that far into the uplands, the heat and mugginess would become unbearable by midmorning.

As she rode, Emriana enjoyed the smells of the ripening fruit—peaches, plums, and starfruit—that permeated the grounds. There

would be a good harvest of them that year, she noted,
and she smiled, thinking about all the preserves and
compotes that would mean. The fresh, sweet scents
almost let her forget about her problems, at least for
a while, but soon enough, she found herself dwelling
on them once more.

Grandmother Hetta had insisted that all the
women of House Matrell spend a few tendays in the
country. "We need some time to recuperate," she'd
said, "to get away from our troubles for a few days."
That logic seemed funny to Emriana, though, for she
discovered that she had spent more time thinking
about the family's difficulties, not less. As she and
Honey meandered between the trees, she felt dread
welling up in her all over again, thinking about
all that had occurred the night of her sixteenth
birthday party.

Stop it, she chastised herself. That was almost
three tendays ago. Get over it. Sighing, Emriana
tried to obey her own inner voice, but it was hard.

Maybe Grandmother Hetta is right, she mused.
But I don't need to get away from my problems. I need
to face them.

It was still hard for Emriana to accept so many
deaths. Uncle Dregaul and Anista Pharaboldi certainly hadn't deserved to die. And though her older
brother Evester and his good friend Denrick, Anista's
son, might have deserved it, she still felt sadness at
their loss—or at least Evester's. Denrick could rot in
the Abyss for all she cared.

She could still see Denrick taking his fatal plunge
over the third-floor railing outside her grandfather's
old study, and there was no remorse. Whenever
Emriana started to feel a little guilty for that lack
of sorrow, she reminded herself that he had tried to
rape her, even going so far as to have that squirrelly
wizard Bartimus magically charm the girl into

cooperating. All in all, it had turned into a rather dreadful sixteenth birthday.

Emriana sighed deeply as she rode on, trying to keep all those feelings of dread from welling up again, but it was difficult. There were still threats from that night running free. The girl wondered where Grozier Talricci and Bartimus the wizard had snuck off to. Just thinking of them on the loose in Arrabar somewhere made her shiver, and she found herself glad that she was far away at the moment. They were supposed to be locked up, she thought bitterly, sealed away from her and her family within the dungeons in the bowels of the Temple of Waukeen.

But they were not, thanks to Grand Trabbar Lavant.

The whole family suspected Lavant, but they didn't have any proof that he was behind it. He was so clever about avoiding any implications, and it made her furious every time she thought of his fat face. Whatever schemes Grozier, Bartimus, and Lavant had been planning with Evester and Denrick, they were undoubtedly still pursuing them. That thought made her stomach roil.

Uncle Kovrim had said they were trying to start a small war somewhere. The only problem was, no one was certain where.

And now, of course, Emriana thought angrily, Kovrim and Vambran have been shipped off on campaign. How convenient. With no one still inside the temple to try to find out, Lavant can do as he pleases.

Vambran and Uncle Kovrim had left only three days before, but to Emriana, it already seemed like a lifetime. They were going to Chessenta for the entire summer campaigning season. Vambran had showed her on a map the night before he'd taken the portal back to the city. Chessenta seemed so far away. She

had begged him not to go, not to leave her there by
herself, but he had made some silly, solemn noise
about duty. It was some nonsense about the Temple
of Waukeen in Arrabar loaning the Crescents to a
sister temple in Cimbar to quell threats from rival
cities, but Emriana knew that was just an excuse to
get them both out of the Grand Trabbar's way. Vambran knew it, too, but he had his orders.

She hated that smug, fat toad Lavant.

The girl shook her head as though to dismiss the
dire contemplations and passed out of the orchard into
another part of the garden, where a broad expanse of
lawn led down from one of the large stone porches to
the pond. Quindy and Obiron, Marga's twin children,
were there, playing along the edge of the water. Mirolyn Skolotti was nearby, watching the twins without
being intrusive.

After everyone came to realize that Grozier, Evester,
and Denrick had been responsible for Jithelle Skolotti's death, Hetta had invited Nimra and Mirolyn to
come live with the Matrells. She had insisted that
Nimra be made comfortable as a way of setting things
right for the woman. Both women had seemed very
grateful, and Mirolyn had even found a way to make
herself useful, taking on the role of nanny for the
twins. It was a far better life than the Skolottis had
ever known before.

They're probably annoying the goldfish again,
Emriana thought as she crossed the grass to join
her niece and nephew.

Obiron spied the girl first and gave her a quick
wave before turning back to peer into the pond again.
Emriana could see that the boy had his crossbow out,
holding it ready. That surprised her a bit.

"I thought your mother told you that you could
not play with that," she commented as she rode up
beside Obiron.

"She changed her mind," Quindy announced on her brother's behalf without looking up.

Puzzled, Emriana glanced over at Mirolyn, who shrugged. "Marga said it was all right," the woman explained. "He's been trying to shoot the goldfish."

"Obiron Matrell," Emriana began sternly, "if you shoot one single fish in that pond, I will take that crossbow away from you and snap it in two!" Obiron turned to gaze at Emriana, saying nothing. The look unnerved the girl, but she refused to back down. "If you want to hunt something, Vambran can take you hunting when he gets back from Chessenta. We have dire-jaguars roaming the woods here," she added conspiratorially, hoping that might interest the boy more than goldfish.

"It's all right. He never hits them," Quindy said, still not looking up at Emriana. The girl was standing on the edge of the pond, gazing down between the lilies and cattails that grew in abundance right along the bank. "You should let him play, or else mother will become angry with you."

Emriana raised an eyebrow in surprise at her niece's warning. Marga had never said a cross thing to Emriana about how she dealt with her niece and nephew. And the twins had never been so brazenly disrespectful to her.

Then again, none of us has been ourselves, since—

"I don't care," Emriana said at last, trying to sound forceful. "If you want to shoot at something, go practice at the targets Vambran built for you." She gave Mirolyn a quick, knowing stare as she finished. The woman smiled back, something of a helpless look, and she shrugged.

"All right," Obiron said at last, though his tone seemed to belie his acquiescence. He and his sister began to move away from the pond, Mirolyn following them discreetly.

Unsettled by her encounter with the twins, Emriana turned Honey away and continued on her ride, and she found herself wishing all the harder that Vambran were there with her. Having her older brother away on campaign had never felt so lonely in the past. She fingered the pendant hanging on the chain around her neck, which he had brought back to her for her birthday. She wanted to use it right then to call to him, magically span the miles between them, just so she could hear his voice, perhaps telling her something humorous, but she knew it was frivolous, and a waste of the magic. Through experimentation, she had come to discover the pendant functioned more frequently than Vambran had believed, but it was still very limited, and she had to be careful how and when she used it.

Besides, Emriana reminded herself, he's busy, and he'll just get annoyed if I trouble him over something so silly.

Reluctantly slipping the pendant back inside her shirt, Emriana passed through a hedge into another part of the estate and found her grandmother also out for an early morning stroll. The matriarch of the household spied Emriana right away and waved for the girl to join her.

"A fine day for a ride," Hetta commented as Emriana moved beside her. "Or for avoiding your lessons."

Emriana snorted, almost laughing out loud. "Grandmother, I don't have tutors anymore," she said, rolling her eyes where she hoped the older woman could not see. "They spend their time with Obiron and Quindy now."

"Not *those* lessons, Em," Hetta replied, sounding, as she often did, as if she were having to explain simple things to a foolish child. "Xaphira returned from the city last night," the older woman said, "and she's about to take Dancer out for a run. I saw she had her throwing daggers with her, so she's probably going to go practice. If you hurry, you can catch up to her before she gets out of sight."

Emriana grinned a little bit in spite of herself. Hetta understood far better than her mother ever would what was in her heart. Encouraging the girl to follow her own path, without regard to the traditional expectations of a young girl in Arrabaran society, was just one of the many things that made Emriana love her grandmother so dearly.

She leaned down and gave Hetta a kiss on the cheek. "Thanks," she said then turned and trotted toward the stable yard, hoping she wasn't too late.

She caught up with Xaphira just as the woman was about to mount Dancer, her sorrel mare. When her aunt spied Emriana approaching, she gave a warm smile and waved the girl over.

"Grandmother Hetta told me you were going for a ride," Emriana said. "Care for some company?"

Xaphira grinned and nodded. "Sure, Em. But first, I want to give you something." The older woman walked Dancer over next to Honey, and Emriana noticed a small wooden box tied to the back of her aunt's saddle. Xaphira undid the ties and lifted the box up, holding it out for Emriana to see. "Open it," her aunt suggested.

The box itself was made of rich, dark wood, smooth and finished so it gleamed in the sun. It was thin and wide, like a container made to hold fine silver. Emriana reached out and lifted the hinged lid.

Inside, the box was lined in shimmering cloth. It held a row of four beautiful daggers, each nestled in its own indentation. The handles were made of carved ivory and were etched and inlaid with adamantine and emeralds. The blades, also of adamantine, were double-edged and had been polished to such a reflective sheen that they could have been mirrors.

Emriana was stunned. "Oh, they're beautiful!" she breathed, tentatively reaching out and removing one. It felt exactly right in her hands, balanced perfectly.

"They're throwing daggers, and they've been enchanted," Xaphira explained. "Once you master the art of using them, you'll be hard-pressed to find their equal."

"Thank you!" Emriana said, running her finger along the blade lovingly. "I don't know what to say!" She felt so happy; she thought she was going to cry.

"Say, 'I will work hard with you to learn how to use them, Aunt Xaphira,'" the woman said, mimicking Emriana's own voice. She closed the box and held it out toward her niece.

"Oh, I will!" Emriana said, taking the box from her aunt and cradling it. "I will! Thank you so much!"

"You're welcome. Now, are you ready to ride?" When Emriana nodded enthusiastically, Xaphira smirked. "Last one to the rope swing is a meazel!" she shouted then put her heels into Dancer, who launched forward, eager for a run.

Laughing, Emriana kicked Honey and charged after them.

The two riders raced across an open field and toward a line of trees, Xaphira perhaps five lengths ahead. There was a trail there leading through the woods toward a swimming hole, and Emriana's aunt disappeared into the foliage along that route. The younger girl was close behind and gaining.

Dancer kicked up great clods of dirt and leaves into the air as Xaphira guided the horse along the wooded trail at a full gallop. Emriana, following closely behind, had to duck low against her mount's neck to avoid the flying debris. Taking such cover slowed her progress, though, and her aunt began to pull away. Grimacing, the girl heeled Honey to pick up the pace when they reached a straightaway along the path, hoping to close the gap and possibly even pass her quarry.

Suddenly, Xaphira drew rein and swerved to one side, sending Dancer through an opening in the undergrowth and across a dry streambed in a single leap. Emriana could not react quickly enough to follow without risking a stumble by Honey, and with only a heartbeat's hesitation, she relented, shooting past the turn and onward, remembering a second crossing a number of paces ahead.

You're not winning today, Emriana thought, glancing through the trees at her aunt, who was on the far side of the streambed and once again paralleling it, a little behind the girl's position. "Come on, Honey," she urged her horse. "Let's go, girl."

As if understanding her rider's urgency perfectly, the dun leaned hard into its gallop, surging ahead a little more. The path narrowed and turned slightly, and Emriana ducked low again to avoid the branches and vines that whipped past her head. The horse and rider became almost one, a single, fluid entity navigating the forest in harmony.

Emriana noted a familiar shadowtop trunk, large and dead, split long ago by lightning, and knew the crossover was only a few more paces ahead. She risked another glance back over her shoulder, hoping that she and Honey had enlarged the gap sufficiently that, when she crossed the streambed, they would be able to cut off Xaphira and Dancer. Her aunt was not in sight.

Emriana gave a subtle smile. That's it, she thought proudly. We've got her.

The break in the bushes and vines appeared ahead, and Emriana slowed her horse the slightest bit, just enough to make the turn safely.

"Em! Stop!" Xaphira called from behind her.

Em darted a quick look in that direction and saw her aunt in the streambed itself, still astride Dancer, though the horse had slowed and was rearing up on its hind legs.

Emriana hesitated, hearing the urgency in her aunt's voice, but Honey knew the route well and didn't respond when the girl began to draw on the reins. The horse slashed through the gap at just the right angle, clearing the bank of the streambed in a single bound. In her indecision, Emriana was not ready for the leap, and she was jostled awkwardly in the saddle, bouncing hard when Honey landed. She felt herself sliding off the horse, losing her grip and flailing wildly.

Her misfortune probably saved Emriana's life, for at that moment a blurred, golden-brown shape sailed silently over her head, fangs and claws flashing through the air where she would have been otherwise.

...

"That could be trouble," Adyan Mercatio drawled, moving to stand next to Vambran Matrell near the bow of *Lady's Favor* and pointing out over the waters of the Vilhon Reach. The lieutenant glanced at his sergeant and saw Adyan grimacing. The expression caused a scar that ran from the middle of the man's chin to the left side of his jaw to crease and glow white in the morning sun. Vambran followed Adyan's gaze toward the horizon and shaded his own eyes as he stared, squinting against the sea spray, at what the sergeant had spotted.

Two ships, fast cutters by the looks of them, had just rounded a spit of rocky shoals jutting out from the Chondathan coast, headed directly for *Lady's Favor*. Vambran put his spyglass to his eye and took a closer look, scanning the rigging for a flag or standard. There were none.

Using his glass to study the decks of the two ships, Vambran began counting men. In addition to the sailors scampering about in the rigging and across the decks, a number of others stood idly, watching. There were perhaps two dozen such individuals on each ship. Vambran even caught sight of a man peering through a glass just like his, seeming to stare straight back at him. The other man, tall and skinny and dressed in a long blue coat and a crimson hat, pointed right at the lieutenant and said something to a companion, a shorter, rotund fellow in a sleeveless tunic.

"Trouble, indeed," Vambran said, turning and handing his glass to Adyan. "Corsairs, it appears, for they show no colors."

Adyan put the glass to his own eye and peered across the waves. "Well, they sure seem to find *us* very interesting," the sergeant said, studying the two ships, which had closed the distance considerably since the two mercenaries had first spotted them. "Damn."

"Exactly," Vambran replied as he spun about, intent on finding Captain Za'hure. "Trouble, indeed," he repeated.

Before Vambran was halfway across the forecastle, someone was already shouting orders from somewhere aft, and sailors were scurrying every which way, running to adjust the rigging and shift the sails. Vambran could already feel *Lady's Favor* lean as she began to change direction, turning so she could catch the wind more fully in her sails. The move was taking the ship farther out into the Reach, away from the coast and the two approaching cutters.

"Captain Za'hure," Vambran called when he spotted the short, barrel-chested man stroking his long, curly sideburns and quietly issuing instructions to his first mate. Za'hure turned to regard the lieutenant, his bushy eyebrows furrowed impatiently. "Aye?"

"Why are you headed into deeper waters?" Vambran demanded. "Our orders are to make best time to Cimbar, and we're still three days out, by your own reckoning."

One of Za'hure's eyebrows shot up in surprise. "And what good will that be doing us, if we slink into port with an empty hold?" the captain asked. "We've got pirates on our tail, Lieutenant."

"Surely you don't think two ships are enough to bother us?" Vambran asked, gesturing back over the starboard side of *Lady's Favor*, where the pair he had spotted earlier were still closing. "I've got an entire company of Crescents on board."

"And while your company be dancing with those dogs, who'll be tending to the louts on the other four ships?" Za'hure countered, pointing back over his own shoulder.

Vambran felt a cold feeling grow in the pit of his stomach as he peered past the captain toward the stern, where four more cutters were visible, pursuing them out to sea. "Six," he breathed, stunned.

"Aye, six," Za'hure said. "They must think that cargo of yours be worth a good spot of coin."

"But it's nothing but campaign supplies!" Vambran said. "Blankets, extra weapons, and provisions for my men!"

The captain grimaced. "Be telling that to them," Za'hure replied. "But I don't think they be listening, so I aim to outrun them."

"Can you?" Vambran asked, eyeing the pursuers worriedly.

"Za'hure shook his head. "Nay, *Lady's Favor* isn't meant for running, Lieutenant. But hopefully, with the wind behind us, those dogs'll lose interest and hunt for easier prey."

The captain opened his mouth to add something, but a shout from the crow's nest cut him off. "Three more ships, two off the port bow, one off the starboard bow!"

"Blast!" Captain Za'hure roared, stomping up the steps to the quarterdeck. Once at the top, the man turned and peered ahead, bringing his own spyglass up to one eye. "They seem hell-bent for boarding us, don't they?"

Vambran didn't bother to answer. He spun away, running for the companionway and calling for his men to roust themselves. "Adyan! Horial! Assemble the Crescents! We've got trouble coming! Sound the call! 'Green Grow the Fields!'" As he reached the stairs leading down into the bowels of the ship, the lieutenant could hear Horial sounding his horn, begining the notes of a signal song, the particular tune ordering his men to assemble on deck and quaff a particular potion included among their equipment.

Trusting that the members of the Order of the Sapphire Crescent would respond quickly and efficiently, Vambran darted down the steps into the lower deck of *Lady's Favor*, headed toward the cabin he and Kovrim had been sharing during the voyage. The lieutenant reached the narrow door and swung it open, stepping inside the tiny room.

"Uncle Kovrim," Vambran said, moving toward the lower bunk and kneeling down beside it. "There's trouble."

The man lying on the thin mattress groaned and rolled over in the dim light of the single lantern, which hung from a hook in the wooden beam overhead. The glow had been reduced to a tiny flame, and it took a moment for Vambran's eyes to adjust sufficiently to the darkness.

"What is it?" Kovrim Lazelle asked. "What's going on?"

"Pirates," Vambran replied, reaching down to try and help his mother's brother sit up. "Nine ships of them, trying to surround us."

"Nine!" Kovrim exclaimed, starting upright. Then the man groaned and sank back down again. "Waukeen, I hate the sea." The older priest swallowed loudly a couple of times then took a slow, deep breath. "What does Za'hure say about it?"

As if in answer to Kovrim's question, the ship shifted to one side, its timbers groaning, and Vambran could feel himself listing against a tight turn. The motion made Kovrim gasp.

"I wish he wouldn't do that," the man said.

"When we thought there were only six, he was going to try to outrun them by turning with the wind, but three more are ahead of us, now. I didn't wait around to see what he would do next, but I guess he's trying to slip past a couple of them. I ordered the company to assemble on deck. Horial's sounding 'Green Grow the Fields.' "

"Probably wise, considering there are nine," Kovrim said. "Don't forget to drink up, yourself."

Suddenly, a horrendous roar deafened the two men, and *Lady's Favor* lurched to one side, as though she were trying to leap out of the water.

"Gods, what was that?" Kovrim muttered, trying to rise to his feet.

Vambran could barely hear his uncle for the ringing in his ears. He staggered against one wall of the tiny room, nearly bumping his head on the wildly swinging lantern. "Up top! Now!" he shouted, spun about, and scooted out through the door again as best as he could with the ship listing so sharply to one side.

Back topside, there was a mad scramble in full force. Men were shouting at everyone and no one, and Vambran could see several of the mainsails scorched and dangling free in the wind, with a number of their ropes flapping in the breeze, burning or smoking. Already the ship was slowing, losing its motivation as the sails were consumed. The Crescents seemed to be gathering in a general group, though there was no space or means for them to assemble into any sort of proper order.

In the next instant, Vambran felt the hairs on the back of his neck tingle, and the next thing he knew, he was facedown on the steps leading to the forecastle as a thunderous crack snapped through the air over his head. He didn't need to see the flash of brilliance to know that it was a lightning bolt. With his hands clamped over his ears, Vambran rose to one knee in time to see one of *Lady's Favor*'s three masts listing awkwardly to one side, tipping over toward the sea. Only the tangle of rigging kept it from going all the way over, but already, several ropes had snapped, and the others were unraveling.

Why in the Nine Hells are they attacking the ship? Vambran wondered. *It's as if they cared not a wit for what we might be carrying.*

Another horrendous blast boomed overhead, and Vambran felt the waves of heat wash over him as the fiery ball of magic burst among the sails. Two men who had been high among the ropes screamed and fell, their bodies singed and black. One hit the deck and bounced along its sloped surface, and the other fell directly into the sea.

At that moment, the lieutenant wished that his newfound sorcerous talents had manifested themselves a bit more strongly, for he would have liked to have slung a magical salvo or two back toward the nearest ship. But his skills were still fledgling in many ways, and he knew that no arcane force he could conjure up would have an appreciable effect against the massed strength of nine pirate ships.

Better to save them for the close-in fighting, he thought.

Lady's Favor pitched sideways with an even more horrendous shudder, knocking Vambran from his feet, and it was followed by two more. When the lieutenant managed to regain his balance and look up, several dark, slimy tentacles, as thick as trees, had snaked up over the side of the ship's rails, holding fast to the doomed craft.

CHAPTER 4

Xaphira watched in horror as a dire-jaguar, half hidden in the limbs of a stout flaming crown tree, leaped from its perch. The woman's warning shout had come too late, and Emriana, oblivious to the danger she was in, barreled directly into the creature's path. Xaphira was certain the girl would be ripped to shreds, but at the last moment, in an awkward tumble, her niece bounced free of Honey's saddle and flipped backward over the horse's rump. The dire-jaguar sailed over her, slashing out with its claws but catching only air.

Xaphira did not waste time watching to see if the girl had intended to dismount in such an undignified manner or not. Digging her heels hard into Dancer's flanks, she pulled her crossbow free of its saddle ties as the horse lunged ahead. The dire-jaguar was already on its feet as Honey whinnied in sudden fright and kicked out before bounding away to the other side of the dry streambed. For her part, Emriana was still half upended, though the speed with which she scrambled to right herself led Xaphira to believe that the girl was aware of her predicament.

Xaphira sighted down the length of the bolt on her crossbow, trying to take true aim despite the jostling of Dancer's gait, but before she could fire at the beast, another blur of motion caught her eye. A second creature had appeared on the scene, slinking through the underbrush. It dashed from its cover, leaping across open ground in great, fluid strides, rushing toward Emriana, who was on her knees, trying to get her bearings. A third one appeared as well, not too far behind. Xaphira jerked the crossbow in that direction and squeezed the trigger in one swift motion.

The shot was not true and merely scratched the lead cat, grazing the great, feral beast. The glancing blow sliced across its spotted golden pelt near the shoulder. It was enough to divert the dire-jaguar's attention, though, and the massive cat leaped and twisted in midair, spinning around to snap at its new perceived threat, the third creature behind it. When it landed, legs splayed and tail twitching, it let out a great, screaming roar, a challenge to its counterpart.

Xaphira never stopped to see what effect her shot had had, though. Discarding the crossbow, she leaped free of Dancer before the horse could follow its frightened mate back up the streambed and landed in a dead run to join her niece. Emriana was struggling to her feet, watching the first of the three dire-jaguars with an ashen face. Xaphira noted that the dire-cat watched the girl warily, waiting its chance to leap in and attack. She moved between the girl and the beast, settling onto the balls of her feet.

"Stay close to me, and keep low," Xaphira commanded the younger girl, never taking her eyes from the cat, while the other two began to circle to either side, prowling on huge padded paws the size of sunmelons. "If one gets too close, try to hit it somewhere on the face. But don't let it bite you."

"You're kidding, right?" Emriana asked, her voice tremulous. "Look at the size of them!"

Xaphira had to admit that the beasts were beautiful, in a deadly, savage way. They were was as large as mastiffs and just as muscular. Their golden eyes glittered dangerously in the morning sunlight, and the mercenary officer could sense a baleful intelligence there, something primal and dark, old like the land itself. One of them opened its mouth wide and issued an ear-splitting scream, a bold challenge to the two women. Its fangs were as long as Xaphira's fingers.

Beside her, she could feel Emriana shudder.

Suddenly, one of the three opposing Xaphira darted in, rearing up on its haunches and swiping at the woman with thick, black claws extended. Xaphira shifted her weight just enough to avoid the deadly talons, while at the same time flicking one fist out to snap against the cat's nose. As if that were some kind of signal, the other two rushed in simultaneously, and Xaphira dropped low, into a crouch, pushing Emriana down into the dirt as she twisted back to face the two of them.

The second dire-jaguar struck low, lunging at Xaphira's ankle, forcing her to kick at it with her booted heel, while the third came in higher, launching itself at her head. Rather than block that third attack, Xaphira sagged backward, over Emriana's prone form. She landed with her hands outstretched

behind her as if she wanted to crabwalk, but as soon
as the cat shot past, its raking claws whisking past
her nose, she was upright again, jabbing a rapid
punch inside at the great beast's ribs.

Almost in the same motion, Xaphira jumped and
spun around, snapping another kick at the first feral
cat, which had shaken off her punch and was darting in close again. She could not completely stop the
dire-jaguar from its lunge, but she used leverage and
its own momentum to redirect the beast, causing it
to collide with the second cat, which was coming at
Xaphira again in a leaping blur, fangs bared. The
blocking maneuver was effective and the two huge
felines collided, spat, and howled at one another. For
a moment, the two creatures were a blur of claws,
fangs, and flying fur; then they parted and retreated,
slinking out of harm's way. The three dire-jaguars
separated themselves from Xaphira and Emriana
and once more began to circle the two women, tails
twitching, waiting to spot a true opening in the mercenary officer's defenses.

Suddenly, all three dire-jaguars rushed Xaphira at
once. As quick as she was, she knew she would never be
able to fend off three simultaneously. As she snapped
another kick in the direction of the closest beast's
head, a flash of motion caught her eye from down
low, near the ground. She landed her kick solidly,
slamming the dire-jaguar's jaw shut, but the great
cat managed to swipe at her leg with one paw. She
almost bit her tongue in pain as she felt the talons
cut through her boot and rake her leg.

Xaphira nearly stumbled off balance as she com-
pleted the motion of her kick, and the dire-jaguar
she had struck twisted in midair from the force of
her blow. It landed with a shriek and darted off,
disappearing into the undergrowth. In the same
heartbeat, Xaphira followed through and snapped

an elbow into the second beast's face, expecting to
have her arm mangled for her troubles, but the
huge beast collided with her, its motion strangely
dull and heavy. The collision knocked Xaphira off
her feet, piling both her and the dire-jaguar on
top of Emriana. The blow knocked the wind from
Xaphira's lungs as the huge cat rolled on top of her,
feeling like dead weight.

The third beast mistimed its leap and sailed over
the top of the pile, but Xaphira felt its hind claws
rake her across one hip, and she would have cried out
in pain had she any breath. As it was, the dire-cat on
top of her flopped over and lay still across her face,
blinding her and cutting off her air. The mercenary
officer felt Emriana struggling beneath her legs,
trying to shift so that she could get up.

In a panic, Xaphira began struggling to get out
from underneath the obviously dead dire-jaguar that
was atop her face. All the while, she was desperately
thinking, this is it. They're going to rip Em to shreds,
and I'm next.

Despite her pain and fear, or perhaps because
of them, Xaphira found the strength to shove the
carcass away from her head. She scrambled out
and up, bringing her fists up, expecting an attack.
But the remaining dire-jaguar was several paces
away, limping as it paced back and forth. Blood
leaked from a wound along its foreleg, saturating
the sandy ground. It screamed a defiant challenge
at the two women then turned and slunk off into
the forest.

Panting, Xaphira peered in every direction warily,
looking for signs of the third cat, which she had chased
off with her powerful kick. She could not see either
one, but she feared that one or both had circled around,
hoping to sneak back in close for another attack. Finally, when it was obvious that the two remaining

dire-jaguars were gone, she allowed her shoulders to slump in relief, letting down her guard.

Emriana, who was seated near Xaphira's feet and breathing just as heavily, was holding one of her new throwing daggers, its blade bloody. Her eyes, which were big and full of fear, looked back and forth between Xaphira and the dead cat lying next to them.

Slowly, Xaphira rose to a kneeling position, resting her hands on her knees. She grinned at her niece. "I guess you found a use for them," she said between breaths, nodding at the weapon. "But you're supposed to throw them."

Emriana looked at the blade in her hand, dropping it as though it were white hot. "I did, the first time," she said, pointing at the dead cat beside the two of them. Xaphira turned to gaze at the creature and spotted the thin wound piercing its chest, just between its front legs. A steady flow of blood was just subsiding. "It was within reach, though, so I grabbed it again." Then the girl shuddered. "I thought we were finished," she added, swallowing hard.

"So did I," Xaphira confessed, grimacing and examining her wounds. The cuts on her leg were not deep, for her boot had absorbed the majority of the damage. Her hip, however, was bleeding freely, soaking her trousers in crimson. "Thanks to you, though, we're still here," she added, reaching into her shirt for the medallion dedicated to Waukeen.

Suddenly, Emriana was beside Xaphira. "You're bleeding!" she exclaimed. "It looks bad," she said, tentatively touching the slash marks with one finger.

"It is," Xaphira replied, wincing. "Give me a moment." Closing her eyes, she began to pray. The pain was making her light-headed, but she pushed the discomfort out of her mind for the moment and concentrated on the orison of healing. Pressing her palm against the wound, she muttered the final words and felt cool, soothing energy radiate into her hip.

When Xaphira opened her eyes, the gashes in her clothing revealed only fresh pink skin and lots of smeared blood. A second spell closed the wounds in her shin.

When she was done, the mercenary officer noticed Emriana sitting next to her with her knees drawn up. The girl was hugging them tightly and watching intently, her yellow-gold eyes wide with concern. "That's a pretty handy talent to have," she said when she understood that Xaphira was finished.

Xaphira nodded. "Only when no one is trying to take my head off," she replied, "or I'm about to pass out from the pain." For a moment, she thought of what might have been, if her injuries had been worse. "Have you ever had to field dress a wound before?" she asked.

Emriana shook her head.

"Well, if you're going to accompany me tonight, you've got to know more than how to throw a dagger."

Emriana giggled, realizing what her aunt was agreeing to. "Tonight?" she said, her eyes shining with excitement.

Xaphira nodded. "But only if you do what I say, beginning with learning how to stop someone from bleeding to death."

"The way you fight, I won't need to do it very often," the girl said. "It was . . ." she paused, contemplating. "Amazing," she said, her face filled with wonder. "I don't think I've ever seen you do that before. And against three of them. You're incredible."

Xaphira chuckled as she got to her feet. "Not so much," she replied as she wiped a forearm across her sweat-soaked brow. "Without you there, they would have taken me down. I'm getting old and slow."

"It was one against three!" Emriana protested.

"Sure, and in that instance, the best thing I could have done is take them out quickly, before they tired me out. But those cats were smart. They were toying with me, wearing me down before they prepared to close in for the kill. I was a fumbling buffoon this morning."

Emriana rolled her eyes, refusing to let her aunt's words diminish her appreciation of the display. "Whatever you say. *I* certainly could not have done any of that."

"Ah, but eventually you can, if you want to learn," Xaphira remarked. "I can teach you."

Emriana smiled, looking genuinely delighted at the prospect. "I would like that."

Xaphira smiled. "Come on, let's get back. Those other two might come back for more, and other things are going to come feast soon, regardless," she said, pointing at the dead dire-jaguar. "I don't want to be around when the quarrels over portions start."

Together the two women began to hike back up the streambed, and it was not long before they found Dancer and Honey, nickering at one another as they feasted on berries.

The ride back to the country estate was less boisterous, and along the way Emriana grew quiet. Xaphira wondered if the morning's attack had unnerved her, but when the girl spoke, her words reminded the mercenary that the impending journey back to Arrabar weighed heavily on her niece's mind.

"Did you learn anything about Junce Roundface last night?"

Xaphira pursed her lips before answering, feeling all her own concerns welling up inside her. "Not exactly, though I might learn something tonight. An old friend of mine promised to do some digging, and if anyone knows someone who can tell us more, he does."

"You mean, *we* might learn something tonight. Right?"

Xaphira nodded. "Right. But we're only going to sit in a bar and talk with Quill. There won't be any rooftop climbing this trip."

Emriana sniffed, obviously a little less enamored of the expedition than she had been previously. "Well, let's hope we learn something, at the least," she said determinedly. "Every time I think about that assassin still running loose in the city, after everything he's done to our family ..." She left the thought hanging there, but Xaphira understood.

"Me, too," she told her niece. "We'll get him, Em. I promise."

"Good," the girl replied. "Because I can't sleep, knowing he's still free."

...

A *kraken!*

By Waukeen, where did it *come* from? Vambran wondered, half in a daze. He shook his head, forcing himself to think. He scrambled to his feet, holding on to a railing for support, and peered all about the ship.

Lady's Favor wasn't long for the surface. She was already sitting much lower in the water than she should have been, and she continued to lean hard to her starboard side, pulled over by the gargantuan squid-thing that clung to her from beneath. Several men were already in the water, including some of the Crescents, though they, at least, had heeded the signal song and were standing atop the waves rather than floundering beneath them. But one unfortunate sailor was high above the waves, held tightly in a barbed tentacle that had coiled around him. As Vambran watched, horrified, the tentacle

whipped the screaming man back and forth rapidly,
slamming him hard against the waves and choking
off his cries.

The creak and groan of the listing ship grew louder,
accompanied by several violent pops. Vambran could
feel the vibrations of those cracking timbers in the
deck beneath his hands and feet. The beast was pulling the ship apart.

Where the hell is Kovrim? He's got to get up here
before the whole blasted ship goes down!

Za'hure went stumbling past Vambran's position,
shouting orders at the top of his lungs even as he
collided with another sailor who had lost his balance
and was skidding across the width of the deck toward
the railing. The captain grabbed hold of the other
man by the arm and swung him around in the other
direction, shouting an order that Vambran couldn't
make out. Somehow, the sailor stumbled in the direction Za'hure had pointed, pulling a cutlass free of
his belt and sliding toward one of the thick, rubbery
appendages that held tight to the sinking ship. The
sailor took a huge swing at the fleshy arm, gouging
a slender hunk out of it. Other men moved to join in,
hacking and sawing at the great tentacles holding
fast to the ship. Vambran wanted to move in to aid
them, but at that moment, one of the huge barbed appendages rose up from the side of the ship. It still held
the sailor from before, though the man hung limply
in its grasp, his head dangling at an unnatural angle.
Using the corpse as a bludgeon, the kraken raked
the deck of the ship, knocking its attackers away in
violent and sickeningly fleshy collisions.

There was another thunderous roar as the ship,
unable to remain all of a piece, splintered violently.
Vambran was pitched wildly up into the air as the
boards beneath him bent and shattered. The lieutenant twisted around in the air, fearful of landing on

the tips of those shards of lumber, but a great gout
of black water burst up from below, slamming into
Vambran and knocking him sideways. The sting of
the cold water took the man's breath away, and he
gasped as he tried to reach out and snag something,
anything, to arrest his fall.

Vambran's hand got tangled in a length of rope,
and he closed his gloved fist around it. He felt a painful jerk in his shoulder as he stopped, swinging from
a splintered spar, dangling out over the water. The
lieutenant groaned in pain as he reached up with
his other hand, trying to pull himself back onto
the ship and praying that the broken boom would
remain intact.

The mercenary officer was almost to the spar when
a splash from below caught his attention. He looked
down and spotted a great barbed tentacle slithering
up out of the water directly at him. In a panic, he
began to haul himself up in earnest, desperate to
evade the grasping appendage, but the fat, bloated
thing was far too swift. He let out an involuntary
cry of panic as the tentacle coiled tightly around his
legs, squeezing them together.

Then the tentacle began to pull.

For a moment, Vambran thought he might resist
the immense pressure of that terrifying tug. He held
fast to the rope, thankful that it was biting into his
gloves and not his bare flesh. His fingers ached from
the effort, but he did not slip even an inch. Every joint
in his body began to burn like fire, though, and he
knew that he could not sustain his resistance. Still,
terror prevented him from releasing the rope, and
he kicked and thrashed as best he could, despite the
growing pain.

There was a sudden and piercing snap of wood, and
Vambran was falling, being rapidly dragged down to
the water. He flailed helplessly, his arms windmilling

about, panic driving him to fight against the descent. When he hit the water on his back and to one side, he felt the wind knocked out of him.

Gasping for air, the lieutenant recalled the dreadful vision of the sailor dashed mercilessly against the waves until his body was battered and broken. Expecting to be pounded to a bloody pulp himself, he began to struggle wildly to pull free. He fought against the terrible grip of the tentacle holding his legs fast, yanking uselessly against its unyielding hold, desperate to escape the other man's horrible fate.

The mauling did not come.

Instead Vambran found himself being dragged under, down and down into the deepening gloom. Further panic made him try to swim back for the surface, but it was a futile effort. The kraken hauled him beneath the ship, coiling more lengths of its tentacle around his body as it drew him toward itself. The salty water stung his eyes, but Vambran could make out the beast's form for the first time in the filtered light.

It was as large as *Lady's Favor.*

The sight of the kraken made Vambran's heart thud in his chest, and he could feel his breath already beginning to fight for release as the beast pulled him closer. He found himself staring at an immense, baleful eye, cold and black. It was larger across than he was tall, and it seemed to be boring right through the man, giving him a chill that went beyond the water engulfing him. He could sense hatred in that eye, feel the loathing for him in its murky depths.

In a flash of equal parts inspiration and desperation, the lieutenant reached for his sword, which thankfully still hung at his hip, flapping half out of its scabbard. Drawing the blade free, Vambran was about to plunge it deep into the huge eye regarding him. Perhaps sensing the danger, the eye was suddenly gone as the creature whisked Vambran away, dragging him rapidly through the water. His lungs were burning by then, and he was fast losing the ability to resist the urge to breathe.

That's when the lieutenant saw the gaping beak, nestled among the bases of the tentacles, as large as he was tall and opening wide.

As he neared the hard, toothless maw, dread filled Vambran. In a frantic attempt to thwart the creature, he swung his sword as hard as he could with both hands. The blade was awkward in his grasp, twisting and turning as he tried to slam it against the flesh of the huge beast, but horror lent him strength, and he managed a couple of solid strikes against the kraken.

Blackness was beginning to rim Vambran's vision by then, but he still had enough presence of mind to switch tactics as the tentacle attempted to stuff him inside the snapping beak. Turning the sword in his hands, he shoved it forward, thrusting rather than slicing, and he felt the tip connect with tender tissue all around the gargantuan mouth. Whatever he hit must have been sensitive, for the kraken shivered violently and jerked him away from itself.

But Vambran did not stop. With his strength waning and consciousness fading, he continued to jam the blade down, stabbing repeatedly into the tentacle encircling him. After three such strikes, the coil loosened. Still he struck, again and again, each blow more feeble than the last.

The lieutenant felt a sudden current of water drive him away, and he found himself tumbling through inky blackness. The kraken had released him, but his victory seemed hollow. He tumbled in the water with no idea which way was up, and his lungs were ready to

explode. He had no doubt that his heavy breastplate
was pulling him deeper into the sea, where he would
settle to the bottom until the fish consumed him.

Consciousness began to recede as his body twitched
and spasmed.

The last thing he felt was numbness, and there
was nothing.

It was several moments before Vambran realized
he was breathing again. He opened his eyes and found
himself staring into another set of orbs, a beautiful
turquoise color with gold flecks. They were inches
from his own, and they seemed to study him intently,
expressing concern and hope all at once. They were
framed by a narrow feminine face of pale blue skin,
the mouth of which was currently locked against his
own in a soft kiss.

Startled at that revelation, Vambran jerked away
from the embrace of the creature holding him. That
act of separation disrupted a smooth gliding motion
he had not been aware of before, and Vambran tumbled away from the other in the ensuing turbulence
and began to sink again through the dim water.

The naked creature regarded him with a combina-
tion of consternation and amusement for a moment;
then she turned gracefully so she was angled toward
him. She began pulling herself down with powerful
strokes of her webbed hands and feet, swimming
easily after his receding form, closing the distance
between them quickly. She was nearly human in
appearance, though she was pale blue from head
to toe with short, darker blue hair, and she sported
gills along each side of her torso, at both collarbone
and ribs. Her only adornments were necklaces and
bracelets of sea shells and a belt made from the skin
of some creature, possibly an eel. A knife made of
what Vambran surmised must be coral was tucked
into that belt at one hip.

A sea elf, he realized, and for a moment, Vambran was dazzled.

When he tried to sigh, though, the mouthful of water he got for his troubles reminded him that he was drowning, and he began to thrash and kick desperately. He struggled to swim up, to follow the trail of bubbles he was making, but his breastplate was too heavy, pulling him down into the depths.

Hands found his shoulders, and at first, Vambran grabbed at them and tried to pull himself upward, fighting against the tug of the deep. But the hands were strong and forceful, jerking Vambran around so that he was once more face to face with the beautiful sea elf, who gave him a stern look before locking him in another kiss.

It was only then that the lieutenant realized she was helping him to breathe.

The sea elf began to swim then, pulling Vambran along with her and occasionally blowing air into his lungs, keeping him alive. Together, they moved through the water like that, gliding down into the depths. He wondered where she was taking him, but he did not care, so long as he could remain close to her.

No! Vambran realized. The ship! Uncle Kovrim!

The lieutenant jerked himself free of the sea elf's embrace. She drew up in the water, reaching for him again. He began to sink, but he ignored it for a moment, holding up his hands to stave off her attempt to catch him. He smiled and gently shook his head, hoping that the expression conveyed both his appreciation and his denial.

The sea elf cocked her head to one side quizzically, but before she could try to approach him again, Vambran reached into a pouch at his belt and produced a small vial. He drew the vial out, thrusting the end toward his mouth. He pulled the stopper free just as he rammed the end against his lips, closing down tight to seal the opening from the water outside.

In one quick gulp, Vambran sucked the contents of the potion into his mouth and swallowed it, trying to ignore the strange mixed flavor of honey and olive oil. Almost immediately, he felt a shift as the magic of the potion took effect. The weight of his breastplate shifted, began to drag in the opposite direction. He was rising to the surface.

As he rose, Vambran looked again at the sea elf. There was a smile on her face as well, a look of goodwill mixed with a touch of sadness. She raised one hand in salute to him, and he returned the gesture then began to pull himself toward the surface, helping the magic, for he was beginning to feel the pressure in his lungs again.

The pain of needing to breathe was just growing severe when Vambran found himself bobbing like a cork atop the pitching sea. He leaned his head back and sucked in a great gulp of salty air, thankful to be on the surface again. In the near distance ahead of him, not far from where he stood, the lieutenant could hear men shouting and screaming.

Vambran looked that way and surveyed the carnage. Everywhere he looked, men floundered in the water, sailors among Za'hure's crew who were either swimming and begging for aid or trying to scramble atop the remains of *Lady's Favor*. The ship itself was mostly beneath the water by that point, shattered into several large pieces that rolled with the motion of the Reach. There was no sign of the kraken.

The Crescents were scattered everywhere in the general vicinity of the destroyed craft. Some of them were trying to help sailors scamper aboard drifting bits of ship. Others were forming up to defend themselves against the attacks of the corsairs, who had drawn their ships close enough to begin firing arrows at everyone in the water. It was hardly a fair fight, and one that would cost so many brave soldiers their lives if they stood their ground.

Vambran made a quick and desperate scan of the men in sight, looking for Kovrim, but his survey was cut short by an arrow clanking off the middle of the back of his breastplate. Cursing, he spun around to see one of the ships only a stone's throw away and closing fast. Already, half a dozen more archers were drawing a bead on him. He lunged to the side as two more missiles sliced into the water near his feet.

Enraged at his own helplessness to do anything else, Vambran turned and ran, sprinting as fast as he could across the open water. He heard the hissing sound of more arrows zipping into the waves behind and to either side of him, but he dared not stop.

Got to get the men to safety, he realized. Only chance is to run for shore.

Vambran scrambled in the direction of a small cluster of mercenaries, one of whom was Horial. "To the shore!" he shouted, motioning in the direction of the coast, which appeared to be a little more than a mile away. "Pass the word, and make for the shore! Horial! Sound the retreat!"

The sergeant nodded, drew his small curved horn from somewhere in his belt, and began to blow the familiar tune signaling the men to fall back. All around, Vambran began to hear the call.

"Retreat! Retreat!" the Crescents shouted, and coolly, like the disciplined troops they were, the mercenaries began to move away from the wreckage of the destroyed ship, making their way toward the shoreline as fast as they could.

Vambran cringed at the wails of despair the other men, the sailors in the water, sent up. There would be no rescue for them, and they knew their doom was upon them. Silently, as he ran, Vambran asked in a

prayer for forgiveness from Waukeen for abandoning
men on the field of battle. But he did not have the
resources to stay and fight to save them, nor could
he carry even a single one of them with him atop the
water. And if the kraken returned....

The lieutenant did not head for the shore straightaway, but rather, he made a quick circle, hoping to
find other Crescents who needed his aid. Hoping,
and yet not hoping, to find Kovrim. As he passed one
particularly large section of ruined ship, he spied
Captain Za'hure, stretched out along a bit of decking,
sprawled on his back, and staring at the sky.

No, Vambran realized, seeing the large gash across
the other side of the captain's neck. Those eyes are not
looking at anything.

Vambran lurched as two stinging darts of pain
slammed into his side. He staggered and turned to
see what had hit him. Most of the pirate ships had
gathered in close by then, and several of them had
set smaller boats down into the water. One such
craft was coming directly toward the lieutenant,
and standing in the very prow, a callous smirk upon
his face, was the man in the blue coat and red hat.
He held a wand in his hand, which he still pointed
in Vambran's general direction.

Snarling, Vambran turned toward the fellow, yanking his crossbow up off his hip. But when he reached
for a bolt, he found that his quiver was empty.

They all must have floated away, he realized
dismally.

The wand-wielding adversary had initially
flinched away at the sight of Vambran preparing to
line up his weapon, but when he realized he was in
no immediate danger, the fellow barked a short laugh
and raised his wand again.

Cursing his ill luck, Vambran turned and sprinted
away as fast as he possibly could. He staggered again

as two more of the magical missiles struck him from behind, arching his back and nearly falling over, but he kept on running, knowing that he had to put some distance between himself and the mage attacking him.

Reaching into his shirt, Vambran pulled his holy coin, which he wore on a chain around his neck, free. He sighed in relief that it was still there and not lying at the bottom of the Reach. Then he offered a quick prayer to Waukeen and cast a spell. Instantly he felt the surge of speed he had prayed for, and he shot forward. Sprinting in strides easily twice as large as would normally be possible, Vambran rushed away from the devastation of *Lady's Favor*, lamenting the loss of every man in the ambush, but knowing he had been given no other choice.

As he ran, he considered what had just happened. Such an attack was more than just mindless cruelty and brutality, the lieutenant realized. Nine ships was a number for sinking, not boarding and pillaging. And the appearance of a kraken could not have been coincidence. It was all a well-measured attempt to kill every man on board that ship. Someone had wanted them all to die. He had a pretty good idea who that might be.

CHAPTER 5

"Blast that lucky son of a bullywug!" Grozier growled, standing behind Bartimus and staring into the image displayed in the large mirror. The two men, along with Junce Roundface and Falagh Mestel, were gathered in the wizard's chambers, observing the results of the sea ambush Falagh had arranged through some of his contacts.

"You should have told me how much magic they had at their disposal," Falagh muttered, standing behind Bartimus and to his left. "They are more stoutly equipped with it than the typical company. If I had known, I could have warned my associates."

"Did you see how fast he ran?" Junce said, laughing. "He shot across the water like a bolt out of a crossbow!" The assassin had strolled away from the mirror and was

in the process of removing a stack of loose papers
from a corner of a bench. "Isn't there any place to
sit in here?" he complained as he just slid the last
of the parchment sheaves unceremoniously onto
the floor.

Bartimus peered around at the fellow, more than
a little anxious about his things being disturbed.
"Please don't do that!" he said crossly, half rising
from his own chair to go and rescue the materials.
They were either the last few pages of a treatise on
the mating habits of the cockatrice, or else they were
diagrams for crafting a new type of siege engine.
The wizard couldn't remember which stack he had
set there.

"Never mind that," Grozier snapped, slamming
his hand down on Bartimus's shoulder. "Where did
Matrell run off to?"

Sighing, Bartimus sank back down and focused
his attention back on the mirror. The image in the
frame rotated to the right, in the direction they had
last seen Vambran as he ran. He was already a mere
speck on the seascape by that point, and Bartimus
had to shift the frame of reference rapidly in order
to bring the mercenary into full view again.

Vambran was just stumbling onto the sandy shore
of the coastline when Bartimus's magical scrying re-
centered on him.

"Where is that?" Grozier muttered. Bartimus
wasn't sure whether his employer meant that to
be answered or not, but he peered at the stretch of
coastline closely to see if he could determine the
location more precisely. All that he could make out
was a long strip of sandy beach backed by an endless
stretch of trees.

"That's the Nunwood, near Hlath," Falagh said,
pointing at the trees. "That's where my associates
were instructed to attack. It's not a terribly welcoming

stretch of coast, something of a no-man's-land between Reth and Hlath. All the endless skirmishing
that goes on between all the mercenary companies
earning their coin, you know. There's little there but
a few villages and lone cottages, most of them long
abandoned. Oh, and lots of beasts feeding on the dead.
We picked that spot because it was unlikely that
anyone else would see the attack." The man shifted
to look over Bartimus's head more directly at Grozier.
"No witnesses that way."

"Ah," Grozier said as he began to count the number
of figures in the image on the shore. "Well, there are
certainly plenty of folks there now who saw the whole
thing," he said sardonically. "So I guess we have some
witnesses after all."

"Now, look," Falagh said, squaring himself and
folding his arms across his chest. "You asked me to
set up an ambush, to sink a ship. Based on what you
and that pregnant priest told me, nine ships and a
summoned kraken should have been more than
enough. But since you never revealed that Matrell
and his men would be so well prepared for such an
eventuality, it wasn't, and that's just coin wasted. I
do not like wasting coin."

"They're mercenaries! What did you expect?"
Grozier answered, shifting around to stare back at
his guest. "I would have thought someone as clever
as yourself, with all of your experience controlling
trade on the high seas, might have considered such
a possibility. But I suppose that was too much to
hope for."

Bartimus wanted very desperately right then
to scoot his chair back from between the verbally
sparring men and get out of their way, but he saw no
easy method of extracting himself without drawing
even more attention down upon his own head. Grozier was just as likely to demand that he summon

a spell and send it at Falagh as to allow the wizard to excuse himself.

Why can't they go argue somewhere else? he wondered. He glanced over at where Junce still sat, his booted feet stretched out in front of him, one heel balanced atop the other toe, and nervously eyed the sheets scattered about the man's legs.

I'd like to finish that treatise before it gets ruined.

"Gentlemen, please," Junce said, rising to his feet once more. "The deed is done, and there's nothing for it but to move forward." He stepped over so he was between the two men, right behind Bartimus's chair, and clapped each of them on the shoulder. "The important thing is that neither Vambran Matrell nor Kovrim Lazelle is in a position to interfere with your business operations for a while. With them both out of the way, you can move forward with your schemes unhindered. And Lavant shall not be pestered with any more ridiculous meddling within the temple."

The assassin's words seemed to placate the two men, for they both turned back toward the mirror and stopped glaring at one another.

"I suppose we could arrange for further trouble for them," Grozier offered as he continued to watch the scene before him. "If they are on the edge of the Nunwood, they aren't too far from part of our own army. Why don't we send a greeting party to intercept them? Since the region is as forsaken as you say, their deaths inland would seem just as circumstantial as if at sea."

"Now you're thinking!" Junce said jovially. "That's a splendid idea."

As the three men began to discuss the logistics of maneuvering a contingent of mercenaries toward the stranded remnants of the Sapphire Crescent troops, Bartimus took the opportunity to scramble out of his chair and rush over to the scattered pages. He began to gather them up, shuffling them into a neat stack.

Oh, he thought as he tightened the stack, it's neither the treatise *nor* the diagrams. These are those notes on that new spell! I had almost forgotten about that. Now, where did I put the rest of that stack?

The wizard began to rummage through several other loose piles on a table near the bench, hoping to find the remaining notes for the new conjuring magic he had been contemplating. When he found the collection of parchment, he placed the stray pages with it. He was just beginning to reread the opening notes when Grozier interrupted him.

"Bartimus! Get over here and show me where they went!"

The wizard started, and nearly dropped the pages he was holding then took a couple of steps toward the mirror again before he realized that the glass had gone dark and was merely reflecting the dim room.

"I'm terribly sorry, but it would appear that the magic has exhausted itself and is no longer functioning. The properties of any such scrying spell are limited not only by their subject, but also by a time factor, which cannot exceed—"

"Bartimus!" Grozier muttered through clenched teeth, making the mage actually drop his papers that time. "I don't care about the theories. Can you show Vambran Matrell to me again or not?"

Bartimus cringed, trying desperately to decide whether to gather up the mess of notes or to look Grozier in the eye. He chose the middle ground, staring at the floor between them. "No," he said, shaking his head. "Though I could begin preparing for another such casting for sometime this evening, if you'd like.

But alas, I did not consider the possibility that you would want more than one viewing, and I did not prepare my magic twice."

"Very well," Grozier replied, his tone exasperated. "As soon as you can."

"Of course," Bartimus answered, stooping down to gather up his dropped notes once more.

The three other men, no longer in need of the wizard's talents, began to walk toward the door leading out of his chambers.

"Oh, I almost forgot," Grozier began as they reached the door, "I found out that Xaphira is on the prowl, looking for you again. She comes to the city every night from that country estate where they're all hiding out, trying to glean information."

"Is that so?" Junce said as they exited. "I'll bet that's frustrating her," he added with a laugh.

Bartimus the wizard did not hear the assassin's reply, however, for he was already engrossed in his notes on a new conjuring spell.

...

"You two look like you spent the morning stuffed in a box with a bunch of angry cats," Hetta Matrell said as Xaphira and Emriana walked into the dining room together. Their riding clothes were soiled and torn, and Xaphira had dried blood caked on her in several places.

"That's not far from the truth," Xaphira said as she took up a clean platter and began to assemble a meal of boiled eggs in cheese sauce, hard bread, and peach compote. "We ran into three dire-jaguars this morning," she explained.

There were several startled gasps around the table. "Oh, by Waukeen! What happened?" Ladara asked, her hand covering her mouth in alarm.

"Em and I took care of them," Xaphira replied. "She's quite handy with a blade, Ladara."

Ladara made a disapproving sound, but Emriana seemed to beam as she followed her aunt's lead and began to fill her own dish. One of the servants of House Matrell brought a fresh pitcher of chilled milk and set it on the table, along with a couple of thick, clay-fired mugs. The two women slouched down into chairs and began to eat.

"Between the dire-cats and last night," Xaphira said between bites, "I *feel* like I was stuffed into a box that was kicked down the garden steps. Now I remember why I don't run with the old crowds anymore. I can't keep up with them."

"Well, I hope your prowling around was worth it," Hetta said, sipping at a porcelain cup of steaming Amnian tea. The elder dame of the house didn't sound the least bit reproachful, merely concerned.

"It was," Xaphira said, smearing some butter and peach compote onto a thick slice of bread. "Quill might know someone who can tell me more about Junce. I'm supposed to meet with him again tonight to find out for certain."

Marga sighed, wishing she were in another part of the house. She didn't want to hear of Xaphira's plans for tracking down the assassin who worked for Grozier. She blamed her brother and his cronies for Evester's death almost as much as she blamed Evester himself. It was bad enough that they had been trying to start a war—especially for the sole purpose of profiting from it—but the tangle of deceit, murder, and greed that Grozier, Evester, and Denrick Pharaboldi had woven in trying to get their business alliance established went beyond making her sick. It horrified her that her own children would have to live with their father's treacherous legacy.

"Well, you be careful," Ladara Matrell said, sitting next to Hetta. "That Junce Roundface is a dangerous character. The way he almost—" the woman couldn't finish, and she swallowed hard as she reached out and squeezed Hetta's hand. "Even the thought of him roaming around out there frightens me," Ladara said, wide-eyed, in a near whisper.

"Calm yourself," Hetta said, giving her daughter-in-law a level look. "Xaphira has hired some very reliable House guards to replace the fools who let Dregaul and Evester lead them astray. We'll be perfectly safe once we return to the city tomorrow evening."

"Did you say Roundface?" Nimra Skolotti said from where she was sitting at the far end of the table, gazing across the room without really looking at anything. She could not see, but there was nothing wrong with her hearing, it seemed. Her daughter Mirolyn sat beside her, looking as surprised as everyone else that the aged woman had spoken.

Xaphira held a bite of food halfway to her mouth. "Yes," she said, a worried look on her face. "Do you know of him?"

"I'm not sure," Nimra replied, bringing her hand up to rub at her brow, which was furrowed in thought. "It seems familiar somehow, but I can't recall."

Beside her, Mirolyn looked at the rest of the group gathered at the table and shrugged. Despite her lost sight, Nimra still seemed sharp in conversations, and if the elderly woman could shed some light on the mysterious assassin who had been plaguing the family, it would be a great boon. Marga knew she wasn't the only one who realized that. Everyone at the table was watching the woman with intent expressions, too. When Nimra shrugged and said nothing further, everyone resumed eating.

Marga continued to watch Nimra for a moment longer. She felt sorry for the old woman, for she could imagine all too keenly the pain of losing a child. Thinking of trying to cope with the deaths of Obiron and Quindy made a lump form in the woman's throat. She tried to banish such notions, but it was difficult.

"I do hope Vambran is well," Ladara commented, breaking the silence. "It's all so terribly unfortunate that they were ordered away while this unpleasant business of war is still unresolved. And so soon after—" the woman paused, suddenly aware of what she was about to say. She sniffed once, her lip trembling, her eyes rimming red with the beginnings of tears. "I'm sorry," Ladara said, dabbing at her eyes with her napkin while another silent pall settled over the table. "I still miss them so much, whatever their faults."

"It's all right to speak of it," Hetta said, trying to smile disarmingly at her whole family. "We can't pretend they're still here. We must accept it and move on."

There was a moment or two longer of uncomfortable silence.

Finally, Hetta turned back to Emriana and asked, "Have you spoken to Vambran since he left? Any mention of how he and Kovrim are doing?"

Emriana shook her head, fingering the opal pendant that hung around her neck. "I thought about it, but I know he's busy, and I haven't wanted to disturb him. I might contact him this afternoon."

Hetta sniffed. "Well, if I know Kovrim, he's likely as not leaning over the railing of that ship right now." Then, in a more serious tone, the elder matriarch added, "Waukeen, keep them safe. Cimbar is no place to spend the summer, and this summer is liable to be particularly unsettling, if Grozier gets his war."

Marga started at the mention of her brother, but she didn't say anything. She hoped no one noticed her reaction, and she very carefully scanned the room to see. No one was even looking at her.

"And you know that's exactly why Lavant sent them there," Emriana said sullenly. "To get them out of the temple so he could do whatever he does."

That uncomfortable silence threatened to return, but Hetta clicked her tongue. "Enough of this morbid talk. Whatever Grozier is cooking up, it isn't happening right here, away from Arrabar. Or even in Arrabar, for that matter. Sammardach is in two nights. I intend to make certain House Matrell celebrates suitably when we return."

At mention of the impending holy day, almost everyone's face brightened.

"Oh, are we going to attend the ball at the Generon this year?" Emriana asked excitedly, sitting forward in her chair. "I want to see the fountain of dancing coins again!"

"Well, certainly we are," Hetta replied. "And we must discuss what you'll be wearing, child."

As the conversation turned to thoughts of festivals and clothing, Marga excused herself and stood up from the table. She noted that only Xaphira was not eagerly joining in the conversation, and she could guess why. The mercenary's last visit to the palace about twelve years before had not been a pleasant one.

The discussion of subterfuge and impending war, the threats to family, all of those were making Marga struggle to breathe. She felt stifled, as though the warm, humid air were crushing her. She had to get out of there.

Slipping away, she practically ran to her chambers and shut the door behind her. Stumbling across the room, she stepped out onto the balcony that overlooked a portion of the garden where her children normally played. She could see the two figures in the morning sun, huddled together around something obscured from her view. She choked on a sob, watching them.

"Hello, Marga," came a voice from the shadows, back inside the room.

Marga didn't turn around, though her back stiffened at the sound of her brother's words. "What are you doing here?" she asked tiredly. "Someone will spot you."

"Not unless you tell them I'm here," Grozier replied coldly, the warning in his tone more than a hint. "I came to see how my favorite sister was faring," he added more cheerfully.

"Stop it," the woman said, still not facing Grozier. "What do you want?" she demanded.

"Fine," her brother answered. "What news?"

Marga sighed, hating herself for what he was making her do. "We're returning to the city tomorrow night."

Grozier grunted. "That's not news. Tell me something I can use."

"There's nothing more to tell," she answered harshly. "Emriana and Xaphira ran into some beasts in the woods this morning while out riding. Everyone is worried about Vambran and Kovrim. What more do you want?" She felt tears welling in her eyes, tears of anger and shame.

"Stop being difficult," Grozier snapped. "I don't have to remind you—"

"You don't," Marga agreed, cutting him off before he could say the words. "I know what's at stake. I'm helping you, not causing you any trouble. So don't hurt them. Please." The woman still stared down at the two creatures playing in the garden below, her heart aching in terror and sorrow.

"Then just keep feeding me the information, and we'll be the happier for it," Grozier replied. "I do all this for them, too, you realize."

"You do this for yourself and no one else!" Marga cried, turning at last to face her brother. Grozier stood beside the doorway leading back into her chambers. Behind him, Bartimus also stood, with that perpetual foolish grin on his face. Marga had hated the wizard since she had been a child. More than once she had caught him prying into her belongings or simply staring at her. She had no doubt that he had often used magical means to watch her undressing or in her bath—his glances were always too knowing.

"I won't dare refuse you," she said to her brother, ignoring the spectacled wizard behind him, "if it means keeping my children safe, but don't pretend you have their best interests at heart! I can't stomach the lies on top of the threats!"

Grozier didn't say anything. He grinned at Marga, a look that had infuriated her all of her life. Finally, he nodded. "Very well," he said. "Straight and to the point. Now, what else do you have to tell me?"

Marga bit her lip, wishing there were a way to avoid giving the man every bit of news. But there was too much risk that he would find out some other way, and if he realized she had been holding out on him—she didn't want to even consider it.

"Come on, I can see you know something. Tell me." Grozier took his sister by the shoulders and squared her to him, making her look him in the eyes.

Marga's stare was baleful. She hated him for what he was making her do.

"Xaphira seems to know someone who can help her find Junce Roundface," she admitted. "She's returning to the city again tonight to meet with her old friend."

"Oh, really?" Grozier said, letting go of Marga's shoulders and rubbing his chin with one hand. "That's not good." Then he got a wicked look in his eyes. "Or maybe it is," he added, smiling. "She might not be returning this evening, Marga, dear." The man turned to go, and Bartimus stood straighter, reaching for something inside his robes with which to create one of his infernal magical doorways.

"Waukeen, Grozier," Marga said, her voice breaking with humiliation and frustration. "Is there nothing you won't do to get your way?"

Grozier turned and looked back at the woman as Bartimus channeled his arcane energy into a shimmering blue portal in the middle of Marga's room. The wizard stepped through, but Grozier glared at his sister for a moment. "I'll see you in a few days. Be certain you have something interesting to tell me." Then he, too, passed through the doorway. It silently vanished a moment later.

Marga turned back to the railing of the balcony. Anger and helplessness welled up inside her, and she pounded her fist against the stone in fury. Then the tears began to flow. She stared down into the garden, watching the two half-sized creatures playing.

As if sensing her observing them, one of the two looked up at her and smiled.

Marga saw Obiron's face, but then, and for only a moment, it flickered and changed, becoming a featureless gray face on a bulbous head with a spindly body. The thing waved to her, still smiling, but she could sense the mockery behind the gesture. Then it was Obiron again, a laughing child running with his sister through the blossoms and orchards.

Marga wanted to retch.

...

Captain Beltrim Havalla, leader of the Silver Raven Mercenary Company, was reclining his chair back, leaning it and himself against the bole of a large tree, trying to take advantage of the limited shade, when he sensed that someone had arrived. He shifted his weight and looked over his shoulder to spot the visitor. In the midst of the open area where the command tents had been set up, Junce Roundface stood surveying the mercenary camp, his back to Beltrim. The mercenary captain sighed at the assassin's sudden appearance and rose to his feet.

Another good nap wasted, he thought.

"What are you doing here?" Captain Havalla called out as he approached his patron. "We're not due to relocate for three more days, yet." Then his eyes narrowed. "My boys had better not have forgotten to let me know you were coming."

Junce began to shake his head, gesturing for the captain to relax. "I didn't send word ahead of time. This is an impromptu visit."

Beltrim sucked his tongue between his teeth and nodded, relieved that his staff had not failed to deliver any urgent messages to him. "All right, then, what are you doing here?" he asked again as the two began to stroll toward the main tent.

Junce grinned. "Happy to see me?" he asked, obviously amused at the captain's abrupt query.

"I've got no quarrel with you being here," the captain replied, "so long as you keep putting coin in my coffers. I just worry that you're here to make things messy for me and my company. As in, maybe you want to command, too."

Junce's grin grew larger. "I'm not here to step on your authority, Captain Havalla," he said. "I just have a special assignment I want you to take care of. A unique mission, a side trip, if you will."

Beltrim let his own scowl deepen as they reached the opening to the command tent and stepped inside. He wasn't about to tell the man that side trips weren't part of the deal, as Junce—or rather,

whomever Junce was representing—paid well enough
to make even five side trips worthwhile. But sometimes, side trips had a way of turning into campaigns
all their own, and as often as not, they created tacti-
cal problems with the original plan later. As the two
men sat down at a table where numerous maps were
spread out, Beltrim grunted, signaling that Junce
should continue.

"There's a small group of mercenaries, a rival
group, if you will, who just landed on the beach not
far from here. Actually, they walked onto the beach
after their ship went down out in the Reach, but that's
neither here nor there," the assassin added, chuckling
at his own humor. "I need you to go remove them from
the field of battle."

"Mercenaries?" Beltrim asked, letting his scowl
fade away a bit. "What's their name? Whom do they
serve?" He was beginning to like the request more
and more after all. His men had been itching to get
into some sort of engagement for most of a tenday, and
instead they had been forced to make camp, sitting
in reserve to guard a larger force's flank.

"These are elements of the Order of the Sapphire
Crescent," Junce explained, and he began looking
at the topmost map on the table, which showed the
region around Reth. "They're here," he said, pointing
to a spit of land only a couple of miles from where the
Silver Ravens were positioned. "There are perhaps
two dozen of them, maybe a few more."

"What are they doing there?" Beltrim asked, already
beginning to formulate strategy. "How well armed?"

"I told you," Junce answered. "They literally walked
up onto the shore after their ship sank. They have
sufficient magic that I would advise you not to take
them lightly."

Beltrim eyed him appraisingly, trying to measure
the man and his words. Thus far in their business

relationship, Junce Roundface had neither exaggerated anything nor led Captain Havalla astray with misinformation. He was inclined to take the assassin at his word, but then again, there was always a first time for everything.

"All right, I'll get my men moving. But what, exactly, do you want done with them?"

At the question, Junce began to rub his chin thoughtfully. Finally, he said, "Capture as many as you can, and kill anyone who won't surrender. The prisoners, you will relocate to Reth, where I will deal with them myself. But don't let any of them slip through."

"Why are they so important to you?"

"I have my reasons. Suffice it to say that there are members of the group that I have a history with, and I can't afford to have them roaming around the area while we're having our little war."

Beltrim shrugged and nodded. "Good enough for me," he said, rising. "We'll be ready to move out within the hour."

"Good. I knew I could get results with you. That's why I made the pay so generous."

At that comment, Beltrim smiled. "We'll take care of it," the mercenary captain said.

"Good. Now I must beg my leave of you. Many other details to attend to."

As Beltrim nodded his understanding, the man across the table from him stood, gave a quick overly dramatic salute, muttered something unintelligible, and vanished. Beltrim snorted at the brazen display of magic then turned to find one of his aides and get his men rousted.

There was fighting to be done.

CHAPTER 6

The shift in temperature between the outskirts of the Nunwood and the Grand Trabbar's private chambers was abrupt, but Darvin was used to it. As the vista changed from coastal grassland to opulent study before his very eyes, the man couldn't help but smile in satisfaction. His magical boots were one of his most prized possessions, and even after all those years of owning them, he still delighted in their use. They had saved his neck on more than a few occasions, and being able to instantly teleport himself to distant places and back with a thought and a word had given him the upper hand in numerous scrapes over the years.

"I wish you would at least find some closet in which to appear and knock on my doors like a proper guest," Grand Trabbar Lavant muttered, not even looking up from the huge desk where he sat, furiously scribbling on a sheet of parchment. "I like you, but I enjoy my privacy more."

Darvin chuckled. "You would protect your privacy at the cost of having someone see me roaming around your grand temple?" he asked. "Spotting someone such as myself deep in its interior, knocking at your doors, would certainly raise some unpleasant questions, don't you think? How secure would your position be if the other high priests knew that you consorted with the likes of Junce Roundface, known scoundrel?"

Lavant sighed. "Enough. Your point is made. Just do not make a habit of showing up in the dark of night. I might confuse you for a burglar and slay you on the spot." Lavant did look up then, giving his visitor a level stare.

Darvin let the smile slide from his face and stared right back, but he did not say anything. He respected the priest sitting before him, for Grand Trabbar Lavant was nothing if not thorough and exceptionally competent, two qualities he appreciated.

He's just defending his territory, as a dog might, the man told himself. As I would, he had to admit, albeit grudgingly.

"I'll do my level best not to startle you during your beauty sleep," Darvin said with a second chuckle. "Or when you're in the midst of a dalliance with one of the maids," he added.

The Grand Trabbar smirked and rolled his eyes but turned back to his writing. "You obviously appeared out of thin air for a reason. Speak of it."

Darvin strolled over to a side table where a crystal decanter sat on a tray, along with several matching cups. He selected one, removed the stopper from the decanter, and poured a bit of the amber-colored liquid into it. The assassin took a single sip and let the flavors roll about on his tongue. There was a hint of honey there, as well as something like toasted almonds, and it was all overlaid with a smoky burning sensation that tickled his throat as it went down.

"The attack on *Lady's Favor* didn't go quite as Grozier and the others had hoped," Darvin said at last, turning back and crossing over to an overstuffed chair opposite the desk. "They sank her quickly enough, and I'd suspect most of the crew went down with her, but the Crescents were better prepared than Falagh realized and used magic to aid in their survival and escape. I'm not sure what he was expecting, but Grozier was not very happy with Falagh."

"Any determination of Kovrim's and Vambran's fates?" Lavant asked, setting his quill down at last and peering across his desk at the other man.

"Vambran lives, but I am not certain of Kovrim. The wizard could not focus the spell on anyone but Matrell, and we watched him run across the water toward shore. Many of the other men with him did the same thing, but I couldn't tell if Lazelle was among them."

"Perhaps I should have given Falagh Mestel more warning; Kovrim Lazelle is nothing if not resourceful, and I would expect nothing less than for him to supply the troops with all manner of useful magic for just such eventualities as today."

"There is more," Darvin said before taking another sip of his drink. "Grozier decided that some of the army could finish the job the pirates could not. The Crescents made it to shore not far from Reth, and we had a company camping in the vicinity, holding as a reserve force. It seemed like a good idea to me, so I spoke with Captain Havalla only a few moments ago and gave him the orders to move on Vambran and his men. They are breaking camp even now, as we speak."

Lavant cocked his head to one side, considering that latest news. Darvin wondered for a brief moment if the high priest was going to oppose his decision. Lavant's biggest shortcoming, in Darvin's eyes, was a rather infantile need to be in charge, to make all the decisions.

But the high priest only nodded. "That seems reasonable ... if we have the resources, of course. This won't hamper our main objectives there, will it?"

Darvin shook his head. "No. They were not due to shift to the front for three more days, and Beltrim claimed his soldiers were getting restless, anyway. So it was a handy diversion."

"Did you order him to kill them all?"

"No. It occurred to me that we might be able to put a few of them to good use."

"How so?"

Darvin couldn't help but grin at what he was about to say next. "Perhaps as soldiers in our new, improved army."

For the first time since the man known to the rest of the world as Junce Roundface had arrived, Grand Trabbar Lavant got a bit of a gleam in his eye. "How clever of you," he said, smiling. "That would be only too fitting." The rotund priest stroked his chin as he considered the implications of Darvin's suggestion, nodding repeatedly in agreement. "Yes, I like that very much. You will make all of the arrangements?"

"Certainly. I'm glad you found the idea as appealing as I did." Darvin let his smile drop as he prepared to change the subject once more. "Grozier told me that Xaphira Matrell is trying to track me down."

Lavant sniffed. "That doesn't surprise me. She always was a very headstrong girl. But I *would* be very surprised if she were able to make much headway. There are only a handful of people in all

of Arrabar, indeed, in all of Faerûn, who know your
true identity. She's not going to be much of a problem,
so long as you remain out of her sight."

"Now, where's the fun in that?" Darvin said, rising
up to replace his cup with the others next to the decanter. "Truthfully, that was my initial reaction, too.
But then I got to thinking, if she's so intent on finding
me, perhaps I should let her. I see an opportunity to
eliminate her from our little game."

"I don't think that's wise," Lavant said, frowning.
"There's too much at stake, and I need you to run my
errands. *He* needs you," the priest added, giving the
assassin a knowing look. "This has been in motion
for so very long, and now, with it so near to fruition,
we cannot risk any unnecessary accidents. We're
too close."

Darvin shrugged. "But wouldn't it be better to face
her on *my* terms, to lure her into a battlefield of *my*
choosing, rather than risk a chance encounter? If she
were to get lucky and stumble upon information that
could reveal more of me than I care for her to know,
is that not a greater risk? *He* certainly wouldn't like
that happening, you understand."

Lavant sighed, and Darvin was almost certain
it was more because he was making good points
than because he was arguing in the first place. But
regardless of whether his logic was sound, Darvin
was itching for that fight. He'd been itching for it
for more than a decade, actually, and the prospect
of finally seeing it become reality was almost too
much to bear. He knew that Lavant was aware of
that, too, and that the high priest could see right
past his arguments.

That didn't make them any less valid.

"Very well," Lavant said at last. "But be very careful. As I said before, she is a very headstrong girl, and
also very resourceful. Do not let her surprise you."

Darvin couldn't wipe the grin from his face as he nodded. "I think I know just the way to handle it. You know," he began to add, seeing another opportunity and not wanting to let it go to waste. "With Xaphira Matrell out of the way, that would almost certainly be the last obstacle to Grozier's plans with their House. Hetta's a shrewd old bird, but she must rely on her children and grandchildren to do most of the work these days. Without Xaphira to protect her and handle the street work, House Matrell is very vulnerable."

"Indeed," the Grand Trabbar admitted. "But don't let Grozier Talricci get too caught up in his thirst for revenge. If he can consummate a merger between his House and House Matrell without losing sight of the main issue, I'm all for it. But don't let him stray too far from his tasks. We need him to keep funneling coin east."

"I'll be subtle and charming, as always," Darvin said. He rose from his seat and prepared to depart. He knew that if he were going to lay a proper ambush for Xaphira Matrell, he was going to have to speak to a few people, and it was already getting on into afternoon.

"Before you go," Lavant said, picking up the sheet that he had been working on when the assassin had arrived, "have a read."

Darvin took the proffered parchment and began to scan the page. The words made him smile. "Your acceptance speech as the new Grand Syndar? We're not getting ahead of ourselves, are we?" he asked, letting the corners of his mouth curl up the slightest bit. "No one has died and left a vacancy to fill, yet."

"No, but it won't be long," the Grand Trabbar said. "Mikolo Midelli speaks with the Merchant's Friend very clearly now, and he will undoubtedly go to join her in the next day or two. Of course," he added, his

tone full of mock concern, "we're all doing everything
possible, drawing on every conceivable magic, both
divine and arcane, to stave off his passing." Then
the high priest let his voice return to normal and
finished with, "It won't be enough."

"Excellent," Darvin said, feeling no small amount
of pleasure at how smoothly everything was falling
into place. "Tymora smiles upon us, it seems. It's all
been almost too easy."

Lavant grimaced. "Perhaps, but good planning
and a strong investment in the future have been
most instrumental. Our deeds favor the Merchant's
Friend, and she favors our path."

Darvin wanted to laugh at the high priest, for
it was so plain to him that the pudgy man, in his
arrogance and stubborn belief in the goddess he wor-
shiped, could not share credit elsewhere, especially
not with another divine force. The assassin held his
tongue, though, for he saw little benefit in riling up
his accomplice, though the pleasure it would give him
was tempting.

"I have to go," he said instead, handing the parchment back to Lavant. "I have a mercenary pest to
catch, and you have a position within the temple
to fill."

"Remember," Lavant cautioned, "don't underesti-
mate her."

"Not on your life," Darvin replied. "I did once
already. It won't happen again."

...

"How many are with us?" Vambran asked, closing
his eyes and lying back, resting his head against the
rocks where he sat. He could hear the tiredness in his
voice, the devastation, and he knew he needed to fight
through that, to put a strong, decisive face on for the

rest of the men. It was hard, though, not knowing what happened to Kovrim.

"Twenty-three, sir," Horial reported. He stood near where Vambran was resting, on an outcropping of rock that overlooked the beach where the handful of Crescents had made it to shore. "Blangarl and Tholis are in need of healing, but the rest are in fine shape, if a little tired."

"Twenty-three," Vambran repeated. "We lost nearly half," he lamented, feeling defeated. "So many." He sat there for a long moment, wondering how many were still out there somewhere, lost, and how many had died.

Or perhaps had gone to some mysterious place deep beneath the waves, he thought wistfully.

Either way, Vambran doubted he would see them again. He let the sorrow of that notion course through him, grieving for every single one of the men and women he would never speak to, would never fight alongside again. Then he sighed and sat up, opening his eyes once more and turning toward Horial. "You have a full accounting of each one missing?" he asked solemnly.

The sergeant nodded. "Adyan is making a list right now," he said. "I'll have him give you a report when he's finished."

Vambran nodded. "How are we doing on supplies?" he asked, changing the subject. Better to deal with what we can control and stop worrying about what we can't, he told himself.

"Thin," Horial replied. "Most of the troops have some sort of weapon, but we are short on bolts, and four are unarmed other than with a personal blade such as a dagger or something similar. Other than that, we've got very little. Almost no one was carrying a pack when the attack occurred, so most of our provisions sank."

Marvelous, Vambran thought silently. "Food?" he asked.

Horial shook his head. "Almost none," he replied. "Foraging shouldn't be a problem, but hunting might be troublesome, with the shortage of ammunition. Of course, some of the men are pretty handy with a sling, so they figure they can make do that way. I've got them gathering stones from the beach right now. Otherwise, we may have to rely on Waukeen's bounty."

Vambran nodded. "If it comes to that, I'll be prepared for the castings. Do we have much of an idea where we are?"

Horial opened his mouth to reply, but a shout from down on the beach cut him off. Both men rose up to peer down onto the sandy shore and saw several Crescents pointing and running. Vambran turned in the direction to which the soldiers' attention had been drawn and spotted a number of mounted figures riding along beyond the perimeter of the beach, near the edge of the forest, coming toward them. They were armed with bows and crossbows, and most of them wore livery of white with some sort of black or possibly silver insignia on it. They were too far away for Vambran to make it out clearly. The figures were strung out, in a long and loose line, and they seemed to be moving warily in the direction of the Crescents' position.

"Scouts," Vambran said as his sergeant began to scramble down the rocks toward the sand below. "Get the men to form up, Horial. Quickly! Double wing formation, backs to these rocks!"

The sergeant scampered down off the outcropping, moving away from Vambran. As he reached the flats of the beach, Horial began shouting orders to the milling soldiers.

Vambran stayed behind, using the superior vantage point to keep watching the scouts maneuver.

Already, Vambran could see more figures in the distance, an orderly column of soldiers marching in his direction from farther along the beach. There were a lot of them, and Vambran found himself wishing he still held his spyglass, so he could get a better look, but like so much else, the lieutenant had lost it among the waves of the Reach during the ship battle.

On impulse, Vambran turned and clambered over a few jagged projections until he was in position to peer in the opposite direction. As he feared, the mercenary officer spotted another group of troops moving toward him from that direction. Again, mounted soldiers led the way, moving in a line right along the edge of the forest. They were light cavalry, the lieutenant realized, strung out to dissuade the Crescents from making a break for the trees, holding Vambran and his troops in place so they could be caught between the two groups of infantry marching from either side.

Damn! They knew we were here, he reasoned, furious at himself for not sending scouts of his own out sooner. Then Vambran's eyes narrowed in suspicion. They knew we were here because they're serving the same curs who sent the pirates against us. The lieutenant's sudden insight made his stomach churn.

No time for worrying about that now, he thought, turning and rapidly working his way back across the rocky point so he could join his men. We're going to get slaughtered if we don't get out of this trap.

Once down on the sand, Vambran sprinted toward the formation he had ordered, which he saw was already formed up. Men armed only with blades were positioned in the middle in a single tight rank, while those with crossbows took up spots on either flank, spaced out a bit more. With only twenty-three men, the formation was pitifully small.

When he joined his soldiers, Vambran knew
what they had to do, and he didn't hesitate for a
moment. "Crescents!" he said, running into a position in front of his troops, turning his back to the
enemy for a moment and facing the remains of his
company. "We're pinned between two larger forces,
coming from either direction." Vambran gestured
both ways along the beach. "This is a lawless land
where anyone you meet is an enemy until proven
otherwise. Their intentions are clear, and there are
too few of us to stand and fight. Once again, I must
ask you to retreat from the battle, though I know it
leaves a foul taste in your mouths to do so." There was
some muted rumbling among the men and women
formed up in front of Vambran, but he held up his
hand for silence.

"We'll make a break for the trees," he said, pointing behind himself. "Keep together as much as you
can because we're going to have to plow through their
skirmish line to get to the woods. They are mounted,
but they are strung out enough that we ought to be
able to punch a hole through them and melt into
the forest. Once there, we can use the cover to our
advantage and convince these bastards to go find
easier pickings elsewhere." A handful of encouraging
shouts issued forth, but most of the twenty-three were
subdued, silent.

Knowing that delaying any longer would cost
them opportunity, Vambran wasted no more time.
He nodded to Horial, who issued the order for the
troops to begin moving forward. Initially the Crescents moved in a smooth, cohesive block, with the
center portion remaining in a straight line and the
flanks, the crossbowmen, trailing out to either side,
so that the whole formation appeared to be something
of a blunt-nosed wedge, moving right toward the thin
line of skirmishers.

As they drew closer to the tree line, Vambran saw
that the lead soldiers among the cavalry had met
up, closing the line, and several had dismounted and
turned toward the advancing Crescents. He saw the
archers among the enemy begin to bunch together
in front of them, preparing for the confrontation.
To either side, the marching columns were also de-
ploying, spreading out into lines and beginning to
advance more quickly, hurrying to cut the Crescents
off before they could defeat the more lightly armed
skirmishers and slip away.

It would be close.

Vambran began to realize his miscalculation as
soon as the first magical effects materialized among
his troops. It naturally occurred to him that some
among the enemy would be able to draw upon magic
to aid them, as he often did himself, but he had not
expected them to be concentrated so heavily among
the mounted skirmishers. But it made sense, he realized, for they could wield their magic from afar
and on the move, much in the same way they often
engaged the troops from a distance with their ranged
weaponry. Plus, the lieutenant realized, they might
have expected the Crescents to make a run for the
forest and needed to be prepared for it.

All of that understanding of military theory did
nothing to change the fact that Vambran's plan to
break for the trees was being thwarted. In the very
center of the line, the coarse sea grass that grew heavily in the sand came alive, growing and squirming
about, wrapping tendrils of plant fiber around the
soldiers' feet. Several men went down, thoroughly en-
tangled in the animated, writhing growth that had a
hold of them. As they tumbled into the sand, more of
the greenery latched on, pinning them helplessly.

At another point, on the left flank where the
crossbowmen moved obliquely, the ground seemed

to become as slippery as a lard-coated floor, causing
several more Crescents to stumble and fall to the
ground. They scrabbled about, trying to find some
purchase on the greasy, slimy terrain, but it was
pointless. They could not maneuver effectively at
all and fell behind.

"Keep moving!" Vambran ordered. "Run!" He hated
the words as soon as they issued from his mouth, but
the lieutenant understood the tactic all too well and
realized he couldn't save everyone. To stop and aid
the other men would only allow the larger forces to
close in and cut them all off.

Just like in the water, Vambran lamented. Damn
you, Lavant!

The remaining Crescents began to charge the
skirmishers' position, and Vambran sprinted along
with them, peering ahead. Beside the mercenary
officer, three soldiers stumbled and dropped to the
ground, apparently unconscious—or asleep, Vambran
decided. He considered stooping down and trying to
wake them, but he had already given the order not
to pause, and he knew hesitating would only mean
his capture or death. His heart heavy for the fate of
the three, Vambran pressed on. He tried not to think
of their names, their families, as he moved away. He
shoved the knowledge to the back of his mind as he
fled. He could grieve later.

When a wave of fear washed over Vambran, he
was able to maintain his composure and ignore it,
but two more soldiers on either side of him froze in
mid-step, turned, and fled back the way they had
come. Even as he lamented the loss of two more
devoted members of the company, Vambran spotted
the spellcaster responsible for the magic. The man
was still mounted and was issuing orders as he prepared another incantation. The lieutenant stopped
momentarily, bringing his crossbow up. He had only

a handful of bolts, having received a share from the remaining ammunition, but he did not hesitate to use it. The cord on his weapon was fresh and dry, and the missile flew true, striking the spellcaster squarely in the chest. The man let out a panicked scream and clutched at the bolt. He lurched in the saddle, drawing back on his reins such that his mount spun away awkwardly, dropping him to the ground.

Vambran ran on.

Other members of the company had slowed in order to fire a bolt or two in the direction of the enemy line blocking their path to the trees, and the missile fire was doing its work well. Already Vambran could see that three or four skirmishers were down, and numerous riderless horses milled about in their midst. The rest of the lightly armed soldiers were moving aside, unwilling to stand before the charging remnants of the Crescents' double-wing formation.

Vambran felt a missile of some sort whistle past his head as he rushed toward the cover of the trees, and when he was a few paces from the initial foliage, one of the skirmishers loomed up before him, a staff held out in both hands threateningly. The other soldier was sallow-skinned, his facial features long and narrow. Absently, Vambran guessed he might have been from the plains of the Shaar. He monitored the man's stance warily as he rushed toward his enemy, and just when the skirmisher shifted and began to bring the staff around to swipe at the lieutenant's head, Vambran altered his direction and lowered his shoulder.

The maneuver sent Vambran plowing into his opponent, who managed to get a single, feeble strike in against Vambran's back, the blow made ineffectual by both his breastplate and the too-close distance between the two. As the lieutenant collided with his adversary, he heard the other man's breath leave his body in a rush, and the pair tumbled across the ground haphazardly.

Vambran wanted to yank his dagger free and deal a killing blow to the skirmisher, but there was no time. Already the main force to his left had closed to within bow range, and a hail of arrows was dropping down among the straggling Crescents behind him. In another few moments, the troops would be on him and his men, and there wouldn't be enough time to disappear into the depths of the forest. Instead of finishing the man off completely, Vambran rolled to his feet again and rushed on, leaping over the heavy underbrush that marked the very fringe of the tree line.

As he crashed into the bushes and began to push through into the taller trees, vines and branches began whipping at Vambran and enveloping him, trying to ensnare him.

Waukeen! he thought, desperately yanking his arms and legs free and trying to surge forward. Can't get hung up here! Must get to cover!

Vambran could hear the frustrated shouts of other members of his company, all around him in the heavy undergrowth, as well as the sounds of enemy soldiers gathering just beyond the edge of the trees. The proximity of the infantry forces closing in lent a desperate fervor to his efforts, but Vambran was unable to make any headway through the enchanted plants.

In one last panicky effort, Vambran managed to yank one arm free. He reached up and took hold of the medallion hanging from the chain on his neck and spoke a beseeching prayer to Waukeen for strength. Immediately, the lieutenant felt a surge of energy course through his limbs, and with his newfound power, he succeeded in breaking free of the worst of the grasping, coiling tendrils of plant growth. He lunged forward, each step a superhuman effort, and finally, he was able to slip beyond the range of the enchanted growth and dart deeper into the forest.

Vambran turned after a dozen or so steps and peered back toward the open ground. He could see several soldiers, armed with crossbows and a variety of bladed weapons, pushing into the trees where he had just been. One of the men spotted him and shouted a warning to the rest, but as they neared the edge of the writhing, clutching plant life, they had to hold up, and they instead chose to shoot at him from where they stood. Vambran turned and slipped away, darting behind the first thick tree trunks to evade their missiles.

As Vambran moved deeper into the forest, the shadowtops that predominated the woods became taller and thicker, their high branches forming a heavy canopy that left him in gloomy dimness. The area around the base of the trees became more open and easily traversed, for little undergrowth could gain the sunlight needed beneath those towering shadowtops.

Knowing he was moving in more open terrain made the lieutenant wary, and he cocked his crossbow and kept a watchful eye all around. At one point, he heard the soft, rustling sounds of movement to his left, but he could not see anyone. Unsure of whether it was friend or foe flanking him, Vambran gave a whistle, a birdcall he had taught his company to signal one another. The answering whistle came back, and Vambran angled his progress in that direction.

After a few more strides, he came upon two other members of the company. Burtis was sitting, his back against the bole of a tree, a nasty gash in his thigh. Filana, one of the handful of women who served in

the Crescents, was kneeling down as though she had
been tending to the wound. Both of them had their
crossbows leveled at Vambran as he approached, but
when they realized who it was, the relief on their
faces was clear.

Vambran gave a signal for continued silence
then motioned that he would circle their position
and watch for any others approaching. Both of his
soldiers nodded, and Filana returned her attention to
the gash. The lieutenant set out again, making wide
circles around the central position where Filana and
Burtis were, and it did not take him long to spot and
signal other members of the group to join him.

After only a few moments, Vambran had half
a dozen mercenaries gathered at the tree. In addition to the pair he had already found, Vambran
managed to round up Horial and Adyan, the two
sergeants from his own platoon, as well as the gold
dwarf Grolo Firefist, who was a sergeant for the
other platoon in his company. The last mercenary
who had made it into the woods was a young man
named Elebrio, who had just joined the Crescents
earlier that summer.

Together, the seven of them huddled together
next to the tree, waiting and watching Vambran for
some sign of what they should do next. The lieutenant
stared back at each of them, feeling numb. From forty
men that morning, his command had been reduced to
six. Each face reflected that same sense of loss he was
feeling. Each person, standing shoulder to shoulder
with what was left of their company, seemed shaken
and defeated. Vambran felt anguish, as though he
had somehow let them all down. He had led them
into the disasters of the ship attacks and the ambush
on the beach.

No! He silently insisted, realizing that letting
those doubts fester would only further damage the

chances they had at survival. Lead them now; accept responsibility for your failures later. If they'll let you lead them, he added dismally.

"Lieutenant?" Horial queried, giving his superior an expectant look.

Understanding that his sergeant was trying to give him an opening to assert himself, Vambran nodded. "Scout back along our trail," he said at last, looking at Horial, beginning to think about strategy rather than his own wretched sense of gloom. "They haven't entered the woods in force, yet, but they will as soon as they can clear out their own magical traps." The sergeant nodded and crept off. Vambran turned back to the rest of his group. "Be ready to move out at a moment's notice," he said.

"Sir?" Adyan said, a nervous look in his eye. When Vambran motioned for the sergeant to speak, he drawled, "You're not planning to cross these woods, are you?"

Vambran sighed heavily. "Not if I can help it," he answered at last. "But there's an army between us and freedom, and we may not have a choice."

"That means leaving the rest behind," Grolo said flatly.

Vambran raised an eyebrow at the dwarf. "Yes, it does," he said. "What's your point?"

"No point, sir," Grolo answered. "I just wondered what your intentions are regarding the rest of them."

"We're seven to a hundred, not good odds. But my intentions are to rescue them," Vambran said.

Not a one of the mercenaries spoke, but Vambran could tell from the determined looks on each of the five soldiers' faces that they still believed in him, were ready to follow him into battle. Especially to save companions. That, if nothing else, gave him hope.

At that moment, Horial slipped back into view. "They're mustering a large sweeping force and entering the tree line," he reported. "It looks like they're coming after us."

"Then the rescue has to wait," Vambran said. "On your feet. We're going deeper into the woods."

With one look back, Vambran set out. He hoped he wasn't taking his remaining command into more trouble.

CHAPTER 7

The first sensation Kovrim Lazelle became
aware of was a steady, painful throbbing in his head, centered on a spot on
the back side of his skull. After that, the
priest became conscious of numerous other
aches throughout his body, as though he
had been beaten and battered by a gang of
club-wielding thugs. He groaned and began
to move his arms gingerly, feeling gritty, wet
sand beneath the palms of his hands. The
sounds of the surf crashing against a nearby
shore brought the man to full awareness,
and he began to remember bits and pieces
of his plight.

Images of great tentacles and a shat-
tering ship flashed in his mind's eye, and
Kovrim remembered trying desperately to
scramble to the deck, stumbling as part of

the flooring beneath his feet cracked in two. As the planking all around him began to snap and split, the priest saw sunlight and seawater rushing at him, and . . . nothing more. Somehow, he had drifted or was dragged to shore.

Kovrim opened his eyes and blinked at the bright, glaring sun shining in his face; then he rolled over, away from the intense light, and tried to sit up. The motion nearly made him retch, and he sank back down, closing his eyes again and panting. His head felt swollen and filled with cotton, and the pain radiated down to his gut, making him queasy. He just wanted to find a quiet, shady place where he could drift back off to sleep, but he knew the risks of remaining exposed too long to the heat of the sun. Taking a deep, calming breath in the hopes that the fresh air would settle his stomach, the priest tried again to sit up, reaching back with one hand to feel gingerly at the painful lump at the base of his skull. Something had walloped him pretty hard, he decided.

Squinting, Kovrim began to peer around and discovered that he was on a beach, right at the edge of the tide line. The waves that tumbled to shore rolled up to a point just a pace or two from his feet, and he could see twin drag lines from there in the drier sand. Someone had brought him to that point. With one hand shading his eyes, the priest began to examine the beach more closely, noting the rough, rocky ground just above the sandy stretch, and beyond that, he could see the tops of a line of trees that stretched as far in either direction as he could look.

There seemed to be no one else around.

Kovrim attempted to rise to his feet and almost regretted the move, as he swayed unsteadily, feeling the pounding increase in his head. He stood very still for several seconds, letting the queasiness subside, and he reached down to his belt and checked a pouch. Thankfully, the potion he had stored there when the Crescents had begun their journey aboard *Lady's Favor* was still safely tucked inside. He drew forth the small vial, pulled the stopper free, tipped his aching head back, and downed the contents. The familiar fiery flavors of pepper oil and burnt meat cascaded down his throat, but he ignored the taste and waited for the effects. A moment later, as he felt the concoction settle in his belly, Kovrim also felt the pain in his skull and joints ease away. Though the potion did not assuage every little stab of hurt, it was enough to relieve the pounding in his head, and he sighed in profound relief and recapped the vial, then tucked it away again.

Once he felt better, Kovrim began to make his way up the beach, toward the line of trees. If nothing else, the blessed coolness of shade was going to be a welcome change. The priest had taken perhaps a dozen steps or so when movement from ahead of him caught his eye. He stopped and peered toward the tree line, trying to get a better view, and he half smiled in relief as he noted a man dressed in the white and blue of the Crescents moving there, crouched over and studying the ground.

Not wanting to draw undue attention to the two of them in case there were threats nearby, Kovrim did not call out, but instead started walking again, intending to catch up to his compatriot. As he drew closer, he noted the identity of the soldier, a younger man named Velati Fenisio, an eager fellow who had signed on with the company in the spring. The trip aboard *Lady's Favor* to Chessenta had been Velati's first assignment.

A fine way to begin his soldiering career, Kovrim thought wryly.

The priest could see that Velati was rooting around in the grass, and as he got closer to the young man, he realized that Velati was foraging for tubers that grew wild in the underbrush. The young mercenary already had an armload full when he turned and spotted Kovrim moving toward him.

A smile broke across Velati's face, and he waved to the priest. "I got you as far out of the surf as I could, then I went looking for food," he said brightly, heading back down onto the beach to join Kovrim.

The priest felt his knees growing wobbly and sank down onto a bit of stone just the right height to serve as an impromptu seat. "Where are we?" Kovrim asked as Velati moved to stand beside him.

Velati shrugged. "Not sure," he said as he dumped the armload of roots to the ground at the older man's feet. "Wherever we are, there's no one else around," he added, settling onto the ground next to Kovrim.

Kovrim closed his eyes and took several long, slow breaths, still feeling weak from his ordeals. His stomach rumbled, a typical aftereffect of magical healing. He eyed the tubers eagerly, almost not even caring that they were still raw and dirt-covered.

No, he admonished himself. Must cook them first, or you'll be squatting in the bushes for the rest of the day.

"Do you have any water?" Kovrim asked the soldier, noting ruefully that his own waterskin had apparently vanished.

"Yes, sir," Velati replied, handing a nearly bulging skin over. "Drink up."

Kovrim took the skin gratefully and tipped it to his mouth, drawing several large mouthfuls and gulping them down. The liquid, though warm, did almost as much to soothe the priest's discomfort as the healing draught had. Finally, he handed the skin back to Velati with a nod.

"So, how did we get here?" Kovrim asked the younger mercenary. "Where are the rest of the Crescents?" Surely they didn't all go down with the ship, he thought, remembering the tentacles and feeling cold in the pit of his stomach. "Where is Vambran?" The fact that he and the young man appeared to be alone on the stretch of beach worried the priest. Then he shook his head, dismissing his pessimistic notions.

Vambran can take care of himself, Kovrim thought. He doesn't need me to look out for him.

Velati shrugged then said, "Lieutenant Matrell gave the order to drink our water-walking potions, and the ship was being ripped apart by that . . . that thing." He shuddered then seemed to regain his composure. "I got thrown into the water when *Lady's Favor* split in half, and you splashed into the drink near me, out cold. I heard the order to retreat, but there were two ships between us and shore, so I hid both of us among some debris until no one was watching, and I began to drag you away from the fight. I had to swing wide of the area to avoid the pirates, and about halfway to shore, the magic of the potions wore out." At that point in his tale, the young man looked forlorn. "I had to remove your breastplate and let it sink, sir," he said ruefully. "I'm terribly sorry, but it was the only way I could keep us both afloat after that."

Kovrim gave the young man a half smile and waved away the apology. "You did fine," he said, though he lamented the loss of the enchanted armor, for it had served him well in campaigns many seasons before, and he had grown quite fond of it.

Nothing to be done about it now, he thought. And I'm alive, so no sense making the lad feel worse than he already does. I just pray that Vambran and the others made it to shore, too. It's a long coastline, and the tide is strong; they're probably just farther along, out of sight somewhere.

"So you swam to shore and pulled me along with you?" Kovrim asked, changing the subject. He was genuinely impressed with the younger man's prowess.

"Yes, sir," Velati replied, beaming. "I was almost done for by the time we reached the shallows. It's a good thing it wasn't rocky along this stretch of coast, or we might both have wound up feeding the fish."

Kovrim nodded, rubbing his chin. "Well, we've got to try to find the rest of the men, soldier," he said, rising to his feet. "No time for eating right now, though those tubers look mighty tasty. Bring them along, though, and we'll see if we can't enjoy them later."

The priest was on the verge of squatting down beside the younger man to help him gather up the food when he saw movement in the distance. He turned in that direction, farther along the beach, and noted several men approaching. In the bright sunlight, it was clear that they were soldiers, though they were not members of the Order of the Sapphire Crescent. Kovrim could not distinctly make out the insignia, but he did not like the look of things.

"Velati," he said as the men spotted him and began to fan out in an obvious maneuver of hostility. The younger man stood up and turned his attention in the direction Kovrim was looking then sucked in his breath. Kovrim began to count figures moving toward them and realized there were at least a dozen. Beside him, Velati pulled his sword free of its scabbard.

"Easy, son," Kovrim said, placing a hand on his companion's arm to calm him down. "There are too many of them," he said. He could feel the younger man's muscles tense and relax as he slipped the blade down again.

"Yes, sir," Velati said dismally.

The enemy soldiers closed the distance and moved to flank Kovrim and Velati, several of them with bows and crossbows out and ready. By that point, the priest could see that the insignia on their uniforms was of a silver raven. He did not recognize it, but he certainly understood that they viewed the two Crescents as potential threats.

"Throw down your arms!" one of the men called out, gesturing at Kovrim and Velati.

Kovrim spread his arms wide to show that he was not attempting to threaten his foes. His crossbow had never made it out of his room when *Lady's Favor* had been attacked, and he carried no other weapons.

Beside him, Velati stiffened again, yanking his blade free in a rush and taking a single, sudden step forward.

"No!" Kovrim shouted, trying to stop the younger man from his foolishness, but the priest wasn't fast enough. He heard the unmistakable twang of several bows firing, and right before him, three missiles lodged in Velati's chest. The young man jerked and stumbled as Kovrim flinched away, fearful that he, too, would be struck by overly eager bowmen. No shots hit him, though, and he turned back to see Velati lying facedown, blood pooling beneath his twisted, still form.

"Damn you!" Kovrim shouted, moving over to where the younger man lay. "Velati!" he shouted, gingerly turning the young man onto his back. Velati's eyes were wide with pain, but he still breathed. Sighing in relief, Kovrim looked up at his potential captors, more specifically at the man who had ordered their surrender. "I'm going to heal him, nothing more," he said, reaching in his tunic for the symbol of Waukeen he kept on a chain around his neck. "I'm no threat to you," he said carefully, hoping the other man would understand.

The soldier eyed Kovrim warily and motioned for him to hold. "No," he said, shaking his head. "You will come with us."

"But he's going to die!" Kovrim shouted, furious. "I'll disarm him first, if that's what you want, but you can't let him perish for one foolish, youthful mistake."

"He made his choice, and now you must make yours, old man," the soldier said, scowling. "If you do anything other than stand up and surrender to us right now, you will be left here to die, too."

Stunned, Kovrim eyed the other soldier, refusing to move. He couldn't believe that a mercenary would be so callous as to let another soldier die, enemy or not. The code of war that most companies in the Reach fought by precluded such barbarous acts. "You can't mean it," he said at last, watching the man's face for some sign of his real intentions.

"I do, and we will," the soldier replied. "Now stand up. It's your last warning."

Kovrim shook his head, still unwilling to leave Velati to bleed to death. The young man's breathing had grown more rapid and shallow, and it was becoming moist. There wasn't much time left.

At that point, another soldier standing next to the leader who had been speaking moved next to his companion and whispered something in the man's ear. The speaker jerked his gaze around to look at the second fellow and shook his head, and there seemed to be a quick argument. Finally, the second mercenary shrugged and moved back to his spot as the speaker scowled for a moment.

"I've changed my mind," the speaker said at last. "You will hold perfectly still while my men search your companion and rid him of any weapons. Only then will you be allowed to heal him. But if I sense even one false move on your part, if I see the barest hint of you casting your magic at me or any of my men, you'll be sporting so many arrows that you'll look like a seamstress's pincushion. Do you understand?"

Kovrim nodded and rocked back on his heels, motioning for his captors to do their work quickly. He sat very still as the men surrounding him drew beads on him. Two soldiers trotted forward, removed Velati's sword from the young man's grasp, and tossed it well out of reach. They did the same with a pair of daggers and they thoroughly searched Kovrim. Once they were satisfied that neither mercenary had anything more hidden, they stepped back.

Kovrim gave the leader an expectant glance, one eyebrow raised. The other man nodded once, and the priest moved close to Velati and began to pray, his hands roaming over the wounds, the arrows and bolts still imbedded in his flesh. Feeling the surge of magic inside him, Kovrim yanked one of the missiles free just as he applied the healing orison.

Velati jumped and issued a half-strangled cry of pain, but the gaping hole in his ribs sealed itself in a moment more. Sighing with relief that the young soldier had survived that first attempt, Kovrim applied a second spell, and a third, withdrawing the weapons a split second before finishing the magic. By the third such healing, Velati was gasping and clutching at his body, obviously still in pain but stable enough to remain conscious.

"Now, you foolish boy," Kovrim said when he was finished, "you will do exactly as I say, or I will let these men kill you and be done with your ridiculous notions of heroics. Is that clear?"

Velati looked at Kovrim, licked his lips in fear and relief, and nodded.

"Good," Kovrim said, backing away and holding his hands up to show that he was not doing anything else untoward. "I'm finished," he said to all within range. "He will need help walking, though. He's still very weak."

"That will be your job, then," the leader said. "Now give me that coin around your neck and get him on his feet."

Reluctantly, the priest removed his holy coin and tossed it toward the mercenary leader. Then he helped Velati up so the young man could stand with Kovrim's help.

"Let's go," the man said, motioning for his two prisoners to begin walking back the way they had come.

As the pair of Crescents began to march in the direction they had been ordered, Kovrim spotted a large column of soldiers, all of them wearing the same silver raven insignia that his captors displayed, coming down the beach in their direction. He frowned, wondering why an entire mercenary company would be in the middle of nowhere.

"Where, pray tell, are you taking us, and why are you treating us as hostiles?"

"My orders were to capture as many of you as I could. Anyone who refused to surrender, I was to kill. I didn't question why. Now be quiet."

Kovrim shrugged but nodded. As he walked along, helping Velati keep a steady pace, he considered why someone would have issued such orders to the men escorting them. It didn't seem likely that they would have known the Crescents would be there—unless *they are in league with the pirates,* he realized. *Perhaps they are working for the same people. But who?*

Then the priest's eyes narrowed. *Lavant,* he thought. *To get me and Vambran out of the way. Why else would I have been ordered to serve as quartermaster at my age?*

The thought that the Grand Trabbar would go to such lengths to eliminate threats made Kovrim's blood run cold. He knew that the high priest had influence, and the evidence he had found suggested that Lavant was putting together an army. But the notion that he would sink an entire ship and destroy a whole company of mercenaries just so he could get two men out of the way was astonishing.

If Lavant ordered our deaths, Kovrim thought, then it's only a matter of time before these men, or those they answer to, realize who I am and try to finish the job.

As the priest considered that, he began to go over other options in his mind. Even without his holy coin, he still had magic at his disposal that could aid him in his escape. But Velati did not, and there was nothing Kovrim could do to assist him that way. No, Kovrim decided, I'll stay with him until there's no other choice. But did I save him only to let him die later?

With such a realization fresh in his mind, Kovrim's thoughts turned once again to his nephew. He wanted to hold out hope that Vambran had somehow escaped, that he had been resourceful enough to evade the pirates and reach the shore, but he feared the worst. The attacks on *Lady's Favor* and the number of troops scouring the beach were so powerful, had been so well coordinated, that it hardly seemed possible that any Crescent had managed to escape.

Kovrim prayed he was wrong.

...

As Vambran moved stealthily through the trees, nearing the edge of the forest, he could hear the sounds of a large gathering of troops, just beyond sight. He picked his steps carefully, trying to avoid

snapping twigs or rustling leaves, but he knew
he was no woodsman, and every time he scuffed
his feet, the lieutenant held his breath, waiting
for sentries to come charging through the underbrush toward him. They did not. Finally, when he
reached a point where he could begin to see beyond
the ground cover that marked the boundary of the
forest proper, he crouched down behind the trunk of
one of the last sizeable shadowtops and just listened
for a few moments.

The typical sounds of an army wafted through the
screen of plant life toward him, of some men shouting
orders and others laughing. He could hear the sounds
of horses whinnying, and those of wagons creaking.
The one sound he did not hear, thankfully, was that of
prisoners being tortured. He hoped it was not because
they had taken no prisoners.

It was growing toward dusk. The seven remaining Crescents had spent the better part of the day
evading the enemy forces, and though the army had
been thorough, its command had seemed reluctant
to drive too deeply into the interior of the forest.
Only after his foes had given up and returned to
open ground had Vambran crept back to the edge of
the woods to scout. The other Crescents had orders
to remain well away from the border. If he didn't
get back to them by nightfall, they were to march
through to the other side and get back to Arrabar
as best as they could.

He decided that he had to get closer, see what he
could determine of the fate of the Crescents who had
not escaped into the woods. He considered trying to
sneak into the perimeter of the gathering, but he dismissed that idea again. There would be sentries. If
the mercenary officers of that army were worth their
salt, they would know that the few who had escaped
might at least try to rescue their companions, and

the soldiers would be ready. Vambran did not like the idea of getting caught by himself in the open, where a handful of spellcasters could easily overwhelm him. There had to be other options.

An idea came to him. Only a few days before setting out upon *Lady's Favor*, Vambran had become aware of a new arcane trick he could perform. The concept seemed to come on him without warning or thought, as a flash of inspiration. He understood what he would need to do to conjure the magic, and it would happen.

He began to rummage around in a small pouch on his belt, producing a tiny vial with a wax-coated stopper. The container held a bit of black, sticky substance. He squatted down and stirred his finger through the dead leaves and other debris at the base of the tree, looking carefully. When he overturned a small stone, a small brown spider scurried out from its disturbed hiding place, and Vambran snatched it up.

Vambran still found the intuitive nature of his arcane power unsettling, but he ignored the sensation and did what came naturally. Eyeing the spider for a moment, he steeled himself and tossed it in his mouth, and followed that by unstoppering the vial and dripping a bit onto his tongue. Ignoring the foul taste of the tarry substance and the wriggling of the spider, the lieutenant swallowed both at once then uttered a phrase that had popped into his head only a few tendays ago.

He waited a moment. Then, when he was certain the magic had taken effect, Vambran turned and began to climb the tree behind which he had been hiding. It was remarkably easy, as he found he could scamper along the surface of the trunk as a spider might, traveling straight up to the top almost as quickly as he could walk the forest floor. When he reached the first branches high in the tree, he stopped and peered out from behind the trunk toward where he believed the mercenary army to be.

Vambran had chosen a good tree, for it was one of the last really tall ones that bordered the woods, and from that vantage point, he could see beyond its sheltering leaves to well beyond the limits of the forest. The army was arrayed below him, groups of soldiers milling about, as though waiting for the order to move out. By Vambran's judgment, there appeared to be perhaps one hundred foot soldiers and half that many cavalry. It was not an overly large force, but certainly sizeable enough to overwhelm the company of Crescents he had commanded, even at full strength.

In a small depression in the land surrounded by armed guards, numerous members of the Crescents sat. They were huddled together, perhaps talking, but it was clear that they were prisoners, for their captors watched them carefully, bowmen with their weapons held casually but ready, and others with swords or axes also watching.

Vambran was both relieved and angry. He wished once again that he had his spyglass with him, so he might get a closer look and determine who was there, but it would be difficult to see faces very clearly in the fading light of day. He could, however, count the figures gathered on the ground, and it appeared that there were approximately two dozen Crescents altogether. That number made him smile, for it meant that others who had not managed to join him on the beach had survived the sinking of *Lady's Favor*. Even if they were prisoners, at least they were alive.

For the moment, anyway, Vambran thought. The pirates certainly weren't interested in taking prisoners. If these soldiers answer to the same masters as the corsairs did, then they must have orders to slay the Crescents, too. But then, why hadn't they?

Vambran considered that bit of information, wondering if his previous assessment had been faulty. Perhaps the mercenary army was not operating under the same guidance as the pirates. Perhaps the Crescents had been in the wrong place at the wrong time. No, that seemed almost as illogical. Something was going on, but he could not yet piece it together.

In due time, he thought. In due time.

Vambran spent a few moments more in the tree, peering as best he could at his men huddled under the watchful eyes of their guards, trying to make out faces despite the distance and growing darkness. He realized he could pick out a few after all, though not all of them were looking in his direction. There was no sign of Kovrim, however, and it was fast growing too dark.

The lieutenant was just about to scurry back down the tree and return to his companions deeper in the forest when the activity of the mercenary army suddenly changed. He could hear orders being shouted, and the soldiers formed up into units. Most of the foot troops began to assemble in column formation, preparing to march, but a handful had stayed near the tree line, milling about and talking. They looked to be the better armed, perhaps most veteran of the troops.

No, not merely soldiers, Vambran realized, trackers and bounty hunters—professionals. They're sending their best back in to get us.

The prisoners also got to their feet, apparently also having been ordered to ready themselves to move. He watched as the Crescents formed a line, still watched over by their guards, and the cavalry mounted up. Together, the cavalry and the infantry began to move off, flanking the prisoners.

Shortly afterward, the trackers began to enter the forest to hunt for the remaining fugitives. The lieutenant was mildly surprised, given the fact that it was nearing the end of the day, but the growing dark did not seem to deter them.

Vambran scurried back down the shadowtop, disappearing into the foliage, and when he reached the bottom, he darted away, weaving through the trunks of the trees in an effort to gain a lead on the impending pursuit. Already he could hear the soldiers beginning to push forward, entering the woods. As he trotted, the lieutenant began to formulate possible plans to evade the new group of hunters. Unlike before, when there were more men hunting, he did not think it would be too difficult to hide from the trackers and wait for them to pass, especially in the gloom of twilight. But Vambran suspected they had effective magic employed to prevent just such an occurrence.

I guess we'll find out soon enough, Vambran thought, nearing the location where he had parted ways with the other six Crescents. They were not there.

Good, the lieutenant thought. They didn't wait around.

Vambran pulled his holy coin free and uttered a quick prayer, visualizing Adyan's crossbow in his mind as he did so. Once his divine magic had taken effect, Vambran could sense the direction in which the crossbow—and by extension, Adyan and the others—lay, and he began to move that way.

Just based on the limitations of the magic, Vambran knew his companions could not be too far ahead of him, and as he drew closer to their position, he could hear them well before they came into his view. There was quite a bit of shouting. Frowning in anger over their lack of stealth, he was ready to scold his sergeants as soon as he caught up to them.

The lieutenant's admonition died in his throat as he rounded a barrier of several tangled suth trees and spotted the six Crescents.

The mercenaries were bunched together, fending off nearly half a dozen very large vipers. Even as he sprinted toward them to aid in the fight, another snake slithered out of the deepening shadows, from beneath the suth entanglement. The serpent blocked Vambran's path as it reared up, towering higher than Vambran himself. As he drew his sword free of its scabbard, the snake hissed and opened its mouth, sending a gout of liquid right at the mercenary officer.

CHAPTER 8

Kovrim and Velati were forced to walk for most of the rest of the day, escorted by their captors along the coast of the Vilhon Reach. Their path followed an old road, presumably an abandoned logging route, for it cut inland after a while, penetrating the forest as it angled almost due east, with the setting sun sinking low behind the group. At several intervals along the way, they came upon other groups of soldiers, more members of the mercenary company that sported the silver raven for its symbol. Each time, new prisoners joined, more members of the Order of the Sapphire Crescent who had made it to shore after the sinking of *Lady's Favor* and were subsequently captured.

Though he was sorry to see the Crescents taken, Kovrim was glad to see them alive and well for the moment. They were ordered in no uncertain terms not to speak, so the priest got little information from any of them. Each time a new handful of prisoners was added to the ever-growing collection of mercenaries and their charges, Kovrim was both relieved and worried that Vambran was not among them.

As nightfall came, the prisoners—who numbered twelve Crescents by then—and their escort arrived at a large encampment. Numerous tents had been set up, gathered in small clumps around campfires. Even in the failing light, it was easy for Kovrim to see that the place was more than just a rest stop for the troops. A large, ruined tower stood in the middle of the open area, most of its stones tumbled and scattered. A newer but no less abandoned cottage, perhaps once belonging to a woodsman or hermit, had been built with some of the stone from the much older tower. It, too, had fallen into ruin, with only one partial stone wall still standing and a chimney leaning haphazardly against it. Stunted trees and tall grasses filled the clearing as the forest did its work, taking back the lands once cleared by men.

The captured Crescents were led over to one side of the camp, near the edge of the clearing. There, an old barn still stood, crafted from rough, natural logs. The building still looked stout enough to keep prisoners confined. The Crescents were led to the makeshift jail and ordered inside.

Once confined, Kovrim sank down wearily in the darkness and sighed, feeling the ache in his feet. The narrow door swung shut behind the mercenaries, and Kovrim watched through chinks in the wall as two burly figures settled a heavy log in place across the portal, effectively locking most of them inside. Kovrim still had options, he knew, but using his little remaining magic would require careful planning. He did not like the thought of leaving the men behind.

"Well, this is a fine mess," one of the Crescents said. It was Hort Bloagermun, known as Old Bloagy to everyone in the unit. He was as old as Kovrim and a veteran of many seasons' worth of campaigning. Though he wasn't quite as spry with a blade as he had once been, he was still a crack shot with his crossbow, which was how he had managed to stay with the company for so many years.

Kovrim nodded, though he knew Old Bloagy couldn't see him in the near-darkness. "Aye, and it'll get finer before it's finished, I'll wager," he said as Hort moved to sit beside him. "Tell me what you know so far."

Hort snorted in the twilight. "Not much, and that's more than most of us," he said. "When the ship went down, we all tried to rally to the beach, but a couple of the lads and I got cut off by one of them accursed pirate ships, which had enough archers on it to stick us all twenty times over. We had to hightail it the other direction, and by the time we had outdistanced them, we couldn't see where the main group had gone. We headed for shore anyway, and hooked up with three more boys, but that's when a whole mess of these fellows' cavalry arrived. We were outnumbered at least ten to one and didn't see the sense in putting up much of a fight, and now here we are."

The rest of the group had similar tales to tell. When they had all recounted their own fates in the attack, Kovrim quizzed the group on how many of their companions they knew had fallen in battle, if any of them had seen or had been with Vambran at any point during the confusion, and what sorts of equipment they had been allowed to keep.

At one point, the priest's information gathering was interrupted as the door was unbarred and opened.

Several soldiers came inside carrying a large kettle of some sort of fish stew and a handful of wooden bowls. "Finish what you want and use the kettle for your jakes," one of the soldiers said. The stew was weak and watery, but to Kovrim, who hadn't eaten in more than a day because of his seasickness, it tasted fine. After everyone had a chance to nourish themselves, the priest continued his questioning.

In the end, despite the total surprise of the corsairs' attack, it sounded as though the company's losses were light. Only four were confirmed dead or mortally wounded at sea, and none of them had seen Vambran fall. Kovrim's hope that his nephew was still alive, and possibly still free, began to grow.

The supplies were not so promising. Most of their equipment, including packs, belts with pouches, and any holy symbols belonging to the priests among them, had been taken. Old Bloagy had managed to keep a small knife concealed, tucked way down in his boot, but it was hardly a weapon, and it certainly couldn't get anyone far in an escape attempt.

"Well, Crescents," Kovrim said at last, "it looks like we'll be biding our time here for the night." When everyone began to speak at once, asking why they had been attacked on the sea and why they had been taken prisoner without having even engaged the enemy in battle, Kovrim had to shout to get them to settle down. "Those are questions we don't have the answers to, yet. But if these soldiers follow any of the code, I'm sure we'll be learning more soon. In the meantime, get some rest, and no one is to try anything foolish on their own. We're still on campaign, and I'm the ranking officer, and those are my orders. Any questions?"

None of the twelve had any issues, so after another bowl of stew for each, the Crescents settled in for the night. Kovrim found a relatively comfortable spot leaning against one wall of the barn and began to try to piece together what he could of the day's events. Assuming that both the encounters with the pirates and the mercenaries were coordinated, he was troubled by the incongruity of their purposes. The pirates had wanted them dead, no quarter offered—he suspected that the kraken was their doing and not just lousy luck. The silver ravens, on the other hand, had seemed loathe to kill them, even going so far as to allow him to heal Velati. Something didn't quite make sense, but Kovrim had a suspicion he would eventually come to regret finding out the answer. He considered whether or not it was an opportune time to slip away unseen and try to hunt for some help, but he decided against it, at least for the time being. He wasn't sure if the guards had taken a head count, and he didn't want to create more trouble for the rest of the Crescents. He would wait to escape until he knew he could get away with it.

The priest fell asleep fretting about many things.

...

"Now remember, this place is real trouble, so be on your toes, and stay out of everyone's way," Xaphira cautioned again as she led Emriana around a corner and down the narrow side street toward the entrance to The Silver Fish.

Emriana tried to contain her sigh of exasperation. "Yes, I know," she said. "You've told me five times already."

"Well, I want to make sure you get it, Em," her aunt snapped back, startling the younger girl with her vehemence. "I'm not kidding around. This isn't practicing in the barnyard. A body or two winds up sitting outside the doors of this place just about every night."

Emriana was more careful to sound respectful and
agreeable. "All right, I'll watch out."

"Good."

Emriana could hear loud, boisterous music and
singing as they approached, and she wrinkled her
nose in distaste. They reached the entrance to the
rathrur and Xaphira led the way inside. Immediately, Emriana could see what her aunt was talking
about. The clientele were of the surliest, roughest
sort she could have imagined, all dirty, sweaty men
and women who performed the most menial labors
of the city. As the two women strolled in, more than
a few conversations halted as many pairs of eyes
turned curiously toward them. Xaphira didn't seem
to notice, but Emriana found herself feeling very
self-conscious. She caught herself crowding in a
little tighter behind Xaphira, almost stepping on
her heels.

I can't believe she used to spend all of her time
here, Emriana thought, vaguely disgusted. It's the
great unwashed all packed together.

The girl wrinkled her nose at the sour smell that
hung in the smoky air and followed her aunt. Xaphira
led her over to a spot along the bar that was unoccupied at the moment and settled against it. Emriana
noticed a dark stain that looked suspiciously like
blood spattered across part of the bar nearest her. She
discreetly placed her hands at her sides rather than
lean against it as she tried to peer around without
actually staring at anyone.

In the far corner of the *rathrur*, a small stage had
been set up, and three musicians played a lively tune
while the patrons sang along. One of the bards had
a swollen, discolored nose. Emriana realized that
there were actually three different sets of lyrics to
the song being performed, and the crowd seemed to
be competing with itself to see which of the versions

was actually correct, the winner being determined by sheer volume. She listened to the version being sung by the table nearest to hers, but after getting the gist of the bawdy words, she blushed and tried to tune it out again.

One of the other patrons stood up and wandered over in Xaphira's and Emriana's direction, and the look in the fellow's eyes made the girl shiver, for it reminded her a little too much of how Denrick had looked at her that night in her bedroom, when he had her tied to a chair.

"Uh, Aunt Xaphira, don't look now, but here comes trouble," Emriana said as quietly as she dared over the music.

Xaphira slipped one of her throwing daggers free from her belt and made a show of jabbing it into the surface of the bar, though she never looked up at the approaching man, who was weaving slightly. Upon seeing the brandished weapon, the drunk fellow paused, tilted his head to one side as if considering whether or not the struggle would be worth the prize, and apparently thought better of it. He adjusted his direction to take himself to the far end of the bar and didn't look back.

Emriana shuddered again. "I can't believe you *liked* coming here," she grumbled, wrinkling her nose again.

Xaphira laughed. "There was a time when all of this was good sport, Em," she said. "There was nothing better than coming down to the dockside of town and slumming with the commoners."

"Why?" Emriana asked, realizing the disgust in her tone was obvious but not caring.

"Because, my dear niece, it made your grandfather unhappy," Xaphira replied. "And I enjoyed making him unhappy, just like you enjoyed making Dregaul unhappy." Then the older woman sniffed once, perhaps recalling some wistful memory about her deceased brother. "Besides, it felt good to be challenged," she added after a moment. "The folks here don't tend to fight fair, but they also don't tend to fight to kill. A black eye or broken hand was worth the experience of learning to brawl." Xaphira caught the eye of the barkeep and motioned for service, then turned back to Emriana. "It was fun," she finished.

Emriana tried not to roll her eyes. "You're lucky you didn't come home with a broken skull," she said derisively. "Actually, you're lucky you made it home at all."

"That is too true," Xaphira said, nodding in agreement. "So now you know why I told you to stay alert. I would be in the deep stable muck if I brought you home tonight with a split lip. I don't think even Hetta could save us from your mother, then."

Emriana tried to scowl at the thought of having to explain such a condition to her mother, but the thought ended up making her laugh instead.

After the barkeep served both Xaphira and Emriana a mug of some sour-smelling concoction and Xaphira tossed a couple of coins on the counter, the older woman led her niece back across the room toward a set of stairs leading up to the second floor. Emriana tried to ignore the stares she drew as she followed her aunt. She couldn't help but overhear more than a few lewd comments directed at her, and she was sure her cheeks were crimson by the time they reached the balcony of the second floor.

Emriana had no idea what Xaphira was planning, but the older woman seemed to know where she was going, so the girl followed her without question. Finally, Xaphira stopped at the open curtains of an unoccupied alcove and slipped inside. Emriana gratefully followed and settled onto the coarse wooden bench opposite her aunt.

"What now?" she asked, sipping at the mug Xaphira had procured for her. The beer inside was weak and bitter, and Emriana set it down and slid it away from herself.

"Now we wait," Xaphira replied, watching the girl with a bemused smile. "Quill will find us. I'm sure he already knows we're here."

True to her prediction, a man appeared a moment later, filling the doorway to the alcove. Emriana started at the sight of him, tall and sinewy, with disheveled hair and more than a few wrinkles. His clothes were just as mussed as he was, but there was a brightness to his eyes that told the girl he was both clever and dangerous. Emriana stared, noting that he eyed her right back, and there was a hint of a hunger in his expression as he appraised her. She wanted to shrink back, but Xaphira was up and taking the man's hand before she could react.

"Quill!" Xaphira said, pulling the man into the booth next to her. "Stop looking at my niece like that. You're old enough to be her father," she said.

The man blinked a couple of times, still looking, and despite Xaphira's admonition, his appreciative stare did not abate. But in the next moment he was all smiles for Emriana, reaching across the table and introducing himself as he took her hand and shook it. Emriana returned the greeting, though she saw that he could sense the coolness of her tone.

"So," Quill said, turning his attention back to Xaphira, "you decided you needed someone to watch your back tonight? What's the matter, don't you trust me anymore?" he asked, chuckling.

"I never trusted you, but no, she's here merely to observe." Then Xaphira's smile faded. "Did you learn anything?"

Quill's own pleasant facade melted away to a deep frown. "Always one to get straight to the point, weren't you?" When Xaphira didn't respond, the man sighed. "Very well. Yes, I found someone who can help you. He's prepared to meet with you right now." Then he glanced over at Emriana and added, "But only you. I didn't tell him anything about a niece, and if we try to change the conditions now, he'll bolt in a heartbeat."

Xaphira nodded, frowning. "Em, stay right here. Don't go anywhere; don't do anything until I get back. You got it?"

Emriana looked across at her aunt reproachfully, but she only nodded. "Not going anywhere, not doing anything," she said, "that's me."

"All right. I'll be back in a little while." Xaphira turned her attention back to Quill. "Lead on," she said, gesturing to the entrance to the alcove. Together, the pair scooted across the bench and out through the curtains, leaving Emriana by herself.

For the first few moments, the girl sat there, studying the rough wood of the table, thinking about how unpleasant the whole excursion had become. She had had no idea just how rough-and-tumble The Silver Fish would be, or she might have decided to remain at the country estate. Then she shook her head, angry with herself.

You get to prowl around the city with your aunt, she scolded herself, and you'd rather be at home, sitting and listening to mother read poetry. The girl rolled her eyes at her own foolishness and decided to get another look at the riffraff below.

Emriana slid out of the seat and peered cautiously through the curtains, checking in both directions before getting up completely. Then she crossed the balcony to the railing and leaned over, looking down. Most of the patrons were busily talking, singing, or drinking, and men were playing dice at one table. It seemed that no one was aware enough to look up and see her watching them, which suited her just fine.

The girl spent a few moments just studying the various individuals in the room, noting the cut and coarseness of their clothing, their unkempt appearance, and the way they carried themselves. Though she found them generally repugnant, she had to admit that they seemed to be enjoying themselves to the fullest. One man, small and wiry with greasy hair tied back from his head, was seated almost directly below her. Her eyes were drawn to him when he began to laugh, for he really guffawed, slapping his hand on the table and sloshing drinks. Across from him, a bulky woman in a bodice that barely contained her ample breasts sat on another man's lap, a huge bear of a fellow with a thick beard and mustache. He was laughing and singing along with the song being performed on the stage, and the hefty dame was bouncing in time to the music and singing right along with him. Though Emriana was embarrassed that the woman seemed to have no shame, the girl was also a bit envious that she seemed so comfortable in the company of the men she was with.

Emriana sighed and was just about to turn back to the safety of her alcove when she noticed a face staring up at her. It belonged to another woman, though she was obviously a bit more refined than the plump matron the girl had been watching. Dressed in purple leggings tucked into supple leather boots and a magenta vest over a white shirt—both of which were unlaced to an indecent level near her navel—the woman had short blonde hair and piercing blue eyes. She was sitting alone on a bench that rested against the far wall and had no table to accompany it, and she was staring right at Emriana intently.

The girl began to stare right back, cocking her head to one side as if to say, "What, exactly, do you want?" When the stranger realized she had been spotted, she shook her head once in consternation and got to her feet. She glanced up once more as she made her way toward the rear of the establishment. Emriana thought the woman had a smug smile on her face. The girl frowned, unsettled by the silent confrontation, and started to follow. Then she remembered her aunt's warning and restrained herself.

No, she trusted me to come with her tonight. I'm not going to make a mess of things.

Emriana returned to her seat in the tiny alcove and waited. After a while, growing bored, the girl began to examine the surface of the table. Countless knives and daggers had carved up the wood, cutting names, simple caricatures, and cryptic symbols over the entire surface. Even so, the wood looked fairly new, not stained and dark as she would have expected.

I wonder how often they have to replace them? Emriana pondered, remembering her aunt's tale of the previous night, when half the furniture in the common area below apparently took a beating. Imagining such a brawl made the girl grin. She could just picture Xaphira in the midst of it all, leaping, kicking, and punching, just as she had against the dire-cats earlier that day. She must have been intimidating, the girl thought.

Emriana began to get restless. Xaphira's meeting was taking longer than she would have imagined, and the girl was growing agitated. She did not want to have to sit there and wait much longer.

When another quarter-hour must have gone by, Emriana realized she was growing genuinely worried. Several times, she half rose from the seat with the intention of hunting her aunt down, just to make certain the woman was fine, but each time, she stopped

herself, not wishing to interrupt whatever delicate
negotiations might have been taking place.

Suddenly, Emriana remembered her pendant.
Fool! she silently snapped at herself. It's been hanging around your neck the whole time.

The girl snatched up the opal dangling on the
chain and withdrew it from inside her shirt. Clutching it, she closed her eyes and envisioned her aunt,
dressed in her telltale red shirt and cloak. Emriana
began to speak.

"Aunt Xaphira, are you well? It's been quite a
while since you left, and I'm worried about you. Do
you need help?"

She paused and waited for a response. There was
nothing but silence.

Growing more concerned, Emriana looked at the
pendant, wondering if it was functioning properly.
She had no way of knowing whether the enchantment had ceased to work or if Aunt Xaphira could
not respond at the moment. Either way, she was going
to have to find out the old-fashioned way.

Rising to her feet, Emriana slid out of the booth
and to the balcony, wondering which direction Quill
had taken Xaphira. She was just about to start down
the row of alcoves, intent on poking her head inside
each one, when a flash of red caught her eye down
below, in the common area.

"Aunt Xaphira!" Emriana called out, but her aunt
had her back turned and vanished beneath the stairs,
never turning around.

Emriana darted down the balcony toward the
stairs, rushing to catch up to her aunt.

What's she up to? the girl thought, reaching the
bottom of the stairs and pushing past the people milling about. Why did she leave without me?

Emriana was so focused on catching the older
woman that she no longer noticed the leering stares

or the crude comments uttered in her direction by
the other patrons. Just beyond the base of the staircase, a narrow hallway ran toward the back of the
establishment, leading to a set of private rooms, including a kitchen or pantry of some sort. Emriana
had to dodge and weave to make her way through the
passage, for it was crowded with serving folk both
coming and going. One skinny fellow with grease
stains on an apron covering his front shouted an
obscenity at her and told her to get out, but Emriana
ignored the man and slipped to the far end of the
hall, where it ended in a doorway leading out into
the night.

Once through the doorway, Emriana had to stop
and let her eyes adjust to the dimness of the evening.
The alley in which she stood was dirt, and it stank of
rotting vegetables and raw sewage. It couldn't have
been more than three paces across, and all the buildings on either side were at least two stories tall, most
even higher than that. But there was no sign of the
other woman.

"Aunt Xaphira!" Emriana called, taking a few
steps away from the doorway and the noise issuing
forth from it. She then stood very still and listened.
At first, she could hear nothing except for the din of
conversation from inside the *rathrur* and the trickle
of some fluids running down the alley, but a moment
later, she caught wind of a faint scuffling noise off
to her left.

Growing suspicious, the girl turned in that direction, slipping into the shadows and padding silently
along the alley, peering into every dark cranny she
came upon, listening still for further sounds of movement. At the juncture of The Silver Fish and the next
building over, she found what she had been looking
for. There was a gap between the two structures, not
really wide enough for a man, but certainly spacious

enough for a more diminutive woman or girl to squeeze into.

Emriana peered cautiously into the gap, but she did not see anyone moving through it. Then a thought occurred to her and she gazed up just in time to catch the silhouette of someone climbing up the gap, using both walls as support. It was too dark to make the person out clearly, but from Emriana's vantage point, it certainly looked like a woman in a cloak.

Convinced that she was not following her aunt, but rather someone who intended to look like her, Emriana hesitated. She was wary of a trap, but her growing fear for Xaphira's well-being pushed her onward. As silently as she could, she began feeling for hand- and footholds, following the mysterious figure above her. She found the going fairly easy, and she had pulled herself halfway up the building when the figure she was pursuing reached the top and disappeared over the side of the roof.

Damn it all, Emriana silently fumed as she continued her ascent. She'll be long gone before I can get up there. She hastened her pace, hoping against hope that perhaps she could make up some ground and keep her quarry in sight.

As Emriana grabbed at the next handhold and began to haul herself up, there was a bright flash of light overhead and a gout of flame roared down from above, directly at her.

CHAPTER 9

Pilos hurried along a dimly lit and rather uninteresting corridor toward the narrow door at the far end. Though the chances of the Abreeant encountering another priest in that particular section of the temple—a seldom-used wing devoted primarily to storage—at that time of the night was unlikely, he did not wish to be seen. Even the suggestion of impropriety on his part would make the young priest lose his nerve and return to his quarters. And his quarters were the last place in which he wished to spend any more time.

True to his expectations, none of the high priests of Waukeen had sent any kind of word to Pilos on the Grand Syndar's condition in well over a day. As the Abreeant had suspected, Grand Trabbar Lavant had had no

intention of keeping Mikolo's attendant informed of
the old man's health or potential for recovery. Though
he had tried to remain obedient, Pilos could not stand
to await news any longer.

Of course, the Abreeant could not approach the
Grand Syndar's chambers and demand an explanation. At the very least, the high priests would order
him back to his chambers with an admonition to
perform some penance for his indiscipline. At worst,
they might permanently remove him from his duties
and assign him to baser tasks as punishment.

If they didn't just decide I was unfit to serve Waukeen altogether, he silently lamented.

With that thought, Pilos nearly halted his progress and spun around to return to his rooms as fast
as he could. The very idea of being denied the opportunity to bathe in the glory that was the Merchant's
Friend was abhorrent, and part of Pilos dared not
even consider the consequences of what he was preparing to do in place of a frontal confrontation.

When the priest reached the end of the small
hallway, where the narrow door faced him, he
paused, taking a deep breath and peering back over
his shoulder one last time to make certain there was
no one there to witness his transgression. Satisfied
that he was alone, Pilos slipped a key into the lock
of the wooden door, twisted it, and half smiled at
the sound and feel of the faint click. Nervously, he
pushed the door open, slipped inside, and hurriedly
shut it again.

In the dark Pilos could see nothing, so he clutched
at his holy coin, which hung from a chain around his
neck, and muttered a quick prayer to Waukeen. Instantly a tiny ball of illumination appeared, conjured
onto the coin. The light was sufficient for him to see
the entirety of the small room, the same as if he had
lit a torch, though the glow of his coin was of a more

pearly hue, like moonlight. He let the symbol settle
back against his breast and peered about.

It was nothing more than a storage closet, a
small room lined with shelves on the walls holding linens that were not in use during the summer
season. In the fall, when the weather cooled once
more, the inhabitants of the temple would very
likely retrieve the warmer bedclothes, but for the
moment, no one would venture into the closet for
any reason ...

Unless they knew something unique about the
chamber, as Pilos did.

When he had first been raised to the level of
Abreeant and awarded, for his pious service in the
temple, the position of servitude to the Grand Syndar
himself, Pilos discovered a few secrets—or rather,
he was taught those secrets by the Grand Syndar
himself—about the architecture of the temple. One
such secret was the numerous concealed passages
that threaded their way through the temple struc-
ture, passing through the thickest of the walls and
following narrow and steep staircases to different
levels. The Grand Syndar seldom used those covert
passageways, but they were there in cases of dire
need. As Mikolo explained it at the time, one never
knew when the Grand Syndar might need to move
from one locale within the temple to another "unmo-
lested," as the old man had put it.

Pilos had never been able to imagine what use
the Grand Syndar might have had for such secretive
modes of travel, but he did not question their exis-
tence, nor did he ever reveal to anyone else that he
was aware of them. Right then, he was feeling more
than a little gratified that the Grand Syndar had
seen fit to share their presence with him.

Moving to the back of the closet, Pilos stared at
the shelving attached to the wall for a few moments,

trying to recall exactly how the Grand Syndar had made them function. He remembered something about a loose stone, but he could not recall exactly which one might be suitable. He shrugged and began to feel with his hands each of the stones that made up the wall. After the fourth or fifth one, he began to grow frustrated.

Perhaps it wasn't a stone at all, he thought, pondering.

Then the young priest remembered. There had been a loose stone at chest height, but it was on the other side of the wall. From the closet side, the trigger mechanism was actually one of the shelves. In fact, Pilos remembered, it was the bottommost shelf. He reached down and felt with his fingers along the bottom of the lowest one. When they brushed across a small stud, he pressed it in and tugged. The entire shelf shifted, and there was a deep click from inside the stone wall. Very carefully, Pilos stood and pushed against the wall, watching with satisfaction when it swung backward, revealing the narrow passageway beyond.

Quickly, before he could lose his nerve, Pilos scurried through the opening and pushed the swinging section of wall back again, until he heard it click shut. Sighing, he wondered if he would be able to figure out how to open it again, but he did not stop to determine which stone was the correct one right then. Instead he turned and began to follow the passage, guided by his glowing coin.

After a short walk down a dusty and cobweb-filled corridor, the passage split into a four-way intersection, and Pilos considered for a brief moment the correct route. When he'd made up his mind, he turned to the right, went down some steep stairs, and turned left at another intersection. He continued to follow that passage for quite some time, passing a couple of different points where he knew other doors were camouflaged in the stonework. Finally, Pilos turned a last corner and found himself in a dead end.

Bolstering his courage, he moved right to the very end of the hallway and stepped on a smallish projection rising up from the floor in one corner. The resulting click was barely audible, but Pilos held his breath anyway, ready to bolt if there was any indication that someone on the far side of the secret portal had heard it open. The distinct sound of voices began to issue through the slender crack that had formed, but they did not change in pitch or volume. When he was at last satisfied that no one had detected his presence, Pilos pulled the door slightly more ajar, peeking through the crack that widened. The door opened into a small alcove in Mikolo Midelli's study where an elegant statue of Waukeen rested.

It was clear to the young man that several people had gathered in the Grand Syndar's study and that they were most likely clustered around Mikolo's desk. Pilos could recognize almost every voice there, realizing that many of the high priests of the temple had congregated in the chamber and were engaged in a heated debate. Their words stung Pilos as sure as if they had slapped him physically.

"And I say that the Grand Syndar has not yet gone on to meet with the Merchant's Friend, and you are blasphemous for even discussing a successor, yet." That was the voice of Grand Trabbar Perolin, usually a soft-spoken priest who was kind to everyone. He was one of Pilos's favorites.

"Surely you are not so naive as to believe his recovery is possible?" asked another, Grand Trabbar Huleea, a diminutive, scowling woman who always seemed to glare at lesser priests unless they appeared busy or in prayer. "You've been a part of the healing

circle; you can sense as well as any of us here that
Mikolo Midelli is not long for this world."

Pilos nearly gasped out loud at that revelation,
understanding for the first time the true cost of his
eavesdropping. He had the knowledge he had feared
to possess, that the Grand Syndar was dying. He could
no longer pretend there was hope.

"Nonetheless," Perolin countered, "I find it noisome
to discuss the Grand Syndar in such terms before he
sheds his mortal coil and advances to the shores of
Brightwater of his own volition. He does not need us
driving him there prematurely."

"It is not a lack of concern for the Grand Syndar's
condition that brings us to discuss these matters," a
third voice said, the smooth, repulsively persuasive
utterances of Grand Trabbar Lavant. "Rather, it
is a due responsibility for the temple, indeed the
faithful among all of Arrabar, that leads us down
the path before we would perhaps be comfortable
exploring it.

"The simple fact is, our blessed leader and guide
has come to the end of his stay here on Abeir-Toril
and will soon leave us. If we are not prepared for a
seamless transition when that eventuality is upon
us, do we not do more harm than good to all of the
works he strove for in his long and illustrious career
at the helm? Do we not shame ourselves in the eyes
of so many if, when we find ourselves leaderless, we
cannot act with assertiveness and confidence? That
is what separates those of us from the flock that fol-
lows us, a sure and indomitable spirit of conviction
that we move in the right direction every moment,
every day."

"And I suppose you believe that you are best suited
to lead us forward down that treacherous path?"
Grand Trabbar Perolin said, his tone making it clear
that he did not favor the suggestion in the least.

"If that is the will of the council, I would humbly accept the appointment," Lavant responded, his tone thickly obsequious.

"You know good and well that the council is filled with your lackeys and confidants, and that, when it comes time for a vote, your name will head the list!" Huleea spat. "Everyone in this room knows your game, Lavant. Do not think us the blindly pious fools Mikolo was. Your position as Grand Syndar is not secured, yet!"

More voices rose up in argument, but Pilos did not hear them clearly, nor did he particularly care. He had already gently pulled the secret door shut again and had turned and fled back along the narrow tunnel in the wall. He was surprised at the number of tears welling up in his eyes, though not the ache in his chest that was causing them.

...

For a moment, time seemed frozen to Emriana as she watched a crackling arc of roaring flame come rushing toward her head. Then the girl was falling, having let go of her perch between the walls of the two buildings where she had been climbing. Rough stone scraped at her knees and shoulders as she slid awkwardly down toward the ground, turning her head to avoid the worst of the heat from the fiery blast above.

Emriana's diminutive stature probably had as much to do with her successful escape as any quick reactions on her part. A larger person would undoubtedly have become wedged between the two walls, stuck in the narrow gap and helpless to evade the scorching blast. But the slender girl dropped easily, barely escaping the worst of the withering heat, though her hair was singed sufficiently

that the odor of it filled her nostrils. She hit the
bottom of the gap and tumbled out, away from
the flames, sprawling, half blind from the flash
of brightness, into the narrow alley leading back
toward The Silver Fish. She landed with a rather
soggy splat in the midst of something moist and
foul smelling.

Emriana nearly gagged when she realized what
she was lying in, and she recoiled as quickly as she
could, holding her breath in disgust. In the darkness,
she could not see the rivulets of filth flowing toward
the grated sewer covers, but she had a pretty good
idea what most of it was from the stench. Though the
smell nearly overpowered her, the girl had to ignore
the nasty stuff covering her front, for it became clear
that she was not alone in the alley.

"Evenin', love," came a male voice from the near-
darkness, off to her right. "'Tis a shame for a comely
wench such as yourself to be out alone, don't you
think?" the man said. Emriana could just make out
his silhouette in the light spilling from the doorway beyond. It was the short, gaunt fellow with the
greasy hair.

"Aye, and I'll bet she's wishing for a handsome
rogue such as yerself to link arms with," came a
second voice, that one female. She stood behind the
wiry fellow, and Emriana could see it was the pon-
derous woman she had been watching inside earlier.
"Maybe we can show her how much more fun she'll
have, spendin' the evenin' with us, eh?" the fat hussy
added, chuckling unpleasantly.

"Get away from me," Emriana said warily, backing away from the pair while trying to fling the
worst of the filth from her hands. "I don't need any
company."

"But of course you do!" came a third deep voice
from the other direction, behind Emriana, cutting

her off from her intended escape route down the alley. "Leastways, you've got it whether you want it or not," the man continued, sounding less friendly.

"You know what to do," came a fourth voice, from above, floating down from the roof. "You've got your gold. Take care of her."

Emriana glanced up and saw her quarry, though she was no longer cloaked and hooded. The girl could see by then that it was the short-haired woman she had spotted before, staring at her inside the *rathrur*. The stranger was standing at the edge of the roof and peering down, a cloak folded over her arm. Then she was gone, leaving the girl with her three unfriendly companions.

Fool! The girl chastised herself, realizing she had blundered right into the trap despite her vigilance. Idiot!

As the two men began to close in on either side of her, Emriana spun and planted her back to the wall, feeling for one of her new daggers, which she had tucked into her belt. She wondered if it was enough to deter unwelcome advances, as her aunt's had been at the bar before. She doubted it, and she hoped her aim would be as good as it had been against the dire-jaguars.

"Now, little monkey-child," the first man said, only a couple of steps away from Emriana, "come along and play real nice, and maybe we won't stick you like a pig for roasting." He was hardly much larger than the girl herself, and he crouched warily on the balls of his feet as he approached.

"I don't think so," Emriana said, just as the man lunged at her. She slashed at the outstretched hand coming toward her, able to follow it by the glint of a ring shining in the dim light of the distant doorway. Her assailant must have guessed at her intentions, for he snatched his hand back at the

last moment, and the girl's dagger sliced through
nothing but air.

The bear of a man timed his attack well, though,
for at that moment, his very large, muscular arm
snaked around Emriana's neck from behind, locking her head firmly in the crook of his elbow. At the
same time, she felt his thick, meaty fingers enclose
her wrist, clamping down and preventing her from
swinging her dagger about again. His grip might as
well have been a steel manacle, for she couldn't free
her arm at all.

Emriana screamed, and when the skinny man
came at her again, she kicked with both feet straight
out, snapping her toes at his face. But he was too
quick and darted to one side, wrapping his arms
around both of her legs in the process. She jerked
and bucked like a wild thing, but she could get no
real leverage, for she was held completely off the
ground. The skinny man worked his way up to
her knees, trying to get a better hold of her as she
thrashed. At the same time, the larger man behind
her twisted her wrist around at an awkward angle,
sending stabbing pains up her arm and forcing her
to drop the dagger.

"Come on," he said, his breath hot in Emriana's
ear, and the two men holding the girl began to move
down the alley, away from the doorway leading into
The Silver Fish. "Let's find a quiet spot where we
can play."

"She stinks!" the smaller man growled. "What's
she been rolling around in?"

Emriana wanted to scream again, but without
her feet under her for support, much of her weight
had settled on her neck, which was still trapped in
the arm lock of the assailant behind her. She flailed
desperately with her free hand trying to pull that
massive arm away from her throat, but it was a

useless gesture. She was gasping for breath as they toted her deeper into the alley. Behind the skinny man, Emriana could still see the capacious woman following, laughing.

As spots began to swim in her vision, Emriana thought frantically of the warning Xaphira had given her, about bodies turning up outside the *rathrur* every morning. Practically paralyzed with panic, Emriana began blindly punching at the man carrying her upper body, slamming her small fist up over her own head at where she guessed his face might be. She felt her pummeling connect with his nose and she struck again, terror lending her strength.

"Ow! You little brat, stop that!" the man howled, nearly dropping Emriana as he turned his face away from her blows. The distraction also loosened his hold on her neck, and the girl gulped a huge breath of precious air.

Just as quickly, though, he had a hold of her again, and he switched hands, shifting his grip so that his arm slid beneath both of Emriana's, between them and her back. With his free hand he took a firm grip on the girl's hair, yanking her head back to face him from upside down.

"You stop squirming," he said, viciously tugging her hair, "or I'll let Lak here slit your throat and be done with you."

Emriana froze, her eyes tearing up from the pain of having her hair pulled. Her hands fluttered uselessly behind her back, unable to prevent the horrid thug from hurting her. Then her hand bumped against a strategic point between the man's legs. Emriana clamped her hand around the telltale bulge and squeezed as hard as she could.

The man's scream was perhaps the loudest thing Emriana had ever heard. It blasted her ears and echoed all around her, bouncing off the high walls

of the narrow alley. More important, he sank down
to his knees, releasing the girl's hair and arms and
bringing both his hands down in a desperate, frantic
attempt to pry her painful grip off of himself.

Emriana landed awkwardly on her arms but quick
as a cat, she was trying to roll over, twisting herself
onto her belly while still maintaining a stout grip
on her assailant. At the same time, she jerked one leg
free from Lak and kicked, slamming the heel of her
boot into his gut.

The skinny man staggered back, releasing her
legs, while the larger man, his hands still prying
futilely at her clenched fingers, doubled over, still
howling in misery. Behind Lak, Emriana heard
the woman swear. Emriana released her grip and
scrambled to her feet. She was just about to dodge
past the larger man, who was still crumpled in
the dirt of the alley, whimpering, when something
struck her hard from behind, right on the back of
her head.

Waves of pain radiated through the girl's skull,
and she dropped to her knees, spots swimming in
her vision. She tried to stand up again, but the whole
world ooomod to be out of balance at that point, and she
staggered to one side, bumping against the wall of the
closest building. As she reached out to catch herself,
the rotund woman stepped into view and planted one
of her puffy fists right into Emriana's stomach.

All of the girl's breath left her in an audible
whoosh, and she sank back down to the ground, gasping. The spots in Emriana's vision only intensified
as she struggled, coughing, to regain her breath, and
she was unable to do anything but crumple where she
had sagged, flopping into the filth.

She felt hands grab her roughly and yank her
to her feet again. Something hard cuffed her hard
upside the head, snapping it to one side and making

her cry out in pain. The blood was roaring in her
ears as she was dragged, stumbling farther down
the alley. A small part of her mind screamed at
Emriana to stand up, to fight back, to stop her
assailants from towing her along, but she was
too dazed to react. She pulled feebly once or twice
against the hands that gripped her by each arm,
but it was a futile gesture and did nothing to deter
her attackers.

Suddenly, Emriana was thrown forward, and she
stumbled to her hands and knees upon something
softer than stone and dirt. She rested there for a
moment, panting to get her wind back, but before
she could figure out what she was resting on, a
hard boot planted itself in her backside and sent
her sprawling the rest of the way down. Without
warning, two or three hard blows struck Emriana
in the ribs, and she vainly tried to bring her arms
down to protect herself.

That, apparently, was what her attackers had been
waiting for, for in the next instant, Emriana felt herself enveloped by the soft material upon which she
lay. She realized it was a carpet, and it was wet and
sour-smelling. She understood that her three assailants were wrapping her up in the rug, and she began
to thrash about again, trying to prevent her entomb-
ment, but she was too dazed and her foes too fast. All
too quickly, she was engulfed in fetid darkness, her
arms pinned to her sides as she was rolled over and
over several times. She could feel the thick material
tightening around her, cutting off her movement and
her air.

"No!" She cried out, trying to jerk her arms back
up over her head. "Stop! Please!" She was panicking,
terrified of the sense of being buried alive, but her
voice was muffled and ineffectual. She frantically
kicked her feet, trying to keep from being completely

trapped, but it was too late. She could already feel
coils of rope being wrapped around her torso and
knees, effectively binding her helplessly inside the
wrapped carpet.

She wound up on her back, and though she continued to kick and fight, Emriana realized that the
trio of attackers was no longer working to contain
her in the rolled-up carpet. She felt herself being
lifted from the ground, and a rhythmic swaying
motion set in, evidence that they were carrying her.
The thought that she was being hauled off, farther
away from The Silver Fish, from any point of reference she knew, frightened the girl even more, if
that was possible. She continued to cry out, hoping
perhaps someone somewhere near her would hear
and investigate. Praying.

At one point, something slammed into the middle
of the carpet roll, walloping Emriana right in her
gut, knocking the wind from her once more. She
gasped and coughed again, trying to take in enough
air to regain her breathing. Tears welled up in
her eyes, tears of pain and fear. The stench of the
wet, molding rug was almost unbearable, and she
thought she would pass out from the suffocating
atmosphere. She stopped kicking and screaming
after that, fearing that she would be struck again
if she continued. She began to sob, shuddering,
shaking sobs, knowing she would never see any of
her family again.

Images of her mother and grandmother, of Vambran, of Xaphira, even of Marga and the twins flashed
through her mind. She could see them all grieving for
her, perhaps wondering what had become of her, why
she had disappeared. The frightening notion made
her chest ache.

No! She insisted, trying to clear her head. You're
not dead, yet! Figure something out! Steeling herself

against the panic, Emriana grew still and began instead to listen, trying to gain some sense of her surroundings. She could hear nothing, but she at least could begin to think clearly.

After a while, she felt herself lowered onto a flat surface, and she could hear muffled voices, though she could not make out what was being said. She realized that her own efforts at making noise had most likely been similarly muted, and the likelihood of someone actually hearing her in the alleys of Arrabar was slim. She would have to save herself.

As she assessed her situation, Emriana remembered that she had a second dagger hidden on her person, tucked into the waist of her pants at the small of her back. She tried to reach it, but her arms were pressed too tightly to her sides, and she was finding it difficult to flex her elbow enough to shift her hand back there. It was maddening. She stopped trying to grab it and considered other methods.

Shrink, she told herself. Get smaller.

Shifting as much as she could to one side, Emriana exhaled and held very still, feeling the blanket sag around her the slightest bit. Then she shifted her shoulder up as high as she could and rolled her arm around toward the blade. She could barely brush the tip of one finger against it. She sucked in air a couple of times, trapping her arm, then exhaled again and tried once more. On that attempt, she managed to touch it with the tips of three fingers, but before she could make more progress, the wagon or whatever she was riding on bounced roughly over something, jostling her. She lost her position and was deposited onto her back again, pinning her arm beneath her.

Before she could try again, Emriana felt the vehicle come to a halt. She strained to listen and thought she could hear the faint lapping of water. Voices began again nearby, still too muffled for her to make any sense of them. The girl felt hands working on the outer bindings of the carpet, and for a moment she believed they were going to release her. She prepared to yank the dagger free the moment she got the chance, but it soon became apparent that her kidnappers were up to something else. She could feel tugging and pulling and grunts of effort.

She was hoisted into the air, and the ropes that had been wrapped around her torso and knees tightened considerably, cutting into her. The shift caused the middle of her body to sag down, tightening the bindings against her arm, still trapped behind her. The roll of carpet swayed back and forth as she was carried a short distance. Then the movement stopped.

"Sweet dreams, little monkey," a voice near her head said, faint and muffled through the wrappings. "Enjoy your swim."

The carpet began to sway back and forth, putting more strain on her. Emriana realized with a flash of panic exactly what had happened. The men had tied heavy weights to her bindings!

The girl began to struggle again, trying desperately to reach the dagger pinned against the small of her back. But the weight of her own body, coupled with the way she was bent almost double, made it impossible. After the third such rocking motion, Emriana felt herself floating free, had the dreaded sense of falling.

She screamed and felt the sudden splash as she hit water. The weights tied to her ropes remained taut, pulling her down. The carpet began to soak through with water, cold and dark saltwater. They had thrown her into the bay.

Emriana squirmed and thrashed, almost insane with terror. She did not want to drown. She did not want to die. She wanted to breathe, to live, to see the light of day again.

Please! she cried out to no one. Please!

The water closed over her face, and Emriana was forced to snap her mouth shut, to stop trying to cry out. She felt the pressure increasing, pressing in all around her. She continued to kick and buck, shaking back and forth in a vain attempt to wriggle out of the rolled-up carpet.

At last, the girl felt herself jerk to a stop as the weights attached to her bindings must have finally settled to the bottom. She floated, almost weightless, feeling her body trying to bob upward, back to the surface, which seemed to be as high overhead as the heavens right then.

Upward!

With her buoyancy lifting her weight free, Emriana realized she could reach the dagger at last. She groped for it desperately, already beginning to feel her chest aching from a lack of air. Her fingers closed around the hilt of the knife, and she jerked it free, brought her arm back around to her side.

Once more, spots were beginning to float in Emriana's vision as she shifted her wrist the slightest bit and jabbed the tip of the dagger into the fabric. She felt it give, and with that tiny bit of hope to cling to, the girl began to saw, trying to rip a gaping hole through the carpet and free herself.

Her hand plunged through two layers, then three, but it wasn't going to be enough. Her air was gone. Her lungs were about to burst. She couldn't do it. Then her hand came free and she could feel the cold water as she cut a bigger hole and began to extract herself from the rug and its bindings, but spasms were shaking her. Her body was fighting against her, trying to make her breathe. Her head broke free of the carpet, but all was dark, all was fading.

The last thing Emriana could feel as unconsciousness overtook her was losing her grip on the dagger and feeling it sink away.

CHAPTER 10

The darkness beyond the windows revealed that the sun had long since set when Marga stirred from where she had been sitting in a large cushioned chair in one corner of her private chambers. Somewhere during that time, servants had come and lit several lamps in the suite, but they had otherwise left the woman alone with her thoughts. She remembered at some point sending Mirolyn away, telling the young lady that she would look after the children for the rest of the evening herself. To anyone entering the chambers where Marga sat, they would have seen a mother watching over her two children, who played with apparent disinterest toward anything or anyone.

The reality was far different.

Marga looked down at the two figures near her feet, wanting to recoil from them. The one that appeared to be Obiron looked up at her and smiled, though it was far from the warm, loving grin she knew.

"You fear us," the boy said. "You want to kill us." Then he laughed, but it was not Obiron's laugh.

Marga had to resist the urge to clamp her hands over her own ears, though she wanted to shield herself from that dreadful, malevolent chuckle, and from having her thoughts drawn out of her head. She hated it, and she squirmed in frustration and terror. Knowing that the two creatures sitting in front of her could penetrate her mind, could know her every thought the moment she did, made her feel violated, alone, helpless.

"Please stop," she said, desperately. "Leave me alone."

"We have our instructions," said the other one, who looked and sounded for all the world like her daughter, Quindy. "We will know if you try to cross us," she added, glowering.

Marga cringed and drew her feet up into the overstuffed chair, pulling as far from that malevolent gaze as she could. The creature mimicking Quindy smiled and returned to her toys.

Marga wanted to pull her hair out, wanted to scream, but she dared not do anything to give away the secret of her situation. So long as she cooperated, so long as she did whatever her brother insisted of her, the real Quindy and Obiron would remain fine. But to cross him. . . .

As if Grozier, too, could read his sister's thoughts, a flash of brilliant pale blue appeared in the corner of her chamber. Marga started at the sudden glow, jerking her head around to see her brother step through the magical portal that had appeared there, followed closely by Bartimus. Behind the wizard, the shimmering, radiating doorway winked out again.

"Hello, Marga," Grozier said in mock warmth, giving her a sardonic smile as he strode across the room toward her. "Spending a little time alone with your offspring, I see," he said.

Marga could feel her eyes well up with tears, but she fought against the emotion. "They will not leave my side," she said. "They lurk next to me constantly, reading my thoughts. Please, make them stop."

Grozier raised an eyebrow in mock surprise and dismay and turned to the two beings sitting upon the floor. Both of them smiled shyly, looking as though they were two children about to be chastised for stealing cookies.

"She has been imagining killing us," the girl said, pointing toward Marga. "And she has considered revealing the truth to the rest of the family."

Marga flinched and turned her face away, hating the fact that she could hide nothing from the two creatures nor, by extension, her brother.

"Really?" Grozier said, turning and looking at Marga.

She could feel his gaze on her, but she refused to look up at him. "But I didn't," she said sullenly. "Ask them; they know I can't, won't."

Grozier laughed and said, "Of that, I have no doubt, sweet sister. And I would expect resentment and resistance from you at the moment."

In two quick steps, the man was in front of Marga, leaning forward menacingly, both hands on the armrests of the chair.

She recoiled from him, though his actions forced her to look up into his eyes. She could see a dangerous glint there. She felt afraid, had anticipated his wrath. She knew that he would be angry when he found out what she had been thinking.

"I don't have to remind you of what will happen if
you decide to act on your impulses," Grozier said in a
low voice. "I'm sure that, should I ask my two accomplices here, they will also tell me why you resisted
your urge to spill the truth."

Marga drew back, until her head was pressed
against the back of the chair, and still she wanted
to draw away even more. "Please," she said, her voice
nearly a whimper. "I know what you'll do. I can't
help my feelings, but I'm not crossing you, I swear
by Tyr's scales. I will not. The thoughts—they just
come, and I—" And she did look away, then, turned
her head to one side and cried, pressing the back of
her hand to her mouth as the fear and pain washed
over her.

Grozier drew back, seemingly satisfied. "You fret
too much," he said in a more jovial tone, countering
Marga's wretched mood. "And you do not see the ben-
efits of our arrangement yet."

Marga sniffed and wiped a tear from her cheek,
feeling angry again. She turned and looked at her
brother with a scowl. "What? You mean all the glory
and wealth that is Obiron and Quindy's to be had,
once *you've* seized control of House Matrell? Oh, yes,
let's allow them to live up to their father's and uncle's
legacies! Let's teach them that the corrupt path, the
path of deceit and theft, will take them far in this
world. Yes, I'm overjoyed at such—"

"Enough!" Grozier shouted, making Marga jump
from his vehemence. "Like it or not, this is the life
before you. You stand at a crossroads, sister. You can
choose to live out your days with your children, watching them grow as I guide them to their rightful places
as the heirs of this House, or you can . . . be elsewhere.
It changes nothing for me, of course, but I would think
you might want to remain living in this world and
be a part of the rest of their lives."

Marga watched her brother's seething face as he spat the hateful words at her, blinking in terror but unable to react at all. She knew Grozier well enough to know that he was not making an idle threat. If she stood in his way, if she tried to prevent him from gaining his revenge upon the rest of the Matrell family for their part in turning his plans awry, he would kill her and think little of it. It was as simple as that.

"She knows you do not bluff," one of the creatures said, but in its own voice then, not that of one of her children. "She knows you will kill her if she does not cooperate."

Both Marga and Grozier turned to look at the thing, standing behind Grozier in its natural form. It was all gangly arms and legs, except for its head, which was large and round, like an egg. The thing's skin was gray and hairless. It was repulsive to look upon, but what unnerved Marga the most were its eyes. They were large and round, yellow orbs with narrow slits. She would have said they looked like a cat's eyes, but such a description was inaccurate. No, she decided, they were the eyes of an octopus. Cold and dead, they seemed, and they stared straight at her. She knew the creature was reading her mind right then, could sense her loathing of it.

"Good," Grozier said, stepping back from Marga and turning to face the thing directly. "She's a smart girl. Because I would, you know," he said.

"Yes," the creature replied in a deadpan tone, its voice strangely dissonant and hollow. "I know you would."

Grozier chuckled. "Of course you do." Then he turned away and began to pace. "But I didn't just show up to taunt or threaten my lovely sister tonight. No, I have most exciting news." He moved beside

Bartimus, who had been standing in the shadows at
the corner of the room, staying out of the way until
needed, as usual. Grozier clapped the mage on the
shoulder in a gesture of camaraderie, then spun and
continued his pacing.

"It seems that various members of the Matrell
family have gotten themselves into some unfortunate scrapes today. Sadly, the family is being whittled
down to nothing, little by little."

Marga gasped, unable to contain her sudden dread.

"Oh, yes," Grozier replied, picking up on the
woman's fear. "Apparently, the ship that was carrying Lieutenant Vambran Matrell and Quartermaster
Kovrim Lazelle sank off the coast of Reth today, and
all hands are presumed dead or missing." His tone
had turned solemn, though it was a mocking gesture,
for the man could not contain his smile as he spoke.
"It seems that neither man will be coming home from
campaign this season," he finished, almost chuckling
in his glee.

Marga wanted to strangle him. Her heart ached
with the news.

"And as it turns out, two other members of the
family have been waylaid in the dark of night in a
more unsavory neighborhood of Arrabar. I'm sorry
to report that Xaphira and Emriana Matrell won't
be finding their way home again, either."

"No!" Marga cried, lunging up from her chair, horrified. "No! You didn't do this! Please tell me you did
not hurt them!" She charged toward her brother, her
hands balled into fists, and began to pound at him,
slamming both fists into his chest, trying to cuff him
about the face and head.

Grozier, in his initial shock, did nothing to stop
his sister at first, but then he began to step back,
away from her assault, and managed to clamp his
hands around her wrists, restraining her. "Stop it!"

he demanded, driving her back from him, driving her down.

Marga crumpled then, sagging to the floor in agony. It had been by her hand that the two women, Emriana and Xaphira, had been harmed. Her betrayal had led Grozier and his accomplices to find them. Marga could not stand that guilt. She buried her face in her arms, right there on the floor, and sobbed.

I did it. I killed them, she thought as she cried. The same as if I'd held the weapon myself. Why has all of this happened to me? Waukeen, what did I do to cross you, to bring this down upon myself?

Marga could feel Grozier step around his sister and continue pacing. He apparently was refusing to be upstaged during his gleeful telling of the horrid tale.

"Regrettably, after the unfortunate events of last month, that leaves only three family members alive, and two of those are ... not of age, yet."

Marga sat up, realizing where her brother was going with his explanations.

He was looking at her, an expectant smile upon his face. "Yes, Marga, dear, I knew you would figure it out. Tonight, the only person who stands between the wealth of House Matrell and your two children is Hetta herself."

"No," Marga said weakly, helplessly. "Don't."

"Oh, I don't intend to," he said, still smiling. "I think we'll leave that for a different member of the family." He turned to the gray-skinned creature, still standing and watching as Grozier had strutted in pride through the room. "I'm sure you have an idea of who might get close to Grandmother Hetta tonight," he said to the thing.

"Absolutely," the creature remarked, and right before Marga's eyes, it began to change, to shift. It grew taller and filled out, adapting a human form

all too familiar to the woman. It was as if she were
looking in a reflecting glass.

"No!" she cried, trying to rise to her feet. "You
cannot do this! Stop it!" Marga demanded, moving
toward the thing, the false version of herself. "Leave
her alone!"

But Grozier stepped between Marga and the imitation of her, grabbed his sister by the arms. "No,
no," he said, wrapping his arms around her when
she began to flail at him, hit him, trying to get past
him and at the false version of herself. "You and I
are going to wait right here, and it'll all be over,"
he said.

But Marga would not be denied. She fought like
a wild thing, for she knew that she could not bear
the shame and guilt of allowing her treachery to the
Matrells to be continued. She had to stop the wretched
creature before it got out of her chambers. She had
to stop it! She began to shout, to scream at the top of
her lungs, hoping someone, a servant, would hear and
expose the plot.

"Bartimus, if you please," Marga heard Grozier
say, raising his voice to be heard over her screams.
"She's going to bring the entire household down on
us, making this noise."

Marga kicked and punched at Grozier, and from
his winces, she could see that she was having an
effect. He released her then, and she lunged forward,
trying to grab her imposter and strangle it, but she
never made it across the floor. In the blink of an eye,
she felt herself lose mobility, felt her body stiffen and
freeze in place, caught in mid-step as she had been
dashing across the room.

Marga's horror was complete then, for she found
that she could still breathe, and could see—though
only in the direction she had been staring, which had
been right at her imposter—but she could not move

a muscle otherwise. The woman could also hear, and
Grozier was laughing. It made her blood run cold.

"Very nice, Bartimus, I must say," her brother
said, chuckling, as he moved in front of Marga. "She
looks quite humorous." Then he turned his attention
away from his sister and toward her duplicate. "You
know what to do," he said to the thing as he handed
it something Marga could not see.

The creature nodded. "Yes," it replied. "She will
die in her sleep, and no one will be the wiser."

"And you're certain you can get to her?" Grozier
asked. "There is only one chance at this."

"Do not worry," Marga's double replied, altering
its voice until it became the perfect likeness of her
own. "I will reach the old woman without trouble
or incident."

Grozier chuckled again. "Of course, I should never
have doubted. Then off with you," he said.

The false Marga turned and departed.

Marga, frozen in place, wanted so desperately to
scream.

...

Vambran felt an exposed bit of root jab him in the
ribs as he tumbled across the ground, desperately
dodging the gout of liquid vomited forth by the snake
before him. The mercenary officer grunted in pain
but refused to stop rolling, jumping to his feet several
paces away from where he had originally been standing. The ground where he had been a moment before
sizzled and hissed where the foul secretion landed,
and he shuddered, imagining what it would have done
if it had struck him.

Though he was intensely wary of the giant snake
turning to pursue him, Vambran also had a thought
in the back of his mind for the men coming behind

him, the professional hunters who were tracking both him and his soldiers through the forest. His agitation that the trackers could catch up to the seven members of the Sapphire Crescent only made it more difficult to concentrate on the battle at hand.

The snake lunged at Vambran, and he shifted his stance to one side and sliced with his sword at the creature's neck. The blow landed true, but the gouge he created was only a narrow furrow, the blade inhibited by the thick scales covering the reptile. Still, the snake did not like that one bit and hissed malevolently as it recoiled from him, swaying and watching its quarry with beady, frightening eyes that glowed in the dusk.

Vambran considered launching a spell that would blind the creature, one of his magical flares aimed right at the snake's eyes, but he dismissed the idea almost immediately, for he did not want to aid the men hunting the Crescents. Instead, he decided to conjure his magical swarm of coins. Reaching into his shirt as he backed away from the advancing snake, he produced his holy medallion and began to utter the words of a familiar prayer. Finishing the petition, he kissed the coin and felt the manifestation of magic form in front of him.

The clump of coins materialized in a low humming swarm, and with a thought, Vambran sent the buzzing cloud right at the snake's head. In the gathering darkness, it was growing more difficult to see clearly, but Vambran knew the cloud of coins struck true when the snake jerked and retreated, hissing and biting at nothing in particular. Maintaining his concentration on the holy weapon and driving it repeatedly at the snake's head, Vambran used the distraction to circle around to a better vantage point. The snake seemed to sense what the soldier was trying to do, though, because it turned several times to keep its foe in front of itself, but each time, Vambran was able to maneuver the swarm of stinging coins in for another round of vicious blows.

The snake lost interest in attacking the man and settled to the ground with the intention of fleeing. It slithered through the dried leaves, rushing away from the repeated stinging bites that it could not see nor retaliate against. Vambran maintained his magic for a few moments more, desiring to make certain that the snake truly fled, but once it was clear the beast was not going to return, he recalled the swarm and turned to see how his companions were faring.

Several snakes were down and lifeless, and the two remaining were badly bleeding. At least one of the mercenaries was also down, unmoving, and two others were writhing in agony, out of range of the battle. Vambran rushed to aid the soldiers, sending his cloud of coins toward the nearest snake.

As the holy weapon struck the serpent across one side of its head, the snake jerked and shifted its attention sideways, snapping at the air. The distraction gave Grolo the opportunity to leap close to the snake and swing his axe with both hands. The dwarf's aim was true, and he lopped the reptile's head completely off with that single blow, sending it bouncing away into the darkness. The snake's body began to buck and writhe haphazardly across the ground, leaking blood and other fluids as it did. Grolo jumped clear of the corpse as Vambran directed his magic at the last remaining snake.

That single opponent was clearly already in its death throes as Vambran's swarm of coins smacked it across the snout. The strike was enough to send it reeling to one side, toppling over into the leaves. Horial and Adyan closed in and finished off the creature.

Vambran turned to the three downed mercenaries. They all had suffered burns from the acid spit by the snakes, he realized. Filana and Burtis were alive but in terrible pain, but Elebrio did not move.

"Help them!" the lieutenant ordered his three sergeants as he bent down to check the youngest Crescent for signs of life. The acid had done its work too well, though, for most of Elebrio's face was nothing but raw, red flesh, his features scoured by the burning acid. As Vambran suspected, the youthful soldier did not breathe.

No pain for you, at least, Vambran thought sorrowfully.

The mercenary officer knew he could not waste a moment grieving for the young man, though, and went over to see what aid he could give the other two wounded soldiers. Both Filana and Burtis were sitting up by then, while the sergeants applied a healing salve to the worst of their burns.

"Elebrio's dead," Vambran said. "Acid got him squarely in the face, it appears."

"Aye," Grolo grumbled as he handed a waterskin over to Filana. "The boy jumped right into the middle of the fight, though," the dwarf said. "Never backed down from the snake for a moment. He would have made a fine soldier."

"We have to get moving," Vambran said, changing the subject. "There are trackers on our trail, hunting us down even as we speak. It won't take them long to find us, with the kind of noise we just made.

"Adyan, strip Elebrio's body of anything useful and bury him in leaves. We can't dig a grave, but we can at least make it a little harder for the bloodhounds to figure out what happened."

"Aye, sir," Adyan replied and moved to do Vambran's bidding.

"Grolo, Horial, help the two of them," Vambran said, indicating the wounded pair. "You get moving northeast, back toward the coast. I'm going to try to mislead our pursuers a little bit by laying a false trail to the south." The other two nodded, and everyone sprang into action at once. Vambran moved to a position in the midst of the snake carcasses and set off through the trees southward, deeper into the forest, doing his best to stir up leaves, snap fallen branches, and scuff his feet into the dirt. After he had progressed in such a fashion for a couple of hundred paces, he stopped near the base of a tree.

It was almost too dark to see anything, so he drew forth his pendant and uttered a soft prayer of light. The resulting glow that sprang from the coin was gentle, like moonlight, and Vambran cupped the symbol in his hand to keep it from shining out in all directions.

Using the magical light to aid him, Vambran knelt down at the base of the tree and began hunting for another spider. He spotted one quickly enough, and he went through the motions of casting the spell again that he had used to climb with before. When he knew the magic had manifested, Vambran willed the soft light to wink out, waited a moment for his eyes to adjust, and scurried up the tree.

Near the top, Vambran began to move out along the limbs of the shadowtop, navigating the narrow branch with ease, thanks to his magical ability. As he neared the end of the branch and felt it begin to sag dangerously low, he transferred his weight to another branch, which happened to protrude from a neighboring tree. Then he scurried across the expanse of that tree's cover and moved on to the next tree.

Vambran continued to maneuver through the forest that way, crossing from tree to tree by means of the climbing spell, never leaving a trail upon the ground. After he had progressed quite a distance and was certain the magic would fade soon, he hurried down. Sure enough, when he was perhaps ten feet from the ground, he felt the spell dissipate, and he half jumped and half fell the rest of the way to the forest floor.

Better not wait so long next time, he thought, dusting himself off. Then he set off in the general direction he had sent his companions, expecting to catch up to them after a little while. Part of his plan also took into account the possibility of his little trick failing to mislead the trackers.

If they don't fall for it, I want them to catch up to me, first, he thought. I can give the others a fair chance to escape by myself.

But his fears did not come to that, and after perhaps an hour of walking, Vambran began to detect motion through the trees ahead. Picking up his pace, the lieutenant issued his telltale bird call. Soon enough, the whistled reply echoed back. Vambran caught up to the rest of the group a short time later.

"Well, we'll see how much we managed to delay them," he said as the six of them settled down to rest for a few moments. "I doubt it will hold them up for long, but every few minutes of time we bought is worth it."

"We tried to tread lightly, sir," Horial said as he began to pass around some hunks of hard bread and some slices of thick, dried meat. "Don't know how good of a job we did, though. We're soldiers, not thieves."

"Don't worry about it," Vambran replied, noticing the ache in his legs for the first time all night. "If we can stay ahead of them, that's good enough." He bit into a slice of meat and tore the mouthful free. His stomach rumbled with appreciation, and Vambran realized he hadn't eaten since before noon that day, when they had all still been aboard *Lady's Favor.* That seemed like such a very long time ago.

Kovrim, where are you? the lieutenant wondered. What happened to everyone?

In the darkness, he could more than see the rest of the group busily consuming the small repast that Horial had doled out. No one said anything, but Vambran could sense the courage and determination from each of them. He could judge it by the carriage of each soldier's silhouette, hear it in the way they ate their food. They were professionals, and he was proud of the way they were handling the bizarre and unnerving circumstances of the day.

"Any idea where we're headed?" Burtis asked between bites.

Vambran shook his head then realized the other soldiers most likely could not see his gesture. "None at all," he admitted, "though I know that Reth lies ahead of us. We keep walking the way we're going right now, we'll wind up hitting either the coast or the road that runs south out of Reth and circles around the Nunwood back toward Hlath. One way or the other, we'll wind up in the city."

"Assuming we can get there before our pursuit catches up," Filana said, her mouth full of bread.

"Well, if you're so worried about that," Vambran replied, rising, "then break time is over. Let's get marching, soldier."

Filana groaned but did not question her superior. As a team, the six gathered up everything they had and set out again.

As they walked, Vambran took the time to listen to the surroundings. Other than the snakes, they had not been visited by any predators, which surprised him.

Don't go looking for more trouble, soldier, he told himself. Be glad the denizens have left you alone.

Vambran recalled then some of the stories of the Nunwood, of how most of the more dangerous creatures had been run off or slain. The forest had been heavily logged for many centuries before the druids of the Emerald Enclave had stepped in and begun making trouble for the folk who lived along its edge. Lumber processing had slowed down considerably once the druids began pushing everyone around, but it had not died off completely. Regardless, both the logging operations—or rather the mercenaries hired by the loggers—and the druids had managed to make the Nunwood a much safer place than other forests in the region.

Of course, that was a relative thing, Vambran realized. Even a safe forest still remained shrouded in mystery and harbored danger. Though the snakes had been unfortunate, he still considered the group lucky to that point not to have encountered more dangerous creatures during their trek.

Vambran's musings were interrupted by the appearance of a glow from ahead. The others saw the emanations about the same time he did, and the whole group drew to a halt. Though they were still too far removed to be certain, to Vambran's eyes, the glow seemed to be the remnants of some dying fires, barely visible through the trees ahead of them Almost as one, the five other mercenaries crouched down and huddled together, waiting to see what their leader ordered.

Vambran leaned in and whispered, "stay here while I move ahead to see what's what. Don't make any sounds because whoever this is might have sentries posted in this direction."

Though he could not see the other mercenaries' responses, he could sense that they understood. Quietly as he could, Vambran rose to his feet and began to creep forward, noting a few conspicuous trees that he could use to navigate back in that direction once he was finished scouting. As he drew closer to the glow, he became more and more certain that it was from multiple campfires, and they were all positioned in a clearing ahead. The lieutenant stopped at one point and peered around, searching for telltale signs that guards stood watch there in the edge of the woods, but he did not see anything, so he began to move forward again.

When Vambran reached the underbrush that marked the edge of the clearing, he saw that it was a military camp. Tents were clustered in orderly groups around the fires, and there were indeed sentries positioned around the perimeter of the encampment, but none of them was stationed very close to the edge of the woods. The lieutenant did notice, however, that several of the guards were standing watch over an old barn near where Vambran crouched. He could see that a fresh door had been built into the side of the barn, and a log was used to bar it shut. The mercenary officer had a pretty good idea that prisoners were inside. He wondered if they were Sapphire Crescents.

Knowing he was risking capture, but burning with the need to know, Vambran circled around until he could approach the barn from the back side and, he hoped, unnoticed. He crept very carefully out of the trees and right up to the wall, which was made only of rough logs, so there were plenty of gaps. He peered inside, but the glow of the firelight was not enough to see by.

Taking a deep breath, Vambran gave a very soft whistle, the birdcall signal he was so fond of using. A form stirred very near where he crouched and mumbled something soft. Vambran whistled again, still keeping the sound very light and soft.

"What the—?" the figure grunted, sitting upright. "Who's there?" the man mumbled, trying to whisper.

"Lieutenant Vambran. What's your name?"

"By Waukeen, Lieutenant, it's sure good to hear your voice!" It was Hort "Old Bloagy" Bloagermun, and he was speaking too loudly.

"Shh!" Vambran warned in a whisper, glancing around to see if the sentries had heard anything. "Keep your voice down!"

"Sorry, sir," Hort whispered back, obviously fully awake by then. "What's going on?"

"A few Crescents and I are in the woods, just beyond the camp here. How'd you wind up in there?"

Hort told Vambran the tale of his capture, along with the others. He did a quick listing of the men included, and when he named off Kovrim, Vambran felt his shoulders sag in profound relief.

"That's great news, soldier," he whispered. "We're going to figure out a way to get you out of there, but sit tight. Don't even wake the rest of the men up, yet. Do you understand?"

"Aye, sir," Hort replied.

"I'll be back soon," Vambran said then turned and crept away. Elation made the man want to move quickly, but he dared not let it get the best of him, so he very carefully backtracked to the point where he had left his companions.

"I found more Crescents," he began, but before he could finish, he realized that the other five were not alone. Numerous figures rose up from behind trees or bushes, surrounding Vambran and his companions. Instinctively, Vambran reached for his sword.

"Don't," came a soft voice from behind him, and a curved blade was laid across his neck at an angle. "You won't make it."

Vambran froze. At first, he thought the trackers had caught up to them, but as he turned slowly to get a better look, he realized that all of the newcomers were covered in plants and branches. The blade at his throat was a scimitar.

Druids!

Before Vambran could reveal his observation, however, a large shout rose up from the camp.

"It's begun," the figure still holding the scimitar against the lieutenant said. "We must hurry."

"What's begun?" Vambran demanded.

"Your doom," the druid replied.

Something slammed hard against the back of Vambran's head, and the world turned upside down before fading away.

CHAPTER 11

Kovrim was startled awake by sudden
noise, but for a moment, he could not
remember where he was. Then the
foggy remnants of sleep began to clear,
and the mercenary recalled how he'd
come to be locked inside a very old barn
with several other soldiers. As he sat up
and peered around, rubbing the sleep from
his eyes, the priest could hear shouting
and the beginnings of some sort of scuffle
just beyond the walls of the barn, and he
realized that the fighting was what had
awakened him.

"What's going on?" Kovrim asked of no
one in particular, standing and stretching
as he observed many of the rest of the dozen
Crescents standing or kneeling, peering
through gaps in the log wall.

"Lieutenant Matrell is out there," Hort Bloager-mun said, turning toward Kovrim. "He said he and some other Crescents were in the forest, and they were going to try to free us!"

"What?" Kovrim said, not sure he had heard correctly. "Vambran's here?"

"Aye, sir," Old Bloagy replied, still pressing one eye to the wall. "He crept up to the wall here and spoke with me just a few moments ago."

Kovrim realized his knees were shaking in relief. Vambran was alive! He was mounting a rescue attempt!

But then, Kovrim began to frown, for he could see no way for such a plan to succeed. The old mercenary knew how many soldiers had been with the company aboard the ship, and how many Vambran was likely to have remaining under his command. It was a pitiful number to take up against the entire army gathered in the clearing where he and the other Crescents were being held. It was foolish to try a head-on assault, and Vambran would know that, too. Kovrim's nephew was no fool.

"No, something else is happening," Kovrim announced, moving to the wall to get a look. "Vambran may be out there, but this is not his work. He wouldn't try to attack the entire silver raven contingent this way. They must have been spotted out in the woods."

"Those aren't Crescents out there," another soldier reported from the opposite wall. "Someone else is attacking the camp."

Kovrim switched positions to get a better look. In the dim light of the embers of the many fires, he could see very little, but the motion all around the clearing was continuous, and he could occasionally make out a figure leaping up from the shadows, pouncing on a soldier of the silver raven group. The sound of the fighting grew louder as more of the attacking force poured into the camp.

Nearby, the guards standing watch at the door to the barn cried out, and Kovrim raced over to see what had become of them. Three silhouettes were arrayed against the pair of mercenaries, all of them dressed in crude, natural clothing and swinging curved blades. One of the figures was an elf.

"Druids," Kovrim said, understanding at last. "They're attacking the logging operation."

"Maybe they'll free us," another soldier said. "We should shout to let them know we're in here!"

Kovrim started to protest such a notion, figuring the druids were well aware of the Crescents' predicament and unlikely to do much about it. The veteran soldier had campaigned against the druids during his years of service, and he knew that the woodland people did not distinguish between rival bands of mercenaries, and the Sapphire Crescents certainly appeared to be a rival band. To them, every soldier was an enemy of the trees, and it was doubtful those attacking the camp that night would have any concern for the plight of the dozen prisoners inside the barn. If they escaped, the woodland folk might even turn on them, as well.

Kovrim was forming up a plan to get the men out himself, but it would require good timing. "Get ready to flee when the right moment comes," he ordered, causing a stir all around him as he moved toward the door. "You'll know when that is," he promised them.

The three druids overwhelmed the pair of guards in front of the barn, but they did not turn their attention to the prisoners, as Kovrim had suspected. Instead, they melted into the shadows again, leaving the men inside to grumble and wonder aloud why they had been ignored.

The fighting raged on, with shouting, horses whinnying in alarm, and the ring of steel on steel everywhere.
Kovrim began to think that the druids would win the
contest, for it seemed to him as he watched that there
were more and more of them and fewer of the silver
ravens. That's when he decided it was time to act.

Uttering a simple phrase, he instantly found himself on the opposite side of the door, standing next to
the bodies of the downed guards. The priest grabbed
the log that had been used to bar the door and shoved
it aside, prepared to open the portal and lead the
Crescents into the woods beyond the camp.

But the blaring sound of horns began ringing out
through the forest. The clarion call echoed from down
the path the Crescents had followed upon arriving at
the camp. Kovrim turned just in time to spot a contingent of cavalry bursting into the clearing, charging
ahead to attack the scattered, ill-equipped druids.
Behind the cavalry, a large force of infantry marched
into view, a wide column of troops who maneuvered
precisely into a skirmish line and moved through the
camp at a steady if not spectacular pace.

Damn it to the nine hells, Kovrim thought, yanking the door open. This may get dicey.

"Hurry!" he said. "Before the reinforcements
catch us!"

The prisoners inside the barn began filing out,
turning and making a beeline for the trees. Before
even half of the Crescents were out of the prison,
though, shouts rose up from nearby. Kovrim spun in
time to see a trio of mounted soldiers bearing down
on him and the men escaping with him.

"Run!" he shouted, urging the soldiers to fade into
the woods. As the rest of the Crescents fled, Kovrim
turned back toward the mounted soldiers, planning
a distraction to slow them down and give the men
time to escape. Slipping a hand inside his shirt, the

priest removed a bit of parchment he had stored in
a secret pocket. He gave it a quick kiss then began
muttering a prayer as he crumpled the scrap and
made a circular motion with it around his body.

The parchment crumbled to dust in Kovrim's hand
while at the same time, a glowing field of protective
energy sprang up, surrounding his body. He ran
toward the cavalrymen, hoping his magical barrier
would be enough to protect him from a stray attack
or two. In the back of his mind, he began to formulate
the words of a final spell, one that he could use to
whisk himself away from the fighting.

When the time comes, he told himself. Not too
soon, though. Must give them time to get deep into
the woods.

The first of the cavalrymen began to twirl a light
mace menacingly, and Kovrim darted in the opposite
direction, hoping to lure the soldier along with him.
The priest huffed and puffed as he zigzagged through
the camp, trying to draw attention to himself while
at the same time avoiding being cornered. The woodland folk had gone into a full retreat, it seemed, for
there were only the dead among them still within the
confines of the camp. It became apparent that he was
alone in his frantic plan, and more and more mounted
soldiers closed in about him, trying to contain him.
He felt a bit foolish, like a lone chicken in a fenced
yard, running willy-nilly all about, trying to keep
himself off the chopping block.

When a mounted soldier approached him with a
halfspear leveled at his chest, Kovrim stopped and
raised his arms out to his sides as a show of surrender.
He began to speak the words of that last spell, ready
to send himself instantly over many miles of terrain
in an instant, all the way back to Arrabar, where he
would regroup and bring reinforcements to aid the
stranded Crescents.

Before he could complete the triggering phrases, though, something struck him hard from behind, on the back of the head, and he sank to his knees, stunned. The words of the spell vanished from his mind, and blackness replaced them.

...

Kovrim slowly came awake with a throbbing pain at the base of his skull. He discovered, to his dismay, that he had a large, leather-wrapped bar of steel rammed into his mouth like the bit of a bridle. The bulging thing pressed back against the corners of his mouth, keeping his teeth pried open and depressing his tongue. It was firmly anchored with leather straps that ran over and around his head, as well as beneath his chin. The entire thing buckled in back somewhere. Furthermore, his arms were stoutly manacled in front of himself, each fist tightly encased in a hinged metal ball that prevented him from even flexing his fingers. Kovrim was helpless to even try to unbuckle the harness. The mercenaries who had recaptured him were apparently used to dealing with enemy mages and priests. All in all, it was a rather effective way to keep the priest from talking. Or casting any more spells.

Kovrim realized to his further dismay that he was back inside the barn, along with most of the Crescents. The men had not made it far into the woods, it appeared, before they had been rounded up and returned to the makeshift prison, and the glum faces made it clear to the grizzled priest that their failed escape attempt had cost more than a spell. They were without much hope.

The larger surprise came a few moments later, though, when Kovrim realized there were more Crescents in the prison than before they had tried to escape. He winced as he counted them, for several were wounded, two seriously enough that they were lying on makeshift stretchers, brought to the camp that way by other members of the company. In all, there were fourteen new members there, nearly a third of the total company. Coupled with the twelve that had originally accompanied Kovrim, that meant well over half of the soldiers had been taken since *Lady's Favor* had gone down and the mercenaries had floundered to shore. With the four he knew to be dead at sea, that meant that at most, Vambran had nearly a dozen men with him. Kovrim strongly suspected there were fewer than that, for the uncertainties of war always left a few more dead scattered on the battlefield than anyone expected.

Less than ten, he surmised. Vambran would never have tried to assault this camp with that few. Perhaps it's good that we did not manage to flee, he told himself, realizing that, had the escape attempt proven successful, it would have meant that the other Crescents would have been left behind. No, the priest decided, it was better to consolidate the troops. Strangely, he felt relief at that.

In addition to the members of the Sapphire Crescent, two of the woodland folk had been captured alive. They both looked sullen and angry, as best Kovrim could tell, for they, too, sported the harsh bit-gag head harnesses and hand-restraining manacles he himself wore. All the old priest could really see of their expressions were their eyes. Both were younger men, dressed in crude animal-skin clothing. Their weapons, of course, had been taken away during the night.

Kovrim sat up and peered about, peeking through one of the cracks in the barn's wall, and he saw that the sky to the east was just beginning to get a little pink. The rest of the reinforcements who had arrived to

The Ruby Guardian   195

turn the tide of the fight were assembled in the clearing. Kovrim reckoned that the group that had taken
him and the other Crescents prisoner the day before
were only perhaps a fifth of the total force of the army
bearing the silver raven that was gathered there.

One of the new arrivals, Tholis, who had served in
Vambran's platoon for several years, saw that Kovrim
was awake.

"Well met," he said, greeting the old priest. "We
tried to find a way to get that out of your mouth, but
they locked it on too well." Kovrim nodded, hoping
the younger man understood that he appreciated
the effort.

"Tell him your tale," Hort said, coming up to stand
beside Tholis. "He might not be able to speak, but he
needs to know your side of things."

"We made it to shore with Lieutenant Matrell
after *Lady's Favor* went down," Tholis began, looking forlorn at what he was having to say. "There were
twenty-three of us. We parceled out supplies and were
just about to get on the move when we were attacked
by that bunch out there. Lieutenant Matrell ordered
us to charge through their skirmish line and make
for the woods, but those bastards put the magic to
us but good, and everyone you see here went down.
We lost two," the man added, bowing his head, "and
seven escaped, or so we hope, including Lieutenant
Matrell." Then Tholis sighed. "They spent most of the
day beating the brush, trying to flush the seven out,
with no luck. By evening, they were sending trackers
into the woods to hunt them down, and we marched
all night. Now here we are."

Kovrim nodded.

"Well, soldier," Hort said, "you'll be happy to know
that Lieutenant Matrell and his remaining companions made it here, too. The lieutenant spoke to me just
before the commotion. Said they were going to try to

break us out, but that attack must have altered their plans. Let's hope they're still out there, thinking of something clever to do."

"So, what's going to happen now?" Tholis asked, sagging down to the ground. "Have they told us why we're prisoners?"

Kovrim shook his head as Hort snorted. "They haven't bothered to tell us anything, soldier," the grizzled old veteran complained, "but we might find out soon. It looks like they're having a serious discussion right now."

Indeed, Kovrim could see what looked to be the leaders of the mercenary army standing in a group near the center of the camp, talking and gesticulating animatedly at the trees, the barn, and various other points. The priest wondered if his identity had finally been ferreted out, and if he had further endangered the soldiers in his charge by not departing when he had had the opportunity.

The priest wished for a moment that he could cast a spell to eavesdrop on the conversation in the distance. Of course, if that were the case, he thought, I could do a lot more than eavesdrop.

After a moment, officers began to shout orders, and soon enough, a contingent of mercenaries approached the barn. The guards jumped to obey as orders were given to open the door leading into the makeshift prison. As the portal was unbarred and swung wide, the commanding officer strode into the middle of the group of Crescents. Several other soldiers followed him inside.

"My name is Captain Beltrim Havalla. I have orders to get you to Reth, so that's exactly what we're going to do. As soon as you've been served breakfast, we'll be setting out."

Several of the prisoners groaned, particularly the newer ones who had just arrived.

Captain Havalla eyed Kovrim appreciatively. "Sergeant," he said in a commanding voice, at which point one of the other soldiers by his side leaped forward, at the ready. "This man gets no breakfast, for we can't afford for him to be speaking. In fact, go ahead and load him into a wagon now. I don't want to torment him with the smell of any food."

The sergeant nodded and snapped his fingers. Immediately, two more soldiers moved forward, grabbing Kovrim by each arm.

Kovrim grimaced and closed his eyes in consternation as his personal escort began to lead him away.

...

Vambran opened his eyes to discover that he was watching the trees drift past upside down, swaying rhythmically. It took him another moment or two to understand that he was hanging that way, hands and feet bound across a stout log carried on the shoulders of two men. All of his belongings, including his breastplate and his weapons, had been taken from him. His neck and back ached.

The lieutenant lifted his head up and peered between his arms, trying to get some sense of what was happening. The other five Crescents who had still been with him during the night were bound similarly, each dangling from a pole borne on strong shoulders. Their escort consisted of perhaps two dozen figures, all strung out in a line, following a trail through the woods. Only some of them were human.

In addition to a handful of men and women roughly clad in the skins of animals and further camouflaged with twigs and leaves interwoven into their clothing and hair, there were a couple of elves in the group—one was a male in a simple loincloth with dark brown skin covered in tattoos, and the

other had more coppery skin and red hair. There
were also a handful of creatures that seemed to be
a cross between an elf and an antelope. Vambran
would have named them centaurs had they had
the bodies of horses, but they were much smaller.
The druids and their companions moved easily
among the trees, practically vanishing from sight
as they glided past shadows and underbrush with
the greatest of ease.

Dropping his head back down for a moment,
Vambran noticed that the sun was beginning to
rise behind him and to his left. That meant they
were heading southwest, at least assuming it was
morning. They were moving deeper into the forest,
to its heart, if he remembered the maps correctly. All
around Vambran, the forest was nearly silent, though
a few early birds were beginning to stir.

A wild-haired halfling carrying a small bow appeared along the trail behind the group and quickly
caught up, passing Vambran. The lieutenant craned
his neck and watched as the halfling began to speak
with a human, the one who had first laid steel to
Vambran's throat the night before. He was a slender
man, with matted dark hair and a strong jaw line.

The leader, Vambran surmised.

As he watched the human listen to the messenger's words, Vambran saw his captor tense. Then he
nodded and barked a quick command to those around
him, and the group halted. Vambran and the other
Crescents were set down none too gently, still tied
to the poles that bore them. The lieutenant found
that an exposed root was poking him in his backside,
and he tried unsuccessfully to shift off of it before
giving up.

"What has occurred?" the lieutenant asked.

The leader looked at him, perhaps angry that the
mercenary had deigned to speak. Then his features

softened somewhat in the dim glow of dawn, and he said, "Our attack on the soldier camp was unsuccessful. Reinforcements arrived and drove us from the field."

"Reinforcements?" Vambran said, surprised. "That's a good-sized mercenary company!"

"Your brethren scour the land all throughout these woods, killing one another and poisoning the land. You are everywhere. Why does the size of this one army surprise you?"

"Because I did not come here to fight," Vambran replied. "We are not involved in the wars of these other soldiers."

The druid sniffed. "I very much doubt that is true," he said.

"What of my soldiers?" Vambran persisted. "They were prisoners, being held in the barn. What is their fate?"

"I do not differentiate one group from another anymore," the leader replied coldly. "You all kill and destroy equally well." Vambran opened his mouth to protest, but the leader gave him a warning look. "Do not mock me with your lies. I would see you dead, but Arbeenok has foreseen some use for you in his visions, so I have stayed my hand—for the moment. Do not try my patience, though, or not even Arbeenok can save you."

Swallowing the retort he would have liked to utter, Vambran instead asked, "Arbeenok?"

The man jerked his head in the direction of another creature before moving off, ending the conversation. The creature he had indicated was accompanying the rest of the group but standing off alone, by himself. Vambran stared, for he had never seen such a beast before.

Arbeenok could almost have been an ape of some sort. His body was completely covered in light-colored

fur, and he had large, tufted ears that rose straight
up from the sides of his head. He was immensely muscular, with his neck as broad as his head. He had a
barrel chest and thick, bulging arms protruding from
a crude leather shirt. His legs were equally robust,
even though they were encased in similar leather
trousers. The mercenary officer noticed beads and
feathers woven into Arbeenok's hair, and he carried
a trio of javelins and a wicked-looking knife that
jutted through a belt around his waist.

Though he was obviously physically powerful, the
creature seemed reserved, almost shy, to Vambran.
The lieutenant studied Arbeenok for a moment. The
creature stood very still, his head cocked to one side,
as though listening. Vambran could hear nothing,
though, and when he noticed the mercenary staring
at him, Arbeenok turned and strode away, vanishing
into the trees ahead.

The rest was brief, and soon enough, Vambran
found himself swaying once more back and forth as
his bearers walked. He pleaded with the leader at one
point to let them down, that he and the other Crescents would cooperate if they were allowed to walk,
but all he got for his offer was a threat of forced silence
if he did not be quiet himself. Sighing, he tried to find
a way to ease the ache in his shoulders and neck.

The entourage's journey took them deep into the
woods, and though Vambran could hardly make it
out sometimes, they were following a trail of sorts.
At two different points along their route, they were
forced to cross a sizeable stream that blocked their
path, but each time, a carefully placed log permitted them to traverse the waterway easily, though for
those hanging upside down, the crossing was nerve-
racking. Vambran noticed that the trees on either
side of the makeshift bridge had many markings
carved into their bark.

Signposts? he wondered. Or messages?

After the sun was well up in the sky, the group stopped for a longer rest. Though the druids refused to untie the Crescents, they did feed Vambran and the others a bit of food. The female elf with the reddish hair came and knelt down beside the lieutenant, a leaf cupped in her hand. Inside, Vambran could see squirming slugs, freshly dug from out of the earth. The elf held one up and brought it to his lips. The mercenary officer did not want anything to do with it. The idea of consuming the still-living thing was repulsive to him, and he turned his head away.

His attendant frowned and shrugged, then popped the slug into her own mouth. "You will not eat?" she asked as she chewed. Her accent was odd, lilting and musical. "The food is fresh," she added, showing him the leaf in her hand.

"A little too fresh, actually," Vambran replied. "There's jerky in my pack. I'll eat some of that, if you don't mind."

The elven maiden made a face. "Dried meat," she said distastefully. "It has no ... goodness," she said, struggling to find the word. "This is better."

Vambran sighed, but he did not feel like continuing the argument. His stomach rumbled and he opened his mouth and allowed her to press one of the wriggling slugs onto his tongue.

If I can eat a live spider, he told himself. . . .

Gingerly, the mercenary officer bit down on the slug and felt its fluids bathe his tongue. He grimaced, but surprisingly, the taste was not as bad as he had thought. Before he could think too much about what it was that he was eating, Vambran chewed up the morsel and swallowed it.

"Another?" the elf asked. Vambran nodded, and she fed him two more. Then she offered him a drink from his own waterskin. Vambran was thankful for

the chance to wash the remnants of the slugs out
of his mouth. Regardless of their taste, he didn't
think he'd ever make a habit of eating them. Once
the rest break was over, the druids hoisted their
prisoners to their shoulders and the group was on
its way once more.

After traveling for perhaps another hour, the entourage came upon a large section of exposed rock
that jutted up out of the ground. The leader guided
them all to a narrow crack that ascended like a ramp
to the top of the formation. Vambran eyed the walls
of the crevice, close in on either side of himself, as
his bearers hauled him through it. More than once,
his shoulders scraped painfully against the stone as
he swayed along, but the two druids carrying him
did not seem to care. Finally, they emerged onto an
open, sunny platform of stone, surrounded on three
sides with rock walls that were dotted with caves.
There were several other individuals there ahead of
the group and signs that the place was inhabited on
a regular basis.

A small fire burned in a shallow pit near the center
of the open area, though the pit was wide enough to
accommodate a much larger conflagration, and apparently did from time to time, judging from the ash
and soot that coated it. Several large logs had been
dragged up to the platform, too, and those served as
benches for a number of folk who sat around the fire,
talking quietly or sipping at steaming mugs of something that boiled in a kettle. Several rugs and mats
woven of rushes and vines covered much of the surface
of the platform, and numerous buckets and skins were
set off to one side, most of them holding water.

As Vambran and the other prisoners were hauled
into the middle of the open area, the folk who had
already been there eyed them with some interest. The
six prisoners were unceremoniously set down on the

rock. Vambran groaned as he settled flat, feeling the strain in his back and neck finally ease. He closed his eyes for a moment and shifted his bound wrists and ankles about, trying to encourage circulation to return to them.

When he opened them again, a woman, a human of middling years with dark brown hair woven into braids that were interspersed with feathers and bits of colored stone on leather thongs, was standing over Vambran, studying him with a critical eye that was a piercing emerald color. She said something to the man in the same undecipherable language the lieutenant had heard previously, from the scouts. His guide answered her with a long explanation of some sort, gesturing more than once at Vambran as he did so. The woman frowned and shook her head, but the man grew animated, even angry, seeming to insist on something.

Just when it seemed that the pair might actually come to blows, another figure approached, hopping down from somewhere previously unseen atop the cliff face. It was Arbeenok who approached cautiously, nodding repeatedly, as though he wanted to speak but was afraid of interrupting. At his arrival, the other two quieted, and the woman gestured for him to speak.

His voice was deep and resonant, rich and warm. He spoke in the same language the other two had been conversing in, which Vambran had come to assume was the language of the druids. Whatever Arbeenok was saying, the other two listened respectfully. At one point, he gestured toward the lieutenant and his companions, then toward the caves lining the cliff walls of the area.

Vambran turned and peered at the openings in the cliffs and noticed for the first time that some of them had been secured with stout cage walls set right into the stone. He could see no visible doors or means of moving the frames, which were constructed of stout saplings. He turned back to the conversation, wondering just what fate the trio was deciding for him and the other captured Crescents.

Finally, the woman nodded and waved toward the caves. The human scowled and shook his head, but she made a sharp, cutting motion that indicated the end of the conversation. The man turned, still scowling, and motioned to his associates, who hoisted Vambran and the others into the air once more.

The druids lugged the prisoners toward one of the caged-off caves. As they drew near, the frowning man muttered something, while at the same time gesturing at one of the saplings. The timber creaked and groaned as it began to magically curl up, and Vambran could see that both ends had previously been set into round holes cut into the stone of the cave mouth. As the slender tree warped, it dropped to the ground, leaving a gap between its neighbors large enough for a man to fit snugly through.

The bearers stepped through the narrow gap, into the cool, dark interior of the cage. Vambran was once again dropped roughly to the stone floor on his back. One of his carriers released the pole running the length of his torso while the other slid it out from beneath the lieutenant's bonds, leaving him free to stretch or sit up, but still securely tied.

The other five Crescents were treated similarly, until all six of the mercenaries were inside the cave, which was just large enough to accommodate them. The druids stepped back out, and the leader picked up the curved wooden pole he had magically bent. Once more, he wove a spell upon the timber then held it in place as it popped and creaked back into its original, straight form, positioned in the holes, effectively jailing the Crescents.

The lieutenant looked out at his jailor, wondering if he was going to learn the reason he and his soldiers had been brought there, but the man seemed uninterested in him any longer, turning and stalking away. The woman, however, approached the prison. She peered through at the six of them there, as though thinking. Finally, she began to speak.

"Arbeenok has studied the portents of the earth and sky and says a great death is coming. He says you may be the key to stopping this great death. Even so, you are a soldier, and all soldiers are the enemies of the woodlands. Thus, we will suffer you to live, scions of Arrabar, but you are our prisoners and will remain so until such time as Arbeenok comes to understand the meaning behind his visions. Should you try to flee, you will be hunted down and slain."

CHAPTER 12

It was the screaming of gulls so nearby that drew Emriana to consciousness, that and the sun beginning to burn her skin. She became aware of the fact that she was half in the water, for the rhythmic bobbing motion of the tide gently bounced her against something hard. Everything stank of fish.

The girl groaned and tried to open her eyes, but the brightness of the light hurt too much, so she just lay there for a long time, trying to remember what had happened, how she had come to be there. Everything was mind-numbingly fuzzy, though, and it hurt to think. Finally, a flash of memory from the night before, a vague sense of danger, jarred her more awake, and she tried to rise.

Emriana discovered that she was tangled in some discarded fishing netting that had been wrapped around a piling at the wharf. Somehow she wound up sitting in the mesh, as though it were a hammock, though her body was half submerged in the filthy water beneath the pier. The sun was canted at an odd angle, catching her face in just the right way so that, though she was actually beneath the wooden causeway, it shone directly on her.

Extracting herself from the ruined netting turned out to be harder than she would have imagined, for she was thoroughly tangled in it, and for a brief moment she wished she had one of her daggers. Then it all came flooding back, the memories of the alley and the carpet, of sinking to the bottom of the bay. She almost screamed right then and there. She stared around herself, wondering how she had managed to escape the confines of the rug and rise to the surface, and even more amazing was how she was able to work herself into the netting so that she wouldn't drown. She didn't remember any of it.

Carefully, the girl disentangled herself from the mesh and settled into the water. She then swam around to the end of the pier and found a partial ladder that she could use to climb up onto the surface of the platform. Once she was out of the water, she surveyed herself and discovered that she was missing one boot and that her left sleeve was torn almost completely off. Other than that, she seemed to be intact, though her head began to pound as she moved around. She cast one last look down into the water and thought she might barely be able to make out an elongated form, like that of a rolled up carpet, perhaps a dozen feet below the surface. The imagery made her shudder, and she was just about to turn away, when she saw a glint of movement.

She knelt down and stared, certain that she had seen a figure moving through the shallows beneath the pier, a slender and graceful form that was more

human than fish. But there was nothing there when
she looked again, though she remained there for several moments more. Wondering if she had imagined
it, Emriana rose to her feet again and tried to figure
out where she was.

In doing so, she failed to notice a head break the
surface for a brief moment, with delicate features that
were angular and tinted blue. Those features watched
the girl stagger away for a step or two; then the head
vanished beneath the surface once more.

It did not take Emriana long to navigate her way
off the pier and onto dry land and before much longer,
she began to see where she was. The section of Arrabar
where she and Xaphira had ventured the night before
was nearby, and even in the daylight, the girl thought
better than to pass through there alone, especially in
her condition. She knew she looked a sight, and she
doubted she could put up much of a struggle should
anyone decide to accost her. Even with the circuitous
route she chose to follow, she drew more than a few
strange looks from the early-morning shoppers and
strollers who were out and about.

As she struggled up the hills upon which Arrabar
had been built, working her way slowly from the dock
area to the nicer part of town, Emriana tried to consider everything that had happened. Remembering
that Xaphira had disappeared worried her greatly,
and she pulled her pendant out and tried to contact
her aunt again.

Again there was no reply for her efforts.

The thought that Aunt Xaphira was already dead
nearly made the girl drop to her knees in the middle
of the street, but she resisted the weakness in her
legs and pushed on, determined to return home and
let everyone know what had happened. She imagined
what her mother would say about her wandering in
after being out all night, but truthfully, Emriana did

not care. Grandmother Hetta was who she needed to speak to right then, and the quicker she got home, the quicker they could begin to figure out how to find and save Xaphira. But as she walked, the pain in her head grew worse, and Emriana felt herself on the verge of passing out more than once. She didn't think she could make the journey all the way back home as woozy as she felt.

The temple, she decided, massaging her skull. It's closer than home, and some of Vambran's or Uncle Kovrim's friends will help me.

As Emriana entered the temple district and drew near the Temple of Waukeen, she saw that a crowd had gathered. She limped closer, reaching the fringes of the throng, and began to try to find a way through the people, hoping she could find a priest she knew. As polite and patient as she tried to be, though, everyone around her gave her cold or contemptuous stares.

Finally, a hawk-nosed woman with severe, beady eyes elbowed the girl, pushing her back a step.

"Know your place, girl," the woman said. "We all want a better look at the new high priest, but this is as close as any of us are going to get, so stop shoving."

The meaning of the woman's words hit her fully. "The new high priest?" she asked. "What happened to Grand Syndar Midelli?"

The hawk-nosed woman gave her a baleful stare. "Haven't you heard?" she snapped. "The Grand Syndar is dead."

"Dead?" she repeated, stunned.

The woman nodded and sniffed. "Aye, he passed last night, they say, though he had been ill for more than that, they say."

Emriana felt the ground tilting beneath her feet as the news sank in. She wondered if everyone at home knew, yet. "Have they named a successor?"

"Where have you been hiding, child?" the woman

asked, shaking her head in consternation. "What do
you think we're all doing here? They're about to an-
nounce it now." With a final shake of her head, the
unpleasant woman turned away, refocusing her attention toward the front of the temple.

At that moment, a hush fell over the crowd, followed by an excited murmur as a line of high priests
began to file out the front doors of the temple and onto
the steps. They were all dressed in their most lavish
finery, and they took up positions in rows along the
steps, creating a dazzling display of the finest white
cloth, sparkling gems of amber and ruby, and plenty of
polished gold. The last priest to appear, dressed most
magnificently of all and wearing a miter upon his
head, waddled in a familiar way due to his consider-
able girth.

Grand Trabbar Lavant.

Oh, Waukeen, Emriana thought, sitting down right
in the plaza. Not this. Not now.

The girl had to draw several deep, slow breaths
to gain her equilibrium back. Lavant was the new
Grand Syndar of the entire temple. It didn't seem
possible for the news to get any worse. She had to let
the family know, but first, she needed desperately to
find someone, anyone, within the temple who could
help her. Otherwise, she would never make it back to
the estate.

"Please excuse me," Emriana said, trying once more
to weave her way through the crowd.

"I told you to know your place, girl," the hawk-
nosed woman said, shoving Emriana back once more.
"Now stop pushing."

"But I want to go inside," the girl said, not understanding why they were being so rude to her. "I didn't
mean to shove."

"Inside?" the woman said incredulously. "Looking
and smelling like that?" Then the woman began to

laugh, a high-pitched cackling that was harsh to
Emriana's ears. Several other people gathered about
joined in. "You know the Waukeenars don't let street
waifs like you in their midst. You've got to have coin
to spend in order to walk the golden halls." The harsh
woman shook her head bemusedly. "Inside," she chuckled, turning away again.

As Emriana looked down at her bedraggled appearance, she felt tears beginning to well up. Her clothes
were ruined, torn in several places. They were soiled
with odiferous gunk from the alley the previous
evening. Her hair, normally so shiny black, hung
limply and smelled of rotting fish. She realized just
how badly she smelled by the way the people around
her gave her a step or two of clearance. No one was
going to believe she was Arrabaran nobility looking
like that. But the only way to prove otherwise was to
either clean herself up or find someone who knew and
could vouch for her, neither of which she could do in
her condition.

Feeling defeated, Emriana staggered to one
side of the plaza and sank down in the shade of a
vender's awning, too tired to even look at what he
was selling.

The man who owned the cart, a fat fellow with
black, bushy hair and huge, flaring mustaches, eyed
her curiously then began to frown. "You can't sit
there," he said, shaking a single pudgy finger in her
direction. "You'll drive away the paying customers."

Emriana nodded and dug out her coin purse, surprised to find it still tucked in a sash at her waist.
"Water," she said, her voice little more than a croak,
handing the man a silver coin. "Please," she added,
hoping her politeness would smooth things over for
the fellow.

When he spied the silver glint in her hand the
man's expression lightened considerably. "Of course,"

he said, helping Emriana to sit up and get more comfortable before snatching up his own belt cup and pouring out a serving of water from a pitcher on his cart. He handed the cup to Emriana, who took it and began to drink thirstily. It tasted of mint and was cool as it went down. The girl hadn't realized how thirsty she was until she began quenching it.

After she finished off a second serving, she sighed and looked up at the man gratefully. "Thank you," she said, feeling better. "What are you selling?"

"Why, hot honeycakes, of course," he said and brought one down for her to smell. "Another silver will get you two," he said, eagerly eyeing the girl's coin purse, which she still clutched in her lap. When Emriana nodded and began to retrieve another silver coin, the man produced a pair of fresh, hot pastries that had been soaked in honey. He set them on a narrow wooden plank, like a shingle, and handed the whole thing to Emriana.

She sat in the shade of the cart's awning and devoured the cakes, then paid for another two cups of water after she was done. After swallowing the last of her drink, she handed the cup back to the man and smiled at him. Feeling much better, Emriana climbed to her feet again. Deciding that the temple was too difficult to navigate with the crowd, she turned for home once again.

Grandmother Hetta needs to know, she reasoned. We have to find a way to stop this madness.

Emriana could not run, having only one boot on her feet, but she walked as fast as she was able, out of the temple district and into the neighborhood where the Matrell estate was located. She arrived there nearly an hour after she had been at the temple and pushed past the guards manning the front gate, who stared at her dumbfounded. She didn't care. She hurried up the front path toward the house.

Bursting through the front door, she began calling for her grandmother. A servant met Emriana near the entrance to the house, and the look on the woman's face made Emriana pull up in abject fear.

"What is it?" the girl demanded, taking the servant by the shoulders. "What happened?" They already know about Xaphira, Emriana thought. The news of her death beat me home. She felt her stomach flutter at the possibility and swallowed hard, afraid to hear the revelation.

"Oh, Miss Emriana, it's terrible," the servant said, a girl named Liezl who worked in the kitchens. "I'm so sorry."

"Sorry for what? Liezl, what on Toril happened?" Emriana said, wanting to shake the fool servant.

"It's Mistress Hetta," Liezl said, her voice barely a whisper.

The blood pounded in Emriana's ears. Her legs threatened to give way once more. She couldn't breathe.

Oh, no. No!

Emriana released the poor girl in front of her and ran to the central room of the house, the main hall. From there, she intended to dash toward the wing where her grandmother's rooms were, but she saw the crowd gathered in the sitting room. She skidded to a stop and changed direction, coming up behind another servant, a man who worked in the gardens, whose name she didn't even know. She pushed past him.

Hetta Matrell had been laid in state in the middle of the sitting room.

"No!" Emriana sobbed, rushing into the room. "Hetta!" she said as she stumbled up next to the table where her grandmother had been arranged. All around her, Emriana could hear the gasps of the people in the room, but she ignored them. "No!" she sobbed again, burying her face against her grandmother's. "It's not true!" she cried, willing her grandmother to still be alive. "Please!"

"Oh, I'm afraid it's very true," came a man's voice from the other side of the room. It was a voice that made Emriana's blood run cold. She raised her head and looked, tears streaking her cheeks.

In the far corner, a sickening smile upon his face, stood Grozier Talricci.

...

"And thus, we mark Mikolo Midelli's passing not in sorrow, but in celebration of his life, his leadership, and his accomplishments," Grand Syndar Lavant said, his voice echoing throughout the grand hall of the Temple of Waukeen. Standing where he was at the great altar, both the acoustics of the chamber and permanent magical enhancements allowed the entire audience to hear him clearly. He was dressed in very formal robes of state, a flowing outfit of cream-colored silk with brocaded gold and maroon highlights, and the whole thing was woven with rubies and yellow sapphires. A great miter sat atop his head, a stiff, almost conical thing of deep red, highlighted with solid gold and ruby decorations, glinting in the light of thousands of candles.

In front of the Grand Syndar, lying within a great gold sarcophagus encrusted with hundreds of gems of every imaginable hue, was the body of Mikolo Midelli, the previous Grand Syndar. He had been dressed in his own finest robes of office, an outfit that rivaled Lavant's, who loomed over him, speaking of the man in his most eloquent and gracious tones.

Pilos wanted to clamp his hands over his ears. He could not stand to listen to the fat, arrogant man who had been named as the successor Grand Syndar to the temple. Not when he knew of the political maneuvering, the wrangling of votes, of support, that had taken place the night before, prior to Midelli's death. Earlier that morning, before the public ceremony on the front steps that proclaimed him Grand Syndar to the world, the council of high priests had assembled, with all other clergy in attendance. They had barely given Mikolo's body time to grow cold before they were nominating Lavant for the position. Of course, there had been others who had coveted the rank, and their names were mentioned in the great council chambers as well, but Pilos knew it was a foregone conclusion, even if many of the other clergy members sitting in audience did not.

As the roll had been called and Lavant had garnered the necessary votes to be raised to Grand Syndar, the priests filling the council chamber had given the man thunderous applause. Pilos could not. He had sat there, feeling sickened and listening dully while Lavant revealed his first edicts. The man had the audacity to begin using the weight of his office right then and there, before the temple had even given the old Grand Syndar a proper, respectful send-off.

Of course, Lavant had waved away his brashness in the trappings of dire necessity, for he spoke of the coming of war in the east, of divinations that all of Chondath would be engulfed in the ravages of conflict if the temple did not act. It was all so necessary, Lavant had explained, that they begin preparing for the coming eventualities he had foreseen. Thus, he had begged their indulgence to allow him to commence running the affairs of the temple immediately, rather than waiting the traditional grace period while the previous Grand Syndar lay in state.

What Lavant had described was a very different temple than the one Pilos had known to that point. The rotund leader was taking them in a decidedly

more militant, aggressive direction than the temple
had seen in many years. Pilos wondered just what
Mikolo would have thought of such changes. He wondered what Waukeen thought of them, returning his
attention to the moment.

"Even during those years of our Lady's absence,"
Lavant was saying, "Mikolo Midelli was resolute,
devout, never faltering in his belief and faith. He did
not turn his back on the Merchant's Friend to bathe
in the holiness of other gods. He sought to continue
Waukeen's teachings, even when Waukeen could not
walk among his flock herself."

That's a dangerous thing to be saying, Pilos
thought in mild surprise. He's all but naming
Mikolo as a surrogate god. What does that say about
those who shifted their allegiance to Lliira when
Waukeen went missing? How many of the clergy is
he alienating?

As if to punctuate the Abreeant's concerns, numerous priests sitting around him began to shift in their
seats uncomfortably or grumble among themselves.

"He will be missed," Lavant said, "but his works
will live on in the glory of the temple for generations
to come."

There was a pause, and Pilos wondered if the Grand
Syndar was finished with his eulogy. What came next
surprised and angered him.

"Mikolo Midelli's time at the helm of the temple
was a time of peace. It was a time of prosperity. Those
days are gone, and we move now into a new era—a time
of danger, of the shadow of war."

He's giving an acceptance speech! Pilos silently
fumed. He's actually going to stand there and talk
about himself during the man's wake! Pilos wanted
to throw something, and he was shocked by his own
vehemence, his own outrage. He wondered if he was
not seeing things properly, seeing them as Waukeen

perhaps did. The thought made him strangely sad, imagining that his own thinking might be so out of alignment with that of his goddess.

"But war can also be a time of prosperity," Lavant continued, "and I humbly endeavor to seek that prosperity in my own ministrations to the temple."

No, Pilos thought, shaking his head, Waukeen has never taught us to prosper through the cultivation of war.

Grand Syndar Lavant droned on for several more minutes, but Pilos lost interest in the new temple leader's words. Instead, he bided his time on happier memories, recollections of the time he had enjoyed serving Mikolo. He would miss the old man, but Pilos realized he wasn't saddened so much by the spiritual leader's passing as he was by being left behind. The young Abreeant felt some pangs of jealousy, for he knew that Mikolo was finding true gratification in Brightwater for all of his years of loyal dedication to Waukeen. There was a small part of Pilos that wished—no, aspired, he decided—to find himself by Mikolo's side there someday. And though he wished to live out a long and full life in Waukeen's service, the chance to rise to that higher spirituality that he knew would come after his death was one he eagerly awaited.

Suddenly, the speech was at an end, and Pilos could feel a pervasive sense of discomfort. He wondered if Lavant's pronouncements had ended with an expectation of applause, but none was forthcoming, if only because of the impropriety of it in the presence of the body resting before the altar. He looked around and noticed that many other members of the clergy seemed to be similarly disturbed, but no one said a thing.

At last, the audience that filled the great hall of the temple began to rise and make their way out into the sunlight of the day beyond, and musicians and a choir arrayed in the loft above began a somber, if cathartic, dirge. The music was gentle and rolling, and it filled the chamber and helped to muffle the quiet conversations that began to hum throughout the gathering.

Pilos would have liked to have moved closer to the dais and kneel before Midelli's sarcophagus, but the flow of the crowd would have made it nearly impossible. Lavant had never even offered the Abreeant a chance to mourn privately in the presence of the deceased Grand Syndar, and though he was disappointed, he was far from surprised. By the time he could have let the throngs of people move past, allowing him to slip up the center aisle and to the resting place of his departed leader, it would be too late. Already, the burial escort was gathering around the sarcophagus, preparing to place the lid on and bear the thing away to chambers deep in the bowels of the ground, below the temple.

Pilos would have to pay his last respects down there, later, when he could be alone.

Sighing, the young man made his way toward one side of the great hall and slipped into a corridor that would lead him back to his own room. There were few others about, for most of the other clergy members were still gathered in the main temple, conversing, no doubt discussing the various revelations of Lavant's speech. Those few who did cross Pilos's path gave him a knowing nod and smile, for they must have seen that his heart was still heavy with grief and disappointment.

He hurried to his room, shut the door behind himself, lit the lone lamp with a taper from the cinder pot, and slumped into the single straight-backed wooden chair that he normally used at his desk. Fatigue and sorrow washed over him, and for a long moment,

Pilos let those feelings course through him, giving
in to them and allowing himself a few moments of
unbridled emotional release. He did not cry, though
his eyes brimmed with tears more than once. It felt
good just to let go of his pent-up sentiments.

When he began to feel somewhat better, Pilos decided to pray. Rising from his chair, the young man
knelt on the oval carpet in the center of his floor
and closed his eyes. He did not voice a specific prayer
initially but instead just tried to find his center, his
focus, and hoped that Waukeen might bless him with
a modicum of her presence. He wanted to feel close to
his goddess for a while, to let the cares and troubles of
the past couple of days wash away in a gentle bathing
of her radiance.

He wasn't sure when he first began to sense that he
was not alone, but Pilos got a cold, prickly feeling on
the back of his neck, as though someone had entered
his room and was peering at him, looming over him
from behind. He opened his eyes and turned, just to
assure himself that it was his imagination, to prove
to himself that his meditations had drawn him far
enough away from his mortal being that his subcon-
scious was playing tricks on him.

The apparition of Mikolo Midelli hovering there,
but a pace behind him, caused a strangled cry to leap
from Pilos's throat.

The ghostly form was barely discernible in the dim
light of the single lamp, or perhaps, Pilos thought, it
was visible only because of the dim light. The image
of the deceased Grand Syndar was dressed as he had
been the night of his illness, when Pilos had first come
upon him. It hovered in the air, its edges insubstan-
tial, and there were no feet visible that could touch
the floor. The thing's body seemed to shine with an
inner glow, a radiant beauty that was something out
of a prayer, a lesson on the glory of Brightwater. But

the face of Pilos's former leader and mentor did not radiate peace. No, Mikolo Midelli's ghost looked decidedly disturbed.

Pilos stifled his yelp and scrambled back, away from the apparition hovering in his room. He pressed his back against the far wall of his chamber, staring stupidly at the thing, wondering, as all who see such things do, if he was imagining the whole experience.

Perhaps it is a test, Pilos thought, an ordeal inflicted upon me by someone who wishes to know my heart.

"Pilos," the ghost said, and though it was Mikolo's voice, it sounded distant, faint. "Pilos, I need your help," it said.

"Who are you?" Pilos asked timidly, trying to determine some way of discerning whether the figure before him was real, imagined, or a conjuration of magic by someone with a terribly inappropriate sense of humor.

"Do you not know me?" The apparition asked, seemingly surprised. "Do you not recognize this face?"

"Yes, of course, but—" and Pilos felt foolish. Asking the ghost to prove to him that its identity was genuine seemed absurd. "I know you, but I do not know if you are real," he finished.

"Ah," the apparition said, nodding. "A reasonable concern." The ghost seemed to be deep in thought for a moment, and its features brightened. "The last time we spoke," it said, "we were walking in the garden."

Pilos nodded, swallowing.

"We were discussing the merits of generosity to the lame and mentally unsteady, and you asked if it weren't better to give coin to the soup kitchens, rather than to the beggars themselves, for you could not abide the thought that they would waste your donations on drink and carnal relations."

Pilos nodded again, beginning to feel overwhelmed. He and Mikolo had been alone during that conversation, and short of magical eavesdropping, no one else could have known that. "I remember," he said at last, hoarsely. "You told me that—"

"I told you that Waukeen found beauty in all coin changing hands, and even though you could not see the beneficence of it, the purveyor of drinks and the prostitute certainly did. All creatures thrive in an environment where coin is freely given and accepted, Pilos. Remember that."

Pilos nodded again, terrified. It really was Mikolo Midelli, hovering there in his chambers. "Why me?"

"Because I can see in your heart that which is also in mine," the apparition replied. "I know you will see the wisdom in crying out, in demanding greater scrutiny against Lavant's misguided rulership of the temple. You must take up a cause that I could not finish, Pilos."

"But Grand Syndar, I do not know what to do! No one will listen to a simple Abreeant. No one will value my words."

"Ah, but Pilos, you are trying to open the eyes of those who refuse to see. You must seek out others, beyond the temple. And it is they who need your aid, rather than you who need theirs."

"Others? But who, Grand Syndar?" Pilos had no idea what the ghost spoke of, nor how he could act on the apparition's instructions. "Who must I find?"

"Return to your home, Pilos. There you will find sympathetic ears. They will help you take up the call against Grand Syndar Lavant. There, you will find the path that must be followed." The ghost began to fade, and Pilos was terrified of being left alone in his room.

"Grand Syndar! Wait!" he cried out, but the glowing figure of his beloved leader was gone.

CHAPTER 13

The wagon was horribly hot and stuffy, and Kovrim squirmed from the itch of rivulets of sweat pouring down out of his hair, past his face and neck, to tickle the skin beneath his shirt. His thirst was severe, made more unbearable by the thick bit still filling his mouth. He had tried to dislodge the gag with his tongue at various times throughout the morning, but it wasn't going anywhere, so he sat there, glum.

Kovrim blinked as the wagon bounced and sent a particularly irritating droplet of sweat right into the corner of his eye. The salty perspiration burned, making him shake his head in frustration. The maneuver only succeeded in causing more rivulets to trickle down out of his damp, matted hair.

"Sorry, sir," Hort Bloagermun said, coming

out of his own stupor. The grizzled veteran leaned forward and, with his own hands locked in more conventional steel restraints in front of himself, used the sleeve of his own shirt to wipe away the worst of Kovrim's sweat, trying his best to help keep it from running into the old priest's eyes. Kovrim was grateful for the gesture, though the beads of perspiration would be running again soon enough. He nodded in thanks.

The old priest looked around the wooden box that he shared with five other Crescents. All of them were secured similarly to Old Bloagy, with manacles locked about both wrists and ankles. Their clothing was soaked through with sweat, and a couple of them looked very much the worse for wear. Kovrim knew that they would begin to grow ill if they weren't given water soon. They had been crammed into the nearly lightless box wagons since early morning, cruelly sealed up inside the heat traps with nothing to assuage their thirst. Kovrim imagined that the Crescents in the other wagons weren't faring much better.

With no way to see the height of the sun in the sky, Kovrim had no clear idea of how long they had been traveling, but he guessed it had to have been at least three hours. And though he did not know exactly where the survivors of the sinking of *Lady's Favor* had come ashore, he knew that they had to be near the city of Reth, just based on old maps of the area he had often studied. Besides, he had overheard one of the soldiers loading them into the wagons mention that they would reach their destination near noon. Though the old priest feared what would become of them after they arrived in that independent city, he welcomed their arrival if it meant getting out of the baking oven of a box in which they rode at the moment.

As if he were a seer, Kovrim detected a change in the sound of the wooden wagon wheels and of the feel of the ride. They had moved off of dirt road and onto stone pavement, a sure sign that they had neared the city. He listened carefully, detecting the unmistakable sounds of crowds beyond the wooden walls of the box wagon, and they were growing louder. Then the wagon rumbled through a shadow, for the sun was briefly blotted out where it shone through the narrow cracks in the wood panels, and Kovrim knew they had passed through the city gates of Reth. It was not long after that that the wagon drew to a halt.

"It sounds like we've arrived ... wherever it is we are," Old Bloagy said, trying to peer through a small knothole. "Looks like a courtyard, but I'm not sure," he added.

Outside, Kovrim could hear a general commotion as orders were shouted and men moved about. Someone began to work on the latch that held the door at the rear of the box wagon shut, and in another moment, the portal swung downward, letting glaring sunlight shine in. Along with that brightness came a blessed breeze, cooler fresh air that wafted in. Kovrim sighed in profound relief.

The six members of the Sapphire Crescents climbed out of the wagons and descended the slanted door, which served as a sort of gangplank. The prisoners congregated in a group, breathing in and exhilarating in the open air, thankful to be out of the box. Nearby, the rest of the Crescents were being offloaded in a similar manner.

Kovrim took a moment to peer about at his surroundings, wondering where, exactly, they had been brought. It appeared, as Hort had claimed, to be a courtyard of some sort, for high stone walls surrounded the cobblestoned area on every side. One wall was pierced with a gated opening, beyond which

Kovrim could see a street teeming with people and shops and carts. In front of him, however, a large edifice rose up, dominated by a high tower in the very center that was four or five stories tall. Kovrim recognized it immediately as the Palace of the Seven, the central keep of the government of Reth.

I guess we'll be guests of the mayor and the senate, Kovrim thought, wondering what sort of connection Lavant might have with the rulers of Reth that he could arrange such.

After all five wagons were unloaded, the entire group of Crescents—plus the pair of druids who had been captured during the attack in the night—were herded together and escorted by a dozen soldiers toward a narrow door set in one side wall.

The prisoners marched toward the door and inside into blessed coolness, each man shuffling along with short steps due to the inadequate length of chain spanning the distance between their ankles. Kovrim nearly tripped at one point, but a nearby guard reached out and grabbed him by the shoulder to steady him.

Inside the doorway, they encountered a somewhat steeply pitched stone ramp leading down, flanked on either side by alcoves occupied by additional guards. The guards eyed the prisoners impassively as they trotted past, and Kovrim could see that a large portcullis could be dropped near the guard post, preventing anyone from descending deeper into the route—or trying to escape, he understood.

The ramp turned a little farther on so that it doubled back. At the bottom, Kovrim and the other prisoners found themselves in the middle of a large, low-ceilinged chamber that was dimly lit by a handful of torches. It smelled strongly of sweat, human waste, and staleness, and the old priest knew they had arrived in the prison.

The prisoners' guards began to rapidly separate their charges into smaller groups again, sorting them into sets of four. Kovrim wound up in the same group with Hort and the two druids. Their guards pushed them off to one side and stood nearby while the rest of the soldiers were similarly sorted. Once the process was finished, they were marched through a narrow doorway and down a hall that Kovrim saw was lined with cells. The lighting in that area was even dimmer than out in the main room, but as far as he could see, the cells in that wing of the prison were empty, for none of the wooden doors had been pulled shut at the moment.

Making sure no one else sees us here, he thought, *or talks to us.*

That notion was ominous in Kovrim's mind, but he shunted it away for the time being and allowed himself to be led into one of the cells, along with Hort and the two woodsmen. As their guard stepped back and prepared to shut the thick wooden door with the tiny, barred window, Kovrim *mumphed* at the man and made a gulping noise while he tipped his head back slowly, miming drinking. The two druids closed ranks with him and began nodding their heads, obviously agreeing with his plea.

"What?" the guard said, staring at the gagged men with no recognition in his face whatsoever.

"I think they're trying to tell you that we haven't had any blasted water since dawn," Hort said, "and they need a drink, lad. What do you say?"

The guard eyed Kovrim suspiciously then nodded once and left, pulling the door shut behind him with a resounding thud.

"I don't know if it got through his thick skull or not," Old Bloagy complained, sitting down in the straw that was strewn across the stone floor. "I'm sorry, sir. I'll try again when he comes back."

It turned out that the guard did come back, only a short time later, accompanied by two other guards and a sergeant. One of them was carrying a waterskin. They all entered the small cell and arrayed themselves in front of Kovrim where he and the two woodsmen sat.

"I have orders not to let you three speak," the sergeant said, gesturing at the harness strapped onto Kovrim's head. "but I'm not one to give a prisoner more than he's due in punishment, if I can help it. They say you are all dangerous sorcerers and will try to ensnare our minds with your devilish tongues, and that we can't listen to you speak."

Off to one side, Hort snorted in disgust. "He's no more a stinking sorcerer than I am a flying pig, son. As for them other two, I can't say, but if you don't give them water, they'll die, sure as the sky is blue."

The sergeant glared at Hort for a moment then turned back to face Kovrim and the other two. "If I have one of my men here release you long enough to drink, I have to have a promise from you that you won't say anything." Kovrim began to nod, and the other two sitting near him did, too, and just as eagerly. "Now, Thak and Jervis are going to keep their blades ready, and if you try anything, they'll run you through in a heartbeat. Is that clear?" Again, all three gagged men nodded.

With that, the sergeant nodded to his men and stood back while one of the guards produced a key and unlocked the harness of the man to Kovrim's left. The other two held their short swords out, each one standing to one side, ready to ram the blades into his neck or gut if he should try anything untoward. Once the druid had managed to work the thick bit out of his mouth with his tongue, he sighed in relief but said nothing, then took the proffered skin in his mouth and drank deeply. After he had gotten his fill, the guard shoved the bit back in his mouth. The prisoner groaned in frustration, but he did not fight as the guard rebuckled the harness and locked it.

Then it was Kovrim's turn, and he waited patiently for the soldier to remove the hated bit. When the nasty leather came out of his mouth, he sighed, working his jaw a few times to get some feeling back into the aching muscles. With his hands still locked inside the steel balls, he leaned forward toward the waterskin and sucked great mouthfuls of cool water in, letting some of it spill over and run down his chin. He even managed to splash some on his head, letting it dampen his hair, before the guard yanked it away again in exasperation and put the bit back against his lips. Kovrim hated the thought of allowing the soldier to restrain him again, but he knew there was no way he could convince them otherwise without getting skewered, so he grudgingly acquiesced, hating the sensation all the more after the bit was back in place.

Once his drinking privileges were over, Kovrim moved off to a corner of the cell and settled down to think. The soldiers let the second woodsman have his drink, and Hort got to finish off the skin.

"We'll be back to try that again with some food," the sergeant said. "As long as you mind your manners, we'll keep this up. But any funny business, and those harnesses stay on." Kovrim nodded and slumped even further against the wall as the quartet of guards departed, locking the cell door behind them.

Hort moved over beside Kovrim. "This isn't right," he said, shaking his head. "They've got no cause to keep us locked up in here."

Kovrim shrugged, unable to speak and explain to the man that he was the victim of political maneuvering, even if he were inclined to reveal such.

The man's been a soldier for forty years, the priest realized. He wouldn't deal well with the idea of a high

priest letting him be killed just to rid himself of a few
rivals, Kovrim thought. Why disillusion him now?
Kovrim considered the possibility of escape again,
wondering if he could verbalize his transportation
spell fast enough for the magic to take effect before
he was run through by the guards. He decided that it
might be possible in a few days, once he showed sufficient compliance, for them to let down some of their
wariness. Of course, it would all depend on the two
druids, he realized. If they tried anything, it could
ruin it for all of them.

Kovrim wanted desperately to make it clear to the
two woodsmen that they had to wait, to bide their
time and not ruin the chance, but he had no way to
communicate with them. He didn't even see any way
to act through Hort as an intermediary.

Filled with despair, Kovrim sighed and tried to
stretch himself out on the stone floor, wondering if he
could get comfortable enough to sleep. Hort, sensing
that the old priest wished to be left alone, wandered
to the far side of the cell and sat. The two woodsmen
had done likewise. In the quiet, Kovrim could hear
other soldiers talking, and he felt somewhat sorry for
Hort, who had been unlucky enough to draw three
cellmates who couldn't converse.

The old priest drifted off to a troubled sleep, interrupted once for a feeding. The process went similarly
to the drinking, except that it took longer, and he was
last in line in that particular case. He was surprised
at how demeaning it felt to have someone else place
bits of food in his mouth, but with his hands imprisoned, he had no choice. Afterward, he returned to his
napping.

A long time later, Kovrim was awakened by the soft
sound of his name being called. He looked up and saw
a face staring at him through the bars of the door.

It was Junce Roundface.

...

Emriana's chest felt like it was bound in iron bands, slowly tightening, crushing her. Her breath came in short, shallow gasps, and her heart thudded rapidly. She couldn't believe the words that Grozier Talricci was telling her.

Vambran and Uncle Kovrim, dead, drowned at sea? It couldn't be! Emriana felt like she was being sucked into a whirlpool, dragged down, down, into the depths of the Abyss.

"So, with Hetta and Xaphira as well as your older brother all deceased," the horrid man said, "Quindy and Obiron, as Evester's descendants, are the rightful heirs to the estate. And since they are not of age yet to properly run the family business, the responsibility falls to Marga. And she," Grozier finished, smiling warmly at his sister, who was sitting in a chair looking positively smug, "has agreed that I should share the responsibilities as guardian for them, administering the household for them until such time as they are ready to handle those affairs themselves."

"You're such a liar," Emriana snarled, trying to stare daggers through Grozier. "You had something done to Xaphira, and your thugs tried to do it to me, too, and you know it!" she shouted, her voice nearly rising to a scream. The girl turned desperately to the other occupants in the room, silently pleading for someone, anyone, to stand with her against the man who was succeeding in usurping her family estate. "Please," she pleaded. "Don't let him do this."

But the only people in the sitting room at that time—other than the house staff, a couple of Grozier's own guards, and the ever-present Bartimus—were Marga, who looked entirely unsympathetic, Nimra and Mirolyn Skolotti, who were in no position to do anything, and Ladara, who was weepy-eyed. Emriana's mother sat near Hetta's body, sobbing quietly and looking miserably at her daughter from time to time. The girl knew Ladara would never lift a finger to do anything, had never done anything except meekly follow Hetta around like a devoted sheep.

"There is nothing for anyone to do," Grozier said, a hint of mocking in his voice. "They all realize that this is proper. With Marga's blessing, I have the right."

Emriana looked at her sister-in-law. "How could you?" she said accusingly. "We gave you a home, always treated you like part of the family. This man is responsible for Evester's death! Your husband. My brother!"

Marga let her smile deepen. "I would not be too ferocious in my accusations, if I were you," she said coldly. "It would not be a difficult matter to have you and your mother thrown out of here."

Emriana let her jaw drop, dumbfounded. "This is *my* house!" she shouted. "It belongs to me more than to either of you!" And the rage got the better of her, and she darted across the room, one arm drawn back, ready to pound the woman smiling smugly at her.

The girl got within a couple of paces, but Grozier's men interceded, preventing her from reaching her target. They latched onto her arms and yanked her back as she kicked and flailed. Oh, how she wished she had learned more of Xaphira's skills. She longed to kick and punch like her aunt had been able to, to strike the two men hindering her from reaching her real quarry. She longed for one of her throwing daggers. They would not block one of those, she was sure. She could not understand how they could have such loyalty to a man such as Grozier Talricci, a man without honor.

"Stop it! Stop it," someone said from behind Emriana, and cool hands were on her shoulders, gently but firmly drawing her back, away from the two men, away from Grozier and Marga. It was Jaleene, using a soothing tone that she had often employed when Emriana was a child. The girl felt like a child right then, helpless, surrounded by condescending adults who said nice things merely to humor her. Emriana gave another hateful glare at Marga; then she looked at Grozier.

"You cannot remove me," she said flatly, as though it were a fact that deserved no argument. "And I will see you undone, before you can ruin my family's name and honor. I won't permit it," she spat.

Grozier lunged forward, his hand drawn back as if to strike her. Ladara shrieked, and Marga had to reach up to restrain the man. Still, he came very close to reaching the girl, and despite herself, she cringed the slightest bit. He saw her reaction and smiled.

"You are nothing," he said at last, jerking free of his sister's grasp and straightening himself. "You will mind your manners, and you will obey my rules in this household every day, without fail. I will know where you are at all times, and you will have guards posted outside of every exit to your rooms at night. There will be no more of this sneaking about, interfering with the work of adults. Oh, and you will hand over that infernal pendant that your brother gave you. I have better uses for it than you ever will."

Emriana felt her eyes widen. Her hand went to her heart, where the pendant hung inside her shirt, nestled between her breasts. Vambran's birthday present. Vambran, who was dead. "No," she said. "You may not have it."

Grozier's eyebrow shot up. "Those are the conditions by which you may remain on the premises," he said, shrugging as if it were the most expected thing in the world. "If you defy me, you *will* be removed, by force if necessary. Choose now."

"No, please don't," Ladara sobbed from her position next to Hetta's body. Emriana thought she was talking to Grozier, that the woman was finally finding the courage to stand up to someone on her behalf, but when she turned to look, Ladara was gazing at her, not Grozier. "Don't cross him, Em," her mother pleaded. "You're only a child. You cannot survive out beyond House Matrell. Do as he says!"

Shock and hurt flooded through the girl all over again. She opened her mouth to protest, to tell her mother just how insulting she was being, but then she snapped it shut again, realizing the futility of trying to get her mother to understand anything beyond her own clinging needs. She shook her head sadly and turned away.

Taking a deep breath, she prepared herself to walk, to turn her back on everything that she had grown up with, had loved, for the sake of pride. The notion of leaving the house forever terrified her. She had no idea what she would do, where she would go, but she would not stay and live under Grozier Talricci's thumb. She'd be damned if she'd ever do *that*.

Em, came a faint voice, Hetta's voice, from inside her head. The girl froze, wide-eyed again, staring at her grandmother's still form. *Em, come to me.* The sound of her grandmother calling to her stunned Emriana, but before she realized what she was doing, she padded across the floor to where her grandmother lay at rest.

Ladara apparently thought that her daughter was coming to her, and she reached out to envelop Emriana in a hug, but the girl shrugged clear and knelt down next to her grandmother's head instead. She gazed at the elderly woman's face, so still, so serene. She couldn't believe that Hetta was dead. She seemed asleep, though there was no rise or fall of her chest.

Em, take my hand, Hetta's voice commanded. Confused, unsure if she was hearing things or imagining them, Emriana slowly reached out and took her grandmother's two hands in her own. They were icy cold to the touch, and the girl almost recoiled in revulsion, but it was her grandmother, her sweet, adorable Hetta. Emriana clasped the two frail, wrinkled hands in her own and squeezed them.

Voices or no, I love you, she said silently, letting the tears fall freely. I miss you already.

Take the ring from my finger, Em, Hetta's voice instructed, and it was clearer, louder than before. Emriana nearly gasped aloud, but she calmed herself and looked at her grandmother's hands. There, on the fourth finger of her right hand, was a silver ring with a ruby set into it. The moment that Emriana closed her own hand about it, she felt a surge of energy, felt another presence inside her body.

Quickly, Em, slide it off my finger. You must take the ring with you, Hetta said as though she were another voice in Emriana's head. Stunned but trying desperately to remain cool and collected, Emriana bowed over her grandmother as though she were offering up a final good-bye. She tucked both of her grandmother's hands into her own and discreetly slipped the ring free.

Don't lose it, Hetta said. *I'm inside it.* A feeling of joy surged up in Emriana then, for she knew she wasn't imagining any of it, that somehow, her grandmother's essence, her spirit, was safely stowed in the ring. *Get out of the house, now,* Hetta said. *It's not safe for you. Defy him, and leave.*

The girl subtly pocketed the piece of jewelry then rose to her feet. She turned to face Grozier. "Go to hell," she said with the most conviction she'd ever felt about anything in her life. Around her, everyone gasped.

"I'll see you there," Grozier sneered, but Emriana

had already turned away, and was walking out of the room. "Guards, make sure she leaves the premises at once," he ordered.

"Em, no!" Ladara called out. "Come back! You mustn't do this!"

The girl ignored them all, though the pain in her mother's voice made her cringe. She realized she had come to despise the woman's timorous nature, but she nonetheless felt self-loathing for hurting Ladara. The woman was, after all, her mother.

You can't help her right now, she admonished herself. You must save yourself, first.

With those words to bolster her courage, Emriana hurried out, practically sprinting to her own room. The guards behind her began to trot to keep up.

If Grozier has his way, I won't even be able to take any belongings, Emriana thought, won't get much opportunity to pack.

In her room, the girl slipped on a different pair of boots, discarding the single one she had on her foot. Then she snatched up a satchel and threw an extra outfit inside. She also dug a pouch of coins out from a cubbyhole in the back of a drawer in her dresser. She was just turning to exit when a box on her bed caught her eye.

It was the set of daggers Xaphira had given her. There were still two inside.

Emriana could hear Grozier down the hall, shouting at the two guards to bodily remove the girl. She glanced at the doorway, where the two guards stood, hesitating to enter a lady's chambers uninvited. Before they could overcome their sense of propriety and cross the threshold, Emriana snatched up the box, stuffed it in the satchel, and turned toward her balcony.

"Get her out of here, right now!" Grozier said from right behind the two guards. "She gets nothing!"

Emriana didn't wait to see if the house guards would jump to their work or not. She darted outside, onto the tiled porch where the smell of blossoms always hung thick in the air, and scrambled down the steps to the grassy expanse below. She heard the sound of footsteps on the tiles behind her and knew that Grozier had ordered the guards to follow her until she was well and truly off the property.

From the lawn, she scurried around the house, through an orchard, and down a side path to the main one leading to the front gate. Once she was there—still followed at a discreet distance by the pair of House Matrell guards—she slipped her hand inside her pocket and slid the ring onto her finger.

Grandmother? She projected. *Is it really you? Are you truly there?*

Yes, child, Hetta replied. *I'm here.*

Oh, Hetta! Emriana silently exclaimed, burbling with both excitement and trepidation all at the same time. *What happened? You died!*

All is not as it seems, Hetta replied. *Magic can do strange and wondrous things, and we Matrells have access to our share of it. I have worn that enchanted ring for a long time. In the event of my death, my spirit would be drawn into the ring, rather than away to the afterlife. I'm a stubborn old bird and have no intention of leaving things unfinished. I'm here with you, and will remain so for as long as you need me, until we settle this.*

Now. Something has happened to Marga, to the twins. I don't know what, yet, but I sense deception. Grozier is up to something, and Marga is not acting herself. Where is Xaphira?

Emriana's heart ached. *I don't know,* she confessed. *She disappeared last night. I was attacked, nearly drowned. I tried to contact her with my pendant, once last night, once this morning, but she would not answer.* She could feel anguish radiate from the presence inside her.

That is truly wretched news, Hetta said solemnly. *But we have no time for that now. Xaphira's a strong girl. She'll survive without our help for the time being.*

I hope so, Emriana thought.

Yes, that is all we can do for the moment. Hope. Right now, we must get away, seek help. I want you to go to the Darowdryn estate. We need their help. I have a lot to tell you along the way.

Grandmother Hetta?

What is it, child?

Did you know that Vambran and Kovrim are lost at sea?

Yes, the woman said, with a kindness and warmth that made Emriana want to cry. *But do not believe it. Grozier Talricci is a snake filled with lies. Vambran and Kovrim may very well be alive. If they can, they'll get word to us.*

My pendant! Emriana thought. *I can reach them with my pendant!*

Before Emriana had a chance to do that, however, a voice calling her name got her attention. It was Mirolyn, hurrying down the path toward the front gate. Emriana was almost to the end of the path, was almost prepared to step outside of her family home for perhaps the very last time. She turned back to the young woman, only a few years older than she.

"I have a message for you," Mirolyn said breathlessly as she caught up to Emriana. "My mother says to tell you that she remembers where she once heard the name 'Roundface.'"

Emriana turned to face Mirolyn, her heart filling with newfound hope. "Well?" she said, thinking that the news could be a lead to finding Xaphira. "Where?"

Mirolyn took a deep breath and said, "Her sister used to talk about a little boy where she worked, a youngster, the son of a courtier named Blackcrown. All the serving staff nicknamed him Roundface, because he had such chubby cheeks. 'Little Roundface,' they all used to call him. She doesn't know what the child's real first name was, but she thought that might help. Blackcrown, she said, and she was very certain."

Emriana tried to keep from sounding exasperated when she asked, "And where did your mother's sister work?"

"Oh, sorry," Mirolyn said, blushing. "It was at the Generon. She was a maid at the Lord's Palace."

CHAPTER 14

Vambran sat peering through the bars of the cage, watching the druids at work on the rock shelf beyond. The five other soldiers imprisoned with him lounged quietly, some of them sleeping. None of them were fettered any longer, having worked together to remove the rope bonds around wrists and ankles. The hardwood saplings holding them in place within the shallow cave were another matter.

"You are a long way from home, mercenary," the woman with the piercing green eyes said, approaching the cave and looking through the bars at Vambran. "We do not see many of the Order of the Sapphire Crescent here."

Vambran returned her stare curiously. "I'm surprised that you know of our order," he replied. "Though we are not here by choice in any event."

The woman raised an eyebrow. "Truly?" she said, sounding skeptical. "Do not all men come here to the shadows of the Nunwood to fight their fights for others? Do the idle rich of the cities not pay you to wage their wars for them out here, where the killing won't stain their precious cities with so much blood?"

Vambran began to shake his head. "Many do, but the Crescents do not."

"You are a soldier," she said, "and you fight at the direction of others. Reth or Hlath, Arrabar or more distant cities, it is always the same."

Vambran gave the woman a level look. "If you're so convinced that we're all alike, then why did your people bring us here, rather than simply kill us where they found us?"

"I have asked myself that question, too," the woman said, giving Vambran a peculiar smile that was a little unnerving. "Edilus thought perhaps that you could be ransomed for prisoners held by the enemy army. He saw the value in holding you, with your three dots."

Vambran blinked, having nearly forgotten that he bore the three symbols of reading, writing, and magic upon his forehead. "He thought I would be valuable to the enemy," the lieutenant reasoned.

"Yes. I told him that we would not negotiate with the mercenaries, that the Emerald Enclave did not parlay. Those of our order who are taken are considered dead and grieved for. He was not happy with my decision."

"Why?"

"Because his brother was among those taken," the woman replied. "I told him we would avenge his brother by spilling the blood of many soldiers again tonight."

Those words were uttered with such force, such finality, that for a moment, Vambran could only stare

at the woman across from him. Her intensely emerald
eyes blazed with a primal fire, and he knew beyond
a doubt she meant every bit of it.

Vambran was going to try, anyway. "It doesn't have
to be that way," he said, hoping she would see his own
earnestness as sincere. "I can help you find a more
peaceful solution. My soldiers and I have no quarrel
with the Emerald Enclave. Indeed, we work toward
similar goals. If you resign us to this cage, then a
resource you have at your disposal will be wasted."

The woman laughed, but it was a bitter laughter,
without mirth. "A resource. I would expect nothing
less from a priest of the Merchant's Friend. The world
simply is, it exists. 'Resource' is but a word your kind
uses to measure what you wish to make your own. I
do not acknowledge your notion of resources. Here, in
the woods, everything belongs to all beings, and no
one takes more than he needs right then, right there.
I drink from the stream, yet there is still plenty of
water for others, both downstream from me and those
who would come later to the same spot I did to drink.
The stream, the water, is not a resource; it dwells as
an integral part of nature. You and your resources
are laughable."

Vambran's jaw clenched in anger and frustration.
"And you and your ilk seem so determined to belittle
others' ways of life, though not all who walk a different
world than yours subvert your ideals so robustly," he
said, raising his voice at the woman. She blinked and
sat back ever so slightly. Vambran doubted she had
been spoken to in such a manner in a very long time.
"I was born and raised in a city of merchants, and it
is the life I know. To expect me to abandon all that I
was groomed for because you see your way of life as
superior to mine is both short-sighted and arrogant.

"I would not presume to tell you that you should
leave the woods behind forever and come dwell in

the city. It is not your element. You, having most
likely never been to Arrabar, would not be at ease
there. You would not be able to find your way from
street to street. The first cart vendor you came upon
would most likely rob you blind and convince you it
was a bargain. But these shortcomings do not make
me a better person than you. I would not see myself
as superior because I better understand the life I
lead than you do. Why must you view me that way?
Our paths may be different, but our values are not
necessarily so separated. Though I may not care and
nourish the forest as the Enclave does, that does not
mean I cannot appreciate the work that you do, that
I cannot value your ideals."

The woman sat and stared at Vambran for a long
time. All around the great platform, no one said a
thing; indeed, none of the other wood folk present
were doing anything at all. They had all stopped
their work at the mercenary's outburst. Vambran
wondered if that was because of the passion in his
words or because they were awestruck that he had
the audacity to challenge the woman so.

At that moment, the pair's conversation was interrupted by a messenger arriving atop the platform.
The woman turned away from the cage and moved to
the new arrival. Together, they squatted down near
the fire and began to converse in low voices.

Vambran turned and looked at the other five mercenaries. "I keep thinking that she looks familiar.
But I've never been in the Nunwood before."

"Aye," Adyan drawled, "I was thinking the same
thing. Can't quite place it, though. Do you suppose
we've fought against her before?"

"I remember her face, too, but I don't think it was
on the field of battle," Horial added. "But if we all
three think we know her, then there's something
to it."

Vambran started to nod, but before he got the words out, a disembodied voice began to speak to him. *Vambran, are you alive?* It was Emriana. *Something's happened to Xaphira and Hetta, and Grozier has taken over the House. Please answer me, Vam. You can't be dead!*

At his sister's startling revelation, Vambran rocked upright, stunned. He found it difficult to breathe. Shaking his head, he formulated an answer.

It's all right, Em. It's a lie. Uncle Kovrim and I are still alive. I'll come to you as soon as I can. Be safe.

He felt the connection break off at that point, and he wanted to shout at the top of his lungs in frustration. There was so much he needed to tell his sister.

"Emriana's in trouble," he said to the confused faces gathered around him. "Something's happened at home." He wanted to pound his fist against the stone wall of the shallow cave. "Grozier Talricci is in control, and Xaphira and Hetta—" and he stopped himself, feeling his throat constrict in sorrow and worry. "I have to get back to them," he said. "Em needs me." Then he closed his eyes in anguish. "But so do the men. I've got to get out of here!" he snarled, grabbing at the bars and shaking them.

A shadow fell across Vambran's eyes, and he looked up to find the woman standing over him, on the other side of the bars. Behind her, the camp had sprung to life, bustling with activity. He did not understand the portent of that, but he did not care. He had to get out. The lieutenant began to speak, to plead for his release so that he could save both his family and his followers, but he snapped his mouth shut again without uttering a word when he saw the look on the woman's face.

There was a very dangerous glint in her eyes.

She looked at Vambran and the others coldly as she said, "Soldiers have slain nearly every member of our order that they captured. They have bloodied the Emerald Enclave, asking for war. Now they will have it. And they will get more than they ever bargained for." She turned to go.

"Wait," Vambran said, willing her to reconsider. "My offer stands. Let us help you."

The woman turned back, rage clear on her face. "Rot in there," she said with a growl. "The Enclave does not negotiate."

...

"Vambran's alive!" Emriana practically shouted. "He answered me!" For the first time that day, she actually smiled. It felt good, knowing that at least part of what Grozier Talricci had told her was a lie. Her conversation with Vambran had given Emriana more relief than she could have imagined, and she began to feel some sense of hope again.

I told you not to believe Talricci's lies, Hetta said, warmth beaming from the presence inside Emriana. *Your brother can take care of himself. I didn't raise foolish grandchildren, or children either, for that matter.*

I know, Emriana thought back. *And I thank you for that gift. But it seems sometimes like the entire city is against us.*

Yes, Hetta said. *Your news of the Grand Syndar is troubling, to say the least. Big things are afoot, that is certain. Now, we must hurry. We still have resources we can draw on, ourselves, but there is no time to waste.*

First things first, Grandmother, Emriana responded. *I'm not beyond Grozier's reach, yet, and I'll be damned if I'm going to let him fool me again.*

Hearing her own words, Emriana felt as though she had aged several years in the course of a single night. She had a debt to pay, to Grozier Talricci and everyone working with him. Still, the girl was homeless at the moment, with nothing more than what she carried on her person. She needed to get to the Darowdryn estate, but she couldn't show up on their doorstep looking and smelling as she did. She had to find a place to clean herself up.

Emriana stepped back out of the alley where she had retreated in order to employ the pendant. She peered in both directions along the street, searching for any signs that Grozier had had her followed. She had no doubt that the man intended to remove her from his life once and for all, whether she had chosen to stay at the estate and obey his wishes or not.

No one walking the avenue seemed the least bit interested in the bedraggled girl, but she waited a moment longer, watching the doorways and rooftops. Memories of the previous evening were still fresh in her mind. She half hoped that she would run into Lak and the other man again.

They won't catch me off guard a second time, she vowed.

She didn't see anything untoward after a few careful minutes of watching, so she turned and headed away from the only home she'd ever known, cutting across the wide street and heading downtown, in the direction of the harbor. She knew the Darowdryn estate was several lanes to the north, but she wanted to find an inn first, a place where she could procure a bath.

Explain to me again how you managed to survive your own demise, Emriana requested of her grandmother as she walked. *What is this ring?*

I had it made shortly after your grandfather died, Hetta began. *Though I was able to carry on the family*

*enterprises ably after his passing, I wasn't so sure that
any of my children were yet prepared to take over,
should I also die. It wasn't that I was worried that,
without my guidance, they would let things fall to
ruin. But I did fear that none of them knew every
nuance of the business—where to find things, which
business partners were truly trustworthy, that sort of
thing. I wasn't trying to stay around past my allotted
time on this world, but I didn't want to leave unex-
pectedly without making sure someone knew how to
pick up the pieces.*

Emriana was impressed with her grandmother's
thoroughness. But then the girl realized that the
matriarch's presence in the ring seemed to be a permanent thing. The thought saddened her all over
again, even though Hetta's spirit was right there
with her. She said as much.

There are ways to return to my body, Hetta said,
*though there is a limit to how much time can pass
and what condition it was in when I left it. I doubt
very much that it will be possible to achieve, given
the state of things back home.*

How can you say that so calmly? Emriana wailed.
I don't want to lose you!

*Child, all things come to an end. But that's a
parting for another time. Right now, we've got urgent
things to attend to, and I'm not going anywhere until
they're dealt with. So stop fretting.*

Emriana wiped the tears that had begun to form
in the corners of her eyes and nodded. *All right,* she
promised. *I'll try.*

By that point, the girl had neared the lane where
the inn she had selected sat. The thought of a hot
bath and clean clothes quickened her steps, so she
almost didn't notice the figure stepping out of the
alley just ahead, blocking her way. The man paused,
facing her, and Emriana took three more steps before

she realized it was Lak. She skidded to a sudden stop, her heart pounding.

Damn it, damn it, *damn it!* the girl thought, berating herself for letting her watchfulness flag.

The skinny man made no move to advance toward her, but he gave her a slight, knowing smile as he folded his arms across his chest. Emriana looked back over her shoulder, confirming what she already feared; that the bear of a man, Lak's companion, was there, perhaps twenty paces back. He had paused as well and was leaning against the stone wall of the building, watching her with a scowl on his face.

Emriana tried to calm her breathing. All of her previous thoughts of bravado faded away at the reality of facing the two men who had tried to kill her the night before. Her daggers were packed inside the box, which was inside her satchel. There was no way she could dig them out in time.

Don't panic! the girl insisted to herself. They won't jump you in the middle of the street like this. They're waiting until no one is around. Keep moving, she told herself. Find a crowd.

The girl turned to cross the street, thinking to head directly away from either of her pursuers, even though that would take her farther from the inn. On the opposite side, she spotted the woman with the short blonde hair, the one who had impersonated Xaphira.

Groaning, Emriana cut across at an angle, watching as the woman began to match her pace, strolling on the far side. Lak did likewise, crossing the street with her, gradually closing the distance. She didn't bother to turn around to see if bear-man was doing the same—she knew they were keeping her surrounded, biding their time.

Where in the nine hells is the watch when you need it? Emriana fumed, beginning to angle back the

other way. She noticed that there were fewer people on
the street right then, a fact that seemed to embolden
the three pursuing her, for they drew ever closer, still
surrounding her position.

Drawing a deep breath, Emriana changed course
again, then darted back the other way, breaking into
a sprint, dashing past the surprised Lak. He lunged
for her, a bold move considering they were not completely alone on the street, but the girl managed to
evade his grasp and scoot past him, charging ahead to
the next intersection. Emriana whipped around the
corner and kept going, all thoughts of the inn and a
bath forgotten.

I have to find someplace safe, where they can't get
to me, she thought. *Grandmother, what do I do?*

*Run, child. To the Darowdryns. They'll protect
you. Hurry!*

Emriana mentally nodded as she sprinted in that
direction, heading toward the massive estate of the
old friends of the Matrell family. Her breath came
in ragged gasps, as much a result of her terror as of
tiring. At the next intersection, there were more folks
out walking, and she slowed to avoid colliding with
anyone. The thought flashed through her head that,
given her bedraggled state, someone might think she
was a thief fleeing the law.

Emriana risked a quick glance back to see if she
was still being pursued. She spotted Lak, his short legs
churning, closing the distance. Behind him, bear-man
lumbered along, not as swift as his partner. The woman
was not in sight, but Emriana had a pretty good idea
that she was using the rooftops to track her quarry.

It's what I would do, the girl thought, turning and
fleeing once more, heedless of the distasteful stares
directed her way by passersby.

As she neared the Darowdryn estate, Emriana
realized the one flaw in her plan. That section of

the city was the providence of the very wealthy,
and their homes were huge, sprawling affairs
that covered several blocks. Few other people had
cause to go there, which meant that the lanes me-
andering between the high walls delineating the
various properties would most likely be empty.
Unless Emriana could outdistance her would-be
captors, they would have no witnesses to hinder
their efforts.

It was a chance she would have to take, for to turn
back would mean heading straight into their arms.

And still no watch, she thought, wishing a squad
would see her running and try to accost her for her
suspicious appearance. What better way to get rid of
those three?

She was only a short distance from the front gate
of the Darowdryn estate when the woman in the
purple pants and magenta vest appeared in front of
Emriana. The girl knew the woman had used magic
to cut her off, and she didn't have to turn around to
know that Lak and bear-man weren't far behind.
They had her cornered.

"Not much room to move," the woman said, strolling toward Emriana. "You're a slippery little minx,
I'll give you that," she added, pulling something
from a pouch at her belt. "But you're luck's run out,
I think."

"Don't bet on it," Emriana said, eyeing her pursuer.
"You haven't caught me, yet." She had no idea why
such bold words were coming out of her mouth; she
was terrified.

"A trivial matter," the woman said, smiling as she
drew closer. The smile was not warm. "Think fast,"
she added, gesturing with both hands.

Emriana did not wait to see what arcane attack
erupted from her foe. She turned and sprinted toward
the wall of the estate, leaping as high as she could at

the last moment. She could not reach the top of the wall, which was more than a full story high, but she had spotted a protruding stone in the work that she just might be able to grab hold of. It was her only chance.

As the girl sailed through the air, a trio of glowing darts shot forth from the fair-haired caster, whistling as they passed through the point where Emriana had been a moment before. She grimaced as she hit the wall and slipped the tips of her fingers over the protruding stone, knowing that the three missiles would double back on her.

She managed to claim a sufficient hold on the wall then hung there helplessly as the three magical darts slammed into her back. The pain from those horrid, burning missiles made her gasp, and she nearly lost her hold as she jerked, tears brimming.

"Bitch," she sobbed.

There was a sudden, soothing coolness flowing through Emriana then, and the pain receded sufficiently that she could concentrate once more on scaling the wall.

Hurry, child, Hetta's voice commanded, though it sounded weak and weary. *I can't do that for you again.*

Thank you, Emriana thought. She began to clamber higher, reaching the top a moment before Lak arrived down below then she pulled herself into a sitting position and glanced back.

"Get back down here!" the diminutive man growled, obviously frustrated. He eyed the wall, looking as though he was going to try to follow, but Emriana's attention was still focused on the female. She began to cast again.

Emriana rolled backward, slipping down the inside of the wall, evading whatever spell had been intended for her.

The girl found herself in a thicket, mostly under-brush and vines, but she could see open field just a little toward the interior of the estate. Behind her, muffled by the wall, she could make out the sounds of people arguing, and she did not want to wait around to see if the trio of pursuers maintained the chase. She pushed through the foliage and into the field beyond, which stretched for quite a distance toward the main house, easily seen atop a central hill.

Perhaps a hundred paces away, a contingent of mounted soldiers were headed straight toward her. They had weapons out.

There was a crash behind Emriana, and she turned back in time to see Lak dropping to the ground at the base of the wall. He rolled to his feet as the woman settled easily to the ground beside him. Both of them began to advance on her.

Run to the soldiers! Hetta insisted. *They will know your name and protect you. Go now!*

Without hesitating, Emriana darted into the open, running with the last reserves of her energy right toward the soldiers, all but one of whom wore red, black, and gold livery. The one exception was an immense man sitting atop a huge destrier, both he and his horse sheathed in polished mail from head to toe. He brought up the rear, his mount laboring to keep up with the smaller, faster horses of the House guards. Behind Emriana, she could hear a hiss of vexation, but she didn't bother turning around to see if anyone followed. Her eyes were focused on those weapons before her, bearing down on her position.

"I yield!" she cried out, keeping her hands in the air as she ran. When she was only a few strides away, she stumbled and knelt in the grass, holding her hands high and to either side. "I yield," she repeated, thoroughly spent.

The soldiers encircled her on their horses, leveling spears at her head or aiming crossbows from the saddle. Emriana flinched, but otherwise all she could do was pant in exhaustion.

"You are trespassing, girl," one of the guards said, eyeing her. "We normally flog for that offense."

"Please," Emriana said, looking fearfully at the guard. "I must speak with Ariskrit Darowdryn. She will know me."

The soldier snorted in derision. "I seriously doubt that," he said. "Lady Darowdryn values her privacy very much, so you can just turn around and hop back over the wall."

"Please!" Emriana repeated. "I promise that I am not lying to you! My name is Emriana Matrell, granddaughter of Hetta Matrell, and I must see the lady!"

The soldier was shaking his head, obviously unwavering in his resolve to keep riffraff away from the lords and ladies of the manor, when the huge mounted knight arrived. He threw a leg over the saddle and slid to the ground, huffing and puffing. The guard leader turned and saluted. "She claims to know Lady Darowdryn, m'lord, but she is obviously just a common street rat, looking for a handout. I was about to give her a chance to bolt, but she is pushing her luck."

The huge man strode past the soldier, staring straight at Emriana, slipping his gloves off his hands before removing his helmet. Great white mustaches settled down past his chin as he gazed intently at the girl kneeling before him. It was Tharlgarl "Steelfists" Darowdryn.

"Em?" the man said. "Emriana Matrell?" He turned and waved away the soldiers. "She speaks the truth. Let her up."

Immediately, the contingent of guards withdrew their weapons and allowed Emriana to rise. She did so on shaky legs, feeling a rush of emotions coursing through her as she approached the man.

"I—I was afraid you wouldn't remember me," the girl said, greatly relieved. "I hoped, but I wasn't sure."

"Goodness, but you're a mess," Tharlgarl said, holding out a hand to help steady her.

The dam of emotions broke then, and tears flooded Emriana's eyes. She tumbled into the huge man's arms, hugging him tightly.

He wrapped his steel-clad arms around her gently and let her cry. "Easy," he said, over and over again. It felt so good to the girl that she stayed there for a long time. When she had regained her composure, Emriana pulled back and drew a filthy sleeve across her face. She sniffed once and looked at Steelfists.

"I've had the worst day," she began.

CHAPTER 15

Vambran followed the woman with the piercing emerald eyes without saying anything. They walked together along a path that paralleled a watercourse through the heart of the Nunwood. The lieutenant still wasn't certain why she had returned later that day and fetched him from the cage, but when she had asked him to stroll with her, he had accepted quickly, though it meant leaving the others behind for a while. He wanted every chance to convince her to avert a war.

She led the way in silence away from the great rock, taking the mercenary down to the forest floor, where her footfalls were nearly silent. She seemed to revel in the greenness of it all, stopping occasionally and drawing deep breaths with her eyes closed in pure contentment. Vambran tried to do the same, though it was hard to appreciate the beauty of the moment when there was so much going on, and so little time to resolve the cascade of events that seemed to be falling all around him.

The thought of running never seriously crossed the man's mind, for he would not leave his companions behind, and he knew that she knew it. He did consider the possibility that he had been led out away from the others so that he would not be a witness to some dire fate for them, but he did not see the druids as being so devious. If they had wanted to kill the other five Crescents, they would have done so.

"You are wrong, you know," the woman said, turning to the lieutenant at last, a hint of a grin on her face. Vambran shook his head, not understanding her, but she added, "I *have* been to Shining Arrabar."

That had been the last thing the lieutenant had expected her to say. He waited for her to explain.

"I went there once, perhaps twenty summers ago. Your Lord Wianar and I were not seeing eye to eye over the encroachment of his population into my woods. I explained to him that, regardless of whether or not the elves had departed toward Evermeet, the humans would not be expanding into the Chondalwood."

Vambran gasped. "You!" he said, dumbfounded. He remembered the incident she spoke of clearly. He had been six years old, and there was a celebration taking place at the Generon. He could not have cared less at the time, but the festivities were to honor a "new era in expansionism." Right in the middle of Lord Wianar's speech, a woman dressed in verdant green clothing had hopped onto the stage and warned him against encroaching into the forest. Vambran still remembered the final warning: *If death is all you can understand after all these years, feel free to pursue the matter.* He had only learned later that the woman was Shinthala Deepcrest, a hierophant druid infamous throughout the Reach.

The realization that he had tongue-lashed one of the most powerful members of the druidic order back at the great rock gave Vambran serious pause. "You," he repeated, barely able to breathe the word.

"Yes," Shinthala said, obviously pleased with the reaction she had garnered from him.

Vambran, flustered, mumbled and stumbled over his words for a moment before managing to get out, "I was simply trying to make you see that you do not know me, my heart, and to make judgments about me based solely on your preconceptions is a dangerous fallacy. I meant no disrespect, Elder Deepcrest."

Shinthala waved his explanation away. "Of course you did," she said. "But I deserved it. Do not fret, Son of Arrabar. I find your passion, your dedication to your ideals, refreshing. And you remind me that I should not label all others by their outward appearances. I offer apology for losing my temper before." She turned then and walked on for a while, allowing Vambran a moment to gather his wits.

When he caught up to her again, Shinthala said in a troubled voice, "Tell me why the killing has begun to grow worse. Edilus thinks that someone is trying to draw the Emerald Enclave into your wars through viciousness and butchery. I say it is simply the nature of soldiers to fight until one side or the other is dead."

"I say that Edilus may be right," Vambran said, to which the woman paused and turned back to him, one eyebrow raised.

"How would you know this, Son of Arrabar?"

Vambran smiled. "Though my soldiers and I are not here of our own volition, we are here nonetheless. I believe that others who have worked against us—against me—back in Arrabar manipulated events so that my unit might be caught up in the midst of the chaos spreading through these woods. I believe they are also in some way responsible for the more vicious turn of affairs here. They scheme and plot for coin, and destroy anyone and anything that stands in their way."

Shinthala grunted and looked to some distant, unseen point. "But the scheming and plotting has gone on since the beginning of time," she said, sighing. "What would make this any different?"

Vambran shrugged. "I don't know," he admitted. "Though I was trying to find out not so long ago, back in Arrabar. Perhaps I can renew my quest here in the Nunwood," he suggested.

The woman laughed. "Again you suggest a pact!"

Vambran shrugged again. "I don't think we work at such cross purposes that we couldn't join together to put a stop to these events. My alternatives do not seem to be all that promising," he added wryly.

Shinthala laughed again. "That is true, Son of Arrabar." She turned to him and drew the slightest bit closer. "Then again, you might find that the alternatives are not so bad," she said, staring at him with those emerald eyes. She brushed his arm with her fingers. "There are many kinds of pacts to be made," she said, running those fingers up to his cheek.

Vambran blinked in surprise, caught totally off guard at her advances, but before he could respond, she turned and continued her casual journey, running her hands lovingly along the bark of tree trunks she passed along the way.

Several steps ahead, Shinthala glanced back at the soldier. "Don't look so surprised," she said. "Every woman has her needs, and you are easy on the eyes; that is certain."

Vambran found his voice and replied indignantly,

"I may have a great need to be released, but I'm not willing to trade my favors for it. I'm not a trollop on the streets of Arrabar, you know."

Shinthala turned back on the lieutenant and snorted. "Is that what you heard? That I was offering a deal? Bed me, and I'll give you your freedom? You must not think as highly of me as you showed before, then. Do I seem that desperate to you?"

Vambran blushed, regretting his words. "Forgive me, Elder Deepcrest," he said, trying to smooth things over. "I—"

Shinthala's anger fled as quickly as it had come. She dismissed his apology with a wave of her hand. "No," she said. "You grew up in the city, as you so passionately explained to me earlier. I should have realized you would read my advances as politic. I should be the one apologizing, for putting you in such an awkward spot." Then her smile softened, became somewhat sad. "I desired you from the moment they brought you before me," she said, blushing. "I do not often act on such impulses, especially with soldiers who destroy my forests, but there was something ... urgent ... about you, and it sparked a fire in me." She looked down, then, staring at the ground between them. "I felt torn, angry with myself for experiencing such feelings. That is why I was so harsh before." Shinthala took a deep breath then, as though gathering her courage, and returned her gaze to Vambran's. Her voice was tremulous. "I would share your bed, but only if you were drawn to me as I am to you, and only for its own reward. I do not play those games, warrior, regardless of our current situation. That is not my way." She turned and hurried along the trail again then, hiding her face from his.

Vambran pursed his lips in thought, then caught up to the woman and took her hand firmly in his own, stopping her and turning her to face him. She struggled to meet his gaze, and he saw that her emerald eyes glistened. "Then you flatter me," he said. "And I have not said no," he added.

Shinthala regarded him thoughtfully, seeming to study his eyes. She smiled, and he wanted to kiss her. "I am a simple woman, Son of Arrabar, and we have met under remarkably complicated circumstances. I don't know what the future holds for either of us, but sometimes the simple pleasures help make the complicated things clear." Then she began to stroll once more, her movements decidedly more lithe than he remembered.

"Vambran," he said, catching up one last time. "My name is Vambran."

...

It was a long time later, well into the afternoon. They lay on a carpet of soft moss, most of their clothes spread out upon the ground beneath them. Vambran was on his back, staring at the bright sky partially visible through the trees, and Shinthala was sitting up, hugging her knees, her back to him. He had not realized how tense he had been until afterward. For the moment, at least, he was allowing himself to relax.

Shinthala's words were sudden, unexpected, like everything she did. "You say that we do not work at cross purposes, but I do not see it. What is your goal, if it is not to fight, as all the other mercenaries battle, further despoiling the woods?"

Vambran glanced at the woman beside him. She was staring off at some distant point again, a sign that she was thinking. "My only ambition, and that of those who serve under me, is the rescue of our companions," the lieutenant answered. "It is not my intention nor my desire to tarry in the Nunwood for longer than necessary."

"Because you did not intend to be here in the first place," Shinthala said, repeating what Vambran had told her earlier. "But you also told me that you are, in fact, embroiled in these vicious displays of brutality in some way."

"Yes," Vambran admitted, "but only indirectly. It is a long tale, suitable for telling at another time, but—"

"We are in no hurry," Shinthala said, looking back at him languidly over her shoulder. Vambran cocked his head to one side, puzzled by her interest in the affairs of House Matrell. He wanted to tell her that he *was* actually in a hurry, but he doubted very seriously that she would share his sense of urgency just then.

So be it, he decided at last. He would tell the sordid truth in all its glory.

Vambran told Shinthala the story in its entirety. The woman stopped him and asked questions of him at several different points, to clarify events or to reveal some bit of information that he had glossed over. It took Vambran the better part of an hour to recount the whole events of the murdered kitchen maid and his family's involvement in the business alliance that had been the architect of the dreadful crime. He finished with the revelation of his sister's communication, and her struggles with events back in Arrabar. Telling that part of it made him feel restless.

I should not be here, he thought. I should be at home, helping my family.

Shinthala was quiet again for a long time. After the silence stretched on for several moments, she returned to her original query. "The soldiers are fighting differently. There has always been war in this region, but it is a pale imitation of true war. The soldiers march about, chasing one another, but they rarely attack. Instead, they negotiate an outcome,

determined by sacks of coin and old debts repaid.
Then they march away, ready to play this game again
another day. It is foolish, but it is not so bloody.

"Now, they kill with abandon."

Vambran saw her shoulders sag, sensed her sorrow.
He understood that, though she had little tolerance
for the world beyond her woods at large, she still suffered to see relentless killing. And though he knew
he personally had little to do with the bloodshed and
violence visited upon the people of the woods, he felt a
sense of guilt wash over him, guilt at his chosen life,
that of a professional soldier. "My uncle and brother
and their partners sought to profit from the fighting,"
he reminded her. "Perhaps they foresaw greater profit
through protracted, total war."

"Perhaps, but I think there is more to this tale,"
Shinthala replied. "The men who kill with abandon
fight on behalf of the city of Reth. They make a point
of claiming so, to all who survive the carnage. It is as
though the leaders of that city wish it to be known
that they push against us, and against all other
armies serving all other patrons."

"Yes," Vambran said, his sense of sorrow and guilt
growing at the woman's descriptions. "Perhaps they
wish to have an insulating layer of anonymity between themselves and the actual armies. They will
profit from the increased control of the woods and the
logging that goes on there after they have secured the
field, but they do not want the populace to make the
connection between the coin they spent slaughtering
all opposition and the coin they gained cutting down
trees."

"Perhaps," Shinthala repeated, but she sounded
doubtful. "But don't you think it odd that these
'businessmen'"—and she spoke that word with great
distaste, reminding Vambran just how vast was the
gulf between their lives—"would choose to back the

government of Reth, formerly a part of your own country, against soldiers serving Chondath? Is not Hlath still under the rule of Lord Wianar?"

Vambran considered the woman's words, trying to make some sense of why Grozier Talricci and Grand Trabbar Lavant would choose to fund an army to go against Chondath, especially in such a conspicuous manner. It was as though they were trying to draw attention to themselves, trying to see what Hlath would do in response.

"They are trying to draw out the army of Hlath," he said, sitting up. "They are trying to goad Chondath into a reaction."

"And what would that reaction be?" Shinthala asked, as though she already knew the answer.

"Wianar would see an opportunity to retaliate," he said. "He might even see a chance to crush Reth's resistance once and for all," he added, realization dawning, "and restake his claim to that city as being part of Chondath. The alliance is working for Lord Wianar in secret!"

"Yes," Shinthala said, turning and looking at him, her emerald eyes sparkling dangerously. "And why, do you suppose, would this alliance you know of go out of its way to involve the Enclave? Why suffer the wrath of two enemies instead of just one unnecessarily?"

"Because," Vambran said slowly, thinking the issue through to its logical conclusion, "if Reth and the druids tear at one another, it weakens both of them, and the armies of Chondath will march into the aftermath and win an easy victory. Wianar reclaims Reth and grievously wounds the Emerald Enclave, long a thorn in his side, all at once."

"You are wise for one so young," Shinthala said, running her delicate fingers along his cheek. "But there is one part of this matter that you have not considered."

"What is that?"

"That you and your soldiers are from Chondath. Further, you serve the same temple that is a part of this alliance, a part of this conspiracy to raise war and retake lost territories. It would be natural to expect Lord Wianar to draw on every 'resource'"—and she gave Vambran a knowing look at the use of that word—"at his disposal to win his land back. That would include a very cooperative Temple of Waukeen, would it not? That would include the armies of the Order of the Sapphire Crescent, true?"

Vambran did not speak. The evidence was damning, and he had no rebuttal other than what he had already claimed.

"We cannot hope to win a two-front war," Shinthala said, drawing her shirt about herself. "And if we allow ourselves to be drawn into this conflict, that is precisely what will occur." Vambran nodded in understanding, beginning to pull on his own clothes. "But if we do not fight," she continued, "then we allow the people of the cities to control the woods, and we have failed in our course. So we are at a difficult crossroads."

At that point, Shinthala turned and looked at Vambran directly. "You have offered your help to us, Vambran," she said. "What do you propose to do to stop this plan?"

The lieutenant paused, considering what he was willing to do. He had offered to help, and he intended to prevent the war, but his methods of doing so might not make sense to Shinthala, who seemed to approach all things in a direct manner. "I will aid you as I can," he offered, rising to his feet, "but I must also look to my own soldiers. They follow me loyally, and I must do what I can to save them. Let me free them from the army camped in the clearing, and I will find a way to diffuse this impending cloud of war that hangs over the Nunwood."

"And what of your family, back in Arrabar? What of your sister?"

"I don't know," Vambran answered, frustration and helplessness rising. "I should go to her, too, but my duty to my soldiers ... I am torn. And every moment I spend here, as pleasant as it is," he said meaningfully, wanting her to know he did not regret their day together, "keeps me from either one."

Shinthala considered Vambran's words. "I believe your sincerity," she said at last. "And I wish for you to succeed, on both fronts."

Vambran reached down and helped her to stand. "Then let me and my soldiers free," he said. "We can stop the killing."

Shinthala stared at him intently, those brilliant green eyes glowing warmly, then pulled him close in an embrace. "I actually believe you can," she said against his shoulder.

...

Emriana was sitting in the formal room of House Darowdryn. The first to arrive in the parlor was Ariskrit Darowdryn, the woman Emriana remembered from many occasions in her youth, most recently her birthday party. The woman took one look at the girl and came right over and gave her a warm embrace. Just seeing the elderly matriarch nearly made the girl cry, for though she was able to speak with her own grandmother, the magnitude of Hetta's disembodied condition still overwhelmed her.

"It's going to be all right, Em," Ariskrit said. "You were right to come to us."

Tharlgarl entered shortly thereafter. Thankfully, he was not dressed in his immense suit of armor any longer, but was instead wearing a comfortable-looking riding outfit. More members of the Darowdryn family soon followed, none of whom Emriana knew.

Once more than half a dozen of them had gathered in the parlor, Ariskrit said, "Now, Miss Emriana, tell us what, exactly, has happened to my dear friend Hetta, and do not leave anything out."

Emriana nodded and began to reveal her tale, including the fact that Hetta's spirit was somehow implanted in the ring she wore. Several times while listening to the girl explain her reasons for being there, Ariskrit's eyes sparkled in anger. When she was finished, the matriarch nodded.

"Hetta has been my friend and confidante for many years," she said, "and though I don't know if she can hear me or not, you assure her that we are going to help you set things right. That whelp Talricci will not get away with this, I promise you."

Emriana smiled. "Thank you so much," she said. "I cannot tell you how much it means to me."

"Well, there is a lot we must do, but before we formulate any plans, my grandson Pilos here needs to add a little to your story." The young man sitting just to Ariskrit's right smiled and sat forward in his seat. Emriana had noticed before that he was dressed as an Abreeant priest of the Temple of Waukeen, and she had glanced at him more than once during her explanations of the family's suspicions about Lavant. In the back of her mind, Emriana had worried that she would offend the young man, but each time she mentioned Lavant by name, she saw him grimace, and the girl realized that he found the obese priest as repugnant as she did.

"As everyone is already well aware," Pilos began, "Mikolo Midelli has passed from Abeir-Toril, and Lavant has ascended to become Grand Syndar of the temple here in Arrabar." He glanced over at Emriana and smiled. "What everyone except Grandmother

Ariskrit doesn't know is that Mikolo Midelli's spirit visited me in my chambers at the temple a short while ago."

There was a unified gasp of surprise from the group gathered in the room, followed by everyone talking at once. Though Emriana was just as shocked as the rest of the folk, her thoughts went to the spirit of Hetta. She knew already that her grandmother's consciousness could hear everything around her, but it still startled her when a surge of comforting emotions radiated through her body.

"Enough!" Ariskrit said, clapping her hands to silence the room. "Let him continue."

When order was restored, Pilos went on. "Mikolo told me that he needed me to stop Lavant from leading Chondath into war. He told me that I would find my path by returning here, to my family." Again, he looked over at Emriana, and for the first time, the girl realized he seemed shyly attracted to her. "I think I know what I am here to do, now."

Emriana smiled back, though she had no idea what a minor priest of the temple was going to be able to accomplish that the rest of his family could not already do. Still, she was grateful for every bit of support she was receiving.

"Well, *I* don't know what to do," she admitted after a moment, when she realized everyone was staring at her again. "Vambran is alive, but far away and embroiled in his own problems, Hetta is—" and she had to stop, to swallow back her emotions for a moment. "—is spiritually bound into this ring I wear. And Aunt Xaphira is missing. Marga and Grozier seem to be in control of my family fortune at the moment. I have nothing to offer this effort."

"Nonsense," Ariskrit said. "You are a very resourceful girl, or you wouldn't be Hetta's granddaughter. You've come this far pretty much on your own, so don't sell yourself short. Now," she said, considering, "we must know what is transpiring in your home. You've already told us that Hetta believes something strange and unnatural has a hold of Marga. Grozier may be manipulating her with magic of some sort. We already know that pesky wizard of his is no good and will do anything to curry favor with the man.

"Tharlgarl," the woman said, turning to the bear of a man sitting off to one side, "you go speak with our own House wizards and see what we can do about finding out the truth—and about establishing a more useful contact with Vambran Matrell. We need to know exactly what's going on where he is and let him know that we have events well in hand on our end." Tharlgarl nodded and rose from his seat to do as Ariskrit had instructed.

"And as for you," Ariskrit said, turning back to Emriana, "I want you to try using that pendant of yours again. See if you can find your aunt."

Emriana nodded and took hold of the opal hanging from its chain around her neck. Almost fearfully, she began to envision Xaphira, praying that the magic would work and that she would get some sort of response. "Aunt Xaphira," she called out. "It's Em. Please answer me. Tell me where you are, so I can help you if you need it. Are you there?"

There was a disorienting sound, something like a groan, and Emriana heard, *Em. Help me... soldier's uniform ... I'm in ... Generon.* And that was it. The girl knew that the magic of the necklace had ended, and she sat there for a long moment, willing herself to repeat what she had heard.

When she was able to relay Xaphira's pleas, Ariskrit Darowdryn's eyes narrowed. "So," she said, "our own Lord Wianar may have something to do with this. We play a very dangerous game, here."

The members of the Darowdryn family began
discussing the ramifications of the revelation, but
Emriana wasn't listening. All she could think about
was her aunt's voice, the pain and disorientation in
Xaphira's words. She knew what she had to do.

"I'm going to the Generon," she said, standing. "I
have to rescue her."

All the conversation stopped, and every pair of
eyes turned toward her. Emriana expected them all
to argue with her, to tell her that she was foolish,
that one young girl could not hope to go up against
the might of the Lord of all of Chondath. But they
didn't.

Instead, Ariskrit nodded. "Of course you are, my
dear," she said. "We all are. We'll visit tonight, for
Sammardach."

Emriana couldn't contain her grateful smile.

CHAPTER 16

Kovrim would have liked nothing better than to reach out and wrap the chains connecting his wrists together around Junce Roundface's neck, but the two guards flanking him never would have allowed it. The pair practically carried him as they walked, for he could not keep up, moving on his own, the way his feet were also restrained. Still, the old priest enjoyed the thought of strangling the hated assassin strolling along in front of him.

When Kovrim had realized who was watching him through the barred window set in the door of the cell, his first thought was that Junce had come on his own, secretly, to dispatch the priest and be done with him. But he soon realized that Roundface was not alone. The door had been unlocked, and guards had moved toward where Kovrim lay, grabbing him and hauling him bodily out of the cell.

The priest and his two escorts followed Junce down the corridor and out into the main chamber of the prison area. From there, they followed a new passage, different from the route by which all of the Crescents had arrived earlier. The corridor Junce selected led deeper into the bowels of the keep, through a doorway and down a set of narrow, spiraling steps that went on for several turns. When they emerged from the staircase, Kovrim saw that they had brought him to some sort of ill-lit torture chamber, replete with hideous devices. His heart skipped a beat at the prospect of what his captors intended, and he dug in his heels, albeit ineffectually.

"Lock him in there," Junce said, pointing toward a barred alcove set in one wall. "He can watch."

The two guards hauled Kovrim to the tiny cell, shoved him inside, and shut the door behind him. The priest could hear the heavy latch click shut, and he turned just as one of the guards threaded a large padlock through the latch and snapped it closed. He stood there watching as the pair of guards strode off, heading back the way they had come.

Junce paced for a few moments, a half smile on his face. Then he turned to where Kovrim was imprisoned. "It's unfortunate I don't have both you and your nephew," he said, "because it would be so thoroughly enjoyable letting you watch him. But since I don't have the luxury of killing him before your eyes, your other companions will have to do."

Kovrim furrowed his brow, angry at how helpless he felt. He wanted to utter a few obscenities in the assassin's direction, but the wedge of leather and iron in his mouth prevented it. Instead, he just turned away, unwilling to give the man the satisfaction of seeing his distress. That's when he noticed the small window on the back side of the little alcove. Like the main opening, it was warded with bars, but it was of a height that he could look through it without having to stand too high.

In fact, the window afforded a view into a larger chamber beyond. The ceiling of that room was the same height as that of the torture chamber, but the floor was well below that under his feet, so the priest was looking down from a second floor. It was square and empty. On one wall of that chamber, on the opposite side of Kovrim's position, he could see a portcullis, down at the moment, blocking a darkened tunnel. On the wall to the priest's left, there was a solid door, also apparently raised and lowered from some remote source. Along the right wall, well off the floor of the room and at the same level as his own window, a balcony looked down into the chamber, or the pit, as Kovrim was coming to think of it. The illumination for the pit came from torches set into sconces along that balcony.

"You see," Junce said from behind Kovrim, "we're fighting a war, as you already surmised back in Arrabar, when you started nosing around in Lavant's affairs. But this war is costly, and we need all the help we can get. That's why we're accepting volunteers to join up and fight the good fight. You and some of your men will be new recruits."

Kovrim turned back and looked at the assassin with the coldest, most baleful stare he could muster, though the other man's words sent an ominous chill down the priest's spine. He wasn't certain what Junce was suggesting, but he knew it did not bode well for him and the other Crescents.

"Go ahead," Junce said, gesturing, "take a look. I know *I'm* going to enjoy this."

He turned, walked to the far side of the torture

chamber, and pulled open another door, disappearing through it and pulling it shut behind himself.

Kovrim shook his head in mute frustration and turned back to the window.

The portcullis began to rise, and a moment later, the two guards who had manhandled him into the torture chamber appeared again, dragging Hort along with them, still in his chains. He was being led along willingly, if sullenly, but when he saw the room, his body stiffened, as though he had gotten a sudden, uneasy feeling. The guards shoved him to the floor and turned back to the exit, where the portcullis was already dropping again. The pair sprinted through the narrowing gap and vanished.

Hort climbed to his feet with a muttered curse and looked around, examining the surroundings. Kovrim made a loud grunting noise, willing Hort to look up, and after a moment, the grizzled soldier spotted the priest looking down at him.

"Well, this is a fine mess we're in, eh, sir?" Hort called up, trying to sound cheerful.

Before Kovrim could grunt a response, there was the sound of a heavy door opening and closing. Hort looked up toward the near side of the balcony, just out of Kovrim's sight, and scowled. Then Junce strolled into view, looking down at his captive.

"Watch carefully," the assassin said, and chuckled. "This is going to be interesting."

The heavy door on the left side of the pit began to rise. Kovrim, panic welling up in him, willed Hort to find a way out, to climb up to the balcony, out of harm's way. But the old soldier turned and eyed the opening portal warily.

No! Kovrim tried to shout, but all that came out was a muffled, nasally whine. Don't do this!

As the heavy barricade reach its zenith, Hort's expression changed from concern to horror. He began to back away, turning toward the portcullis and running to it as fast as his chains would allow. "No!" he cried out, yelling down the blackened hallway. "Raise the gate! Raise the gate!"

Kovrim stood, transfixed in a state of helpless horror, as something began to emerge from the interior beyond the barricade. A man shuffled out, or what once must have been a man. Its movements were awkward and jerky, and Kovrim could see that it was undead.

The thing's skin was discolored, like one continuous bruise, all purplish yellow with tinges of blue at the joints. Pustules of yellowish ichor also covered its sagging, lifeless flesh. Muscles moved beneath the surface like burrowing grubs, and its clothing, that of the guard there inside the Palace of the Seven, hung filthy and loose, torn and deteriorating.

A zombie.

As soon as the nasty thing was fully into the room, a second and a third followed it out of the tunnel. They shuffled without pause directly toward Hort, who was bellowing and banging his manacles on the bars of the portcullis, pleading to be let out of the deathtrap in a voice that rose ever higher in panic-induced pitch.

Kovrim screamed, too, or tried to. He pounded his steel fists against the bars of the window, trying desperately to distract the zombies, all the while furiously but futilely attempting to dislodge the thick wad of leather so firmly clamped between his teeth. If he could only speak, he could help, cast a spell or drive the undead things back, away from Old Bloagy, or he could—but it was useless.

The priest watched in horror as the zombies closed in on his companion, watched as Hort turned, screaming, and began to pummel the walking dead things his fists. The soldier used the length of chain

stretched between his wrists to good effect, like a
garrote, wrapping it around the neck of one of the
zombies as though he were trying to strangle it. Being
undead, it did not need to breathe, but Hort held it
firmly there anyway, shifting it back and forth, using
the creature as a shield against the slow, witless attacks from the other two. For a moment, Kovrim
thought that perhaps the man would survive the
horrible assault, that Hort might destroy the zombies before they rent him to pieces.

But eventually, the chain sawed clear through
the held zombie's neck, and its head went bouncing
away while its body slumped to the floor in front of
Hort, twitching uselessly. The other two ignored the
downed corpse and pursued the man. Hort backed
away, waiting for an opening while licking his lips
in desperation, but he looked strange to Kovrim, slow
and ill at ease.

What's the matter with him? the priest wondered.
He looks ... unwell.

Truly, Hort's complexion had paled considerably,
and his breath was coming in ragged gasps. Kovrim
could see no wounds, no marks upon the man, but all
the same, the soldier acted as though he had been
mortally wounded. As the zombies backed him into a
corner, he went down to one knee, coughing, clutching
at his sides.

No, Kovrim thought desperately, no! He wanted to
turn away, and yet he could not.

The zombies drew closer, pummeling their prey.
Hort cried out, then slid down, and the zombies con-
tinued to beat on him long after he stopped moving.
The sounds of their blows turned wet, pulpy.

Kovrim's throat constricted in anguish. The brutality of the fight made his anger burn hot inside.
He turned and stared malevolently at Junce, but the
assassin had his elbows resting on the railing of the

balcony, watching with bemused interest. He didn't even notice the gaze, or if he did, he ignored it.

The priest had felt hatred for few people during his long life, but the fury, the savage enmity that coursed through him right at that moment for the man standing on the balcony was beyond compare. His blood pounded in his ears, and his vision was tinged in red. He swore to himself, to Waukeen, that if he got the chance, he would kill Junce Roundface, would strangle him or bludgeon the man with his restraints, even at the cost of his own life. He would never hesitate.

Bathed in his anger, Kovrim did not realize that Junce had started speaking again.

"Normally, we restrain them," Junce commented casually, "because otherwise, they put up such a fight, and we lose as many new recruits as we create. And that's not productive, obviously." Junce departed from the balcony then, moving out of Kovrim's field of vision momentarily to the sound of a door opening and closing. He reappeared again within the torture chamber, strolling over toward the cage wall behind which Kovrim seethed.

"But I decided to make an exception, just this once," Junce said, picking up where he had left off. "I wanted you to get to see a little sport, think for a few minutes that your friend down there had a fighting chance. It was kind of funny, actually, watching him get the disease all over himself. That's really ironic, don't you think?"

Kovrim glared at Junce, not deigning to give the horrid man the satisfaction of any sort of reaction.

Junce shrugged. "Well, *I* think it is. After all, what's the point of fighting something that's already killed you the moment it gets near you? Your friend was already dead the instant he first bumped up against one of them; he just didn't know it, yet."

Realization began to dawn on Kovrim, and his eyes widened in horror. No! he thought again, banging his steel-encased fists on the bars of his cage. No, no, no! Not this! You cannot! You're a madman!

Junce laughed. "Yes, I see that you understand now. Ingenious, don't you think? We spread the plague with the zombies, and even though the people think they've destroyed the creatures, they get sick themselves. And it's only a matter of time before our army is replenished. Go on, see for yourself," he finished, gesturing toward the window at the back of the alcove.

Slowly, horror making his limbs feel wooden, Kovrim turned back around. Gazing down, he saw that the two zombies had moved off already, shuffling back into their lair. But Hort's body was clearly visible. It was battered and bruised, and already, bulbous, puss-filled bumps covered his skin.

Then the dead man began to move.

...

The Generon was, as usual, remarkably beautiful. The entire palace had been decorated in silver and gold, the color of coin, in honor of Sammardach. Silver lanterns, pierced globes that swung gently in the evening breezes, hung from every available point. Magical golden streamers of light, conjured by House mages periodically during the festivities, flitted from porch to porch and through the gardens. Inside, Emriana saw the amazing fountain that sat squarely in the center of the main entry hall, transformed for the evening so that coins, rather than water, seemed to dance and splash down its sleek sides. The girl stood transfixed for a few moments, just gazing at the wonder of it all.

But her interest was not held for long, for her

nervousness made her restless. She knew she could not truly enjoy the celebration within the lord's palace so long as her family was at risk. She knew that she had to find her aunt, and that the search itself could very well be her undoing. Still, she lingered a moment longer, staring at the illusory fountain. It wasn't so much that the effect was that breathtaking, the girl decided, it was the nostalgic remembrance of her delight as a younger girl.

A more naive girl, she thought. She missed those carefree days, when nothing mattered but whatever interested her at a given moment.

The mages of House Darowdryn had tried several different magical tricks to see if they could locate or even retrieve Xaphira from her undisclosed location, but all their efforts proved fruitless. Wherever Emriana's aunt was being held, magic had been employed to keep her there, and to keep the site a secret. However, the wizards had been able to guide Emriana in the use of a scrying crystal, which she had then used to locate a few of the older woman's belongings. Peering through the crystal, the girl could see that Xaphira's weapons had been carelessly left lying upon a crude wooden table in a dimly lit stone chamber. At one point, a shadowy figure had passed near the table, and Emriana caught enough of a glimpse of the clothing to realize it was that of Lord Wianar's House guard.

Xaphira was, indeed, imprisoned in the Generon.

The wizards had also considered further scrying and possibly trying to magically transport someone to the chamber, but they ended up dismissing it as too dangerous. Besides, they had explained to Emriana, Lord Wianar's own wizards had the entire palace well shielded from such magical intrusions. She would have to get inside the walls of the Generon before she could employ any magic to track down her aunt.

After the discussion of how best to go about doing that very thing was concluded, Ariskrit had insisted that Emriana let the house staff pamper her royally. It was amazing to the girl what a hot bath could do to wash away the stench of dead fish, and she had settled in for a well-deserved nap. She had had no idea just how tired she was from her various ordeals over the course of the past day, but when she woke up, it was late afternoon, and she felt much better.

Emriana had chosen a red dress for the evening, subtly but symbolically representing her goal of finding Xaphira. Still, it was a wonderful outfit, pulled from the deep and varied wardrobes of a distant Darowdryn cousin who matched her in size. The dress was trimmed with thread-of-gold highlights, and it had a matching cape and cowl in a steel gray with red and gold highlights. Over the dress, Emriana wore a traditional Chondathan golden chain-and-gem bodice, the whole thing covered in yellow sapphires. And she had also donned one of the customary masks that all the women within the Generon would be wearing, an old symbol of a forgotten time when one's identity was best kept to oneself. Emriana doubted anyone who knew her well would have any difficulty recognizing her, but the mask made her feel a little more secure, a bit more anonymous.

Pilos had decked himself out in his most formal priestly garb for the occasion. His white silk trousers and shirt shone in the moonlit night, and the doublet he had donned over that was a deep crimson color. He wore a slender circlet of gold atop his head, a symbol of his rank as Abreeant. Together, they made a rather fine couple, Ariskrit had proclaimed, causing both Emriana and Pilos to blush furiously.

The family members attending the celebration had traveled to the Generon in splendid covered coaches, arriving to much fanfare, for House Darowdryn

was one of the half dozen or so wealthiest Houses
in all of Arrabar, and its comings and goings were
constantly heralded. Emriana and Pilos stayed close
to the family initially, blending in with the crowd
during the family's formal announcement. Shortly
after that, they entered a grand ballroom, filled with
guests. A high balcony sported a sextet of musicians,
and many of the partygoers were dancing to the lively
tunes.

On the far side of the chamber, up on a dais, Lord
Eles Wianar sat with his guest of honor, the Grand
Syndar Lavant, by his side.

Emriana wanted to spit, and she felt Pilos stiffen
beside her. "Come on," she said. "Let's get some air."

Together, they drifted off by themselves at a
natural pace, wandering in and out of the palace's
open chambers, casually strolling about the grounds.
Just getting away from the sight of the hated priest
seemed to lift Pilos's spirits, and Emriana felt much
better.

After perhaps half an hour or more of pretending
they were just a happy young couple seeing the splen-
dors of the Generon, Emriana began to keep watch
for a means of slipping away from the party and into
the less-trafficked sections of the palace. It was not
going to be easy, she realized, for despite the festive
nature of the celebration, Lord Wianar's guards were
still in abundance and still discreetly stationed at
just about every ingress that led into more private
areas.

"We're going to have to climb over a wall somewhere," she whispered as they strolled along a
balcony that followed the curved wall of a great
central dome. "Someplace where we won't be seen,"
she added.

Emriana noticed Pilos glance at the girl, startled.
"I think not," he replied, never breaking stride as a

couple approached them coming from the opposite
direction. "I'm hardly dressed for climbing," he
whispered.

Emriana gave the other pair her best innocent
smile, and once they were past, she whispered, "Then
what do you propose?"

At that, Pilos pulled the girl into a small alcove
set into the wall, a spot where there had possibly
been a statue or something similar at one time, but
that was empty at the moment. "These," the young
priest said, withdrawing two small vials from an
inner pocket of his doublet. "With them, we transform into mere clouds of mist, able to go just about
anywhere—through cracks, under locked doors, over
walls. Much more elegant than climbing."

Emriana smirked at the jab, but she eagerly took
the vial Pilos held out to her and examined it. Inside,
she could see a smoky gray liquid. *Grandmother,
what do you think?*

I think you've got one clever partner, Hetta replied,
and that you should hurry.

Emriana nodded then asked, "Do you have two—
wait, we'll need three—three more of those for getting
back out again?"

Pilos started to smile and nod, but when the girl
corrected her statement, his face paled. "No," he said
forlorn, "I didn't think to bring a third."

Emriana grimaced but said, "Don't worry about it.
We'll figure something out when the time comes."

Pilos looked relieved. "Then let's not waste any
more of it," he said. "Where are we going?"

Emriana pointed to a high wall that connected
with the circular building they were in. "See that
gate?" she asked, pointing specifically at a large
closed double-portal. When Pilos confirmed that he
did, she said, "My guess is that there's a stable and
barracks through there, where Lord Wianar's guards

operate. If there's a prison in the palace, I bet we can reach it from there."

"I can't argue with your logic," Pilos said, "but do you really think it's wise to head into the teeth of the palace's defenses? I thought we were trying to avoid the guards."

"Trust me," Emriana said, half smiling. "I'm guessing the yard beyond will be almost deserted this time of night. Most of the guards are either serving as sentries for the celebration or else off on leave. Anyone who stayed behind is probably trying to get some rest."

"How do you know all this?"

Emriana laughed. "Because I spend enough time avoiding my own House guards to figure out their patterns. It's the only way I can sneak out at night."

Pilos stared at the girl with a mixture of shock and admiration on his face; then he shrugged and gestured for her to lead the way. Emriana smiled and left the alcove, heading in the direction of the large barred gate.

The two of them made their way down a winding flight of stairs and into a garden. At the far end was a wall about twice the height of a man. By her bearings, Emriana reckoned that the large wall with the gate was on the other side of the garden wall, across from a narrow lane that ran between the two.

Giving a quick glance around to make certain no one was nearby, she turned to Pilos and said, "How does this work? What will it feel like when I drink this potion?"

"It's hard to describe," the young priest replied, "but you'll know what to do."

"How long will it last?"

"Perhaps ten minutes. Make sure you aren't in a tight area when it expires, or you'll be in serious trouble."

Emriana nodded and unstoppered the vial. Taking a deep breath, she swallowed the entire contents in two large gulps. The taste was strange, sort of smoky, but the liquid itself sapped the moisture from her mouth, as though she were sucking on a thick piece of gauze. She started to complain about the sensation, but she realized that she was no longer able to speak. Her body felt completely weightless, and she found she could see in every direction at once, which was quite dizzying. Once she overcame her initial surprise, she got her mind back on the task at hand and willed herself to float to the top of the garden wall. It happened so fast, she almost drifted right past it and up into the sky.

There was no one in the narrow lane, and sure enough, just as Emriana had silently predicted, the thicker curtain wall was standing on the opposite side. She drifted toward the gate, looking for a gap in the doors through which to squeeze. At the last moment, she decided to go under the twin panels, and even as she thought of the motion, it was happening.

There was, indeed, a courtyard beyond, with a riding area and practice field, judging from the various accoutrements set up throughout the open area. On one side sat a large barn, and next to it was what appeared to be a low barracks where the Generon's soldiers lived. Emriana turned in the other direction, which headed back toward the main part of the palace. There was a long porch on that side, and several doorways leading into darkened interiors.

As she drifted, Emriana began to realize the shortcomings of traveling in such a fashion, for she could not go nearly as fast as she wished, and she was constantly having to compensate for drift caused by the evening breezes. Still, they made good progress. At one point, a pair of guardsmen emerged from one of the doorways, talking softly to themselves as they began to cross the open expanse of courtyard, headed toward the barracks. Emriana instinctually froze.

Go low, Hetta commanded. *Remember, you're a mist now. Cling close to the ground.*

Emriana willed herself to spread out, low to the ground, mimicking the evening mists that often sprang up in her own gardens at home. The two soldiers moved past her position, still deep in conversation, never giving the patch of wispy mist a second glance. After they were beyond her, Emriana wanted to breathe a sigh of relief, but her vaporous condition prevented it. Still, she felt Hetta's sense of relief echo her own thoughts.

The girl began to move forward again, seeing Pilos moving right along beside her. She led him through a doorway she had picked out upon first entering the courtyard. She had no good reason for the choice. It was a gut reaction.

The space beyond was a narrow, torchlit hall that led deeper into the palace. The first chamber off the passage was a kitchen, though not a large one, and Emriana wondered if it was for staff. At the moment, it was empty and dark, so Emriana drifted inside and toward the back, away from the light of the doorway. She waited as Pilos joined her, wondering how much longer the magic of the potion would last before she had to return to human shape. Apparently, even the thought of materializing was sufficient to undo the enchantment, for Emriana found herself weighed down again. It felt both strange and reassuring at the same time.

Pilos materialized beside her. "Why did you do that?" he whispered. "Why didn't you keep going?"

"Because," Emriana replied just as softly, "I don't know which way to go, and I didn't want to get caught in the open when the potion's magic vanished. I didn't know how much longer we had."

The young priest nodded. "Probably wise. All right, I think it's time for me to do a little divination. Wait just a moment." With that, he extracted a pendant from inside his shirt. It was a coin, a holy symbol just like the ones she had seen Vambran, Xaphira, and Uncle Kovrim wearing. Pilos wrapped his hands around it and closed his eyes, bowing his head in prayer. He began to mutter something, so softly Emriana could not make out the words.

After a moment, the Abreeant opened his eyes again and motioned. "You picked a good route," he whispered, beginning to head back out of the kitchen and into the hall. "We can get into the lowest levels by following this around and to the left."

Emriana smiled and began to follow her companion, feeling a strong sense of hope that they would soon find Xaphira.

In a small room elsewhere in the palace, unbeknownst to either the girl or the young priest, a bespectacled wizard watched the pair dart out of the kitchen through the glass of a small mirror. He smiled and went to tell his employer the news.

CHAPTER 17

Your companions have been taken away, hauled out of the forest in great wooden box-wagons," Shinthala said, seated in the middle of the great rock, facing the fire pit. "They were bound for the city of Reth itself."

Everyone began talking at once. Vambran sucked his breath in. At any other time, he would have believed that his soldiers were being treated like any other prisoners of war, and that, in time, they would be released, once the temple funded their ransom. But knowing that Lavant was somehow behind the series of events in the area changed his perceptions dramatically. There was no doubt in his mind that the priest wanted him and Kovrim dead. If what the lieutenant and Shinthala had deduced was true, then the company, and Kovrim, were still in danger.

And now they're farther out of reach, while I've dallied in the woods.

Vambran and Shinthala had returned from their tryst in the forest after highsun, and she had ordered the release of the other members of the Sapphire Crescents. That had caused some consternation among the other druids, especially Edilus, but she had been adamant. Then they had all gathered together upon the great rock, druids and mercenaries together, to decide what must be done.

"I have to get inside the city," Vambran said then repeated himself loudly to quiet the din of so many voices talking at once. "I have to save my uncle. They will kill him to keep him from revealing what he knows. All of them will be slain to preserve the illusion that we died at sea or in battle, the victims of piracy or simple warfare. I have to go to them."

Shinthala shook her head. "No," she said. "You have a greater duty. You must return to Arrabar and let your people know what is happening. You must find proof that Lord Wianar is manipulating these events for his own ends, then you must show the city. Your companions are not as important as the truth."

"I cannot abandon them," Vambran said, though inside, a part of him wanted to, just so he could return to Emriana. "I cannot just leave my uncle and my troops to die there. We must find another way."

"Let us return home," Adyan said in his drawl. "We can go back to Arrabar and spread the word, and you can go to Reth."

"No," Vambran said. "My family needs me, too."

Adyan shook his head. "We'll help Em, Vambran, and with your family safe, we can stop this before Wianar marches half of Chondath east. You go to Reth. Six is no better than one against a whole city, but by yourself, you can still save them. Waukeen herself seems to smile on you."

Vambran looked at Shinthala, who nodded encouragement. "All right," he said, knowing he could not be in both places at once. "You five return home. I don't have to tell you to be careful once there. You're walking into a pit of vipers, it seems."

Adyan snorted. "And you aren't?" he said sardonically. "As long as we've known you, Lieutenant, you've done nothing but lead us into trouble." Vambran could hear the humor in his sergeant's voice, and when he looked at the man, Adyan winked.

"You know we'll find her," Horial added. "We'll get to Em in time."

Vambran took a deep breath and nodded his thanks. "In the meantime," he said, "I'm going to Reth."

Arbeenok stood then, walking to the center of the gathering from his spot on the fringe. He looked first at Shinthala, speaking to her in the language of their order. Then he turned to Vambran and said, "I wish to accompany you to the city. My divinations tell me this is right."

Vambran was taken aback, and when he looked at Shinthala, all she said was, "Arbeenok makes his own trail, even among those of the Enclave. I have learned not to question him, but to trust his visions and know that he will find his own path regardless of my efforts. If he believes he should go with you, I would take that as a boon to your journey."

"But how will we ever get him inside the walls?" Vambran asked skeptically. "He will not pass for a human, no matter how much clothing we pile on him."

At that, Shinthala laughed. "You still have much to learn of us, Son of Arrabar. Go and trust that Arbeenok will know a way to succeed."

Vambran could only shrug. When it was obvious that the lieutenant had accepted Arbeenok's

proposal, the creature put a hand out to the man.
Vambran took it and accepted the handshake.

Once the decision had been made, Shinthala
promised Vambran aid from the Enclave, including
a number of magical potions and oils that might be
of use during both excursions. It did not take long for
either group to pack, and soon enough, they were all
saying their good-byes.

Shinthala followed Vambran and Arbeenok to the
edge of the clearing, away from the rest of the druids
and mercenaries. The lieutenant noticed that a look
from her sent Arbeenok ahead a few paces, out of
earshot. Then she turned Vambran to face her.

"The blessing of your goddess go with you, Son of
Arrabar," she said, smiling wistfully at him. "I'd like
to see you again, preferably alive."

Vambran nodded. "I'll try to get word back to you
soon. If I can free my men, then I—"

Shinthala pressed her fingers against his mouth,
quieting him. "I know all that," she said, "and my
prayers go with you for success in stopping this
war. But what I meant was that today, in the woods,
wasn't enough." Her emerald eyes shone brightly at
him, and Vambran realized it was a little more than
mere lust that made them glow. "Come find me again,
warrior, one way or another, when this is over." Then
she turned and sped back along the path, not giving
him a chance to answer.

Vambran watched her go, wondering if he would
ever get the chance to fulfill that request. Then he
turned and caught up with Arbeenok, and they were
on their way.

The alaghi, as Arbeenok claimed his kind called
themselves, traveled lightly, with little more than
what Vambran had seen him carrying that morning.
For his part, the lieutenant had changed out of his
uniform, which was stored in a satchel he carried, and

he was wearing simple garb, that of a laborer, so as not to draw notice to himself. They spent the rest of the afternoon traveling, though they covered most of the distance by means of a portal that passed between two great oaks. Both trees—the one near the heart of the forest and the one closer to Reth— seemed at first blush to be ancient, lightning-shattered trunks, hollowed out on the inside. But Arbeenok led the lieutenant into one, and just as quickly, they were stepping out of the other. From there, it wasn't much farther to the border of the woods.

At last, they came to the edge of the forest lying alongside the road leading into Reth. Vambran crept forward the last few feet and peered out of the underbrush, screened by tall grasses. The city was not visible from that vantage point, but Shinthala had assured him that it was not much farther beyond that. Beside him, Arbeenok also peered out, studying the path in both directions.

"No one comes," he said, his voice deep but gentle. "We should continue, for darkness will fall before we reach the walls of the city."

Vambran nodded. "Well, if you have some idea how to sneak past all the gawking stares, now is the time to reveal it," Vambran said. "Once we're out on the road, you will be noticed."

Arbeenok smiled, an expression that was surprisingly human in appearance. "I will not be able to speak, but I will understand you perfectly," he said. "So it will be important for you to realize that I will be trying to communicate to you in other ways and to pay attention to me. Do you see?"

Vambran grinned, beginning to appreciate Arbeenok's company more and more. "My soldiers and I have hand signals we sometimes use for communicating on the battlefield, so I am used to such," he said.

"Good. Then let's continue our journey." And with that, he stood and began to transform right before Vambran's eyes. The alaghi dropped down to his hands and knees, and his clothing and other items seemed to melt inside his body. When the change was complete, Arbeenok was a large, yellow dog. He wagged his tail and barked once at Vambran, who only stood there grinning.

"Very clever," the lieutenant said, reaching a hand out to pat the dog. Arbeenok played the part, panting and rubbing his head against Vambran and wagging his tail all the harder. "And you can understand me, yes?" Vambran inquired. Arbeenok barked and nodded.

"Then you are a fine traveling companion," the mercenary officer said and stepped out of the brush into the open. "Let's go."

The two of them set off together, and to everyone they passed, farmers in their wagons, loggers and craftsmen, and especially soldiers setting out toward the battle lines, they looked like a peasant and his dog. They hiked along at a steady pace, and Arbeenok ran ahead periodically. Though it appeared that the mutt was simply frisky and stretching its legs, Vambran began to see the advantage of having his companion able to scout ahead.

At one point, Arbeenok came running back and grabbed at Vambran's pants leg, dragging him off the road and into the bushes. A few minutes later, a large contingent of soldiers wearing the silver raven on their tabards went marching past. Though he couldn't be certain, it was entirely possible that some of those soldiers had engaged him in fighting, and he was thankful the alaghi had had the presence of mind to help him avoid a confrontation.

As the afternoon drew on toward dusk, Reth came into view in the distance. By the time Vambran and his hound reached the gates, darkness was coming fast. The guards were preparing to close the great portals for the coming night, and Vambran had to hurry to get inside the city before they were completely shut. The guards didn't give him a second glance.

Once they were away from the main thoroughfare and moving down a smaller side street, Vambran said, "I'm taking us to the home of an old acquaintance. I haven't seen her in a year or so, but I think she will help us. Her name is Elenthia, and she runs in the right social circles to hear all the latest news and gossip, so she will know where the Crescents have been taken. Elenthia's father is a senator in the government, so if they're in the prison, she might also be able to get us inside."

Arbeenok wagged his tail by way of answer, and taking that as a sign that the alaghi thought it was a good plan, Vambran led the way to the woman's house.

Elenthia Gelterion's home was as the lieutenant remembered it, a second-story apartment above a soap and incense shop in a rather upscale area of the city. Though the Gelterion family was wealthy, she had chosen to move out of the familial estate before she was actually ready to marry, and in the intervening years, had found that she liked the life of an eligible socialite. Vambran was one of her many distractions, he knew, but he didn't mind playing that role. She was a kind-hearted woman who never expected anything more from him than an occasional dalliance.

When the mercenary and the druid arrived and knocked upon the door, Vambran said, "You ought to continue pretending to be a dog until I find a good way and time to explain to Elenthia who you really are." When Arbeenok cocked his head to one side quizzically, Vambran added, "They'll probably

take you into the kitchen and feed you scraps from
the evening's dinner. I will try not to take too long
talking with her."

Arbeenok barked in understanding and a moment
later, a servant opened the door and let them both in.
Once he had been announced, Vambran did not have
to wait long before Elenthia came gliding into the
entryway, all glowing smiles. She was a remarkably
beautiful woman, Vambran thought, reminded again
when he saw her flashing amber eyes and voluminous dark hair. She was wearing a casual dressing
gown, something to pad around the home in, but she
looked stunning nonetheless. She hesitated when she
saw the lieutenant's outfit, but the pause was barely
noticeable, and she greeted him with a rather florid
kiss.

"Vambran Matrell, what a surprise! What are you
doing in Reth?" she asked, beaming as she led him
into the parlor. "And you have a dog with you," she
said with a hint of distaste. "I must say, this is not
how I expected to see you again." The question of his
current condition and stature hung there, hinted at
but unspoken.

The lieutenant chuckled. "Many things are not as
they were, Elenthia, but I am still serving with the
Crescents. But this is not a social call. I have come
seeking your help."

"Ooh, a call for aid," she said, teasing him, motioning for him to sit with her on a couch. "Judging from
your current outfit, I would guess you don't need me
to play at soldier with you," she said, a mischievous
sparkle in her eye.

Vambran had to grin, remembering a time not
so long ago when she had playfully donned his uniform, or rather, parts of it. She had been particularly
fetching in the get-up. "No," he said, banishing the
thoughts before they got the better of him. "I need

your connections. And it is a large favor I ask. You will need to be discrete."

"Ooh, a mystery," Elenthia said, letting her voice drop.

"I'm serious," Vambran said, letting his smile go. "This could be dangerous for you."

Elenthia sat up straighter and tried to appear serious. "Anything for you, my love," she said. "Whatever it is, I'm eager to assist you."

"Good," Vambran said. "Then I need to find out where my soldiers are. They have been brought here as prisoners."

Elenthia's expression did turn serious then, and she frowned. "Vambran, I cannot ask my father to release prisoners. To begin with, his position is not one of handling the city's defenses, and besides, that would just not be possible. I—"

The lieutenant held up his hand to stop her. "I'm not asking you anything of the sort," he said. "I simply need to know where they are. I will get them out myself."

"What? You mean you intend to try to break them out of prison?"

"Yes, that's what I mean."

"Vambran, you can't be serious! You'll never succeed, and they'll throw you in the dungeon right alongside your soldiers, and I will never see you again! I'm not going to help you do something mad!"

Vambran shook his head. "I don't have a choice, Elenthia. Men have taken them and intend to kill them to ensure their silence—men who are behind the war that's occurring."

Elenthia's frown deepened. "That is unfortunate," she said. "The war is bloody, and Father has stated in no uncertain terms that the senate is up in arms over the whole affair. Half the senate approves of it, and the other half—"

"Elenthia, please," Vambran pleaded. "I don't have time for this. My companions are in danger, and I have to find them right now."

The look on the woman's face broke Vambran's heart, for he realized that he had hurt her with his harsh words. But he dismissed his feelings, promising himself that he would make it up to her later. Right then, he had more important issues to attend to.

"All right," Elenthia said, rising. "Let me get properly dressed, and I will take you to see Father."

Before she was able to walk three paces, though, alarms began to sound outside in the streets. As Elenthia gasped, Vambran moved to the window to see what the commotion was about.

"That's the call to arms!" she cried, a tremor in her voice. "The city's under attack!"

...

"I'd really love to stay and watch all of this," Junce was saying from a distant corner of the room, "but I have to get back to Arrabar. There's some unfinished business I must take care of at the Generon involving your niece. That little Emriana's becoming quite the lovely lady, don't you think?" he said, smiling. "I believe she and I might find something suitable to talk about, a mutually enjoyable way to spend our time together."

Kovrim jerked against the bonds that held him strapped down to a table, wanting with all of his being to get his hands around the assassin's neck and throttle him. But he was completely immobilized and finally gave up, letting hopelessness begin to wash over him. The guards who had removed him from the alcove and restrained him there had disappeared, leaving him alone with Junce.

"A word of advice, though," the assassin said, crossing over to loom near Kovrim's head, a smug smile on his face. "Fight the transformation. It won't make a difference, but I can imagine the desperation you'll feel while it's happening will be truly agonizing. So resist it with everything you have, just for me."

Kovrim gave a throaty shout at the man standing over him, but Junce backed up a pace or two, spoke a phrase, and vanished. When he had gone, the old priest broke down, sobbing in his loneliness and fear. He wasn't afraid to die, but he was terrified of becoming an undead thing. Watching Hort rise up from the floor and stare with glassy, unrecognizing eyes straight ahead as he shuffled off to join the other zombies was the most difficult thing the old priest had ever had to witness.

And he knew he would be joining his longtime companion soon, transformed by the magical plague into another mindless, disease-spreading creature, part of Junce's new army. It sickened him, made him want to retch. He began to thrash again, fighting the restraints that held him on the table.

A door opened, and Kovrim twisted his head around, trying to peer in that direction to see who it was. A man strode into the chamber where he lay, but his face was hidden by a deep-cowled hood, part of a long robe he wore. There was a strange glow radiating all around the stranger, and Kovrim guessed that it was some sort of protection against infection from the plague.

"You see," the stranger said, his face turned away from Kovrim as he stood at a workbench, doing something Kovrim couldn't see, "my cousin doesn't want to have to battle the armies of Reth and the Emerald Enclave at full strength. In truth, he doesn't want to have to fight them at all. He would much rather let the ravages of disease take their toll, and Chondath can arrive with healing magic and save the day, allowing Reth to return to the fold, where it rightly belongs."

Kovrim listened to the man's cryptic words, not understanding them, but not really thinking about them, either. It was the stranger's voice that captivated him. It was vaguely familiar, someone he had known, many years ago. But he couldn't quite place it.

"Of course," the man continued, "my cousin must make certain that Chondath is not seen as having released the plague itself. That's everyone's worst fear, that Shining Arrabar will bring the Rotting Plague back. So he developed a plan. The plague would come from elsewhere, and he would be seen as a savior rather than a devil. And who better to release the plague upon a hated city than the druids of the Emerald Enclave? When they begin to track the zombies' origins and head down into the sewers, they will find the bodies of two promising young wood folk who both gave their lives so that the 'hated city folk' could be devoured in disease."

At last, the man turned to face Kovrim, holding a small alembic, which contained a thick, yellow substance. He approached where the old priest lay, holding the alembic well away from himself. "It was a long plan, a slow one, and one that I didn't have much say in," the man said. "But then, that's always the way my cousin operated, so I guess I should feel fortunate that I was included at all."

Kovrim wanted to scream, not because the man was about to pour the thick, sludgy substance onto his face—that in and of itself was too horrible to contemplate. No, the old priest's anxiety reached a fever pitch because he remembered the face, knew the man.

Slowly, as the man let a bit of the disease-ridden pus slide out of the alembic and dribble around Kovrim's mouth and nose, he lost his faculties, his mind seeking shelter by receding from consciousness.

Rodolpho Wianar finished the application of the disease to the priest and smiled.

CHAPTER 18

Emriana held her breath, trying to hold perfectly still. It was hard, hanging as she was with her knees drawn up and hooked over a timber and her torso folded in half, both hands clinging to that same beam along either side of her knees. She would have pulled herself up the rest of the way and found a more comfortable perch, but there hadn't been time. She felt very undignified with her rear end jutting downward like that.

Below the girl, a lone guard stood in the midst of the room, his head canted slightly to one side as though listening. One hand rested on the hilt of his short sword while the other gripped the scabbard. Emriana knew that any movement on her part would disturb the dust coating the top of the beam, causing it to sift downward—right on top of the man below her.

"Anyone there?" the guard called out, uncertain, craning his neck to peer into the shadows of the library. There was no answer, of course, because when Emriana and Pilos had entered the chamber to flee the guard and his companions, it had been perfectly dark.

Which is why I managed to bump into a shelf and knock over a whole stack of books, Emriana recalled. Oh yes, Emriana Matrell, you are a first-class sneak, she silently taunted herself.

She wanted to throw up from fear.

From the shadows beyond the guard's torch, there was a slight scuffling sound.

"Who's there!" the guard demanded, more forcefully.

A cat appeared, its eyes reflecting the torchlight, a mouse caught in its teeth. It let out a low growl as if to warn the human away from its meal, then slunk back into the shadows.

The guard snorted and his shoulders sagged, obviously relieved. "Stupid cat," he mumbled, turning to go. "Scared the demons out of me." He stomped out of the library, pulling the door shut behind him, leaving Emriana in blessed darkness. She heard the click of a lock turning, and all was quiet.

The girl sighed in relief and thanked Tymora for the luck of a cat. She then eased herself back down from the timbers in the ceiling, dropping to the floor. She began smoothing her dress in the darkness, knocking the dust from it, just as Pilos reappeared, dispatching himself from the nearby wall. His pendant still shone with a soft, pearlescent light. The glow had vanished when the guard had first interrupted them and the young priest had magically melted into the wall. The way in which he had done that fascinated Emriana.

"I need to cast spells like that," she muttered as the young man moved beside her. "I bet you were a lot more comfortable in there than I was hanging half upside down."

Pilos grinned. "You looked like you were having fun," he said wryly. "I thought for a moment that his torch was going to scorch your backside."

Emriana groaned at the possibility. "I guess it's a good thing the ceiling's so high," she remarked.

"Or that he was so short," the young man came back.

Emriana chuckled then took a deep breath. Her heart was still pounding. "Where are we?" When she saw the glint in her counterpart's eye, she added, "And don't say a library. You know what I mean—how close are we?"

Pilos paused with his mouth open then nodded as he let his grin fade. "Close," he said. "We're at the right depth, at any rate."

"Why would there be a library down here, so far below the surface?" Emriana wondered aloud.

"Maybe the guards in the prison get bored and need something to read," Pilos quipped. Emriana shot him a glare. "I'm sorry," he said, straightening his features once more. "I'm very nervous. I tend to joke when I feel that way."

"It's all right," the girl said, understanding all too well how he felt. "But it won't be very funny if we get caught."

"I know," he said, and she could sense that his seriousness had returned. "Truthfully, if Lord Wianar is as powerful a wizard as the rest of Chondath fears, the Generon is probably loaded with libraries, all filled with spellbooks."

Emriana had been about to reach for one of the musty tomes on the closest shelf, but upon hearing the priest's comment, she jerked her hand away.

No telling what magical traps are laid on these books, she thought.

Turning back toward the man accompanying her, Emriana said, "We're running out of time. Let's see about getting that door opened."

Together, they moved toward the portal that led back out into the hallway from which they had arrived. While Pilos held his pendant close, Emriana examined the latch. She slipped one of her enchanted throwing daggers free of the place where she had secreted it in the small of her back and went to work. With a few subtle twists of her wrist, the blade of the dagger manipulated the latch perfectly, and there was a faint click as the catch released.

Emriana motioned for stillness; then she pulled the door open just a crack and listened. All was silent and nearly dark in the hallway beyond. She put her eye to the crack and peered about, but there seemed to be no one there. Carefully, she pulled the door open a little more and stuck her head out. The passage was indeed empty, dimly lit by flickering torches spaced at distant intervals.

"Let's go," she whispered to Pilos, and as one, they slipped out of the library. Emriana pulled the door shut behind them.

As Emriana followed the route Pilos had divined was the correct one, she studied the walls. The architecture was familiar, and she realized that she had seen its like when she had used the scrying crystal to locate Xaphira's possessions. That revelation both soothed and frightened her.

On the one hand, it means we're getting close to the prison, she thought, listening for sounds of others. On the other hand, it means we're getting close to the prison guards.

The pair of interlopers reached an intersection, and Emriana turned to Pilos expectantly. The young priest scratched his head, frowning, and he shrugged.

Emriana groaned. Pilos's spells had proven quite useful to that point, but without another divination of some sort, they could become lost, wandering aimlessly through the bowels of the Generon. But standing in the open while he cast another augury was risky. She was just about to whisper a suggestion that they retreat to the library and perform the divination there when sudden motion caught her eye.

Emriana's heart nearly skipped a beat.

Junce Roundface stood in the middle of the intersection, having simply appeared there. Blessedly, he faced away from the two intruders, and the moment he showed up, he began walking, his boots clicking loudly on the paving stones of the hallway.

He had not seen them.

The girl held her breath as the assassin strode away from her, down the hall and out of sight around a corner. It was only after she let herself exhale again that she realized she had one of the throwing daggers in her hands. She decided to keep it out.

"Come on," she hissed to Pilos, who looked as pale and shocked as she felt. "That's Junce. We have to follow him!"

The Abreeant nodded, and silently the pair darted forward, cutting through the intersection with a cursory glance in either direction. Emriana tried to remain as quiet as she could, but behind her, Pilos's every footfall brought a scuff or click that was driving the girl crazy.

He's even breathing too loud, she thought.

He's doing the best he can, Hetta chided, nearly making Emriana jump. Her grandmother had been strangely silent for so long, the girl had almost forgotten she was with them. *Without his spells, you would never have made it this far.*

Chagrined, Emriana answered, *I know. I'm just scared*.

She turned, halted Pilos, put her mouth to his ear, and whispered, "Try to roll your feet with each step, heel to toe, heel to toe." She felt the young man nod, and she continued on her way. After her advice, the priest's steps were quieter.

When they reached the turn Junce had taken, Emriana pulled up again. She peeked around it cautiously, afraid to expose too much of herself to anyone watching. The new passage ended only a short distance away, as an open doorway. Beyond the wide doorframe, Emriana could see the bars of several prison cells. The whole place was lit with flickering torches.

It was the same chamber from her vision.

Emriana drew her head back and looked at her companion. "That's it," she mouthed to Pilos, motioning around the corner.

The young priest nodded and peeked around; then he drew back. Holding up one finger as a sign for Emriana to wait a moment, he reached inside his doublet and removed a scroll. He glanced at it then nodded in seeming satisfaction. He leaned close, putting his mouth to Emriana's ear and said, "A spell to handle pesky guards. Very quick."

The girl smiled appreciatively at Pilos and turned back. Taking another deep, calming breath, she peered around the turn once more then stepped out. She padded step by step closer to the doorway, her arm cocked back, dagger at the ready.

Don't miss.

At the doorway, Emriana pressed herself to one side, peering in all directions. The room was square, but the central corridor that ran among the cells was laid out in a **T** shape. The entrance where she stood would have been at the base of the **T**. There was no sign of Junce, a fact that almost filled her with dread more than relief. She tried to scan every corner, every cranny in the prison, but the whole place seemed empty. Even the cells appeared to be unoccupied, though she couldn't be sure, for they were cloaked in deeper shadows.

Frowning, Emriana stepped into the room.

In one corner, she spotted the table from her scrying. Xaphira's clothing and equipment were still haphazardly scattered across its surface. The girl's heart raced, filled with hope.

She pointed to it, and Pilos nodded. He still held his scroll in his hands, unfurled, ready to be used in an instant.

Summoning all of her courage, Emriana took another step into the room, then another. She made her way to the table, her dagger still held high, drawn back for throwing. When she reached the wooden slab, she tentatively reached out, feeling the items, wanting to make sure they were real.

A groan, soft and muffled, issued from a cell to the girl's right.

Emriana spun, staring in that direction. "Aunt Xaphira?" she called out before she could stop herself. She froze, listening. Beside her, Pilos craned his neck forward, trying to see into the corner cell.

"You might as well come in and join us, Em," Junce said, his voice carrying from the shadows in the deepest part of the cell. "That's what your aunt calls you, isn't it?"

Emriana froze, her heart sinking. She half turned to flee again then stopped, rage filling her.

No.

"Show yourself, you worm," she said aloud. She stormed forward, trying to spot the assassin where he hid. "Or are you really scared of one helpless girl?" Do something, Pilos, she thought desperately as she moved toward the cell, before he thinks to pay any attention to you.

Junce laughed, and she saw him, reclining against the corner, inside the cell. Another form lay at his feet, pale and naked in the dim light of the torches.

Aunt Xaphira.

The dagger was sailing forward, passing between the bars of the cell, before Emriana even realized what she had done. Her aim was true. The blade was spinning directly toward Junce's chest.

He reached up and snagged the blade out of the air.

"Actually, you have proven to be the most resourceful in your family, Em," Junce said, his voice filled with mirth. "I've had more trouble dealing with you than the rest of them combined."

Using the very dagger that Em had unwittingly provided him, Junce reached up and sliced through a thin cord that ran through the cell. As it snapped, the girl saw motion out of the corner of her eye. A black cloth was rising, itself being pulled by a cord attached to counterweights. Behind the cloth, she caught a flash of light, though it was not magical.

A reflection.

In the heartbeat of time it took Emriana to realize she was looking into a mirror, she found herself in the grip of its magic. There was the briefest of tugs, and suddenly she was in a small, lightless space. Four walls, a floor, and a ceiling, all surrounded her, all within arm's reach. She was trapped in a box.

She huddled, naked, alone, imprisoned.

Everything—the Generon, Pilos, her clothing, the ruby ring with Grandmother Hetta inside—was gone.

There was the faint sound of Emriana's name being called then a window appeared, at first very far away, overhead. It seemed to enlarge, to zoom

close to her, becoming one wall of her tiny prison.
She could see Junce through that clear, solid bar-
rier, still standing in the cell of the jail room in the
Generon, looking at her.

Emriana tried to push against the window, but it
was still as solid a barrier as the darkness before it
had been.

Junce laughed. "It's quite a mirror, isn't it? I hope
you like it, because you're going to spend a long, long
time in there."

And the window was receding, growing ever so
tiny, until it winked out completely, leaving Emriana
alone in the darkness once more.

The sound of her scream echoed in her own ears.

. . .

Vambran and Arbeenok dashed out into the street
to find people running in panic. As one man went
sprinting by, a look of horror on his face, Vambran
grabbed him by the arm and spun him around.

"What is it?" the lieutenant demanded. "What's
wrong?"

"The plague!" the man cried, yanking his arm
free and running off again. "The Rotting Plague
has returned!"

Arbeenok, who had remained in dog form until
that moment, transformed back into his natural
shape. "The great death," he said.

"What?" Vambran said, spinning to look at his
companion. "What do you mean?"

"My vision. Remember? I foresaw a great death,
and in my divinations, I saw that it began in a great
city. It seemed that I might find a way to prevent it,
but I did not know what it would be, so that is why I
have come here with you. Now I know. We must find
a way to stop this plague before it spreads."

Vambran was shaking. "My uncle," he said. "The Crescents. We have to find them, free them, before the plague can get to them."

Arbeenok nodded, and together they ran down the street, moving opposite of all the fleeing citizens.

As they rounded the next corner, Vambran skidded to a stop, not sure he was seeing clearly. In the half light of evening, shambling forms appeared out of the deepest shadows, chasing after running, screaming people. The figures' gaits were slow, unnatural, and Vambran understood with horror that they were not alive.

"Zombies!" he cried. "They might be what's spreading the plague! We must turn them back!" Fishing his medallion out of his pocket, Vambran stepped forward, preparing to turn the undead away with the might of his holy courage and faith. He extended his hand, displaying the coin, and began to pray.

Beside him, Arbeenok began to chant, pulling a small totem free from his belt as he did so. When his chanting reached a crescendo, a small ball of flame appeared in the palm of his hand. He hurled the tiny conflagration at the closest zombie, scoring a direct hit. Another handful of flame instantly appeared in its place in his palm. He flung again, striking the same zombie, and it went down, becoming a roaring bonfire that lit the street.

Bolstered by his companion's skill, Vambran proceeded to advance down the road, calling on the power of Waukeen to aid him in driving back the shambling undead. Suddenly, to his right, another shuffling, limping creature stepped out of the shadows of an alley. Vambran spun, ready to drive it back. Then he faltered, the prayer dying on his lips.

The zombie shuffled closer, reaching for him, plainly visible in the light of the fire behind

Vambran. Its eyes were lifeless, its skin pale and tinged, and it came closer, a low growl issuing from its throat.

It was Uncle Kovrim.

R.A. SALVATORE'S
WAR OF THE SPIDER QUEEN

THE EPIC SAGA OF THE DARK ELVES CONTINUES.

New in hardcover!

EXTINCTION
Book IV
Lisa Smedman

or even a small group of drow, trust is the rarest commodity of all. When the expedition prepares for a return to the Abyss, what little trust there is crumbles under a rival goddess's hand.

January 2004

ANNIHILATION
Book V
Philip Athans

ld alliances have been broken, and new bonds have been formed. While some finally embark for the Abyss itself, others stay behind to serve a new mistress—a goddess with plans of her own.

July 2004

RESURRECTION
Book VI

he Spider Queen has been asleep for a long time, leaving the Underdark to suffer war and ruin. But if she finally returns, will things get better… or worse?

April 2005

The New York Times *best-seller now in paperback!*

CONDEMNATION
Book III
Richard Baker

he search for answers to Lolth's silence uncovers only more complex questions, allowing doubt nd frustration to test the boundaries of already tenuous relationships. Sensing the holes in the mor of Menzoberranzan, a new, dangerous threat steps in to test the resolve of the Jewel of the Underdark, and finds it lacking.

May 2004

Now in paperback!
DISSOLUTION, BOOK I
INSURRECTION, BOOK II

FORGOTTEN REALMS®

GO BEHIND ENEMY LINES WITH DRIZZT DO'URDEN IN THIS ALL NEW TRILOGY FROM BEST-SELLING AUTHOR R.A. SALVATORE.

THE HUNTER'S BLADES TRILOGY

The New York Times *best-seller now in paperback!*

THE LONE DROW
Book II

Alone and tired, cold and hungry, Drizzt Do'Urden has never been more dangerous. But neither have the rampaging orcs that have finally done the impossible—what for the dwarves of the North is the most horrifying nightmare ever—they've banded together.

June 2004

Now in hardcover!

THE TWO SWORDS
Book III

Drizzt has become the Hunter, but King Obould won't let himself become the Hunted and that means one of them will have to die. The Hunter's Blades trilogy draws to an explosive conclusion.

October 2004

THE THOUSAND ORCS
Book I
Available Now!

TWO NEW WAYS TO OWN THE PATHS OF DARKNESS BY *NEW YORK TIMES* BEST-SELLING AUTHOR

R.A. SALVATORE

New in hardcover!
PATHS OF DARKNESS COLLECTORS EDITION
A Forgotten Realms® Omnibus
February 2004

•

PATHS OF DARKNESS GIFT SET
A new boxed set of all four titles in paperback
September 2004

Contains: *The Silent Blade, The Spine of the World, Servant of the Shard, Sea of Swords*

Wulfgar the barbarian has returned from death to his companions: Drizzt, Catti-brie, Regis, and Bruenor. Yet the road to freedom will be long for him, and his path will lead through darkness before he emerges into the light. And along the way he will find old enemies, new allies, and someone to love.

FROM *NEW YORK TIMES*
BEST-SELLING AUTHOR
R.A. SALVATORE

In taverns, around campfires, and in the loftiest council
chambers of Faerûn, people whisper the tales of a lone dark
elf who stumbled out of the merciless Underdark to the no
less unforgiving wilderness of the World Above and carved a
life for himself, then lived a legend...

THE LEGEND OF DRIZZT

For the first time in deluxe hardcover editions, all three volumes of the
Dark Elf Trilogy take their rightful place at the beginning of one of the
greatest fantasy epics of all time. Each title contains striking new cover
and portions of an all-new author interview, with the questions posed
none other than the readers themselves.

HUMELAND

Being born in Menzoberranzan means a hard life surrounded by evil

March 2004

EXILE

But the only thing worse is being driven from the city with
hunters on your trail.

June 2004

SOJOURN

Unless you can find your way out, never to return.

December 2004

CHECK OUT THESE NEW TITLES FROM THE AUTHORS OF R.Á. SALVATORE'S WAR OF THE SPIDER QUEEN SERIES!

VENOM'S TASTE
House of Serpents, Book I
Lisa Smedman

The New York Times Best-selling author of *Extinction*.
Serpents. Poison. Psionics. And the occasional evil death cult. Business as usual in the Vilhon Reach. Lisa Smedman breathes life into the treacherous yuan-ti race.

THE RAGE
The Year of Rogue Dragons, Book I
Richard Lee Byers

Every once in a while the dragons go mad. Without warning they darken the skies of Faerûn and kill and kill and kill. Richard Lee Byers, the new master of dragons, takes wing.

FORSAKEN HOUSE
The Last Mythal, Book I
Richard Baker

The New York Times Best-selling author of *Condemnation*.
The Retreat is at an end, and the elves of Faerûn find themselves at a turning point. In one direction lies peace and stagnation, in the other: war and destiny. *New York Times* best-selling author Richard Baker shows the elves their future.

August 2004

THE RUBY GUARDIAN
Scions of Arrabar, Book II
Thomas M. Reid

Life and death both come at a price in the mercenary city-states of the Vilhon Reach. Vambran thought he knew the cost of both, but he still has a lot to learn. Thomas M. Reid makes humans the most dangerous monsters in Faerûn.

November 2004

THE SAPPHIRE CRESCENT
Scions of Arrabar, Book I
Available Now